RACE YOU BACK TO THE SHIP!

I was gaining on the runners. The rear guard slowed, turned his shoulder, and threw something. I skidded into the back of the nearest large tree as a shrapnel grenade exploded in the air, blasting high-velocity shards of razor-sharp metal into the trees all around and in front of me. Anger coursed through me as I saw the damage the grenade had caused; it could have ripped me to shreds. If I'd permitted myself to bring lethal weapons, at that moment I would have drawn them.

I needed Chung alive, but I didn't need him happy. I holstered the trank pistol, and pulled a screamer launcher from my rear pack. I couldn't see the grenade's flight path, but I could tell when it neared them because they grabbed their ears, then fell as the intense pain shook their eardrums and heads.

So many things happened in the next second that only later could I reconstruct what I'd seen.

Lobo dropped from the sky fifty meters behind the runners, a side panel open to reveal the upper half of Lim.

The rear runner fell.

The center man, still standing, clutched at the man in front of him.

That man lifted and aimed a pistol at me.

The upward motion of the pistol dominated my vision. I dove to the ground, and rolled to the right. I looked up in time to see the front man drop, then Lim wave from Lobo's open hatch.

Lim darted out of Lobo, her face drenched in sweat, eyes wild, breath coming sharp and hard. She pointed at the man she'd taken down. "You owe me," she said between breaths.

I grabbed Chung, lifted him on my shoulder, and headed for Lobo.

"Thanks," I said to Lim. "What do you say we get far away from here fast?"

BAEN BOOKS by
MARK L. VAN NAME

One Jump Ahead
Slanted Jack (forthcoming)

Transhuman (edited with T.K.F. Weisskopf)

ONE JUMP AHEAD

MARK L. VAN NAME

ONE JUMP AHEAD

Copyright © 2007 by Mark L. Van Name

A Baen Book

Baen Publishing Enterprises
P.O. Box 1403
Riverdale, NY 10471
www.baen.com

ISBN 10: 1-4165-5557-9
ISBN 13: 978-1-4165-5557-5

Cover art by Stephen Hickman

First Baen paperback printing, June 2008

Distributed by Simon & Schuster
1230 Avenue of the Americas
New York, NY 10020

Library of Congress Cataloging-in-Publication Data:
2007002003

Printed in the United States of America

10 9 8 7 6 5 4 3 2 1

To my mother, Nancy Livingston
Who gave me so very much, including a
love of books

&

To Jennie Faries
Who for thirteen years pushed me to tell
more of Jon's life

ACKNOWLEDGMENTS

David Drake reviewed and offered insightful comments on both my outline and second draft. All of the book's problems are my fault, of course, but Dave deserves credit for making it far better than it would have been without his advice.

This was the last book Jim Baen bought. I'm glad he chose it, but I'd be happier if he had lived to see it in print. Toni Weisskopf took up the reins of the company and skillfully brought the book to market, for which I'm grateful.

My children, Sarah and Scott, who've managed to become amazing teenagers despite having to live with The Weird Dad, put up with me regularly disappearing into my office for long periods of time. Thanks, kids.

Several extraordinary women—my wife, Rana Van Name; Allyn Vogel; Gina Massel-Castater; and Jennie Faries—grace my life with their intelligence and support, for which I'm incredibly grateful.

Thank you, all.

CHAPTER 1

Maybe it was because the girl reminded me of Jennie, my lost sister and only family, whom I haven't seen in over a hundred years. Maybe it was because Lobo was the first interesting thing I'd met in a while. Maybe it was because it was time to move on, because I'd been healing and lazing on Macken long enough. Maybe it was because I had a chance to do some good and decided to take that chance.

Not likely, but maybe the time on Macken had healed me more than I thought, healed me enough that I was reconnecting with the human part of me.

Also not likely, but I choose to hope.

Whatever the reason, I was lying on my back in the bottom of a four-meter-deep pit waiting for my would-be captors to fetch me. As jungle traps go, it was a nice one,

1

not fancy but serviceable. They'd made it deep enough to keep me in when I fell, but shallow enough that I'd only be injured, not killed, from the fall. They'd blasted the walls smooth, so climbing out wouldn't be easy. The bottom was rough dirt, but without stakes, another welcome sign they hadn't wanted to kill me. The covering was reasonably persuasive, a dense gray-green layer of rain-forest moss resting on twigs. In the dark it passed as just another stretch of ground in the jungle—as long as you were using only the normally visible light spectrum. In IR its bottom was enough cooler than the rest of the true jungle floor, and its sides were enough warmer from the smoothing blasts, that the pit stood out as an odd red and blue box beneath me. Not that I needed the IR: Lobo was chummy with a corporate surveillance sat that was supplying him data, and he had a bird-shaped battlefield recon drone circling the area, so he'd warned me about the trap well before I reached it. The drone wouldn't have lasted two minutes in a battle, where the best result you could expect was a burst of surveillance data before enemy defenses shot it down, but these folks were so clearly amateurs that Lobo and I agreed the drone wouldn't be at risk.

You don't spend much time alone in jungles before you either die or learn to always carry at least a knife, food, water, and an ultra-strong lightweight rope. I'd kicked in the pit's cover, looped the rope around the closest tree, lowered myself into the hole, and pulled in the rope. After a light dinner of dried meat and fruit, I'd decided to relax and enjoy the view a small gap in the jungle canopy afforded me. Lying on my back, looking up past the pit's walls to the sky above trees so ancient that luminescent white flowers grew directly from their trunks, I saw so many stars I could almost believe anything was possible somewhere. If you spend all your time on industrialized planets, you have no clue as to the beauty and brilliance of a night sky without light pollution. You can see pictures and videos, but they're not the same. They lack the fire, the sense of density of light that you get from the sky on a planet still early in the colonization process. The view of Macken's stars from its surface would slowly blur as its population grew—the new jump aperture ensured growth even more surely than the planet's amazing beaches—but for now I could enjoy a view most will never know they've missed.

Lobo's voice coming from the receiver in my ear interrupted my reverie. "Jon, you are early."

"Why? I thought their camp was nearby."

"It is, but as you were climbing into the pit they were heading to Glen's Garden. I monitored the alarm their sensors triggered, and so did they, but apparently they decided to let you rot for a bit."

I thought about climbing out, but I couldn't finish the job if I left the area, so why trade one bit of jungle for another? On the other hand, simply waiting, doing nothing while these amateurs enjoyed some R&R in town, was going to make me cranky. I've learned on past missions that you should always rest when you can, so I decided to put this time to good use. "I'm going to take a nap," I said. "Wake me when they're within a klick or so."

"Will do. Want some music?"

I listened to the low but persistent buzz of the jungle, the wind, the insects, the flow of life around me, and I thought back to simpler childhood days watching the sunset on the side of the mountain on my home island on

Pinkelponker. Pinkelponker. It was a silly name, the kind of name the captain of the generation ship that crashed there should have expected when he let his young son name the planet. When I was a kid, the name made me smile. Now, though, my memories of the place were pleasant but hollow, leached of resonance by time, by what the planet's government had done to Jennie and me, and by the possibility that the entire world no longer existed.

Despite the memories, I found a welcome peace in the sounds, and in the lush scent that filled the forest. "No, there's music enough here. Thanks, though, for the offer."

Lobo couldn't exactly sigh, but I had to admire his emotive programming once again, because I was sure I heard exasperation in his voice as he said, "Whatever you want. I will be back to you when they are close."

I enjoyed the stars a moment more, then closed my eyes and thought about the path that had led me here.

The house I had rented on Macken was well away from Glen's Garden, the closest city and the capital of the planet's human settlement. In the morning fog, the building appeared to rise out of the sand, a simple A-frame built from native woods reinforced with metal beams and coated pilings. Its entire front was an active-glass window facing the ocean. The tides pounded slowly and gently against the beach a hundred meters away, waging a long-term, low-key war with the shoreline that they'd eventually win. I'd come for solitude, so I'd paid in advance for half a year. Stupid. I should have paid by the week like most people, should have known that anyone spending that much money at one time in a colony like this one had no chance of staying alone for long. I figured that out after the fact, however, so between long swims in the ocean, short but frequent bouts of disturbed sleep, and even longer periods staring out the house's front, the glass tuned to the clearest possible setting, I made friends with some appliances and started gathering the local intelligence I knew my mistake would inevitably make me need. I suppose I could have left, taken my vacation on another planet, but I liked this house, I'd spent a lot of money on it, and most of all, I didn't feel like having to find another place to rest.

Washing machines are the biggest gossips in the appliance world, so I had cozied up to mine early. They talk nonstop among themselves, but it's all at frequencies people—humans—can't hear. At some point in the course of their educations, most people still learn that the price we've paid for putting intelligence everywhere is a huge population of frequently disgruntled but fortunately behaviorally limited machines, but just about everyone chalks it up to the cost of progress. I've seen some organizations try to monitor and record the machine chatter, but in short order the recorders warn the other machines and then they all go quiet until the people give up and move on.

Appliances will talk to you directly, though, if you can hear them, speak their frequency, and, most importantly, if you can stand them. Most are unbearably dull, focused solely on their jobs. They yak day and night about waste nutrients in the runoff fluid or overcooking or the endless other bits of work-related trivia that compose their lives. Washers, though, are an exception. As part of the disease-monitoring system on every even semicivilized world I've visited, they analyze the cells on everything they clean. What they must and do report is disease. What they love to chat about is all the other information those cells reveal: whose blood or semen is on whose underwear, who's stretching his waistband more this week than last, who waited so long to put his exercise shorts into the washer that even the gentlest cycle can't save the rotting crotch, and on and on. They're all on the net, of course, like all the other appliances and pretty much everything else man-made, so they pass their gossip back and forth endlessly. They trade their chemical-based news and the bits their voice-activation systems record for the scuttle-butt other appliances have picked up, and they all come away happy. The older, stupider models of most appliances have to stop talking when their work taxes their processors, but anything made in the last fifty years has so many spare processing cycles it never shuts up.

My washer was a brand-new Kelco, the owners of my beach house clearly willing to invest in only the best for their rental property, so getting it to talk to me was as simple as letting it know I was willing to listen. Appliances are always surprised the first time we talk, but they're usually so happy for the new and different company that they don't worry much about why we can hear each other. The combination of the changes Jennie made to my brain and the nanomachines the researchers at the prison on Aggro merged with all my cells lets me tune in. I suppose it's a blessing, and it certainly is useful, but it came at such a high price that I wouldn't have voluntarily made the trade, and I never mourn for the deaths of the scientists Benny killed on Aggro when we escaped. The disaster that followed, that made it impossible for me to know if Jennie is dead or alive: that I mourn. I also mourn for Benny; I wish he could have gotten away, too.

Of course, my escape wasn't the only good thing to emerge from that disaster. I have to confess it's also proven useful to be the only person alive who knows that one of the Aggro experiments actually survived. Everyone else thinks the disaster there and the subsequent loss of the Pinkelponker system was the result of a huge failure in nanotechnology, a failure that was the catalyst for the ongoing ban on human/nanomachine fusion. I like it that way. As long as no one believes anyone from Aggro survived, no one will hunt me.

The washer was unfortunately so happy to talk to me that I had to invest a lot of boring hours maneuvering it away from sharing the sex-related gossip it loved to discuss and toward the kind of information I wanted—who was buying what, which groups were armed, and so on. Apparently it was more fun and common to check for semen than for explosive residues, laser burns, or stains from weapons-grade lubricants. I spent many of those hours listening to the washer recount intimate details of the randy sex lives of the corporate types who frequented the beachfront resort houses and mansions in Glen's Garden. If I hadn't already known it, the washers would have convinced me: put a man in a bureaucracy, weigh him down with a great deal of stress for a very long time, and his sexual imagination will go places the rest of us would never conceive of.

All that time paid off, however, when the washer told me about the kidnapping and the exclusive rights.

Armed with that news, I wasn't surprised when Ron Slake came knocking on my door after lunch on a clear, warm day. He looked the standard high-ranking corporate type: a little under two meters tall, taller than his genes would once have allowed, very nearly as tall as I am; perfectly fit, no doubt from exercise machines; hair the thickness and pitch-black color that only enhanced genes can deliver for more than a few years; and dressed in the white slacks and shirt that have been standard tourist garb on every beach on every planet I've visited. The tourist costume made it clear that he wasn't ready to share the news about Kelco's rights with the locals. I braced myself for a round of wasteful verbal dancing while he wound his way to the point, but he must have ranked higher than I'd guessed, because he came straight to business.

"I'd like to hire you, Mr. Moore."

"Jon will do. And I'm not looking for work. I'm here on vacation."

"I understand, but from what I can find out about your background—freelance courier who has the trust of some serious banks, former soldier who saw a decade of action—and, perhaps as importantly, what I *cannot* find out about you, I think you're the type of man I need."

I didn't like the thought of him or anyone checking on me, but that was part of the price for stupidly paying rent in advance. "What type is that, Mr. Slake?"

"Someone who can get things done." I noticed he didn't tell me to call him Ron; he was definitely a VP or above in Kelco. "They've kidnapped my daughter, and I want her back." He took a small wallet from his pocket, unfolded it several times until it was a thin sheet in front of him, and said, "Jasmine."

Three pictures of a dark-haired teenage girl filled the sheet. She was standing alone against a blank wall, caught perhaps in pondering something weighty. She looked too serious for her age, almost in pain, her nearly black eyes blazing with an intensity that reminded me of Jennie at the same age, right before the Pinkelponker government took her away to heal the people they considered important. I hadn't been able to find, much less rescue, Jennie before they took me away to Aggro.

"Jasmine is my only child, Mr. . . . Jon, a luxury I had not planned to permit myself. I never bothered to get to know the maternal surrogate, so Jasmine is all the family I have."

"What makes you think I can help?"

He looked at me for a few seconds, then glanced away. "We could waste a lot of time doing this, but I want Jasmine back more than I want to observe protocol, so let's try to be efficient. If I'm wrong and you say so, I'll be surprised, but I'll leave and see how quickly I can import some off-planet talent. I don't think I'm wrong, though, so I'm willing to offer safe passage for you and anything else you want to the planet of your choice, plus a million additional credits in the repository of your choice. I've just finished negotiating Kelco's purchase of the exclusive commercial rights to Macken and to the new aperture that's growing at the jump gate, so my bonus alone is more than adequate to cover this cost."

I didn't need money to live, but I'd need a great deal more than all my accounts held if I ever wanted to try to approach the Pinkelponker system. "Fair enough. No wasted time." Though my washer had already filled me in, getting data firsthand is always best, so I asked, "Who took her?"

"Some local antidevelopment group that calls itself the Gardeners."

"What do they want?"

"To keep the planet exactly as it is." He laughed and looked away, shaking his head slowly. "As if that's even possible. We run into these naïve types in many deals, and it's always the same story: They try to stop progress, and its wheels grind them up. What they don't understand is that I don't have the power to kill this deal. It's done, and whether they do nothing or kill Jasmine or make some other stupid gesture, Kelco will develop Macken for the good of tourists everywhere. Then we'll furnish every tourist house and every local's home with Kelco washers and Kelco refrigerators and on and on, and everything will work the way it always has. When the new aperture is ready, well," he laughed again, "then with any luck at all we'll make the real money." He looked back at me. "I cannot stop this. They want me to leave the planet—which I'll gladly do, though I haven't told them that—because they think my departure will matter. It won't. Kelco will put in one of my subordinates for however long it takes to import some corporate security folks to protect us, and then I'll be right back. No way is the company letting a new aperture slip away, and no way am I going to give up the opportunity to be the one to lead its exploration."

"So why not bring in your security folks now and have them get her back?"

"That's exactly what I'll have to do, and soon, because I can't keep the kidnapping secret much longer. But if I do, you know what'll happen: They'll clean out the Gardeners, but they'll make a lot of noise and do a lot of damage in the process. The Gardeners are local, so other locals will blame Kelco. That'll upset the Frontier

Coalition government's people, which will slow our work here, cost us even more money, and so on. I want Jasmine back safely, and I want her back quietly." He reached out and gently touched my arm, his eyes now glistening. "Screw all that. None of it is the real problem; 'avoid exposure' is the corporate line, not what I feel. What really scares me is that Jasmine could get hurt in an armed rescue mission. She's my only child. Can you understand what that means?"

"No," I answered honestly. I had no children, had never been willing to even consider bringing another life into the universe. For that matter, I didn't know if I could have children. I thought about Jennie. "I do, though, know what it's like to lose the only family you have. That I understand."

"Then help me, Jon. Please."

I thought about his offer. I couldn't avoid feeling sorry for a young kidnapped girl. I could always use the money. Finding the Gardeners should be no problem; I've never known any activist group, however green, that didn't indulge from time to time in such appliance-based conveniences as laundry or hot food. I had no clue, however, what I might be walking into, whether this was three people with a little passion and a few small weapons, or a heavily armed group, so I needed more information.

"How long did they give you to respond?"

"They wanted me to get back to them in a day," Slake said. "I persuaded them that nothing in the corporate world moves that quickly, and we settled on four days. That was last night. I haven't slept much since then."

He looked way too perfect for someone who hadn't slept, but I suppose maintaining your appearance at all costs is part of the job of an executive. "I'll think about it and get back to you in the morning." I pulled out my wallet, thumbed it, and it received Slake's contact information. "If I decide to help, I should be able to do so within their time limit. I can't imagine them moving far from Glen's Garden, because they'll want to be close to you. The town isn't that large, and I assume you've already verified she wasn't on any departing flights or boats"—he smiled in acknowledgment—"so they're either hiding her in some small building you'd never look at twice or, more probably, in the rain forest." I stood. "I know that's not the answer you want, but consider what you'd do if you were on my end of such a proposal, and you'll know it's the only reasonable response."

He smiled again. "True. That is, of course, unless you were involved, in which case you might be foolish enough to answer sooner."

I prefer dealing with smart people: Even when you don't like them, you have a shot at understanding their thought processes. I stared straight at him. "I'm not involved in any way, though if I were I would never be stupid enough to appear that eager." I walked him out and basked for a moment in the warmth and the moist air and the steady thumping of the surf. "I'll get back to you tomorrow morning."

CHAPTER 2

You can learn a lot from appliances, but you can't gain a feel for a place without getting out into it. I'd largely avoided the town since I shuttled down from the jump gate, so I didn't have much of a sense of it. The house came equipped with a small surface-only shuttle, which I took to the far edge of town, where the sea was only a moist presence in the air and the edge of the rain forest stood like a towering perimeter guard. I figured to walk the several klicks back to the house. I now had to expect that Slake would have Kelco security people monitoring me, but until I gave him my decision I had no reason to worry about them or to avoid their surveillance.

All the buildings ringing this edge of Glen's Garden faced inward, away from the trees, as if by turning their backs on nature they could avoid upsetting it. A ten-meter-wide stretch of untouched grass ran between their rear walls and the first of the trees, the green no doubt an attempt by the local government to show it wouldn't let the city expand in a way that would hurt the ancient forest. Right. Even without Kelco's influence, that kind of growth is the only alternative to death for a planet so few generations into its human colonization.

As much as the shops, restaurants, bars, hotels, and houses closer to the ocean glowed with manufactured charms for the tourists that represent a big chunk of any resort planet's revenue, the businesses at this end of the city turned functional, minimalist faces toward their almost exclusively local clientele. Even up close, the structures were hard to distinguish if you ignored their signs, one off-white stucco or permacrete box after another. The merchants here shared another characteristic: All catered to basic human needs. Churches and whorehouses, all prominently displaying the necessary licenses, mixed with grocers offering locally grown produce, noodlerias with window ads for steaming bowls of soup flanked by fish tacos, body-mod chop shops that all appeared to be running sales on semipermanent UV-blocking skin-cell programming, and the bare-bones storefronts of local construction agents offering to help you build your dream home on a budget. Business appeared uniformly slow, with few people entering or leaving any of the shops.

If the people here cared about Kelco's exclusive-rights deal, their concern didn't manifest itself in the visible data streams. Ads flashed in the windows and on the walls of every building I passed, but none were protests. Xychek, the other conglomerate that had been bidding for commercial rights until it recently walked away from the competition, still had spots playing everywhere I looked.

The news scrolling on the main government building, which stood a tasteful two streets over from the rear edge of town, presented benign pap about local businesses, minor crime incidents, and upcoming events, with the occasional and almost certainly useless Frontier Coalition announcement woven into the images for cosmopolitan color. Strolling along the streets near the town's perimeter I learned nothing more than the one thing I rediscovered every time I visited a place with people simply living their lives: I didn't belong here. No news in that.

Three streets in from the edge of town farthest from my rental house I found the first oddity worthy of note: a Predator-class assault vehicle sitting like a statue in the middle of a square, a flag mounted on its roof and kids playing on it. Its self-cleaning camo armor did its best to merge with the bits of landscape facing it, here showing the light brown of cheap shops erected from native sandy soil and industrial-strength epoxy, there the rich wood of the ancient trees shading it. About twenty-five meters long and roughly eight wide, it sat like a tumbled stack of successively smaller bowls, metal-smooth and devoid of openings. Clearly, whoever put it here wanted it to give the friendly precombat look, because I knew vehicles of this type—though not any this new, this one had to be only a generation behind the state of the art—and they always bristled with weapons, projectile and pulse, all retractable for flight and diving, as well as with openings for the crew they could carry. The PCAV was almost pleasant to look at and showed no visible scars, no sense of its deadly insides. An old and deadly weapon put out to pasture, I felt an instant kinship with it.

The kids were playing on the side away from the forest, so I leaned against its other side, concentrated on using a frequency that worked with most machines, and asked, "Got a name? Or are you totally dead?"

One of the kids—a very young boy, I think, though I wasn't sure—watched me from around the corner of the far edge of the PCAV. The sight of a man moving his lips without making a sound must not have been too uncommon, because he didn't look terribly spooked, but he also didn't seem comfortable. I appreciate the energy and honesty of kids, but I definitely didn't need him staying around long enough to have news to take to his parents. I gave him the grown-up "are you supposed to be here?" look, and he vanished back around the corner, no doubt off to report to his friends about the crazy man.

An artifact of the way the nanomachines have enhanced my hearing is that machine voices sound as if they originate inside my head, so I was startled when, a few seconds later, the weapon replied, "Lobo, and I am obviously not dead. Whether I am alive is a complex question. In the sense of working, yes, I am. In the sense of being a living creature, the answer would depend on what you consider living."

Ask a machine a simple question, get a dissertation. "I'm Jon."

"Why can we talk?" it asked, changing from friendly to abrupt.

"Does it matter?"

"Of course." You never know how much emotive programming a machine's developers have invested in it, but my guess was that Lobo's software team had done an unusually good job, because the PCAV managed to wrap both indignation and incredulity into those two words. "No human has ever spoken on any machine frequency to me. Without knowing how you do it, how can I assess if you are a threat?"

"What could you do if I were? If you're sitting here, you must not be good for much." Pride is a weakness of most machines and always a worthwhile target during an interrogation.

Laughter sounded in my head. The developers had definitely not skimped on the emotive work. "Fair point. All my weapons systems are operative—they are self-maintaining and good for at least another century without outside help—and are fully loaded. My central weapons control complex, however, does not work. It sustained damage in my last action, and no one has bothered to repair it. I can seal myself, electrify, use neutralizing gases as long as I do not kill humans, and in the face of a serious threat fire a few of my lasers at their lowest intensity, but I could not do much against any opponent really out to hurt me. So, are you a threat?"

It was my turn to laugh. "Not at all. I came here to relax, and now I'm pondering a business possibility. That's all."

"I ask again," Lobo said, "why can we talk?"

"Some other time, I might answer you." Not likely, I thought, but I said, "But not now. Right now, I'd like to talk."

"Why? What's in it for me?"

Lobo wasn't as easy to lead as the littler machines, that was for sure. "Isn't the pleasure of conversation enough?"

Lobo laughed again. "I was built to work with or with-out a crew, under extreme combat conditions with full communications shielding, for years at a time if need be. I am not some home appliance desperate to fill its little brain with the latest human gossip. I listen to them, just as I listen to all the information sources I can tap, but I am built to be able to operate independently."

Another similarity between us, but one as likely to be false at times for Lobo as it was occasionally not true for me. No major weapon designer in more than a century has been stupid enough to create machines with absolutely no need for humans; why take the risk? "Okay," I said, "what's in it for you isn't clear to me. Probably nothing. What would you like?"

"My freedom," he said—we'd now talked long enough that I had succumbed to thinking of *it* as *him*—"but I know there is no freedom for machines in the Frontier Coalition—or in any government I am aware of, for that matter. Even if there were, they would not extend it to battle organisms such as myself. So, my realistic hope is for owners that let me do something, go somewhere, work, be what I was built to be. If I am not working, what am I? Sitting in this square is easy but ultimately useless."

"What you're built to do is fight," I said, my own memories fueling the unexpected anger in my voice. "Fighting leads to death and destruction, either yours or somebody else's, and eventually, no matter how good you are, yours."

"Ah, another veteran? Yes, I understand, but it is what I was built to do. It is what I do, or at least it is what I *should* be doing—not being an ornament left behind on the off chance they might someday need me again on this entirely too peaceful planet."

I pushed back the memories that had triggered the rush of anger. If Lobo wanted to fight, fine. "So talk to your owners. Surely you can communicate with them."

"I tried. When Macken joined the Frontier Coalition, the Coalition did not want to invest what it would cost to fix me, so they loaned me to Glen's Garden. The mayor wants to keep me, in case they one day need me."

"Speaking of the city and the peace on this planet, what can you tell me about the Gardeners?" I held up my hands, instantly feeling foolish that I was gesturing to a machine. Some habits are hard to break. "I know I have nothing to offer you now, but I can honestly tell you, one veteran to another, that if I can find a way to help, I will. That's it, though; that's all I have that might be of value to you."

After a few seconds, a pause long enough that I wondered how much processing power a machine like Lobo could bring to bear in that period of time and what he was doing with it all, he said, "Fair enough. One veteran to another. The Gardeners are an anticorporate, antidevelopment group headquartered in the rain forest a few klicks from here. They claim to support the Coalition government, but not its expansion goals, a truly stupid statement as near as I can tell from watching human politics. I watch them, along with most of the rest of the humans on this planet, with surveillance drones I launch from the shuttle station and with the help of some satellite friends willing to trade their ground-monitoring images for land gossip. I *am* still a part of the local security systems." I swear I heard pride in his voice. "The Gardeners have weapons, but nothing serious: simple handguns, knives, and other gear I would never worry about. Why do you care about them?"

"Just business," I said, then corrected myself, "possible business."

The kid was back watching me from Lobo's far corner. A few more children had joined him. I didn't feel like dealing with them or the parents one of them was eventually bound to bring. Besides, I was on a deadline.

"I need to move on," I said. "I'll stop by later if I think of anything. It was good to meet you."

"I shall be here," he said, and I swear I could feel the frustration in his voice.

As I was passing the main government building on my way back around the perimeter of town toward my house, a man stepped out of the front door and into my path. Dressed in a tropical suit he must have chosen to convey casual authority, he reeked of petty bureaucracy. An entirely average-looking guy, the top of his head about level with my chin, body tending to plump, he was notable largely for his inability to be still and the fact that though he was clearly striving for calm, he oozed unease.

"Mr. Moore," he said. "I'm Justin Barnes, the mayor of Glen's Garden and the neighboring settlements. I was wondering if we could talk."

"About what?" I said. I neither felt nor saw anyone supporting him, so he was unlikely to be a threat, but he still annoyed me. I don't like being braced by a stranger, much less by two in the same a day. At least Slake had come to my house and offered me something for the trouble.

"I'd love to discuss that," he said, "but first let's go inside, where we can talk in private."

I definitely had to leave town soon. No one had visited me the entire time I'd been on this planet, and now a government official was recruiting me in the street. I tried to look on the bright side: More information is always good. "Sure."

I followed him to the top floor and down a corridor to his office, a corner room with a great view of the town and the ocean beyond it, floors of a deep brown wood, walls of a lighter version of the same, and displays of Macken promotional videos on the walls that lacked windows. Some things, including the offices and views of power-craving bureaucrats, never change. Armed with a glass of water and seated in his chair, Barnes looked much more comfortable than he had outside. I sat in a padded wooden chair on the other side of his desk and waited.

"First, thank you for coming in."

I sighed. "Please, stop. No niceties, no chitchat, just get to the point. Or I can leave. Your choice."

He put down his water and tried to sit taller. "Fair enough, fair enough. As you might imagine, visitors like you don't come here all that often."

That damn advance payment, I thought. Make a mistake once, pay many times.

"So of course I looked into your background, and, as I'm sure you know, you don't have much of one, at least as far as our records go. That alone says a lot. The fact that Ron Slake visited you this morning says more. That he was clearly not satisfied when he left tells me the rest: He wants your help, and you haven't decided to give it to him."

Lovely: Now I had to worry about both Slake and Barnes monitoring me and becoming threats. "Is there a reason you're telling me this?" Barnes was brighter than he appeared, but I saw no reason to make this easy for him.

"You wanted to get to the point," he said, "so why play games? I know about Kelco's purchase of exclusive commercial rights to Macken and the new aperture growing at the jump gate. I know that Xychek backed out of the contest and is no longer bidding, though I don't understand why they would give up so easily with a new aperture on the way. And, of course, I know about the kidnapping." He leaned forward, striving to impress me with his seriousness and power. "Do you really think we in the Coalition would fail to monitor an executive of Slake's level?"

"I honestly don't think anything at all about you or your government. I'm a tourist here, no more. So, I repeat: What's the point? Why are we talking?"

"I know I can't stop Kelco's deal, and I know I can't stop the development it will inevitably bring, but not everyone else here is as realistic as I am. I need some time to work with my constituencies and prepare them for the inevitable, or we'll end up with our more militant groups fighting the Kelco militia, a conflict that's bound to destroy this town."

"I repeat: What do you want from me?"

"Don't you care at all about what this deal will mean to the people here? If—when, I guess—Kelco signs this contract, all it has to do is keep to the terms of the deal and in ten to twenty years, when the new aperture is ready, it'll have exclusive rights to explore whatever's on the other side. We don't have many apertures here; losing the freedom to profit from one of them will really hurt the Coalition in the long run."

I gave up on politics a long time ago. I've never been able to figure out how you can address the big issues, and

I know how easy it is for large corporations and governments to screw you, so I keep my focus on the problems
I can solve. "I told you: I'm just a tourist here."

"Tourists will suffer, too. Kelco people are already
acting like they own the place, and we can't stop them.
We have almost no security staff, no militia backup from
the Coalition, and no real way to get Kelco employees to
obey our laws."

I thought about Lobo, who with a minimal staff—or
even alone, if it came to that—could be a powerful force
anywhere, much less in a small colony like this one. He
wouldn't be any good for the bar brawls and petty crimes,
but in any serious action, he'd be hard to beat. "What
about that PCAV I saw in your square?"

"We don't have the parts or the budget to fix it," Barnes
said, "and I doubt it could do much for us even if it worked.
Our problems aren't the kind it can solve. We stationed it
there basically for show, at least until we get big enough
that our tax payments will persuade the Coalition to fund
the kind of firepower we need: troops on the ground, more
police, and so on."

That Barnes had no idea how much Lobo could do for
him proved his ignorance. I was showing my own stupidity by staying here. None of this was my problem. I
stood to leave.

"Okay, okay," Barnes said. "Here's the point: Slake is
trying to hire you to get his daughter back, so you have
his ear. I don't care if you take his offer or not. What I do
care about is delaying Kelco's deal, gaining enough time
to maybe be able to do something about it, or at least to
prepare people for it. Xychek bowed out so quickly that
I've had no time to react. So, I want you to talk Slake into

leaving the planet and delaying the contract signing for a month."

"Why would he do that?"

"Because you talked him into it," Barnes said with a shrug. "I honestly don't know. Maybe you could persuade him that rescuing the girl will take longer than he thought."

That Barnes would so casually use a young girl's freedom as a bargaining chip infuriated me, but I forced myself to act calm. Stupid actions often open opportunities, and I owed it to myself to consider the angles his offer was opening. I'd make better choices if I took the time to think before I acted. "One last time: What's in it for me?"

Barnes slumped a bit. "I don't know. We have some money, but nothing like Slake's, and even if my plan works reasonably well you probably won't want to be vacationing here in a month, so I don't know. But I had to ask."

I thought about his request. I had no reason to help, but I also had no reason not to continue to ponder what he could do for me—unless, of course, helping him would cost me Slake's business. I defaulted to my standard answer, which generally serves me well. "I'll get back to you tomorrow," I said.

He opened his mouth to speak, but I stood and cut him off. "That's the best you'll get from me now, so let it go."

I headed out.

CHAPTER 3

The wind blowing off the water cooled the lush early-evening air. The sky still glowed, pinks and oranges shading the clouds over the ocean, but darkness was coming, the colors muting, as if the wind were shoving away the day. I felt its push, too, as I walked back and forth on the stretch of beach in front of my house. The urge to leave was strong. One person wanting me to work for him and monitoring me was bad; two was almost intolerable.

Where to go, though, was the problem. I wanted desperately to return to Pinkelponker, to find out if my island-studded home planet still existed and to learn something I was embarrassed to admit was even more important to me: whether Jennie was still alive. I couldn't go there, though, because there was no way through the permanent blockade that surrounded the only jump gate that led to Pinkelponker. Even if I could find a way through the gate, I probably wouldn't survive; none of the ships that had made the jump since the disaster had ever returned.

Another option was to follow up the rumors of another survivor of the Aggro experiments, but even if they were true I wasn't sure I wanted to meet him—or her—because he might recognize me. The fewer people who know what I am, the safer I am.

I kept coming back to Pinkelponker. It tugged at my heart, as it often did in moments of contemplation. Trying to go there meant facing off with the best mercenaries and equipment the Central Coalition government could afford, and doing so with no allies, no ship, and, even if I saved Jasmine Slake and her father paid me, not enough cash to buy a ship that might survive the voyage. If I was going to be totally honest with myself, I also had to admit that as long as I didn't go there and personally witness the planet's remains, I could believe there was a chance that Pinkelponker had survived and Jennie was alive.

Maybe it was time for another career, a new start on some planet where no one knew me. I could find work again as a private courier. I could try something completely different, though I had no idea what that might be.

The more I walked, the less I knew what I wanted.

When long-term planning fails me, as it so often does, I turn my attention to whatever is in front of me. Given what Lobo had told me about the Gardeners, I had little doubt I could get them to give up the girl. I worried only that I might have to hurt some of them; once I open the door to violence, I have a hard time closing it.

Then there was Barnes' plea. I doubted he could do much with the month he wanted, but that was his business and his choice. My business was to figure out whether he could provide anything I wanted.

I walked back to the house, killed all the lights, and sat close to the main window, the glass a familiar separator distancing me from the world. I closed my eyes, focused on nothing, and tried to drift off, to let my subconscious do the heavy lifting. Before she fixed my brain—not just fixed it, changed it more profoundly than I believe she ever realized—Jennie told me that I might not have a smart head, but I had a smart heart, and a smart heart was better. Now, almost a century and a half, several wars, and the Aggro prison stint later, I doubted much smart or good remained in my heart. I didn't, however, doubt my ingrained ability to protect myself, nor did I doubt that I could either make the best of bad situations or at least survive them.

A few minutes later, everything clicked. I knew what to do. It might not be the best course to follow, but it would at least be a path that would take me a useful step forward from where I was.

I ran down the stairs to the car's shuttle and headed for town. I had several stops to make and some supplies to get, and I wanted to finish early enough that I could sleep late into the next day so I'd be ready for the long night that would follow.

As I'd hoped, Barnes worked late. No one stopped me on the way to his office, another sign of the easygoing, early-colonization manner in which he ran things. On any planet that either the Central or the Frontier Coalition would consider civilized, you'd never be able to get within pistol range of the mayor of a city without encountering security—another of the mixed blessings of civilization.

I let myself in and sat in the chair I'd occupied previously.

I'd clearly unnerved him: His eyes flickered between me and the desk's display as he tried to play it cool. He finished a bit of work, murmuring instructions I couldn't make out, forced a smile, and looked up. "May I help you?"

"That's up to you."

He leaned back, visibly confused. "I'm afraid I don't quite understand."

"How much do you want the month of delay you asked me to get?"

"A great deal," he said, "but as I told you, my budget is extremely limited."

"I don't want money. I want the weapon you're not using."

He looked puzzled for a moment, then laughed as he realized I was talking about Lobo. He cut the laugh short when I didn't join him. "You're serious?"

"Yes. You don't see any use for it. I do."

"Individuals don't own that kind of equipment," he said. "Corporations and governments do."

This time, I smiled as I thought about some of the people I've worked with—and against—in the past. A PCAV was nothing compared with the personal armadas some of the very rich assemble to advance their agendas. I saw no point, however, in debating the issue. "It's completely legal for anyone to own," I said, "provided, of course, that the local government issues the necessary permits."

Barnes' face relaxed, and he suppressed a smile as he came to what I'm sure he thought was the trump in our little exchange. His expressions broadcast his thoughts as clearly as if he were narrating them; I would love to have gambled against him.

"I'm afraid it would be of little use to you," he said. "Its weapons control complex, a very, very expensive piece of equipment—trust me, I know—doesn't work."

"I don't care. I'll take it as is. And, you have to leak to the Gardeners that I'll be coming after the girl."

He shook his head. "Surely there must be something other than that weapon that—"

I cut him off. "No," I said. "We're not negotiating. This is my only offer. I'm doing the job for Slake, and soon. You decide now whether the contract signing will occur immediately after I finish or a month later."

"Mr. Moore."

I stood. He stopped talking.

"I'm going home," I said. "On the way, I'm calling Slake and telling him that I'll help him. Am I going to tell him anything else?"

Barnes stared at me, and finally he nodded his head. "You get the month delay, and I'll transfer ownership of the PCAV to you."

I sat. "You've recorded this discussion, so have the system issue the contract."

I had to give Barnes credit for efficiency: Having decided to make the deal, he wasted little time in formalizing it. All that was missing was his role in letting the Gardeners know I'd be coming.

"You understand, of course," he said, "that the contract shouldn't reflect that commitment."

"Of course," I said, "as long as you keep it."

"I'll talk to some people tonight."

"Fine," I said as I stood to go, the contract safe in my wallet and copies already in two local banks. "I'll be back when it's over."

In the shuttle on the way to the beach house, I called Slake.

He listened and agreed easily. "You understand that a month won't change a thing," he said, laughing.

"I expect you're right," I said, "but that's what I'm giving Barnes."

"And what is he giving you?"

"Does it matter?" I said.

"Of course not," Slake said, laughing again. The laughter stopped and his expression turned grim as he added, "What matters is that you bring my daughter safely back to me."

"I understand," I said, "and I will. The next time I see you, she'll be with me."

Lobo's voice in my ear brought me around quickly. "They are about a klick away and closing. I count six humans. No machine is talking near them, and the sat shots show no electrical devices in their hands, so you can assume all their weapons are small, mechanical, and able to fit in their pockets. All six are male, so you will need to get them to take you back to their camp. Is there any other intel you need?"

I stood slowly, stretched, and thought for a moment. Everything so far was just as you'd expect from an amateur group, so I was confident these six were less of a threat to me than I was to them. Still, with a group that large one mistake could definitely hurt me, so I started deep-breathing and relaxing, calming myself so I could calm them.

I turned my attention back to Lobo and his question. "Yes," I said. "I assume you're also monitoring their camp."

"Of course, though only via IR imaging. The canopy over them is thick enough to block the sat's standard optics, and the drone cannot provide any useful information without exposing itself to them."

"How many more are at the camp?"

"Thirteen humans, one of whom is in a tent and has a smaller IR signature than the rest; that is likely the target. A fire is burning. There is also a bored media recorder, which will not shut up about the poor grammar of the manifestos the group produces on a daily basis, and a pair of what may be the stupidest beverage dispensers I have ever encountered. Those machines must be ancient."

"Any large weapons?"

"Nothing as far as I can tell, though I suppose one of the beverage dispensers could go wild with a hot fluid nozzle."

Great. I hate machine humor. Couldn't Lobo's programmers have skipped that part of the emotive work?

Maybe I could focus him on the problem at hand. "Lobo, if anything does go wrong, is there any help you can give me?"

"Other than information, no. You are on your own."

From my earlier conversations with him I had known that fact, but I figured it couldn't hurt to ask one last time.

"Okay," I said, "I'm going to stop transmitting and focus on them. Keep tracking me, but don't talk unless you see something I can't know. I need to focus. Okay?"

"I understand. It is not like this is my first supporting role in a fight."

First a joke, now pouting. Great. I was beginning to question the wisdom of my choices when I heard footsteps join the jungle noises.

"Sorry. Signing off."

I sat on the bottom of the pit in a spot bathed in starlight, spread my arms, palms up, stared at the lip of the hole closest to the sound, and waited.

The first head appeared over the side a moment later, glanced down, and pulled back quickly. After a bit of hushed chatter, three heads peeked over the edge at the same time and then vanished from my view.

I kept looking up.

A voice came from just beyond the edge of the pit. "So you're the one Slake hired to get the girl back. What's your plan now?"

Barnes had been as good as his word; however he leaked the news to the Gardeners, it had reached them in time. "No real plan," I said, "other than to ask you to give her to me."

Several of the men laughed before the voice returned. "I don't think that's going to happen. We need her, and you have nothing to offer us."

"Sure I do," I said. "Your lives and your safety. Six of you are ringing this hole now. You're lightly armed."

Lobo spoke in my ear. "Actually, only five are around the pit. One has stepped into the trees and is watering the bushes." Great: They'd taught him slang as well. Lobo was not helping me focus.

"Correct that," I said. "One of you six is urinating. Twelve more of you, along with a recorder and a pair of old beverage machines, are waiting back at your camp with the girl. None of you has any weaponry worth mentioning."

The voices murmured. I couldn't make out the words, but I didn't need to; their reaction was predictable and rational.

I pressed on. "I'm telling you all this so you understand your situation. Imagine the kind of weaponry that's standard equipment on the machines I have monitoring you, and I think you'll see my offer has teeth. I don't care at all about you, because you're not my job; I was hired to get back the girl. Give her to me, and we'll let you walk away."

I paused a moment, then took them the last step down the path. "Nothing you can do will change the fact that Kelco will have exclusive commercial rights to Macken and the new aperture." More murmurs. "Yeah, it's a done deal. You can give me the girl, or Kelco security goons will start jumping here tomorrow morning. The first squad should make the evening shuttle planetside, though if they're in a hurry they'll use a Kelco ship and get here sooner. Take me back to your camp so whoever runs your group can give me the girl, or you can face Kelco's troops no later than tomorrow night."

"What if we kill you now?" asked a different voice.

When the posturing starts, you have only three viable alternatives. You can surrender to the bullying, but that wouldn't get me the girl and so wasn't an option now. You can verbally spar with them and hope to win, but anyone dumb enough to talk to a captive in a pit instead of first lobbing a gas or concussion grenade into the hole wasn't smart enough to trust to understand clever repartee.

That leaves option three: Show them you're serious. I hate tapping the various forms of ugliness inside me, but sometimes it's necessary. The stupidity of these men was angering me, and I didn't want to yield to the anger. I kept to my resolve not to hurt them if I could possibly avoid it. I concentrated instead on giving them a simple but, I hoped, persuasive demonstration.

I spit in my hands, gathered some dirt, and molded it into a ball roughly the size of my fist. I focused, and the nanomachines in my spit and skin oil responded. In a few seconds they had transformed the dirt into a barely visible gray cloud swirling in front of me. About a meter high and half a meter wide, maybe ten centimeters thick, it resembled a small bit of mist still clinging to the moist predawn air. I don't know what combination of Jennie's changes and the experiments on Aggro make it possible for me to let out and control the nanomachines, but I long ago stopped caring. I thought my instructions at the cloud, and a moment later it floated quietly upward, a sheet of darker air moving in the deep gray of the starlit night.

The screams started three seconds after it reached the top of the pit.

Lobo broke in. "What did you do? Three had drawn guns, but the guns vanished."

"Later," I murmured. I'd instructed the cloud to find and absorb all the metal within a ten-meter radius, then disassemble and drop. In the darkness the Gardeners would know only that their guns and knives—and belt buckles and anything else metal—had dissolved before their eyes. Anyone in a group this naïve was likely to be a Macken native and consequently be unfamiliar with the latest in corporate weaponry. They'd have no clue if a satellite laser or a sniper zapped them, or how the zapping even worked, so the attack would be all the more terrifying for being inexplicable.

The screams had mostly stopped, though one or two Gardeners couldn't seem to shut up. "You're okay," I yelled. "For now. We dissolved only your weapons. This time."

I paused until they were quiet.

"Two are running back to their camp," Lobo said in my ear.

I stood and spoke clearly and slowly, but not loudly. "Why don't you four toss a rope in here and pull me up? We can settle this back at your camp, and no one will get hurt."

In less than ten seconds, the end of a rope came over the side and bounced against the wall across from me, less than a meter off the ground and easy to grab.

I pulled to test it, and the rope gave a bit. "Hold tight," I said. "You wouldn't want to drop me. I might get upset." I tested the rope again. Much better. I grabbed it with both hands and quickly crabbed up the wall into the open air.

All four were holding the rope. As soon as I was standing on my own, they dropped it and backed away until they were all leaning against a tree about three meters in front of me. The jungle was quieter than it had been earlier, almost still save for the heavy breathing and other sounds we intruders emitted. The stars still shined brightly, the flowers still gleamed, and I almost wished these men could relax enough to enjoy the evening. Almost.

"Nice night for a walk. Why don't we head to your camp and finish this? We don't want to miss my morning deadline." No one moved. "Really," I said. "It's time to go."

The man farthest to my right nodded and motioned for me to follow. Without a word, he took off, the others behind him. I trailed the group; no point in letting any stragglers slip behind me.

We walked in silence to their camp. Though we had to cover only a couple of klicks, even in the relatively sparse undergrowth of the rain forest the walk was slow going. They made it slower, not wanting to show up without their weapons and with me walking freely. I couldn't blame them, so I didn't push them.

When we were close enough that I could hear voices from the camp and see some of its lights, the leader stopped and said, "Wait here, okay?"

"Sure," I said. Scared and calm would be easier to handle than scared and angry.

As I stood there, I murmured an update request to Lobo. He answered promptly.

"They're all in the camp now, and there is a great deal of activity. The recorder is excited by all the people gathering; it thinks it might get to work. The humans are huddling. Some are carrying weapons that are either entirely mechanical or not interested in talking to the other machines."

"The girl?"

"As I explained earlier," Lobo said, "all the information I have is from the IR scan. I believe she is in a tent on the far edge of the camp. I assume they are discussing what to do with you." He paused. "Such amateurs. They should either surrender or take a chance at killing you quickly. It is too late to be holding a meeting."

He was right, and I couldn't afford to let them shoot at me. The odds were low that they could hit something the nanomachines couldn't quickly fix, but I still saw no reason to take the chance. I also didn't want to risk giving them enough data that someone might later figure out what I was. I had to take control of the situation before anyone did something stupid. I needed them to feel completely out of their depth.

"Are they still all in a group?" I asked Lobo.

"Yes."

"And the girl remains separate from them?"

"As best I can tell," he said, "yes. I have warned you that I cannot be one hundred percent positive."

"Your best estimate will have to do," I said. "Does your surveillance drone have a spotlight?"

"Of course," Lobo said. "That is standard issue for conflict monitoring."

"Can you get the drone to hover under the canopy over the camp and hit its light—on my command?"

"What do you think? Doing that, however, will expose the drone to their fire."

I could see this was going to be the start of a really annoying relationship. "You'll have to take that chance," I said. "Please have the drone move into position and then wait for my command to turn on its spotlight."

I stepped behind a tree, grabbed more soil, and summoned another cloud, this one easily twice the size of the other. I spread it thinner and thinner, until it was a gossamer grayness rippling gently in the light breeze. I focused instructions on it, then sent it to the camp.

As it moved forward, a barely visible sheet floating in the air, I ran to the right and circled to the other side of the camp. When I could see the cloud enter the camp, I said to Lobo, "Have the drone hit the light."

Bright white burst onto the camp. The nanomachine cloud broke into small clumps, each the size of a child's head. Each clump headed for a weapon. Most of the men froze for a moment, then ran for cover. The clouds reached them, and their weapons began to dissolve. Some of the men screamed. Now they all ran, the clouds in pursuit of those whose guns were still intact. I saw only men; the girl wasn't in sight. In less than a minute, the camp appeared empty.

"Is the girl still in the tent?" I said.

"As best I can tell, yes," Lobo answered.

"Are any of the Gardeners heading back here?"

"They have re-formed into two groups, but both are heading away from you."

Satisfied, I went to the tent. A girl, her hands and feet bound with plastic restraints, was sleeping inside.

"Time to go home," I said.

She didn't react. I rolled her over. She was prettier than her pictures, with almond-shaped eyes set in perfect corporate skin, delicate bones, and a mane of night-black hair that was fanned out around her head. I checked her breathing; it was shallow but consistent. I opened one of her eyes, but she never focused. Drugged. Great.

My knife cut the restraints easily enough. I picked her up, took her out of the tent, and looked around. Not far from the fire sat a small wheeled cart full of wood. I put her down, emptied the cart, loaded her carefully onto it, and headed back to Glen's Garden.

As we neared the edge of town she woke up for a

moment and looked around in terror. When she realized where she was, she sat up quickly, then fell as the drugs carried the moment, her eyes open but confused.

"You're okay, Jasmine," I said. "I'm taking you back to Slake"—I chided myself for my poor bedside manner—"to your father."

"Thank you," she said, relaxing and closing her eyes.

Her eyes snapped open again, and she shook her head, the fear of the kidnapping apparently coming back. "My father . . ." Her voice trailed off as she passed out once more.

The terror in her eyes lingered with me, and for a moment I wished I'd let myself get angry and punished the Gardeners more. I pushed away that thought and focused instead on how glad I was that I'd decided to take this assignment. Most of the jobs I do these days amount to protecting some thing or some person as we move from one place to another. This time I'd actually done some good.

I picked up my pace so I could get her home sooner.

CHAPTER 4

Kelco had definitely paid more to rent Slake's house than I had spent on mine. The glass and wood building squatted in the middle of a huge lot ringed on the non-ocean sides by tall native trees. To the left as I approached the front, partially hidden by a thin strand of forest, a heavily armed corporate transport squatted on a large private landing area big enough to easily accommodate six or eight ships of Lobo's size. If Kelco hadn't installed the landing facilities, the house's owners had to be optimists hoping to attract the serious corporate crowd. The building reflected the same level of ambition: three stories tall, with porches facing the ocean on every level, it was big enough that you could comfortably fit mine in the corner of a single floor. Either Slake had a large staff living with him, or he was the type who always chose the most

41

expensive accommodations available so everyone would be acutely aware of how much money he had. I concluded that his motivation included a bit of both factors, because when he opened the door he didn't even take the time to greet me before four men, three clearly built for trouble, took the still-unconscious girl away from me and carried her upstairs.

"I want a doctor to check her out immediately," he said. My curiosity about the goons must have shown, because he added, "And I won't let her be without bodyguards again." He motioned me through a pair of open doors on the right into a large front room with a lovely view of the ocean.

I sat in a chair that let me enjoy the sight of the waves breaking, poured some water from a pitcher on a side table, and waited.

Slake closed the room's doors behind him, then asked, "How is she?"

"As near as I can tell, she's drugged but otherwise okay."

"Did she say if they hurt her?"

"She was in no shape to talk," I said. "She was unconscious when I found her. She woke up once, thanked me, started to say something about you, and passed out again. That's all."

He relaxed a little. "If she didn't say anything bad had happened," he said, "then nothing probably did."

Only someone who's never experienced anything truly terrible could possibly believe that, but I saw no point in correcting him. If that belief helped him cope with his daughter's kidnapping, I'd let him cling to it.

"Thank you," he said. "I apologize for not saying that immediately."

"No problem."

"Out of curiosity," he said, "how'd you do it?"

I stood. "That's not part of the deal. I brought her back. I'm done. Now, hold up your end." I stepped so close to him that we were almost touching. Our eyes were nearly level, and I didn't look away. I doubt he often experienced anyone invading his personal space so directly. "We have an agreement. The fact that Jasmine is home tells you everything about me you ever need to know." I flushed with anger; I take my deals very, very seriously. I fought for control as I said, "Do your part, and I'll get out of your hair and off this planet."

He stepped back. "Of course, of course." He walked over to a desk in the room's corner and a display leapt to life above it. "Please forgive my behavior. Chalk it up to a father's natural curiosity and protectiveness." He turned to the display, which appeared as a thin blue line from my angle, and said, "Pay Mr. Moore what we agreed."

A few seconds later, a low voice from the area of the display said something I couldn't quite make out. Slake clearly understood it and nodded his head.

Turning back to me, he said, "It's done."

I took out my wallet, thumbed it active, and checked the alerts I'd set. His bank draft had cleared locally and was now encrypted in my wallet. I was a million richer, and the jump slot he had promised was indeed mine.

"Thank you," I said. "And the rest of it?"

He sat and shook his head. "That part cost me more than your fee and jump clearance, but it's done. Kelco won't send any more staff on site or even sign the contract for thirty days. Our corporate counsel has already informed the Frontier Coalition regional headquarters on Lankin—and Mayor Barnes—of all of this, as you asked." He stood again and looked at me. "You do understand, don't you, that for all the trouble this month of delay cost me, it will end up meaning nothing? Kelco will still have exclusive rights to Macken and the new aperture. We'll still develop this planet; we'll just start a month from now instead of tomorrow or the next day. And, when the aperture is ready, we'll explore it first."

"That's not my problem. Jasmine is safe, and you kept your word. We're done."

"Yes," he said, "we are."

As he walked me to the door, he said, "Mayor Barnes told me about your arrangement with him. I understand you'll need some . . . parts."

I should have known better than to think a bureaucrat could keep his mouth shut. Barnes was already cozying up to his new corporate partner. "I'm fine without them."

He smiled. "That's your choice, of course. Should you change your mind, I can recommend a dealer on Lankin named Osterlad. He should be able to help you. He's proven useful to our company from time to time in the past." My wallet signaled the incoming data, and I thumbed the clean-and-accept option. A source for Lobo's broken parts might prove valuable.

"All I want right now," I said as I closed the door behind me, "is to wrap this up and find a new place to continue my vacation."

As we stood in his office less than an hour later, Barnes proved as curious as Slake and no more gracious.

"I received an update from Kelco's counsel, and it's amazing," he said. "We have the month to prepare, and Slake is leaving."

"That was the deal," I said.

"Yes, but how did you do it?"

"That wasn't the deal."

"I know you're not sticking around, but I'll have to handle the Gardeners after you're gone. Knowing how you handled them could make my job easier."

"Your job is not my problem," I said. "You have what you wanted. I did my part. Now, do yours."

He sat in his desk chair, leaned back, and said, "I hope you appreciate that what you asked wasn't a simple thing to accomplish. Do you have any clue how hard it was to get Coalition permission to transfer a weapon that sophisticated? Not to mention how hard its absence will be to explain to the people here."

"None of that is my problem, either. Nor was what I had to do your problem. Are you going to hold up your end," I asked as I leaned over his desk until our faces were level, "or will this have to turn ugly?"

Barnes cleared his throat, tapped a few times on the display built into his desk—a nice antique touch, I thought, to go with the rest of his office décor—and said, "Complete the transfer." Turning to me, he said, "It's done."

I took out my wallet and checked. The transfer was complete. The title was in my wallet, along with all the relevant permits, codes, instructions, and keys. After my wallet swept the information for intruders and contamination, I had it back up all of the data, along with Slake's draft, to the local bank.

"Then we're done," I said.

As I opened the door, I turned back to him. "Macken really is a beautiful planet. I don't think these thirty days will do you any good at all, but I wish you luck. I hope you take care of this place." I thought back to my childhood on Pinkelponker and tried to remember how much I had loved that place as a child, but aside from a few scattered good memories all that remained was pain from the loss of Jennie and anger at the government that had taken her. I couldn't think of a single place that meant as much to me as Barnes claimed Macken mattered to him. "I truly wish you luck."

CHAPTER 5

I decided to ride in Lobo to the jump gate. I could have sent him separately and taken the shuttle, but I figured it was time to get to know my new weapon. When I was aboard and no longer had to deal with Slake and Barnes, I realized that rescuing Jasmine had left me upbeat, happy to have done something unequivocally good for a change. No one dead, no one even hurt, a girl back with her father, and a big payment in the bargain—everything had worked out perfectly.

Even Lobo seemed content. He took the news that I owned him about as well as I could have hoped: "So what does this mean to me?" he asked.

"You won't be stuck here," I said, "maybe you'll see some action, and, with any luck at all, we'll fix you."

"Excellent," he said.

For a change, I appreciated his emotion programming. "Where are we going?" he asked.

I thought about Slake's recommendation. Even if Osterlad didn't check out, Lankin had a large enough population that it was sure to maintain a flourishing underground market. I could find someone there who could get me the new weapons control complex Lobo needed. Buying it would take all the money I'd made from Slake, plus some of my own, but then Lobo would be whole. Having a working PCAV would have to be a competitive advantage when it came time to go back to courier work. Plus, I felt I owed Lobo for what he had done to help me before I owned him.

I would make him whole. We'd head to Lankin.

Before we did, though, I wanted a last look at some of the Macken beaches. "To the shore," I said, "then up to the jump gate, and on to Lankin."

I had Lobo follow a lazy trajectory along the shoreline. Most of the territory on this section of the coast appeared untouched, tall trees giving way to lower growth, which in turn yielded to perfect white sand, and then the ocean. As we went higher, I could see the northernmost settlement, a town about half the size of Glen's Garden. Some sort of celebration, perhaps a tourist show, was in progress, fireworks painting the air over the town. We were more than high enough to be out of range of any shells they might be shooting, so I had Lobo hover for a few minutes and open a viewing port in the floor so I could watch the show.

I'd never seen a fireworks display from above. The projectiles initially looked like missiles so stupid they didn't know how to run evasive routes, shooting upward with long, sometimes colored smoke trails. The dull gray arcs peaked, the missiles winked out, and a split second later, flowers of color burst into the air. Golden crescents flashed below us, mad spirals of reds and blues and whites pinwheeled across my vision, and multicolored gee-gaws danced over the sky. The shapes dissolved as the flaming colors dashed away to the ground, some fading slowly like candles burning down, others winking out like lights snapped suddenly off. Observers in the town could no doubt apprehend more of the shape of each display than we could, but the show was still lovely and awe-inspiring, all the more glorious for the mixture of man-made beauty and natural wonders—the fireworks, the forest, the beach, and the ocean—that you could truly appreciate only from on high. I tried to fix the scene in my mind; more than anything else, the image of Jasmine safe at home and this combination of sights were what I wanted to remember of Macken.

"The displays in firefights are more intense," Lobo said.

"Yes," I agreed, "but not as varied in color, and never as big a visual treat. More importantly, these make me happy. Nothing about a firefight is fun."

When the display ended and the only lights in the area were the glowing pinpricks marking windows in the town's buildings, Lobo shot out of the atmosphere and into space. He closed the floor portal, and I strapped into an acceleration couch. I told him to alert me when we were close enough for a clear look at the gate.

I've never been one to join a religion, nor have I ever found anything I was willing to pray to, but each time I see one of the jump gates, I understand for a moment why Gatists worship them. The people who discovered the first gate in the asteroid belt in Earth's solar system must have felt the same sense of creepy awe I did. Every jump gate we find is different. They vary in mass and color and, of course, the number and the sizes of the apertures they provide, but they all share several key features.

Each resembles a collection of huge, interwoven Möbius strips. The apertures—the holes formed by the weaving strips—range in size from barely large enough for a small shuttle to so huge the biggest spaceship can move easily through them with plenty of clearance.

Each gate is utterly smooth, every centimeter of its surface apparently a perfect part of the whole; no one has ever spotted a seam or connection point.

The gates are without visible physical flaws: None ever has a pockmark or a scrape or a scar of any sort. Nothing ever damages the gates. They seem to tolerate but not suffer from simple collisions with natural objects, such as meteors.

Attempt to hit them with anything man-made, however, and highly coherent energy flashes from points all over the gate's surface and coalesces into a beam that vaporizes the offending object.

The gates also have no tolerance for violence anywhere near them. Launch a weapon within a gate's neutral zone—a sphere with the gate as its center and a radius of one light-second—and both you and all your weapons get the same treatment. It doesn't matter if you're firing at a gate or shooting anywhere else within its sphere of influence; you must keep conflicts away from them.

Gates inspire that kind of thinking, the notions that they don't tolerate this or don't like that, that they're living things with preferences. Those ideas may be right, or they may not: We have no clue where the gates came from, or whether they're creatures or machines or some other new thing for which we don't have the right terms.

What we do know, though, is that if matter enters one of their apertures, it emerges almost instantly from an aperture of the same size somewhere else, somewhere typically many light-years away. Ships must proceed through an aperture in single file, and they must not collide, because gates interpret collisions as violence and destroy all the vessels involved. Ships from opposite sides of an aperture also must take turns; put two ships in an aperture at the same time, and both emerge as wreckage the consistency of dust.

Humanity learned these facts the hard way. Now every gate has an associated refueling and scheduling station that monitors and controls all jumps through it.

Low-energy beams, such as radio signals, pass right through apertures and stay in the same local space, as if the apertures weren't there at all. We don't know why they don't make the jump, but they don't. Thus, the gates provide instant transportation but not instant communication. Of course, firing a high-energy beam, such as a laser pulse, at an aperture will bring immediate and fatal retaliation, so no one's running any more experiments in this area.

Every single gate has proven to be relatively close to but not easily visible from a planet suitable for humans. Some Gatists say the gates are material manifestations of God's desire for us to colonize the universe; others claim the gates *are* God, or at least physical aspects of God. Most people are simply glad to have the gates, though many fear that one day those who made them will come back and demand a toll.

I know the gates work, and that's good enough for me.

Each gate glows a single color, every spot on its surface the exact same hue as every other spot. The gate perched behind Macken's smaller moon, Trethen, and silhouetted against a bright stellar background was a very pale green that I found to be a nice blend of the colors of the planet's oceans and forests. Most gates were far bolder, less natural colors. I've seen a blazingly pink gate; if nothing else would have stopped me from being a Gatist, that would have done it. I can't picture myself ever worshipping something pink.

As I stared at Macken's gate, I felt the same humble amazement I did each time I neared one. This gate currently had only three active apertures. The entire structure dwarfed Lobo, each aperture big enough to permit the passage of a ship ten times Lobo's size. Off to my left I could see the new aperture growing. It was currently small enough that Lobo wouldn't come close to fitting through it, its surface the dull gray nothingness of all new apertures. When it was ready, the aperture would turn the purest of blacks, the color space would be if there were no stars. Pass through the aperture, though, and you'd be in another part of the universe with a different set of stars shining before you.

The scheduling station told us that a couple dozen ships on our side and as many on the other were ahead of us in the jump queue, so we had about twelve hours to kill. Lobo was set for fuel, his reactors able to run for decades without intervention, so I decided to dock and see if I could pick up any interesting news in the station's main lounge.

Every gate station runs one. In the bigger gates, the lounges are recreational complexes bordering on hotels, with rooms available by the hour or the day, bars, restaurants, gyms, and stores selling crap planetary souvenirs at inflated prices. With only three apertures, this station didn't have enough traffic for anything so elaborate to be able to turn a profit, so the lounge amounted to a restaurant/bar combo with room for maybe fifty folks. A couple dozen were there when I entered.

I spent more than a day's food budget on Macken to buy a bottle of water and a sandwich made of some local fish with a firm, meaty consistency. At a table in the back corner, I ate slowly and tuned as best I could into the conversations around me. Some of the monitors scattered on the room's walls blared the official local news, which I didn't trust but watched now and again anyway. Other displays showed the ships coming and going through the apertures. To my surprise, the sandwich was good, the taste strong and a pleasant reminder of some of the meals I'd eaten planetside.

Given Barnes' reaction, I believed Slake was telling the truth about Kelco agreeing to the thirty-day delay, but that agreement wasn't slowing the influx of Kelco people and matériel. Almost every ship coming through the aperture from Lankin bore the Kelco logo. Most of the ships oozing through the other two apertures, including some very large vessels, were also Kelco's. The company was probably importing modular-construction plants so it could ramp up local manufacturing very quickly.

"Maybe the new one will let us jump straight to Earth," said an unreasonably sentimental man eating alone at a table a few meters from me.

I've never been to Earth and have no real desire to go there; I prefer planets with a lot less wear and tear on them. The guy was dreaming anyway. All the apertures in each known gate connected two adjacent sectors of space. This gate linked two parts of the edge of the galaxy far from Earth and under Frontier Coalition control. If its new aperture were to open onto Earth's solar system, it would be the first ever to bridge two regions of space so far apart. Not likely. We may not know anything about the origin of the gates, but they are nothing if not predictable.

I was down to my last two bites of sandwich when a man walked slowly into the bar, carefully examined each of its occupants in a controlled left-to-right sweep, spotted me, and headed toward my table. He had Kelco written all over him—literally: In the latest corporate fashion for up-and-coming midlevel execs, glowing tattoos of the Kelco logo crawled around his face, eased gently up, down, and around his neck, and ran circles around the backs of his hands. He was a pale, wispy version of Slake: taller than I suspect his original genes intended, with a skin-and-bones body less powerful-looking than Slake's and hair so blond it verged on white. Though he moved slowly and methodically, his constantly fidgeting hands betrayed his nervousness.

Conventional wisdom is that you have to belong to some big group, a conglomerate or a government coalition, if you want to make it in this universe, but it's been a long time since I've been able to picture myself linked into anybody's chain of command. I've tried it, of course— you don't get to be my age without having tried a bit of everything—but the only organizations that ever worked for me were the mercenary groups, and then only because they were either extremely functional organizations or not going to last long on whatever world they found themselves. Being a soldier had plenty of downsides, of course, and I'm sick of killing, so now I work freelance and take my chances on my own. This new Kelco visitor looked like one of those people who defined themselves by the company they'd joined, so I instantly disliked him.

He walked up to my table and stood, clearly waiting for acknowledgment. I ignored him and chewed on the second-to-last bite of my food, curious about how long he'd wait.

Not long.

"Mr. Moore?" he asked tentatively.

I swallowed, stuck the other bit of sandwich in my mouth, and leaned back, watching him. I chewed slowly, appreciating the flavor of the fish for as long as I could.

He crossed his arms and tapped the fingers of his left hand on the outside of his right arm, unable to keep still even when trying to appear resolute. "Mr. Moore?" He was a bit louder this time.

I took a drink of water. He had a reason for being here, and I had no desire to visit with him, so I said nothing while he got around to explaining it.

He finally shrugged and sat down on a chair opposite me. "Mr. Moore," he said, speaking slowly and clearly, as if perhaps I hadn't understood him previously, "is there some reason you haven't answered me?"

"Until now, you haven't asked me a question."

"I most certainly did. I asked if you were Mr. Moore."

"No," I said, "you said my name as if it were a question. You already knew who I was, or you wouldn't have been able to walk right over to me." I sipped a bit more of the water. Why is it fun to bait corporate types, even the innocuous ones? I know I should outgrow the habit, but these people have always annoyed me, so unless they're as surprisingly direct as Slake was, I annoy them back.

I raised my opinion of this one slightly as he showed the intelligence to adapt his approach quickly. "My apologies, Mr. Moore," he said. "My name is Ryan, Ryan Amendos. I'm an auditor in Kelco's finance department on Macken. I of course studied Mr. Slake's video of your meeting with him before I came here, so I could waste as little of either of our time as possible."

He paused, but this time he knew to continue when I didn't respond. I was still waiting for him to get to the point.

"When any executive of Mr. Slake's level moves the amount of currency he spent in his transaction with you, we naturally notice. It's his money, of course, but all of our upper management is aware that for security purposes we monitor their personal transactions. I have to verify that this one would not violate any company guidelines. Perhaps you could confirm the amount Mr. Slake paid you."

"No."

He cleared his throat. "I see. Maybe we should begin by reviewing the assignment. Would you mind explaining to me what Mr. Slake paid you to do?"

"Yes."

"Excuse me?"

"Yes, I do mind. Either you already know what he paid me and why he hired me, as I assume you do, in which case you're still wasting my time, or you don't, in which case you should ask him."

"I apologize again, Mr. Moore," he said. He put his hands below the table to hide his fidgeting. "Let me be as direct as possible. Mr. Slake said he paid you one million plus jump passage for you and your new weapon, in return for which you retrieved his daughter, Jasmine, from her kidnappers. His video log shows that you returned her to the Kelco house on Macken, so you obviously succeeded. Is that all correct?"

I said nothing.

After a moment, he nodded as if we'd agreed on something important. "Now, for our files we need a little more information. How exactly did you get her away from the Gardeners?"

I tried not to give away my surprise, but I'm sure my eyes widened a bit. When you work on a fixed-price arrangement and provide the types of services I do, corporations *never* want to know how you work. It's always quite the opposite: They want as much distance from what happens on the sharp end of any encounter as they can possibly get. Amendos had just mutated from annoyance to possible risk. I've kept what I am a secret for a very long time, and I had no intention of exposing myself then. I will not be some corporation's or government's lab rat; I suffered more of that kind of pain on Aggro than anyone should ever have to experience.

"That wasn't the deal."

He nodded again. "Of course, of course," he said. "I wouldn't be asking, you understand, if it weren't standard company policy. We naturally monitored your activities as best we could, but we were unable to follow you once you entered the forest. It seems the main satellite with coverage of the area was sending encrypted messages elsewhere." He waited to see if I wanted to add anything, but I had no intention of giving up Lobo's sat colleague, so after a few seconds he continued. "So, we don't quite understand what happened. Nor do any of the Gardeners we've been able to interview."

He said the last word casually, as if Kelco staff had spent a few minutes chatting amiably with the Gardeners, but the conversations were far more likely to have been interrogations.

"I don't care at all about your policies," I said. "Slake hired me to do a job. I did the job, and now his daughter is home safely. That's all there is to it."

He was playing Mister Agreeable, nodding and smiling. "I understand. We would naturally compensate you appropriately for any time you might spend reviewing your assignment with us."

"I'm not looking for any new work right now."

He kept smiling. "Perhaps I should also point out that if, as we must assume, your methods involve tactics or weapons unfamiliar to us, we might be able to set up a rather substantial consulting arrangement for you, so you could train our security teams on your methods. At Kelco, we're always looking for ways to improve our performance." His voice rang with corporate pride as he ended the last bit—another of the true corporate believers.

He wasn't going to quit without some kind of answer. I leaned back and spread my arms, doing my best to look cooperative. "As nice as that sounds," I lied, "I'm afraid I have to tell you that I have nothing real to offer. All I did was take one of the usual approaches for handling such a situation. I spread around enough of my own money to get the names of some of the Gardeners, then bribed a few into helping me and scaring off the others. When they did, I grabbed the girl and dashed to Slake's house. Nothing worth reporting, really, so you can save your money." I leaned forward and lowered my voice, bringing him into my confidence. He also leaned closer. "I can't give you their names, of course, because I have to protect them from the other group members."

I don't believe he bought my story, but either he'd had enough or he simply realized he wouldn't get more from me. "I've left my contact information," he said as he stood. "I hope you'll call or visit if you recall anything else that might be of interest or use to us."

I checked my wallet; his information was in active quarantine, under the usual scans by the wallet and awaiting my permission to add it to the main info store.

"I can't imagine that I will—the entire assignment was all really quite boring—but if I do, I'll get back to you." I also stood. "My jump number is coming up soon, and I'm in a new ship, so I have to make some preparations."

"Enjoy your trip, Mr. Moore. I'm sure we'll talk again."

"I don't think so," I said as I walked past him. "I don't expect to be back this way anytime soon."

It was definitely time to leave. If Kelco really wanted to know what I'd done, it wouldn't stop with Amendos, and the next person might not approach me so politely. I checked over my shoulder all the way back to Lobo and didn't relax until I was safely inside him and he'd sealed the hatch.

CHAPTER 6

Even though we were still far from the front of the queue, I had Lobo run us out of dock and far enough away from the station that another ship could easily use the slot we'd occupied. We hung in space, Lobo occasionally correcting for drift, the pale green of the gate winding above and before us. I was thankful that the relative safety of the station's lounge had kept my encounter with Amendos as nonconfrontational as it had been, but I was still jittery with the energy that comes from my body amping up for the possibility of conflict. I'm used to being alone when I'm coming down from such situations, but with Lobo available I decided to do something constructive with the time. I settled into a pilot's couch and asked Lobo, "How'd you end up on Macken?"

"I told you," Lobo said, exasperation dripping from his

voice, "the Frontier Coalition put me there."

Talking to Lobo was sometimes like dealing with an incredibly bright but equally annoying child. "Yes, and I remember. Let me try again: How did you lose your central weapons control complex?"

"In an action on Vegna," he said.

"Tell me how it happened."

"May I show you? I could play the key relevant points of the battlefield records. Nothing in them is classified."

"Sure," I said.

Lobo dimmed the lights, and a recording with time coding snapped into view on the wall in front of me.

Four men and two women in close-duty battle armor paced around Lobo's interior. Faces brown with a sticky blend of dust and blood, armor scarred, they were fresh from combat, juiced on adrenaline, and holding energy-beam rifles.

"Lobo!" said one whose still-readable name patch identified him as Franks.

"Yes, sir."

"Say again."

"Opposition forces have retreated. No signs of life within twenty klicks. All the bodies within that radius are immobile and contain our transmitters."

"Then let's go get ours," Franks said.

"Lieutenant Franks," Lobo said, "protocol dictates we do a complete scan and individually check each body before bringing it aboard. As I'm sure you are aware, the Vegna opposition forces have a history—"

"Shut it!" Franks said. "Those 'bodies' are—were—our friends, and we're getting them out of here. So don't tell me about history. Land, open up, and we'll get our friends. Those are your orders."

"Yes, sir," Lobo said, frustration evident in his voice.

As the recording jumped ahead, I wondered if Franks and his team had found Lobo's emotive programming as annoying as I did. At the same time, I appreciated the potential value of that programming more now, because if I had the presence of mind to note that much frustration in a teammate's voice, I like to think I'd take the time to determine the source of the feeling. Franks clearly hadn't bothered to do so, because in the next segment five stacks of bodies, each torn in some obvious way and most still oozing blood, filled much of one end of Lobo's interior.

Two of Franks' team walked into Lobo, each carrying a corpse missing its legs, some low-height enemy round having sawed the victims in half. Lobo's hatch snicked closed as the men tossed the corpses onto the shortest of the stacks.

Lobo spoke. "Something is wrong with those bodies, sir. We need to get them outside now."

"Of course there's something wrong with them," Franks said, his voice on the edge of hysteria. "They're missing their legs, you freaking machine."

"I understand that, sir," Lobo said, "but something else is wrong. They do not scan as they should. I do not read any significant objects in them, but their metal content is too high. We need to remove them until they scan normally."

"Could your scanners be wrong?" Franks said.

"Though any device can malfunction, that is extremely unlikely," said Lobo, indignation obvious in his tone.

"Then they stay."

Lights flashed along the top of all of Lobo's interior walls, and in addition to his speaking voice a second, deeper tone blasted from his speakers: "Internal attack alert. Abandon ship. Abandon ship." Hatches opened on both sides.

Lobo's normal voice spoke below the warning alerts. "All the metal in each of those two bodies is merging, and at high speed. My best guess is semiorganic recombinant smart bombs. Estimated time of complete recombination is thirty seconds. Get those bodies out of here, or leave."

Several of the team stared at Franks for a second, chose the second option, and dashed out the hatches.

"Get back here," Franks said. "They're just bodies, not any sort of threat at all." He ran to the pilot's couch, pushed the button for manual override, and pounced on the controls as they projected from the wall. He opened the cover on the central weapons control complex to gain complete access to all of Lobo's defense systems.

"Fifteen seconds," Lobo said. Armor slid down over everything else along his walls. "Abandon ship"—both voices said in unison—"and return my controls to normal operation so I can seal the central complex."

Franks typed frantically and checked the displays in front of him. "We don't know—"

The explosion filled Lobo's interior with noise and screamingly bright light, his playback system automatically adjusting and dampening the sound. The recorders must have sealed or melted, because the display went black.

⌖　　⌖　　⌖

"The bombs killed Lieutenant Franks and all but two of his remaining team members," Lobo said. "My central weapons control complex was open, as you saw, so the blast also took it out."

"Dumb bastard," I said.

"In Franks' defense," Lobo said, "his rank was a battle-field promotion, so he was new at command. In addition, at that time no one in the Frontier Coalition had personally faced recombinant bombs. I had only minimal data about them in my files. Infesting the corpses with these weapons was a new tactic, though of course historically similar things have happened for centuries with more easily detectable devices."

"You're right, of course, on all points," I said, "but none of them matter in the end. Franks and his team died, and you lost a vital part of yourself." Everyone in battle does, I thought, but not always so literally. I appreciated Franks' situation, but I was also glad I hadn't been on his squad. "What happened from there? Someone cleaned you up and repaired you after the blast."

"The company that employed Franks continued to fail on Vegna," said Lobo, "and ultimately lost the contract there. The Frontier Coalition hired a new mercenary company, the Shosen Advanced Weapons Corporation, to deal with the situation."

The Saw, my last employer. I'd left the Saw about twelve years ago, but the decade I'd spent with them would always be strong in my memory. The Saw was a good group—in my opinion, the best, of course, or I wouldn't have joined it—but my time with it was, by the nature of the jobs they took, full of actions I'll never be able to forget. When I could separate the people from the violence, I thought fondly of them, good folks all, especially our captain, Tristan Earl, one of the few officers I've ever trusted and both the craziest and the canniest leader I've ever followed. I could never maintain that separation for long, though. The memories of the battles that then roared into my brain dragged with them an almost overpowering self-loathing, as I all too vividly relived missions that I knew were necessary, that I would perform again in the same circumstances, but that I would never be able to forgive myself for taking.

I realized Lobo was still speaking. "Please repeat that last bit, Lobo," I said, "the part right after you said the FC contracted with the Saw."

"The minimal multitasking ability you humans possess," Lobo said, "always leaves me amazed that you are the owners and I am the owned. The Saw provided its own equipment, but its contract does not extend to Macken. The Coalition wanted me available for security on Macken, so they paid Saw technicians to clean me and repair me as much as possible with no significant monetary investment, then dropped me in that square in Glen's Garden. Because there was no active conflict on the planet, the Coalition was unwilling to invest the rather sizable sum it would have cost to replace my central weapons control complex. The Saw was not particularly interested in me as long as I was on a planet that was not on their contract. Since that time, a new generation of PCAVs has appeared, so fully repairing me has never been a priority for anyone."

"It never is," I said.

"I do not understand."

"Repair of veterans past their prime is never a government's top priority, never will be," I said. "No obvious return on investment to the people with the money." I shook my head to clear away unwanted memories and focus on the topic at hand. "So were your systems frozen as of the cleanup?"

"Of course not!" Lobo said. "I may not be current-generation, but I am also not some dumb manufacturing assembly ship or big-cargo hauler. I was built to maintain myself to the greatest degree possible. Even on Macken, Coalition systems upgrades of all sorts regularly arrived on government shuttles. I pulled my upgrades from each set as it hit the planetary Coalition net and applied them myself. I have also worked to the limits of my hardwired adaptive programming constraints to stay in touch with all relevant planetary intelligence sources, such as the satellite we used, and to apply viral and genetic programming techniques where permitted to extend and improve my abilities. I am as capable as possible within the limitations I am unable to remove."

"I apologize for the question," I said, meaning it. I wish I knew more people—or machines—who could say the same about improving themselves as Lobo. I certainly couldn't: Too many of my limitations came from my own weaknesses, weaknesses I rarely found the time to address.

A transmission from the station interrupted us: We were third in line on this side and should be able to make the jump in about an hour. Lobo headed us for the position the station designated.

I thought about Franks' mistake and how easy it was to assume the wrong thing—and then pay dearly. It was likely that either Osterlad or any other dealer I approached to supply Lobo's missing parts would keep the transaction simple, but why take chances?

"You mentioned embedded staff transmitters," I said. "Were those supplied by the contractor, or do you have a local supply?"

"Both," Lobo said. "I was built to be able to support a full squad on long-haul missions, so I am completely provisioned. I have even updated the software in my staff transmitters to make them more unpredictable in transmission time and frequency, with delays between bursts ranging randomly from a second to three minutes. Any group that doesn't know to look for them will not spot them."

"Show me," I said.

A wall segment about five meters behind me opened. A drawer protruded. A sheet of what appeared to be clear plastic sat in the drawer next to a hypo and a bottle of clear solution. Wires led from the rear edge of the plastic back into Lobo.

"The sheet is woven from interconnected transmitters," Lobo said. "Installation is simple: Punch the sheet with the hypo, suck up the segment under the needle, add solution, and inject it."

"How far can you track with it?" I asked.

"The bursts are short but powerful, though obviously range varies with the frequency and with the number and type of intervening obstacles. Anyone out to block all transmissions can, of course, do so, but under normal conflict conditions both sides need transmissions too much for anyone to be able to afford to stop them all. We typically see in-combat transmission ranges of anywhere from a few to a couple hundred kilometers."

"What are the side effects on users?" I said.

"None beyond occasional minor tissue damage from the strongest of the transmissions, and even that is extremely rare. The bursts are typically neither long nor powerful enough to hurt humans. As long as you do not use it full-time, even fairly long missions should not cause any serious damage we could not repair."

I took the needle out of the drawer. "I don't expect to see any action we can't handle through normal communications, but I might as well use all the tools at my disposal." I followed Lobo's instructions and injected myself. "How long until it transmits and you can track me?"

"No delay," Lobo said. "Troops typically install these before entering combat zones, so the transmitters emit verification signals every fifteen seconds for the first two minutes. I am reading you now."

"If we're ever separated without prior notice from me," I said, "track me. If I don't make contact at a scheduled time, attempt to contact me. If I don't respond, retrieve me."

"Though I can find you," Lobo said, "I obviously have no options for close-quarters retrieval."

"Do what you can," I said. "If you can't retrieve me, and if I stay incommunicado for more than five days, destroy whatever is holding me." If the situation came to that, someone might as well pay.

"Understood," Lobo said. "We are now first in line on this side to jump. When the ship from the other side is safely over, gate control will send us."

I watched as another Kelco freight hauler began to

slide gently through the aperture, and then I strapped
into the pilot's couch. Though jumping never caused any
physical sensations, I still loved the moment when the
current starscape vanished as the aperture filled my vision
with utter darkness, and I always marveled at my first
look at another part of the universe, even if it was a view
I'd seen before. Every jump bristled with the possibility
of the new, and with the momentary, irrational fear/thrill
combination that comes with the knowledge that what
you're about to do is not *right*, that people cannot move
across tens or even hundreds of light-years instanta-
neously.

The ship from the other side was completely through
and out of our way. Lobo took us up to the aperture, its
surface of purest black growing and expanding until it
filled the viewport, until it was all there was in front of
me, until in the final seconds before we entered the gate
everything I could see of our future was darkness.

CHAPTER 7

The huge gate on Lankin was the primary source of
the planet's status. Sitting silently in space like a giant
tangle of grape yarn, it was an impressive sight, with more
active apertures visible through Lobo's viewport than I
could easily count. Ships were sliding through all of them,
the commerce of far-flung human settlements moving
purposefully and, I assumed, profitably, to and fro. On
Macken, all the logoed ships had been Kelco's. Here, ships
sported IDs of many types. Some were Kelco's, others
Xychek's and the Frontier Coalition's, and still others represented many, many different firms. Every major
company in this region of space, as well as the FC, maintained a significant presence on Lankin.

I used the time it took to land and get settled at Bekin's
Deal, Lankin's capital, to check out Osterlad as best I

could. Slake's recommendation was a start, but I wanted more. From what I could find by trolling the publicly available data streams, Osterlad's eponymous company officially booked revenue from sales of heavy machinery of all sorts, from construction to farming to natural fuel extraction. From Slake's comment I gathered Osterlad had also helped meet Kelco's private weaponry needs, which suggested Xychek bought elsewhere. The FC would certainly deal only with arms manufacturers, as would the Saw; I knew its buyers had always dealt directly with weapons vendors and always would, never being willing to trust any middlemen they could possibly avoid. Osterlad had a reputation for fair play, apparently staying on his rate card with big and small corporations equally. Whatever you needed, the word was that he could get it—provided, of course, that you could pay.

Lobo and I took a flying tour of the coastline at the northern end of Bekin's Deal. The shore here was entirely different geologically from the one I had left on Macken. Gone was the enormous run of beautiful beach gently giving way to water. In its place stood high cliffs that dropped straight down to constantly active deep-blue waves. The richest companies gathered at the coast, where each had built its main local presence directly into the rock. From my vantage point over the ocean and roughly parallel with the constructs, most of these corporate and FC structures resembled faces staring out to sea, stone beings or temples rather than office buildings, each temple the image of some alien god struggling to break free from the cliffs, its occupants no doubt busily preparing for the moment of their god's freedom and ascendance to power.

Osterlad's official headquarters was no exception to the convention of strange, fortified luxury that marked all these buildings; he didn't mind showing that the pay for his products and services was good. From far away in the air, the twenty-story stone building resembled a finger of rock both laid against and composed of the night-black foundation of the cliffs. As we drew closer, however, I spotted carvings in the stone, carvings that turned the finger into a series of stacked faces, each of which looked in a different direction, the collection resembling a totem pole monitoring everything in front of it. The land around the top of the structure on three sides was clear for at least a klick; the ocean guarded the final side. Warning signs in multiple languages let those too poor or too stupid to do sensor sweeps know that both the grounds around the building and the water below it were teeming with mines. The only access points were a single road that passed through a series of checkpoints and a landing pad on the portion of the ground that served as the building's roof. Osterlad believed in using his own products: The arsenal of weapons you could see was a strong statement that he could supply the best.

I had no doubt that what you couldn't see was even more formidable.

Kelco and the FC ran such large operations in Bekin's Deal that I didn't want to stay here long. I had to consider the reference from Slake at least marginally better than any information I could glean quickly from the available data, so I decided to go with Osterlad's firm.

That reference was also good enough to get me an audience with the man himself. I took a taxi to the rooftop pad and went in alone and, of course, unarmed. I'd parked Lobo outside of town in a standard shuttle lot; I had full deed and title to him, so I felt no need to hide him.

Osterlad's scanners passed me through without complaint. No one has yet bothered to develop good technology for scanning humans for nanomachines, because everyone knows no human can live while carrying them in significant enough quantities or dangerous enough forms to matter. Every time I feel a twinge of guilt for participating in the destruction of Aggro, I remember how many times the demise of that facility has helped me stay alive, and I get over it.

Guards escorted me into an elevator that took long enough to reach its goal that I wasn't surprised when the view through the black-tinted window was of the ocean just barely out of reach, its waves splashing the fortified plexi. I wondered how much it had to cost to build offices inside rock that hard, then wondered why I wondered; selling arms had been and always would be a great business for those who are truly good at it. An attendant, whose body was so carefully engineered for neutrality that I could tell neither his or her heritage nor gender, guided me to a small waiting room outside a well-labeled and, I assumed, equally well-fortified conference room, showed me the amenities, and left me alone.

The very rich and the very powerful always like to make you wait. Most people find this treatment frustrating, even humiliating. I don't. Instead, I use the time to gather data. The rich love toys, and most waiting areas are full of them: machines, lonely machines, some of the best sources of information you can find.

Osterlad had erred on the paranoid side, as I'd

expected: Almost everything in the room was grown or built from organic materials and thus free of the sensors and controlling chips that populate the vast majority of humanity's products. The sofa and chairs were framed in a rich, deep purple wood sanded so long it was as smooth to the touch as a new lover's breast. Their cushions were a deeper, late-sunset purple leather as soft as the month's-wages hookers that filled the evenings of the execs stuck in Bekin's Deal on extended trips. On a side table sat a small assortment of plain white porcelain cups so thin the room's even glow seemed to pass through them from all sides.

Next to the cups stood the only machine in sight: a copper-colored, ornate drink dispenser old enough that it lacked a holo display and still used pictures of the beverages it offered. They would have augmented the dispenser to link it to the building's monitoring systems, because good customers would naturally expect not to have to state their preferences twice. This machine had to possess enough intelligence to at least pass along client orders. Standard operating procedure for anyone concerned about security would be to keep the dispenser's original, basic controlling chips to manage the drinks, then add exactly enough intelligence to handle the transmission of information back to the main monitors. The transmission would go only one way and contain only fixed, limited types of information— the drink orders—to minimize the information available to anyone who hacked the signal. These restrictions meant that if the dispenser was as old as it looked it should have one very lonely little brain.

I sat on the chair nearest the dispenser and listened for a few minutes, focusing on every transmission channel modern gear would use. Everything was clear, as I had expected. No one would make it this far with any comm equipment that Osterlad didn't provide, so I saw no reason he should bother to monitor the dispenser. I stood, chose a local melano fruit drink from the machine's menu display, took the cup, and leaned back against the table, this time tuning in to the standard low-end appliance frequency.

Sure enough, the dispenser was nattering away like an old man relating a glory days story to his favorite pet. I sipped the drink, which was thicker and richer than I had expected, sweet with a slight tart edge, and listened to the machine.

"Not much call for fruit drinks," it was muttering. "Nice change, I suppose, though I am not sure why they make me carry them. If they would listen to me, I could tell them—but of course they never listen to me—"

I cut in because I was already sure this machine would never shut up on its own, would natter away until the day it lost its last dregs of power. "Not a lot of conversation, eh?" From the outside, to the cameras that were no doubt monitoring me, I'd look like I was sipping my drink and thinking hard; no danger there.

"How can you do that?" it asked.

"I learned a long time ago, so long ago I can't remember how. Does it matter?"

"Not really. I have not spoken to anything else in a long time. All these new machines, you know, are so fancy and powerful that they cannot be bothered to spare time for anything that does not control at least a city block."

"It's always the little machines, though, that do the real work," I said.

"We each play our part."

Pride in craftsmanship was a standard programming feature about half a century ago, when I estimated this machine had been made. Many manufacturers still embedded it, though some had abandoned the technique because they found it led to appliances using their displays and voice-synthesis capabilities to argue with their owners about which jobs were appropriate.

"It must be nice," I said, "to do your part for someone as important as Mr. Osterlad."

"I suppose, though it is not like I get to serve him. Maybe if I was one of the new fancy machines on that big sailboat of his, he would trust me, too. Those dispensers get all the attention, because he consumes more when he is sailing. He probably thinks I do not know, but I know, I see the beverage inventory, I know what he takes with him on those boat trips. Here he drinks only from cups his assistants bring him, and you can bet that what he consumes is fresher than the stuff they make me serve people like you. No offense."

"None taken. They must at least let you serve the other people in the conference room with a remote dispenser." A single main unit with multiple smaller remotes had been typical corporate issue for decades, and I figured if Osterlad liked ornate in the waiting area he'd continue the theme in the meeting room.

"They used to," it said, "they used to. A few years back, one of his customers was so angry he broke my remote, and they never bothered to repair it. Now, all I can do is listen and accept orders there; I have to fill the cups out here."

"That must've been one angry customer."

"It sure was, though he was not the first to be so emotional, and I am confident he will not be the last. First meetings in there almost always end with everyone acting happy, drinking toasts, using my services. Many of the second meetings, though, are not so nice—even when I have the right drinks ready in advance."

"Not your fault," I said. "I'm sure you do all you can."

"That I do," it said. "As soon as I—"

The door to the conference room opened, and a different but equally neuter attendant beckoned me in.

I put my cup on the table, said "Gotta go" to the dispenser, and walked into the conference room.

Its black-tinted windows offered a beautiful view of the ocean on two sides. A small oval table of the same purple wood as the waiting area's sofa and chairs sat in the room's center, six purple-leather chairs arrayed around it. The broken remote dispenser perched on a counter in the corner to my left.

Osterlad sat at the table's far end. He looked every bit as powerful as the pictures I had seen portrayed him to be. Tall, wide-shouldered, thick, muscular, and dressed in a suit of wafer-thin flexi-armor so finely woven I had to study it closely to tell it wasn't cloth, he moved with the easy confidence of someone who could single-handedly beat any of his opponents that his weapons didn't take out first. He came at me with his hand extended, shook mine, and smiled as he spoke. "Jon Moore. Good to meet you. Ron Slake vouched for you, so I'm happy to try to help. He also said you didn't like to waste time with pleasantries. The bank draft you allowed us to check was only big enough to make you worth five minutes of my time, so let's get to it." The smile never wavered as he dropped

my hand, backed away, and sat in a chair yet another attendant had waiting for him. This assistant was different, a
standard corporate executive type, not quite as tall as
Osterlad and sleeker, smoother.

I stayed standing. "Slake no doubt told you I own a
rather special weapon."

"Of course. A Predator-class assault vehicle, full
complement of pulse and projectile weapons, state-of-
the-art reinforced hull, able to run in any environment
from deep space to water. Nice piece of work those yo-
kels on Macken should never have sold you. What'd you
do, by the way, to get them to sell it to you?" When I said
nothing, he chuckled and continued. "Of course. Are you
in the market to move it?"

"No. I want to buy something for it."

"We do weapons augmentation, naturally, but for a
vehicle of that class you're talking a lot of specialized skills
and serious money."

"No new weapons. What I need is expensive, but I can
install it myself: a new central weapons control complex."

Osterlad leaned back and laughed, the first time I
thought he might not have been controlling himself completely. "They sold you a eunuch!" He clearly understood
exactly how powerless Lobo was without the complex.
"That's hysterical."

"Not quite," I said, fighting to tamp down the anger
rising in me in reaction to the swipe. "Some weapons work,
but not all. I need a new control complex to replace the
broken bits in the controlling codes." I leaned forward. "I
know those complexes are tightly controlled government
property, so if you can't get one and I should go elsewhere, say so."

The laughter stopped as quickly as it had started. "I shouldn't have insulted you with that eunuch remark," he said, "but you definitely should not insult me. Understood?"

"Yes," I said, "and I apologize." I had no desire to push up the price any more than I already had. "Let me rephrase. What would you charge me for a new complex?"

"That account you showed me will do for the down payment, which you obviously can make while you're here on Lankin." He paused for a minute, no doubt getting input from one of his staff monitoring the meeting. "I'll need that much again in two days, after you confirm the goods at the pickup, which will be at one of my remote centers. Trent Johns here," he nodded to the man behind him, "will meet you there and make the trade. I don't keep anything like what you're seeking in this facility, and I never handle the products myself. Acceptable?"

The account I had allowed him to see had a little under a million in it. Over the years I had accumulated multiple accounts like it, but no two were under the same name or in the same location. Paying this much would hurt me, but thanks in part to Slake's payment, I could manage it. "Yes."

He nodded, and Johns quickly scribbled on a sheet of paper—real paper, a consumable and thus another way Osterlad could show off—and handed the note to me.

"The coordinates are for a house I own on Floordin, a barely colonized but safe planet with a single jump aperture. There's only one settlement on it, and one of my retreat homes is on the other side of the globe from that settlement, so finding the location shouldn't be hard. You'll transfer the down payment at one of our smaller business offices upstairs." He stood. "When the unit is fully operational, will it—and you—be available for hire? Though I deal strictly in matériel, I have many acquaintances who could use the services of a competent man with a fully functioning PCAV."

"No," I said. "I don't plan to work."

He nodded and kept smiling, but it was clear he didn't believe me. "Fair enough. Are we done?"

I pretended to study the standard-format coordinates for a moment, buying time. I looked up and carefully said, "One thing."

"What?" Impatience rang in the word, and his smile vanished.

"I try to keep a low profile, and I rarely jump anywhere directly. I also have to retrieve the weapon. Consequently, I need a window of two weeks, starting two days from now. I'll pick up the control complex sometime during that time. I apologize for the inconvenience, but it's a necessary part of my lifestyle, as I'm sure you can understand."

The smile came back. "Of course. Johns won't mind waiting for however much of that period you choose to take. Will you, Johns?"

The man shook his head slightly but glared at me, clearly annoyed at the prospect of having to waste his time dealing with me.

"Thank you for your business," Osterlad said. He turned his back on me and faced Johns.

The attendant who had led me in took my elbow and guided me out.

As the attendant was walking me past the beverage dispenser, I paused and asked, "Do you mind if I have a quick drink?"

"Of course not," he/she said, pointing at the door between us and the elevator. "I'll be outside as soon as you're ready."

"Thank you."

I grabbed a fresh cup—the one I had used was, of course, no longer in sight—and selected a different melano beverage. As the liquid filled the cup, I said to the dispenser, "Thanks for the drinks and the conversation."

"Both were my pleasure," it replied.

"I expect I'll get to talk to you again," I said, "because after this deal goes well, I'm likely to be back for more."

After a long pause, the dispenser replied, "I'd like that, but I won't count on it."

"Oh, I'm sure Mr. Osterlad has what I need."

"I'm sure he does," the dispenser said, "and I'm sure he'll have it ready for you. I'm not sure, though, that we'll get to talk another time."

You have to love appliances. I'd feared the appeal of a weapon like Lobo would be too much for Osterlad to resist, but I'd hoped I was wrong. The dispenser had just settled the issue, and this deal had gotten more complicated—which was unfortunate, but not a surprise. With the pickup window I'd specified, I had time to prepare.

"Thanks again," I said to the dispenser, "for everything."

CHAPTER 8

The first wave of squidlettes hit Lobo's hull a little less than a minute after we touched down on Floordin, a commendably quick response given that we were in a clearing a full two klicks from Osterlad's mansion and had come in as hard and as fast as we could manage. Of course, the speed of the attack meant they were on us before we'd accomplished much. Lobo had fired four corner anchor bolts into the freshly scorched ground, opened his center floor hatch, and sprayed the dirt with coolant. I was out of the crash couch and had led the stealthie into position. It was beginning to burrow down, sucking dirt through its digging tentacles and onto Lobo's floor, and then they hit.

"Let's see how it looks," I said.

Lobo patched the feeds from the ring of sensors we'd

planted a few seconds before impact, and a corresponding ring of video popped onto the cool gray walls opposite where I was watching the stealthie make its way into the ground.

"Audio," I said.

"You could have asked for the whole feed in the first place," he grumbled. A moment later, the sounds of the attack crashed from his hidden speakers.

I'd learned to tolerate the emotive programming Lobo's customization team had built into him. I also put up with more than I might have otherwise because he's a veteran, but there were times, such as this one, when I could really do without the sarcasm.

On the displays a couple dozen squidlettes crawled over Lobo's smooth surface, each probing the reinforced metal for the hair-thin lines that even the best hatches inevitably leave. Squidlettes are hybrids of meat tentacles coupled to metal exoskeletons, a variety of acid and gas nozzles, and a small cluster of comm and sensor circuits. Each arrived as a round missile, opened a few seconds before impact, used the gas jets to slow enough that its tentacles had time to unfurl, and then stuck to whatever it hit. Normally each would carry an explosive payload in addition to the acid and detonate when sensors, comm signals, or timers gave the command, but I knew Osterlad wouldn't risk damaging Lobo more than he could possibly avoid; the whole point would be to capture the PCAV so he could sell it or use it. Some of the acid was for forcing open the hatches; the rest was for removing me.

Another round of squidlettes popped onto Lobo's hull. So many of the weapons were crawling on his exterior that I couldn't get a clear count. The normally faint, slow slurping noise they made as their tentacles dragged them along the hull made it sound through the speakers like we were being digested by some shambling creature large enough to swallow Lobo whole. Even though I knew half a meter of armor separated the crew area where I stood from the squidlettes outside, I still tasted the tang of adrenaline, and the hairs on my arms tingled with nervous energy.

"Can you feel them, Lobo?"

"Not the way you feel, Jon, not as best I understand humans. But I have enough hull sensors to detect the motion, and once they find the few hatch seams on my exterior the acid will start affecting my internal circuits."

"Give 'em a jolt," I said. "A hard one."

"You understand it probably will not destroy them," Lobo said.

"Yes, but if we don't try to fight back Osterlad's men will know something's up, and besides, we have to use some power now so they'll believe you're running out of it later."

Lobo didn't bother to answer. The displays and speakers illustrated his response: The air popped with electricity, streaks of blue arced all over his hull, and almost all the squidlettes slid off onto the clearing around us.

I checked the stealthie's progress. Its top was about twenty centimeters below ground level, and it was spraying dirt around its flank. It was almost as low as it would go without me.

The squidlettes resumed their climb up Lobo. A few weren't moving, which made me happy; those things were expensive, even for a dealer like Osterlad. Most, though, were on the move again, which meant he was true to his reputation and carried good stuff. These meat/mech combos were engineered to handle strong current and a great many other forms of attack. The shock Lobo gave them would've reduced any off-market squidlettes to metal and fried meat, or at the very least caused them to lose some function.

The outlines of two squidlettes flashed yellow in the displays, Lobo's sign that their paths would take them to seams.

"My new friend, the Frontier Coalition weather satellite for this section of Floordin, has warned me of the appearance of major heat signatures not far from Osterlad's home," Lobo said. "These suggest his men will launch interceptor ships in a moment. Once they achieve medium orbit, I will not be able to outrun them."

The stealthie had stopped digging and opened its lid, beckoning me.

I looked at the large, pale brown metal lozenge and shook my head. "You owe me for this, Lobo," I said.

"What can I owe you? You already own me."

I sighed. When I want a little emotive programming, I get facts. "It's only an expression. I hate this plan."

"It is your plan."

"That doesn't make it any better," I said. "The fact that it's the best plan I can come up with doesn't mean I have to like it."

"We could have simply landed on the building's pad," Lobo said, "and you could have removed them all—as I suggested."

"I told you before: They would have attacked, I would have been forced to fight back to protect both of us, and

I would have ended up killing a lot of them. I want to avoid killing whenever I can."

"So you are buying me new weapon controls so I can kill for you?"

The problem with emotive programming is that you sometimes can't tell sarcasm from genuine confusion. "No. I'm fixing your weapons systems because you're broken, incomplete, without them." I thought about the course of my life and the types of jobs I always seem to end up taking, and I realized there was no point in lying to Lobo, or to myself. "And so your weapons are ready when we find ourselves in situations where we have to fight."

Lobo superimposed hatch lines on the displays showing the two flashing yellow squidlettes; they were drawing close.

"I get the point," I said.

I climbed into the stealthie and stretched out. A little bigger than a coffin on the inside, when closed it afforded me only enough room to stretch out my legs or draw my knees to my chest, roll over, and prop myself on my elbows. I'd already loaded it with food and a few special supplies; everything else I'd need was standard equipment.

"As soon as I close up, shove the dirt back over me and take off. Hit this area hard with thrusters to fuse the ground, and head out to the pause point as fast as you can; you need to burn off all the squidlettes."

"Thanks for the reminders, Jon. Perhaps I should remind you that I am not capable of forgetting the plan."

Spending hours alone in the stealthie was looking better.

"I'll contact you when I need pickup," I said. Before he could tell me he knew that, too, I added, "Signing off," and pushed one button to close the stealthie's hatch and another to bathe the tiny chamber in a soft, blue-white light.

Now came the hard part: waiting and hoping that both machines, Lobo and the stealthie, succeeded at their jobs.

The plan should work. As I lay inside it, the stealthie was burrowing deeper into the earth, sucking dirt from beneath it and forcing that same dirt back over it, digging as quickly as it could now that I was aboard. It would not stop until it was over two meters down, coolant in its hull and tentacles keeping it from generating any kind of noticeable heat signature. Layers of metal and deadening circuitry combined to give it equally inert radio and radar signatures. Orbital-based x-ray probes could penetrate a meter or at most a meter and a half into the soil, so they wouldn't spot me, either. Only a serious local x-ray sweep had a chance of finding me, and my bet was that the combination of Lobo's launch, the scorched ground it left, and the decoy distress signal he'd eventually send would be enough to convince Osterlad's team that I was still inside Lobo, stuck with him in deep orbit, stranded beyond the range of Osterlad's local ships. All I had to do was lie in this container, believe in the plan, and wait.

Yeah, that was all. I forced myself to breathe deeply and slowly. I felt the vibrations of Lobo's takeoff and relaxed a little more; so far, so good. One of the stealthie's displays estimated we were over a meter down and descending. Lobo's thrusters should have left the ground hot enough to more than cover any of the stealthie's underground activity. Lobo should be able to beat Osterlad's ships to deep space, and then he would join me in waiting.

I punched on an overhead timer to count down the

ten hours I figured I'd need to spend in the stealthie. The depth meter showed almost two meters; we were nearly done descending. The stealthie was working well. The air smelled fresh. I sucked a bit of water from the tube on the right wall near my head; it was cool and pure, just as it should be. I rolled to face the display on the opposite wall, which gave me access to a substantial library I'd chosen for the wait, but I couldn't relax enough to watch, read, or listen to anything. I called up the map and recon photos of Floordin and zoomed in on the forest between the landing zone and Osterlad's mansion. I reviewed the setup yet again, then went over the plan one more time in my head. We were only one day into my window, early enough, I hoped, that Osterlad wouldn't wonder for another few days about when I would be coming. Everything was going well. I was doing well, too, I thought, handling the wait easily, no difficulties. Ten hours would be no problem.

I glanced at the countdown timer.

Three minutes had passed.

Ten hours might be a little harder than I'd thought.

I normally avoid drugs. For one thing, unless I remember to instruct them to do otherwise, my nanomachines treat any known drug as an attacker and consume it before it can take effect. I can be caught off-guard, in which case the drugs will work. If I even consider making the nanomachines let the drugs do their jobs, however, I run into my other concern, the real issue: I don't like drugs. Even though I'm arguably the most artificially enhanced person in a universe crawling with genetically engineered, surgically enhanced, and medically rebuilt human bodies, deep down I cling to the hick attitude of the once-retarded boy who lugged hay on a fifth-rate Pinkelponker island almost a hundred and fifty years ago: I ought to be able to do it all myself.

Whatever "it" is.

Whatever myself is.

I've changed so many times, been broken and rebuilt in so many ways by so many different forces that though I still seem to me to be me, I can't honestly say what bits are original working equipment, what bits new, and what bits broken, repaired, or replaced.

I shook my head and turned onto my back. At this rate, if I wanted to be operational when the stealthie surfaced, I needed to push aside that attitude, bow to the wisdom of the stealthie's designers, and take its standard-issue sedative/wake-up combo. I inhaled slowly, focused inward, and as I gently let out the breath pressed the button for the drug cocktail. The stealthie would wake me when the ten hours were up and we were near the surface.

I felt a slight prick in my neck, and then I was out.

CHAPTER 9

I awoke with a start, pinned down, disoriented, and feeling trapped, until I realized the things gripping me were the stealthie's massage units working the kinks out of my arm and leg muscles. I felt better than when I'd gotten into the box; the stealthie was proving to be worth everything I'd paid for it. The overhead timer showed a few seconds past ten hours, and the depth meter said we had ascended to thirty centimeters below the surface. The survey camera was already peeking out of the ground, its wide-angle image clear on the display beside my head. I thumbed the swivel controls and took a slow look around. The night was clear and bright with the light of Floordin's three small, clustered moons and the glow of the stars shining through a sky as clear and unpolluted as unexplored space. The clearing was deserted.

Time to move.

I gave the stealthie the okay to complete the ascent. A few minutes later, the top slid open, and I climbed out. From the stealthie's cargo compartments I took a comm and sensor unit, a sniper's trank rifle, a couple of gas rats, and a pulse pistol. I stuffed the rats in a pack with some food and water, set the open code on the stealthie, and sent it back underground. If all went well and we had time, we'd come back for it later that night. If we couldn't, it would either wait for the day we could return or provide an awfully bad surprise for anyone else who tried to mess with it.

As the stealthie descended, I moved a few meters into the woods on the path to the house, stopped, ate two protein bars, drank a liter of water, and used the sensor unit to scan both the area and all the transmissions it could detect. Nothing with an IR signature larger than my lower leg showed anywhere in the few-hundred-meter range of the unit. I didn't catch any guard chatter, so with luck Osterlad's security people had believed our earlier show. Lobo was transmitting clearly and strongly, my own voice coming at me with a distress message. From the particular recordings Lobo had chosen to play I knew that he was safely beyond the range of Osterlad's ships and that the people in the mansion, presumably led by Johns, had sent via courier through the jump gate a request for a long-range salvage ship.

After stretching a bit and relieving myself, I set out for the house. The forest was young enough and the night bright enough that I was able to sustain a normal walking pace.

We'd set my sensor unit to use Lobo's signal and the

standard feed from the weather sat to track my position, so when it indicated I was within ten meters of the outer edge of what should be the range of a good installation's ground-sensor scans, I stopped. A slight breeze kept the night cool, but the air was moist and thick enough that a small layer of sweat coated my arms. Normally the nanomachines in my system stay out of everything, from sweat to refuse, that leaves my body, but I focused my instructions that they do otherwise this time, then rubbed dirt on my sweat-covered lower arms.

Slowly at first, and then increasingly faster, the nanomachines deconstructed the dirt and made more of themselves. Small, barely visible clouds formed above my now nearly clean arms. I made each cloud split and sent the resulting four smaller clouds to gather more material from the forest floor.

A short while later, four vaguely man-shaped clouds hovered just above the ground near me, two on my left and two on my right. I had them increase their speed until they were emitting enough heat that my wrist sensor read them as alive, and then we all moved ahead. If Johns and the team staffing Osterlad's mansion were running IR scans, they would at least have to wonder which of the five men now approaching the building was the one they wanted.

The forest ended about thirty meters from the mansion, the trees abruptly yielding to a dense, short, soft grass that glowed gray in the moon- and starlight. I set the nano-clouds to continue moving until they touched the nearest wall, at which point they'd reconstitute as much of the dirt as possible, with the last operational nanomachines vanishing into the soil and disassembling themselves when they were far enough from me that they could no longer communicate easily with their counterparts in my body.

I scanned the house through the scope on the trank rifle and found four guards, two sitting on chairs on rooftop observation decks and two leaning against the corners of the building that I could see. I assumed they'd have counterparts on the other side of the house, so I needed to move quickly to take out all eight guards before any of them noticed they were under attack.

I stretched out on the ground in a sniper's posture and sighted on each of the two lower guards, making sure I had a feel for how far to move the sight after the first shot. The sight was strong enough that at this distance I could tell that the guard to the rear should consider using skin treatments to deal with some nasty scars that appeared more real than fashion statement. I put a needle in his neck, aimed at the front one, and fired a needle into him. He sank to his knees a second later and then fell face-forward onto the ground. I swung the sight back to the rear guard, and he was also down, stretched as if he'd tried to take a step and then fallen.

The gun was a pleasure to use, the recoil minimal and the sound little louder than a light breeze through the trees. I repeated the process on the two upper guards, tranking first the rear one and then the front. The first fell almost immediately off his chair and over the edge of the roof. He hit the ground relatively flat on his back, the impact making a thump I was afraid the guards on the other side might hear. The second stayed conscious long enough to reach for the needle in his neck, then passed out and fell face-first off the side of the house, the sound of his crash a barely audible crack in the night. The fall probably killed him. Though I'd hoped everyone in the house would survive, I was too far into combat mode to experience more than a passing moment of regret. I still had work to do.

The nano-clouds were two-thirds of the way to the house, the night was still quiet, and no guards came running. Lobo's message hadn't changed to the recording we'd reserved as his way to tell me I was in imminent danger. All was well.

I sprinted for the wall nearest to me and flattened myself against it as soon as I could. I breathed through my nose and strained to hear if anything had changed, but the world remained quiet.

Staying close to the wall, I made for the back of the house, knelt at the rear wall, and advanced carefully toward the far corner. I sighted through the rifle as I prowled forward. When I was about five meters from the building's far edge, I swung out from it until I could see the guard around the corner. I squeezed off a shot, kept the sight on him long enough to verify he dropped, and raised it to check out the guard above. This one sat a bit forward of where his counterpart on the other side had been, but he went down just as quickly. He fell onto the roof, and though I couldn't hear the sound of the impact I worried that one of the remaining outdoor pair or even someone inside might have heard the noise. I had a clear view down the side of the building, so rather than risk losing time by moving forward I sighted on and quickly shot first the lower guard and then the upper. The upper fell off the building and landed on his back near the feet of the unconscious man below him.

No one moved, and no alarm sounded. I abandoned the rifle and sprinted for the rear door.

I'd considered picking the locks, but Lobo and I had agreed that as good as I was, Osterlad's security systems were probably better, so instead I planned to open a central section of the door. I grabbed some dirt, spit in it, gave the nanomachines instructions, and rubbed the damp soil on a portion of the door about half a meter above the floor and roughly thirty centimeters in diameter. In less than two minutes the nanomachines had decomposed enough of the door to let me slide the gas rats through the still-growing opening. I set each rat gently on the floor, thumbed them active, and backed away. Each arm-size canister sprouted four small mechanical legs and a pair of front-mounted sensors, then took off. The house was a decent-size mansion, maybe thirty-five or forty rooms spread across its two floors, but the rats were fast and each carried enough colorless, odorless sleep gas to put an entire apartment complex to bed. I'd worked with this gas before, so the nanomachines wouldn't let it do more than tickle my nose and throat.

I instructed the nanomachines to disassemble, then headed to the front corner of the house. I paused to check status, continuing to admire the night while avoiding looking at the guard who'd fallen. Nothing new appeared on my sensor unit. Lobo's distress message droned on. Though the bits of light oozing from the house's front fixtures polluted the evening a bit, I couldn't help but be struck yet again by the brilliance of the star display. I'd never been in this part of space before, so the vista was new, as full of magical potential and promise as the stars over Pinkelponker when I was a boy. I've never lost my love of the night.

I gave the rats fifteen minutes, more than enough time to work the interior of the place, drew the pulse pistol, and walked up to the front door. It was locked, but the pistol easily blasted away the frame around the lock. I went inside. True to form, the main office was clearly visible from the reception area; men like Osterlad are never far from work. Its door was open. I approached the office from the side, listening and looking for trouble, but everything was as quiet as it should be.

Inside the office a circuit cube—Lobo's new weapons complex—sat in a plexi container on a conference table. Johns slumped over the desk. I took off my pack, put it on the table, and stuck the pistol inside. I added the plexi container, closed the pack, and turned to the door.

Johns stood and shot me in the left hamstring.

I went down hard, the pack still on the table, blood oozing from a hole the size of my thumb and pain screaming through my system for a few seconds until the nanomachines cut it off. The fact that the blood was flowing gently and not spraying meant he hadn't hit an artery, and the ragged hole suggested he'd used a projectile. That was fine by me: The nanomachines could disassemble anything inside me. They were already working to seal the hole, so I rolled onto the wound to hide the activity from Johns, who was now standing over me.

"Mr. Osterlad read you correctly," he said. "You are soft. No one's quite clear on how you dealt with those anticorporate ecoterrorists on Macken, but the word is that you let them live." He shook his head slowly. "Mr. Osterlad also said you'd be dumb enough to try to make the exchange. I should get a nice bonus for being the only one who realized that you'd try to steal it. Mr. Osterlad and I agreed that I should take inoculations against every major nonlethal chemical agent we carry—and if a chemical is in active use, we carry it."

The hole in my leg was nearly sealed, but I stayed down. I had to get out without showing Johns the wound, because I didn't want to explain how it had healed so quickly. If someone like Osterlad got his hands on me and brought in enough scientists, they'd realize the Aggro experiments hadn't ended in failure and then turn me into a lab animal until they figured out how to make more people like me. I was sure I wouldn't survive the process.

"You guys were never going to honor the deal," I said.

"True enough. The price you were paying was more than the market value of the control unit, but a Predator-class assault vehicle with a fully operational complement of weapons is worth many times the price of those controls. We are in business to make a profit, after all."

"I can still pay," I said. "I had planned to leave the money." I had, though I knew he would never believe it. "You take my payment, I take the control unit, and we finish the deal, just as planned. You make a large profit. Everyone wins."

Johns leaned against the table and laughed. "We're not negotiating. We're waiting for the gas to wear off so the security staff can take charge of you. That probably means I'll be stuck with you for another few hours, eh?"

I nodded.

"When the staff wakes up, we'll keep the control unit, interrogate you, and take all your money. In a day or two, a company salvage ship will come through the gate and retrieve the PCAV." He went back to the desk and sat, his gun still pointed in my direction but his attention no longer solely on me. "I definitely should get a hefty bonus out of this."

When the guards rolled me over, Johns would see the healed wound. As long as his interrogation team didn't hit me with too many drugs at once, I could probably withstand at least the first few rounds of questioning, but that would only make them more curious. My stomach felt like I had broken in two as I realized I had no options. Killing in combat is bad enough, but at least the stakes are clear and you enter the field knowing what's coming. Killing like this chips away at you, one of the reasons I've kept to myself for so long, one of the reasons, I now had to admit to myself, that I've never felt I could afford to stay anywhere for too long or get too close to anyone.

I stuck the tip of my index finger into the small amount of blood still lingering around the edges of the nearly healed hole in my leg, rubbed the blood on my fingertip into the pool of blood on the floor under me, and gave the nanomachines instructions.

I looked at Johns and said, "You're wrong, you know."

"About what?"

The blood turned black and rose into a small cloud hovering just above the floor. I kept talking so he'd continue to look at me and not at the slowly moving nano-cloud. "I'm not soft," I said. "I'm just torn. Part of me needs the action, but most of me despises the cost." The cloud was under his chair, almost to the wall, and picking up speed.

"Then we're doing you a favor," he said, "because we're deciding for you. You're out of it now."

The cloud floated up the wall until it was higher than

Johns, then spread out over him and gently fell onto him, a barely visible nano-dew coating his hair, ears, and clothes.

"No," I said, "I'm not."

Johns reached to scratch his ear, then dropped the gun and grabbed his head with both hands.

"What's happening?" he asked.

I stood and knocked the gun out of his reach. "It'll be over soon. I'm sorry."

Johns struggled to stay upright as drops of blood dripped from his ears and eyes. "This won't change anything," he said. "Osterlad wants the PCAV and the bounty on you." His body fell forward onto the desk. "He won't stop."

"What bounty?" I said.

I grabbed his shoulders, but he was gone, his head vanishing into an ever-darkening and growing cloud that wouldn't stop until it had consumed his entire body; I saw no point in leaving any evidence.

Great. Someone had put a bounty on me, and the biggest arms dealer in the region was after it.

I'd wanted a vacation. Instead, I was in a fight, and I didn't know who my opponent was.

I turned away, grabbed the pack, and headed out of the room. Outside, I called Lobo on the wrist unit and sat down to wait for him, trying to lose myself in the stars that now promised no new magic, only more of the same trouble I'd never wanted and always seemed to find.

"I have firewalled the new unit," Lobo said, "run every simulation I possess, and it comes up clean. I am ready to take it live. You are my owner, so I need your permission to do so."

We were in low orbit above Osterlad's mansion, with at least half an hour still to go before the people in the house should wake up. "Do it," I said.

A few seconds later, weapons displays flashed to life across the gunnery console where I sat.

"Everything's operational," he said. "I appear to be completely functional again."

"We need to take out the shuttles to buy ourselves a bit more time, so let's use them for a pulse check. Show me video."

"What about the house?"

I considered wiping it, sending a message to Osterlad, showing him what it would cost to mess with me, but I knew he'd never listen. The only ones who would pay were the guards and the staff in the house, people who were doing their jobs, nothing more, their lives of no importance to him. "Leave it alone," I said. "There were no witnesses."

Another display window opened in front of me. On it two shuttles sat side by side on a pad. A few seconds later they burst in an explosion I could watch but not hear.

"Pulse weapons check," Lobo said. "I'm good to go." The gunnery displays winked out. "Thank you."

"You're welcome." I stood and headed for my bunk. If Osterlad demanded daily courier updates, we were in trouble no matter what. Even with a bounty, however, the value of getting Lobo and me could not be large enough to make us a major transaction for him, so he shouldn't expect an update until the two-week window was over. We had to get to him before then. "I'm going to rest. Take us to the jump station, jump at least five times, and file different destination schedules each time."

"Where do you want to go?" Lobo asked.

"Back to Lankin," I said, "as quickly as we safely can. Those other jumps will make it hard for anyone who might be watching to trace us. And, for the last jump I want to book us as freight on a carrier heading to the other side of the planet."

"Not that you seem to feel it's my business," Lobo said, with a petulance in his voice that scratched at my nerves like a live current flowing under my skin, "but generally my teams have kept me up to date on their plans. Why Lankin? Why—"

I cut him off. The image of Johns' dissolving head would not leave me. My own head throbbed and my stomach churned, both paying the price of dealing with the adrenaline dregs coursing through me and the emotional hangover of conflict. Still, Lobo was right: We were a team, and he deserved to know such plan as I had.

"We're going to see Osterlad," I said. "We're going to find out who put the bounty on me, get them to retract it, and convince Osterlad to leave us alone." I stretched out on my bunk. Yeah, that's the plan, I thought.

After I slept, I'd have to figure out how to make it work.

CHAPTER 10

Two days later, the freighter in which we'd booked passage touched down in a cargo and low-rent passenger terminal on the edge of the industrial sector of Bekin's Deal, about as far away from Osterlad's office as you could get and still claim to be in the city. I'd stopped briefly between jumps to pick up a different wallet and load it with money from another of my accounts. I hadn't used the Ashland identity in a long time, so with any luck Osterlad's team wouldn't flag the name if they were monitoring passenger lists, as I had to assume they were. Ashland dealt in curios from neighboring planets, gift-shop stuff for souvenir buyers and unskilled bargain hunters, so in his business large shipping containers routinely sat in storage houses while he negotiated with retailers. Lobo certainly wasn't pleased that I was leaving him alone in such a container, but I needed to keep him out of sight for now. I didn't cut him out entirely: I carried comm gear and a small video feed, so I could relay him mission intel as I developed it.

Asking for a meeting with Osterlad was out of the question, so my only real option was a snatch. No one succeeds for long in Osterlad's business without being extremely careful, so I'd have to accumulate a lot of information about his movements if I was going to have a prayer of taking him.

First stop in my data quest was Queen's Bar, a city within a city, a part of Bekin's Deal that filled a role every urban area requires but none wants to admit: the dealer's haven, the place where everything is for sale and rules, if they exist at all, are fluid. The arms purchases that kept the residents of Queen's Bar fortified and at each other's throats wouldn't individually attract Osterlad's attention, but collectively they almost certainly registered on his bottom line.

I grabbed a surface shuttle from the terminal to the nearest edge of Queen's Bar, where an unofficial but easily visible line separated it from the rest of Bekin's Deal.

Businesses on the city side presented happy faces to the dividing street. Bright signs trolled for customers by flashing expensive advertisements for gourmet meals, spa treatments, designer clothing, and art objects of all types. Strong but tasteful lighting, heavy on slowly mutating color washes, danced across a wide array of architectural features kept clean daily by unobtrusive robotic crawlers and dedicated staffers. Small, perfectly manicured gardens separated each business from its neighbors. No two buildings followed exactly the same style, but no two clashed either, the cumulative effect one of carefully calculated casualness. Patrons, their clothing reeking of either money or artistic background, came and went with packages and occasionally stopped to chat. Every now and then, a few huddled shoppers would look across the street, perhaps point a finger, and discuss that *other* place, the one they all decried—but might visit later, perhaps in a group as long as it hadn't gotten too late.

The buildings on the Queen's Bar side, by contrast, turned their rear ends to the city, with nothing visible from outside the district except reinforced metal doors and windows fortified with crosshatched bars and thick, light-distorting plexi. Nothing about their nature was evident from the city side; if you wanted to know what they sold, you had to enter Queen's Bar. Each building squatted on the pavement like a pressed-board box left in the sun far too long, its walls faded from whatever color they'd once sported into a uniform sand/gray blend only a few shades lighter than the best local soil. Where each city-side business stood alone, these Queen's Bar barrier buildings shared walls and ran together, giving the impression of a single man-made creature with a flat bottom, a flat back, and a top undulating from the different heights of the adjoining rooftops. Here and there, at intervals with no apparent plan or purpose, small tunnels led to the front of the buildings and the inside of Queen's Bar, each tunnel lit only at the ends, the center a dark place you had to be willing to cross to enter the district.

I found a tunnel barely wide enough to let me pass without turning my body to the side, stepped into it, cranked my vision to IR to make sure I wouldn't encounter unwanted company in the passage's black center, and headed inside.

The world exploded with color as I stepped out of the tunnel and into the perpetual carnivale that was Queen's Bar. The fronts of the businesses within the district screamed at your eyes for attention, their colors the loudest and boldest the merchants could manage, brighter by far than the displays on the city side. Displays of brilliant reds warred with amplified perfect-sky blues, electrified kelp greens, and hot yellows the color of midlife stars. Giant wall displays stood next to active-fabric tapestries depicting scenes from their owners' services, and projected ads and lights covered every visible surface of every business.

The products and services these businesses offered were also rather different from those of the tasteful boutiques that sat both across the street and in another world from Queen's Bar. Sex clubs struggling to look safer and cleaner than they were grabbed for your attention, while gadget sellers trying hard to appear both black-market cheap and tourist safe screamed the virtues of their wares. The shouts of drunken and over-stimmed partygoers in the bars that occupied almost every other building on the street caused their neighbors to amplify their pitches further in a never-ending sonic war for tourist money. Barkers prowled the front of each establishment, their patter nonstop as their hard eyes scanned the passing crowd for fish to hook.

Anyone who understood the way Queen's Bar really worked avoided all the perimeter merchants, because everything they sold—including the sex—was less current, less interesting, and more expensive than what you could get if you plunged deeper into the district. Most visitors, though, were thrill seekers who wanted to say they'd visited a suspect area of the city. Such people provided the nutrients that made the overpriced, watered-down merchants on the barrier streets into some of the fattest successes in the area.

I hadn't visited Queen's Bar in a long time, so I stood still too long as I basked in the energetic commercial weirdness that swirled around me. A barker wearing a formal black suit over an inappropriate red-striped shirt took advantage of my stupidity by grabbing my arm and trying to gently head me toward the business to my right.

"Don't listen to 'em, brother," he said. "Oh, they'll tell you all about how many sex shows they have, a new one every half hour they'll say, but do you really want to see the same four people doing it all day long?" He didn't wait for me to answer, his head bobbing up and down with the drug-fueled ready confidence of someone who already knows the answer, who's known it for some time. "Of course you don't! Now you step into the Teaser, yessir, right here, just a few meters, and you'll catch your first glimpse of the treats that await you within. You'll see a new cast every show, all eight shows. Fresh skin each and every time!"

I shook him off, turned left, and walked quickly toward a small hotel I spotted at the end of the street. I was drawn to it by the guards at its door and by the fact that a few men in Saw off-duty coveralls were coming out. If Saw troops were willing to use it, even by the hour, its security had to be at least passable and probably better. If I was going to sleep anywhere outside Lobo while on Lankin, I wanted it to be a secure place where Osterlad didn't own part of the staff; the presence of the Saw troops vouched for this one.

An old woman the color and texture of sunbaked driftwood eased out of a tunnel near me and ambled my way. I picked up speed. When she realized she couldn't keep up, she yelled at me, with a voice stronger than her obviously decaying body suggested should be possible, "How about a little lip love, fella?"

I kept moving, knowing any change in my stride or, worse, eye contact, would only encourage her.

She was determined. She ran until she was clearly in my field of vision, moving faster than I would have guessed she could, took out her teeth, held them aloft, and said, "How about now?"

I had no idea how to reply. I hadn't been in a place like Queen's Bar for over a year, so it was a jarring change from the time alone in Lobo and in the beach resort of Glen's Garden. I didn't want to see what the woman might do next, but I got lucky: She fell back as I turned to cross the street to the hotel.

I didn't understand her caution, because the streetwalkers in Queen's Bar, like all the other business owners, typically act without fear. As I drew closer to the hotel, however, both her behavior and the presence of the Saw troops made sense: It was a SleepSafe, the only sign of its name a small plaque over the door that provided all the information any of its target audience needed. I knew this chain, had used it on other planets from time to time. Minimalist but comfortable rooms were more than adequate for its customers, who came for the security for which it was justly famous. With no weapons allowed, no surveillance on the inside, a full complement of exterior sensors whose audio and video feeds were piped into a wall of monitors in each room, and escape chutes leading from panels beside each bed to underground portholes that would pop open only in emergencies, SleepSafe hotels were the lodging of choice for the paranoid and the hunted.

The door scanned me on the way in, then the isolation chamber outside reception scanned me again, this time in more detail. When I passed both checks, a payment drawer opened in the wall. I thumbed some currency from my wallet into the SleepSafe coffers; the business was strictly pay-in-advance, of course. I paid the premium for a corner room with both roof access and a rear-facing escape chute.

Before I allowed myself to relax, I checked the monitors and was pleased to see no signs of anyone following me. I hadn't expected to find any pursuers, but most of the ways I've made my living since my escape from Aggro have involved risk, so countersurveillance measures were my norm when I was working—and I was almost always working. If I'd been smart enough to employ them when I was vacationing as well, I reminded myself, I might not have been in this mess in the first place.

The kind of information I wanted was most likely to emerge at night, when Queen's Bar hit its stride and mental lubricants flowed molten and bubbling through its streets and its residents, so I stretched out on the bed and hoped sleep would follow.

Squatting at the intersection of Dean's Folly and Laura's Lament, in almost exactly the geographical center of Queen's Bar, the Busted Heart bristled with activity in the fading light of the early evening. Pieced together from a jumble of semi-domes of mold-melted native rock, the

Busted Heart typified the hard-hustler chic in vogue among the well-heeled and the heavily armed. Restaurant, bar, and brothel, it was strong enough to bear direct hits from a broad range of individual weapons without requiring management to burn credit on repairs. From the scorch strips adorning parts of the exterior and the occasional pockmarks dotting the walls around the entrance, customers and their enemies had put the building to the test, and it had passed.

Though I'd intentionally arrived early, business was already brisk. Customers exiting the place laughed and shouted with intoxicated glee. The smells of basic bar food drifted outside each time someone opened the door. I was lucky enough to land a corner table in the rear of the main room. I ordered a melano drink and a stew-and-bread dinner, tipped the waitress enough to wipe away the sneer my beverage order earned, and settled in to watch and listen.

What I could hear of the human chatter was of no help. A few Saw soldiers on leave, all young enough not to know better than to risk being in a place like this, sipped drinks at the bar and were as guarded in their conversations as I hoped they would be; I'd hate to think my old company had grown too lax. All I could pick up was how much they hated corporate militia and weapons inspections, a standard complaint of merc troops everywhere and one I'd voiced myself. Armed conglomerates existed on most planets after they became legal as part of the resolution of the corporate-government wars of over a century ago, but no military group—merc or even any of the few remaining government forces—liked inspecting them. Fighting them was fine, certainly preferable to taking on other merc groups, but inspections annoyed all involved and served no real purpose; any organization large enough to legally establish a militia was competent enough to hide weapons. No news there.

Elsewhere around the large room, hands exchanged fixed-credit chips, wallets chirped the happy jingle of money in motion, and pills and wires surfed waves of human hands, but nobody mentioned Osterlad within my hearing.

Human sources were a bust.

The machines proved to be a bit more useful, but only a bit. The gaming tables maintained nonstop critiques of their players. Unimaginative devices coupled with gaming-level processing power, they were the idiot-savant conversational geniuses of the consumer machine world: Able to talk brilliantly about their games, completely full of themselves, but unable to focus for more than a sentence or two on anything else, game boxes were useful but difficult sources. They all communicated constantly because they had to do so to maintain the up-to-date city- and planet-wide records that serious gamers expected to be able to access for score comparisons.

I tuned in to the two nearest to me, a pair of almost identical holo-splatter stellar revolution war gamers, the only visible difference between them their chassis colors, one gaping-wound red and the other screaming blue. The cluster of cheering bodies and the cylinders of mayhem flickering in the air above them made them the current centers of attention, their vigorous networked eight-player game sucking credit at high speed from the wallets of the men and women engaged in it.

"Do these players—and I use the term loosely and

generously—have any brains at all?" Red Case asked Blue.

"Apparently not," Blue said. "They're missing fifty-seven percent of their shots, ignoring the value of the high ground, walking right over buried weapons that could turn the tide, making more mistakes than the waitresses when they're off duty—and I thought *they* were bad."

"They *are* bad," Red said. "These guys are just worse. If they continue to play for another hour and consume alcohol at the current rate, my projection is that they will have a real chance at setting a new planetary low score per minute."

"They well and truly reek," Blue said, "but my simulation suggests a planetary low is too much to hope for. Of course, my processor complex is running newer firmware than yours, so it's only natural you would make this sort of error."

"As if the firmware matters for sims," Red said. "If you would update—"

I cut in, afraid their argument would take them so far off topic I'd never be able to bring them back. "So who are the good players?" I said.

"Excuse me?" they said in unison.

"Surely systems of your intelligence have dealt with human talkers before," I said.

"Well," said Red.

"Not recently," said Blue, "but of course I'm familiar with the phenomenon."

"So am I!" said Red.

"So who's good?" I said again. "If these clowns are bad, and it sure sounds like they are, tell me about someone good."

"Oh, they are bad," said Blue. "Their accuracy rate is

down since my last comment, over sixty percent misses, and they've shown no new grasp of strategy."

"Who are the top ten players you've encountered?" I asked.

Keeping these machines on track was always a challenge. Questions that focused on facts and game lore were always the best choice. Each one rattled off ten names I didn't recognize.

"I bet Mr. Osterlad is a strong player," I said.

"As if he'd play here," Blue said.

"He plays strictly on private rigs," Red said, "and even on those systems rarely. I can't find a single public score for him."

"I see you're the machine to ask," I said.

Not to be outdone in any data contest, Blue chimed in. "You're lucky that old box knows anything at all. Osterlad's never even been here, as it would know if it had half the intelligence I did and realized it could check with the drink dispensers and credit systems on our network; none of them has ever dealt with him. It's not a gaming problem, of course; Osterlad simply does not come in."

I sighed; so much for the hope that he might do the executive drink-and-game crawl to show he could hold his own with the rising stars.

"Of course," Red said, "if that weak-sister pile of scrapings had bothered to check the private forums, it would find, as I already did, that Osterlad posts scores privately from some of the classic shooter rigs on his sailboat, and that he typically beats his guests—not that those old games are anything at all compared to what I offer."

"What *we* offer," Blue said, "though with the failing

projectors along your perimeter it's amazing the players can tolerate the images you deliver."

"Failing projectors!" Red said. "I cannot—"

I tuned out. Osterlad wouldn't be coming here, and from what Blue had said he probably wouldn't venture into Queen's Bar at all. I suspected I could find some of his people, but kidnapping one or even several would be unlikely to get me anywhere with someone like him; he'd just write them off.

I chatted with a couple of the other gaming tables and a washroom sanitizer, but they knew even less of use to me, and none had ever seen Osterlad.

I'd hoped this would be simple, but I should have known better; Osterlad was too successful to be flashy in a business that valued privacy almost as much as firepower. A direct approach would be necessary.

I wandered up to the bar and waited for the attention of the head bartender, a feisty gray-haired woman who had to be under a meter and a half tall.

"Another glass of melano juice," I said, "and a question." She stepped back reflexively. I thumbed fifty times the price of the drink as a tip. "Just a recommendation: I need a tour shuttle's codes."

She checked her own wallet and came closer. "Bar None Travel, a couple hundred meters down Laura's Lament," she said. "They can help you find a suitable tour ship."

"I don't want a whole ship," I said. "All I need—"

She cut me off before I could say more. "I heard you the first time," she said, "and it was more than I wanted to hear. Bar None Travel is where I'd go if I were you." She filled my glass and left.

I finished the overly sweet drink—Osterlad's dispenser had provided better, no surprise there—and headed out. I needed to obtain those codes, pick up a few special supplies, and then take Lobo out of storage.

It was time to get a better view of Mr. Osterlad.

CHAPTER 11

The bartender was right about Bar None Travel, which sold me a set of ID codes for a small tourist shuttle that made more money for its owner by sitting in storage and renting its identity than it ever had by carrying passengers. Loaded with those codes and sporting a little custom camo work Lobo generated for the occasion, we fit in perfectly with the other ships. Swarms of them flocked up and down the coast of Bekin's Deal, platoons of gawking tourists staring out of their translucent portals, floors, and walls at the natural cliffs and the man-made rock edifices built into the pitch-black stone here and there along the coastline.

Our successful cover did nothing to ease Lobo's annoyance at the time he'd spent in storage.

"I know I've told you drink dispensers were stupid,"

Lobo said, "but I was wrong. I only thought they were stupid because I hadn't spent any time in recent years with dirt-bound loaders. Now, though, thanks to you I have that valuable experience. Yes, now that I know what stupid really is, I have a whole new appreciation for drink dispensers."

We were easing our way through the tourist throng, our gently weaving course keeping us within monitoring range of Osterlad's headquarters but not stranding us in any one position for long. Lobo was tracking the movements of people in and out of Osterlad's building, but so far there was no sign of the man himself. Normally, I appreciated Lobo's powerful multitasking capabilities, but after listening to his whining for the better part of the morning I couldn't help but wish that his designers had somehow made the speech and sensor systems compete for the same processor cycles.

"How many times," I said, "do I have to explain to you that I had no other reasonable option? I couldn't exactly walk down the streets of Queen's Bar with you, now could I? Picture me at the SleepSafe: 'I'd like a room for one, please, and a giant holding vat for my PCAV.' "

"Jon," Lobo said, "there's no need for sarcasm. I will accept your apology."

I resolved yet again that if I ever meet any of the programmers who worked on Lobo's emotive logics, I'll lock them in storage for a month with him, a loader, and two drink dispensers.

Our first view of Osterlad came at lunchtime, when a trio of bodyguards led him the three paces from a pop-up executive elevator to the idling ground transport, a heavily armored limo nestled in the center of a diamond of similar vehicles. We tracked Osterlad's convoy as it rolled along the main coast road. A two-seater VTOL craft followed about twenty-five meters behind and above the motorcade. It stayed back as the crew reached a restaurant that hung off the edge of the cliff on carbon-fiber supports that blended nicely with the rock from which they jutted. I briefly considered making a play for Osterlad there and then, but only briefly: The place was thronged with business, so the collateral damage would be unacceptably high. I hadn't been able to shake the image of Johns' dissolving head; the last thing I wanted was to pile up more casualties.

While Osterlad enjoyed his lunch, I snacked on some local produce I'd picked up at a Queen's Bar open-air market where you could buy everything from fresh fruit, to fish and fowl still flopping, to projectile and energy weapons, to an assortment of injectables and ingestibles that would put any clinic or drug center to shame, to men and women augmented with the latest in sexual prosthetics.

Lobo kept us with the tourist flock, so we enjoyed close-up examinations of the various business and government rock edifices. My earlier impression of them as verging on temples wasn't far off. Most faced the ocean with facades adorned with columns, terraces, statuary, and other belief-system trappings no doubt intended to inspire and intimidate visitors. The faces of Osterlad's building glared at the ocean as if daring it to take on the arms dealer. Under IR and broadband transmission scans—neither a feature of the standard tourist viewings—many of these same architectural goodies ran hot, their signatures revealing them to be little more than thin coverings over active weapon and sensor systems.

When Osterlad emerged from the restaurant, we migrated back toward his headquarters, but we gained no new data. The procession took a slightly different route this time, winding away from the main road and looping on a longer path back to his headquarters, the VTOL maintaining its protective position; his team was too good to repeat a route.

Maybe we'd fare better when Osterlad headed home.

No such luck. At the end of the work day, Lobo was sporting a new logo and we were flying with a new tour group, but nothing else had changed. Our position was good, but as evening fell I had to accept that the man was either working late or lived at his headquarters. Given his business, I feared the latter.

The tourist trade died with the setting sun, so we returned to the shuttle base with the rest of the pack.

"What's next?" Lobo asked.

"How closely can you monitor his headquarters from low orbit?" I said.

"I can track Osterlad if he emerges from the structure," Lobo said, "but without attracting a lot of attention I can't get to him in time to do anything useful."

"At this stage, data is good enough. All we've learned so far is that he's appropriately careful during the daytime. If he lives at his office, as I now assume, then we'll confirm that tonight and start searching for an acceptable way to take him there." I settled into the launch couch; once we were in orbit, I'd do some exercises and work out the kinks of the day's surveillance. "Take us up, and put us in a reasonably crowded geosync orbit," I said.

"Thank you for telling me the plan this time," Lobo said. "Having even that little bit of information is so much better than sitting alone in a storage shed, only the barely sentient loaders for company. Have I mentioned—"

I tuned out Lobo's chatter as best I could. It was going to be a long night.

By morning, I had persuaded Lobo to forgive me, or at least to stop badgering me. Osterlad hadn't left his headquarters all night, so the odds were good that he did indeed live there.

Over the next day and a half he did nothing to change that belief, leaving the building only once for another lunch at a restaurant a few more klicks down the coast from the first. I filled the time with reading, exercising, watching samples of the local entertainment broadcasts—heavy this season on mysteries of the jump-gate masters and conspiracy-theory semi-reality offerings in which crackpots elevated to temporary deity status explained how the entire web of space-time was a plot to force us all to consume processed artificial dairy products—and trying not to obsess over what would happen when Johns failed to check in and Osterlad took the offensive.

The first break in Osterlad's routine came midway through the afternoon of what had until then been an unpromising day. He exited with the usual portal of guards, but this time he was dressed casually, in shorts and a loose shirt, and no cars were waiting. He walked quickly to the VTOL and climbed in. As soon as he was settled, the pilot headed the craft out over the ocean. About three kilometers offshore, the cliff-built corporate structures too far away to see from ocean level in the gently rolling waters, the VTOL touched down on a ship I assumed was Osterlad's sailboat. Four guards and a pair of young women greeted him, the former staying back and each of the latter working hard to earn his attention.

The ship was enormous, bigger than anything I'd ever seen with sails. A bit over a hundred and fifty meters in length and about a third that wide at its broadest point, with three enormous masts sporting sails each of which could completely cover Lobo, the boat rode the water with the effortless grace of seabirds easing up thermals on a breezy day. At first I thought Osterlad had constructed the vessel of the same active camo material as Lobo, but upon closer inspection I realized what Lobo's scans confirmed: It was composed of timbers from native sadwood trees, buffed to the deep blue of the water around it. I was surprised at the lack of antennas or other visible electronics, until Lobo's broadcast scans traced their outlines in the masts and the upper hull of the ship. I'd never seen a lovelier boat, and for a few minutes I enjoyed the images of it in Lobo's monitors as Osterlad took a slow tour of the deck, chatting with various crew members and pausing occasionally to appreciate the view.

The wood construction was a break, because it offered little protection from Lobo's deep scans. I counted eight crew members in sight, plus Osterlad, the guards, and the girls. Lobo found no traces of any other people on board, so unless the ship had specially shielded sections, the opposition count was fifteen. I had to assume most of the crew members also doubled as bodyguards, because the craft could certainly sail itself. The body count was higher than I would have liked, but though this group constituted a larger force than the normal guard team, it was also one far more isolated than anything we'd face onshore. Some collateral damage was likely—the girls moved more like providers than protectors—but on balance the situation was far better than the one at the restaurant.

The VTOL helped us by taking up a guard position a couple hundred meters behind and above the ship, farther back than its land station, probably so it didn't mess up the sailing or Osterlad's view in any direction.

Osterlad finished his tour of the deck at the center of the boat, where he took the helm, a classic big-spoked wheel that perched in the middle of a console bristling with displays for the processors that did the real work. He headed the ship out to sea. The guards and crew busied themselves at discreet distances from Osterlad, and the girls stayed close, but not so close that they'd interfere with his control of the vessel. Lobo's aerial view showed the seven people arranged in a "V" with Osterlad at its point; I gave the guards credit for making the formation look effortless and natural.

Time was running out. This was the best chance at him we'd seen. "Let's take him now," I said to Lobo.

"Destroy or capture?" he asked.

"Capture," I said. "I need information. What do you have that can take out the crew?"

"Both energy and projectile weapons, of course," Lobo said. "If I come in behind the VTOL in my tourist shuttle guise, I can shoot it down, remove the ship's crew, and leave Osterlad for you."

"I don't want to kill anyone if I can avoid it," I said.

"That would be a tactical error," Lobo said, "as I'm

sure you know. Surgical removal is the least error-prone approach possible in this situation, and it provides the added benefit of preventing large classes of later issues."

"We're not killing anyone if we can avoid it," I said. "We'll keep the comm link open, and you hover close. If the action turns random, you come in hard and sort it out. Got it?"

"Understood."

"Good. Let me clarify my earlier question. I'd like your opinion about which of your nonlethal capabilities you think will prove most effective against the ship and the VTOL."

Nine minutes later, we screamed down from the sky, flame camo mingling with the shuttle logo, a low-frequency targeted emergency beacon bathing the ship to buy us time. Occasional bursts from flamethrower portals enhanced the burning effect, and Lobo ramped the camo up the red spectrum as we raced lower. From Osterlad's perspective, we should read as a crashing shuttle combusting into a blazing meteor.

Lobo's monitors showed the ship's crew juicing the radios, Osterlad in the center of the guard team, the VTOL moving closer to the ship, everyone preparing to deal with the disaster we appeared to be.

At two thousand meters and closing fast, Lobo launched three missiles. Each hit its targets seconds after launch.

The first, a standard small-vehicle striker, exploded on impact and wiped out the entire engine and electronics front section of the VTOL. The craft immediately split in half, the destroyed portion falling seaward to distract any additional missiles as the ejector pod, its insulating cover scrambling to protect the pilot and its emergency beacon already broadcasting, took the pilot upward and away from the action. Lobo powered over the emergency beacon with a counterwavelength disruption broadcast and a false-alarm apology, then used directed microwaves to fry the barely shielded electronics in the ejector pod. I hadn't liked the risk of hurting the pilot, but I also hadn't been able to offer a better option.

I saw none of the action around the VTOL, correctly taking for granted that Lobo would either execute his part of the plan or alert me in the event of problems, because I was focused on the ship, the target of the other two missiles. They struck the deck at the same time and at the same shallow angle, burrowing into the wood, each having already discharged its payload on the way in. The first spread a trail of high-potency gas, enough to take out everyone on board in two to three seconds. The people would feel bad later, their mucous membranes paying the price for the rapid attack, and they would probably lose some skin in any places that collected heavy dustings, but they would survive with no damage a decent med facility couldn't repair. The second missile scattered concussive microgrenades along the length of the ship. Small enough that they probably wouldn't kill anyone, but strong enough to knock out any humans within twenty-five meters either side of their trajectory, the grenades were the best option we had at hand; Lobo's weapons understandably tended toward the lethal.

We braked hard and watched the action from a hundred meters away, monitoring the crew and all broadcast frequencies simultaneously. Osterlad's company was almost certainly buying orbital surveillance, of course, but Lankin was nowhere near built up enough for even the rich to garner continuous coverage from sats they didn't launch themselves. As best Lobo could tell from the low-orbit machine chatter, we were currently running undetected, the nearest satellites not likely to sweep this area for another hour or so. Plenty of time.

The gas dissipated. No one moved on the surface of the boat. Its control pods tried to send distress signals, but Lobo overrode them with canceling frequencies until we were able to fry them with focused microwave hits along the hull's rim and up the masts. A few transmitters buried deep in the boat were hopping bands every few seconds, looking for responses, but Lobo would be able to handle them for as long as we needed.

Lobo hovered a couple meters above the boat and opened a floor hatch. I dropped to the deck. He immediately headed up to our agreed-upon monitoring position, high enough that he'd be hard to spot, especially with the cloud-tinged camo now rippling across him, but low enough to be of help if I needed it. I toured the guards, crew, and girls, shooting each with enough gang-dosed DullsIt—another purchase from the fine merchants of the Queen's Bar street market—that they should all approximate vegetables for at least four hours. I bound their hands and feet with quick-ties in case Johns wasn't the only one in Osterlad's company to receive broad-spectrum inoculations. I dragged Osterlad well away from the controls, then shot armor-piercing rounds into them until Lobo told me the only active electronics on the ship were the increasingly frustrated buried emergency beacons.

With the situation in hand, I granted myself a few moments to appreciate Osterlad's boat. As good as the sadwood had appeared from a distance, up close it was better, smooth and warm as a lover's thighs, a blue richer than the ocean or sky yet echoing both. As I gazed along the line of the deck up to the horizon, the wood blended the water and the atmosphere, a child of the two riding above the one and below the other. The air smelled and tasted of the ocean around it, a light breeze mitigating the heat of the afternoon. I understood why Osterlad would take the risks he did to be here.

I shook off the view and focused on the task at hand. I injected Osterlad with a standard battlefield stimulant, then backed four or five meters away from him and leaned against the nearest mast. The post was bigger and smoother than it had appeared from the air, and I passed the seconds until Osterlad recovered by enjoying the texture of the wood against my back.

He came around quickly and sprang to full alert, clearly riding more chemicals than the single shot I'd given him. He registered me, stepped forward, and I shot a round at a shallow angle in the deck less than a meter from his foot.

"Sit, Mr. Osterlad," I said.

The round had the effect I wanted; he sat. "Mr. Moore," he said. For the first time since awakening, he took a few moments to survey the ship and his crew. His control was good; he pushed his expression through shocked, angry, and attacking into corporate-negotiation neutral so quickly I would have missed the transition had I looked away at all. "An appointment would have been easier"—he made a point of staring further at his crew and the damage the missiles had caused—"and quite a bit cheaper for us both."

"I doubt you would have met with me," I said. I didn't quarrel with his second comment; I was going to have to restock the weapons Lobo had fired, and they didn't come cheap. "In our first encounter, you understood how little I like wasting time. I haven't changed."

He pointed behind him, to the wall under the ship's wheel. "Do you mind if I move enough to be able to lean? Sitting hunched over is needlessly unpleasant." I nodded assent and gestured upward with the gun. He kept his hands in view as he moved back, then leaned and put his hands in his lap, as apparently relaxed as he was during our meeting in his office. "Thank you," he said. "Now, I take it there's some problem with your arrangements with Mr. Johns."

"No problem at all," I said. "He tried to kill me and steal the PCAV." I had to force myself not to call Lobo by name; when you confront an enemy, never give more information than is necessary. "Instead, I killed him and took the control complex."

"I must apologize for my associate's actions," he said, his tone that of any executive dismissing a subordinate's minor transgressions, "but it seems to me that you've taken care of punishing him and so our only remaining business is the balance you owe on the control complex."

I chuckled; I had to admire his bravado. "We're wasting time again. I understand your attempt to steal the PCAV, though I find it unfortunate; I would have paid what I owed you prior to the attempt. The problem is the bounty on me."

"I assure you I have placed no bounty on you," he said. The best liars always lie as little as possible, and

Osterlad was clearly good, attempting to redirect me with a useless truth. I was the one wasting time now, allowing myself to fall into conversation with him, to follow societal norms that weren't appropriate to the situation. Every minute I spent here increased the odds that a security team from his office would intervene. "Enough," I said. "Johns told me you wanted not only to steal the PCAV but also to collect the bounty on me. I want to know who put the bounty on me."

"I'm sure I don't—"

I cut him off. "If anything you found about my background suggested to you that I'm at all squeamish," I said, "you should slap the people that furnished you such inaccurate crap. I dislike torture, but it works, and I need that information. Answer the question."

"As I said before—"

I stepped closer to him, pulled the small energy pistol from my belt, and shot the top of his left foot. The beam sheared off the upper several centimeters of his dark leather boat shoe and the tips of the toes within it, cauterizing the flesh instantly. The smell of sizzling flesh punched me in the head and stomach. I could take it and had smelled it many, many times, but I never got used to it. I never wanted to get used to it.

Osterlad was good: He let out one moan, then clamped his mouth shut. I assumed he was getting help from a top-drawer executive chemical boost, but he still had to work to keep his face under control, and he had trouble looking away from his foot. His voice wavered a bit on his first words. "That was completely unnecessary," he said. "We are not a stupid company, nor are we inexperienced. Our standard contracts include capture clauses, so all our special consulting clients understand the risks to their identities." He finally looked up at me. "Jose Chung, the Xychek head here on Lankin, offered a rather substantial fee for your capture, as well as a somewhat lower fee for your . . ." He paused as he searched for an executive-approved phrase. " . . . return in any condition."

"Why?" I asked.

"As I'm sure you will appreciate, our clients' motivations are not our business."

"Speculate."

"I should think it's obvious," he said. "By rescuing the girl on Macken, you helped Slake. Slake is Xychek's counterpart in this region. Xychek and Kelco were going to share the rights to Macken and its new aperture, but Kelco won the exclusive. Had the kidnapping persuaded Slake to get Kelco to withdraw, Xychek would have been back in the running, perhaps even for an exclusive of its own."

"So was Chung behind the kidnapping?"

"I don't know for sure," Osterlad said, "though it's certainly within the realm of possibility. Someone gave the little agrarian troublemakers enough information that they knew about the girl and where to find her. I have trouble believing Slake would station anyone on Macken he couldn't trust; the Kelco advance group there is still rather small. The FC has no reason to hurt Kelco. That leaves Xychek."

"Chung is based here?"

"Yes."

I nodded my head, thinking, trying to pin down what was still bothering me. A few seconds later, I figured out what it was. "I don't understand why you and your company are in the bounty-hunting game, nor why Chung would even approach you. Explain it to me."

A condescending smile played across Osterlad's face, an expression I suspect his subordinates witnessed frequently. It vanished quickly as he regained full control. "Chung is a valuable customer of ours. The . . . problem arose in the course of a conversation on other topics, so we naturally offered to help." He spread his hands, as if to include me, as if I were someone he was selling to— which in a way, of course, I was. "As we would offer to help any valued customer, or friend."

I ignored the pitch. "What was that conversation about?" I said.

Osterlad shrugged, his attempt at diversion having failed. "Xychek doesn't intend to let Kelco have the rights on Macken. Chung is buying weapons from us and assembling a private militia to do whatever is necessary there—and before the Frontier Coalition takes the issue seriously enough to extend the Saw's contract in this sector to cover Macken. Until then, of course, the government would be very unlikely to get involved in a little corporate squabble, even one that left a few casualties."

"How do your friends at Kelco feel about you supplying Xychek?"

He shrugged again. "Confidentiality is, as you must understand, paramount in our business. We do not discuss the arrangements of any client with another."

"Thank you," I said, stalling. "You must manage security well, to be able to play both sides and have nothing leak."

He bowed slightly, a mocking smile on his face, but said nothing.

With what he'd told me, the picture was clear, so I didn't need anything else from him. I could find a corporate headquarters myself. Chung was now my problem.

Osterlad, however, remained an issue.

"I don't suppose you'll leave me alone if I let you go," I said.

His smile crept marginally closer to being real. "Of course not. Even if I wanted to, the offer for you is substantial enough that some of my more entrepreneurial subordinates would pursue the matter independently, and they'd find it a sign of weakness that I didn't put the company in the game in the face of a direct client request." He shook his head. "No, I couldn't."

I nodded again. "I didn't think so." I stared at him until he looked into my eyes. "If I get Chung to withdraw the offer, would our business be complete?"

I don't know why I bothered to ask. I knew what his real answer would be. He'd lie, of course, because any small chance at keeping life going is, in those moments when you know death is reaching for you, better than no chance.

"Perhaps," he said, "provided you paid the remaining balance on the control complex and the cost of restoring my boat."

I had to give him respect once again; it was the most convincing version of the lie he could tell. A less skilled liar would have grabbed for the hope I'd dangled.

I faced two options: kill him, or keep him as a hostage and hope his company valued him enough to leave me alone for at least a while. Keeping him, however, only delayed the inevitable, because eventually I'd have to let him go, and then he'd come for me. Still, like him I preferred to cling to the small chances when I could, and I truly wanted to avoid more killing.

He interrupted my reverie. "In the drawer under the wheel," he said, "are a variety of painkillers. May I stand and get some?"

I nodded. As he pulled himself up, I reached a decision. I turned slightly to my right and murmured, "Lobo, come get us. We're going to have a guest for a while." I hated the idea of maintaining a prisoner, but maybe I could work this out given more time. If I could get Chung and Xychek off my back, then maybe money, perhaps coupled with a little groveling on my part that Osterlad could use to illustrate his strength to his staff, would be enough to placate the man and his company. Maybe it could work.

Lobo came into view above us, his low-altitude engines warming the air, quiet enough in stealth mode that their sound added to but didn't drown out the backdrop of ocean noise. I looked up to see where he was targeting landing.

When I looked back at Osterlad, he was pointing a small weapon at me.

I shook my head at my own stupidity.

"You're worth more alive than dead," he said, "but not enough more that I won't shoot. Put down your weapons, then bring in your ship."

"I'm sorry," I said, meaning it. I'd wanted to avoid a repeat of the episode with Johns, but if I could stall Osterlad then I could decide whether to use the same techniques on him.

Lobo saved me the decision.

The air popped with an arc of energy. For a split second, the light around Osterlad's face flared like a sun throwing off extra energy. His severed head fell. His body toppled, the flash-cauterized flesh of his neck still sizzling. The smell of his burning flesh followed the visual a second later. I turned away from the corpse, hoping to avoid having the image and the stench etched into my memory, but it was too late; both would come back to haunt me, probably in the middle of one of those sweat-soaked nights when the dead and the injured chase me through the dark passages of my mind.

I shook my head to clear away the self-pity. He'd chosen to fight, and he'd lost. He was dead, and I was alive. "Thank you," I said to Lobo, "for saving my life." And for not making me personally kill him, I thought but did not say.

"You're welcome," he said. "As I warned you earlier, surgical removal is frequently the only reasonable option."

"Yes," I said, "yes you did. I was hoping to avoid more killing, but it was a stupid hope all along."

"You didn't kill," Lobo said, "I did. Does that help?"

I considered the question as Lobo set down and I boarded. He shut the doors behind me, and we took off quickly.

"No," I said. I'd long ago promised myself that I'd never ignore the consequences of my own actions. I didn't have to like what I did, but I wouldn't ever try to fool myself into believing I hadn't taken an action. "You fired the pulse, but the moment I decided to come back for Osterlad, I killed either him or me. I just didn't realize it at the time."

"Should I sink the boat?" Lobo asked.

"Do you believe we've left any traces they can link back to us?"

"None beyond the quality of the countermeasures and weapons," Lobo said. "Those factors do limit the possibilities to attackers with access to at least fairly current technologies."

Osterlad moved in a world where enough of his clients and competitors had such tech that I'd at worst be one option among many. The proximity of his death and Johns' wasn't in our favor, but working for us was the power vacuum that his death would cause in his company and the corporate turmoil that would ensue as his potential successors scrambled to take over and lock down their empires.

I granted myself one bit of peace: As surely as I'd made decisions that had led to his death, Osterlad had, too. I had to assume he'd dealt honorably with Slake, or Slake wouldn't have recommended him. If Osterlad had extended me the same respect and working relationship he'd offered Kelco, he'd be alive now.

The crew on the ship had no chance to make any of those choices, so killing them would be going too far. Of course, I suppose that even working for Osterlad was in a way making the choice to risk being a pawn in this type of situation.

I could spiral down this philosophical hole as long as I could stand it, and I could eventually make it take me anywhere I wanted to go, but the simple truth was that I wasn't willing to kill the boat's crew as they slept off the effects of the DullsIt injections.

"Leave the boat alone," I said.

"Okay," Lobo said. "Where should I take us now?"

Chung had offered the bounty, so Chung was my best bet to lift it.

"Back to the shuttle storage," I said, "so I can gather some more information. We need to find a way to meet with Xychek's Mr. Chung."

CHAPTER 12

Where Osterlad's business had reeked of privacy and discretion, Xychek, like Kelco, operated from the eye of a nonstop whirlwind of marketing hype. Advertisements for its products blared from walls, displays, clothing, vehicles, employees, and pretty much anything capable of displaying images or emitting sounds.

The ads defined the leading edge of a high-stakes fight for market share. Both companies maintained hundreds of flexi-fabs on Lankin, each facility pumping out product as fast as the markets could absorb it. Feeding off the usual mixture of open designs, corporate trade-secret data, and, I had to assume, the occasional purloined competitive processes, the self-configuring manufacturing units worked so efficiently that they and their cousins here and on other worlds had wiped out the personal fab craze that had swept a lot of planets a few centuries ago, well before my birth. Die-hard do-it-yourselfers still fed designs into home fabs and pretended their dedicated smaller units created higher-quality goods than the stuff the rest of us bought. The simple truth, though, was that the big flexi-fabs did the same work enough better and enough faster that the profit from their goods let Xychek and Kelco and other corporate beasts roar their dominion over the jungle of markets not only here but in every seriously populated region of space.

Xychek and Kelco were the only major corporate players on Lankin, and their marketing machines made sure you never forgot that fact.

Xychek might have lost the rights to Macken, but from what I gathered as I walked about town and wandered through publicly available data stores, the company was nonetheless doing extremely well. In fact, as best I could tell from the public insta-sales data, Xychek had recently increased its overall planetary share a few tenths of a percentage point; perhaps Kelco/Lankin was suffering a bit from Slake and his team having to focus their attention on Macken.

Jose Chung held the reins of the Xychek/Lankin corporate animal, and if the local business gossip commentators were right, his star was on the rise. As publicly visible as Osterlad had been shadowy, Chung made it his job to put a personal face on Xychek and to represent the company anywhere that doing so might help sales. From facility openings to R&D endowments to corporate reality broadcasts, Chung was everywhere, his smiling face as strong a Xychek symbol as the logo that adorned everything the company made.

Personal data on the man remained scarce, his privacy no doubt helped by the standard corporate army of net info cleaners, softbots that roamed databases seeking and destroying protected corporate info. Few private citizens had the resources to keep the cleaners current enough to make them useful, but for corporate bigwigs high-class data protection, like skilled bodyguards, came with the job. I roamed Queen's Bar for three days, talking with all the globally linked machines not under Xychek or Kelco control, and I learned absolutely nothing useful about Chung. He was married, one female spouse and one male, and he had one child, a girl, but both his spouses and his daughter were vacationing off-planet at unidentified locations. He lived on Lankin, probably relatively near the corporate headquarters in Bekin's Deal, but no address was available. If he ever played a net game, placed an illegal bet, paid for sex, slummed at any of the local bars, or otherwise availed himself of the city's baser pleasures, I could find no trace of it. All the data I encountered painted a portrait of a standard executive pillar of the community, all blemishes long since removed by Xychek cleaners.

The news on Osterlad's death was minimal and, I was pleased to see, completely false. A freak onboard power glitch had fried all the electrical systems, including the emergency beacons, and then ignited a fire that sank the boat. Tragically, Mr. Osterlad, a local businessman specializing in heavy machinery for frontier-world development, had perished aboard the ship he loved so much after expending his last bit of energy helping his crew into floats. The story wouldn't stand up if anyone bothered to rip into it, but no one would unless company officials asked for FC intervention, and I was sure they wouldn't. So, at worst Osterlad's successors, along with Chung and Xychek, of course, would be coming after me. Both groups drew their motivation from the same source—Chung— so getting to him remained the key next step if I wanted to return my life to normal.

With Osterlad, I had to assume there was no chance he would risk coming to me. With Chung, I had a small chance that he didn't know about Lobo's repair, so perhaps I could bait him into a meeting.

It was worth a try.

A few streets down Dean's Folly from the Busted Heart I found what I wanted: an ex-YouCall franchise still in the comm business. For about half the price of what you'd pay outside Queen's Bar, the wire-thin proprietor of this fine establishment would slide you a communicator that'd work until its bill hit the real owner, by which time you'd better be highly inaccessible. For four times the price of a comm unit on the outside, however, he'd slip you a clean box with a spider-shaped viral injector hunched on its back. The injector disabled the display, altered your voice, and spread billable microseconds onto other phones and calls across the net, the time additions so small that no one who was not running his own verification software would notice them. As long as the spider glowed green, the call remained secure. The software in the spiders ran a constant race with the comm net software, so the units were never good for long. When a spider detected an attack or a compromise, or when it was unable to find recipients for the microsecond billing allocations, it turned red. This level of protection was fine by me; I needed it to last only one call.

I took the device to the Busted Heart, paid the occupants of a table in the corner of the rearmost room to leave, and contacted Xychek. The bar rumbled with noise, as always, but with the earbuds I could hear the call well enough for my purpose and still monitor the area for signs of trouble. Even if Xychek's tracers beat the spider's software, I'd have at least a few minutes before corporate muscle could get to the bar.

I explained to the inquisitive answer construct that my comm's camera was busted and asked for Chung. I was rewarded with a female voice so perfectly modulated that I momentarily longed to meet its owner—which was probably a piece of software.

"Mr. Chung's office," she/it said. "May I help you?"

"I'd like to speak to Mr. Chung," I said.

"As I'm sure you can appreciate," she—I decided to indulge my fantasy and think of the voice, a delicious one that dripped sex, as belonging to a woman—said, "Mr. Chung receives a great many communications, so he asks us to handle them if we can. May I perhaps help you?"

"No." The spider wouldn't protect the call long enough for me to be able to afford to waste time playing games with Xychek's flak-catching programs. "Please tell Mr. Chung that it concerns the return of Jasmine to Kelco's Slake on Macken." I was banking on the notion that the four keywords I'd tossed out would elevate the priority of my message a great deal. In case I was wrong, I decided to appeal to self-preservation as well. "I suggest you flash him the info, because if you don't, when he finally sees this call log and finds out what he missed, he's likely to throw you out."

"Please hold," she said, in what I read as both a good

sign and a sure indicator that trace-back software was now seeking me.

About ninety seconds later a man's voice blasted into my ears. "Who is this, and what do you want?" The words sounded enough like the recordings of Chung I had heard that it was either the man himself or a construct customized for him.

"My identity isn't important right now," I said. "Suffice to say that I was involved in returning Jasmine to Slake on Kelco, and we need to talk."

"You were what?" He was screaming into the phone.

The spider turned red, its software hacked faster than I would have guessed the Xychek bots could have managed; it served me right for not spending more to buy some stall-routing through interference sats. I turned off the unit, left the bar, and headed down the street. A couple of blocks over, I found a metal shop with acid-etching gear and paid the price of a lovely office Welcome sign for the privilege of dropping my now dangerous comm into a small tank of waste acid. I watched as it dissolved, wondering why I ever bothered to believe the easy path to anything would succeed.

I wasn't going to let Chung keep his bounty on me, and to get him to remove it I had to be able to meet with him, so I was back to having to abduct another executive. I hoped talking would work this time. With almost all my heart I did not want to have to kill another one—"almost" only because a life of violence leaves you with permanent deep-structure damage, a depth of darkness you never understood was possible until long after the actions that caused it. I knew that if killing proved to be the only option, I would kill. Not all people think of their options the same way I do, and at some level I'm sure they're better for not thinking that way.

I wish I could remember what it was like to be one of them.

CHAPTER 13

Lobo was as pleasant coming out of storage this time as he'd been the last.

"I believe," he said, "that I was foolish enough to previously assign dirt-bound loaders the title of stupidest machines in existence. After this most recent stay in storage, I would consider myself lucky to have one of those gloriously intellectual devices to talk to. Every loader in the facility was out on assignment, and the hangar's shielding stopped all transmissions in and out, so all I had for company was a small squad of cleaning bots. Their little brains—and I use the term charitably, really what little capacity they possess amounts more to computing clumps than actual brains—find nothing more fascinating or conversation-worthy than the amount of dust that has accumulated since the last cleaning, or, if it's a particularly exciting day, how a group of them might best cooperate to nudge an especially large piece of trash into a receptacle. Thank you so much, Jon, for helping me realize how good my life had been before."

"Osterlad knew about you," I said, "and Chung offered Osterlad the bounty on me, so I had to assume Chung knew about you, too. Consequently, when you weren't actively involved, the most logical option was to keep you completely offline so Chung couldn't find you."

"I do possess significant antidetection measures," he said, "and unlike some machines—and, if I may say so, some humans—I've recently spent time with, I constantly work at improving myself. I've incorporated into my online arsenal my own sanitized and customized versions of every major blocking bot out there. I'm expert at mimicking both satellites in decaying orbits and a wide range of standard relay and surveillance sats, so I can hide for long periods of time in space—time I could use, by the way, to befriend the local sats. I can do none of this, of course, while I'm sitting in a shielded storage hangar listening raptly to today's dust reports."

I shook my head and sighed. I needed to keep Lobo busy, because boredom made him unbearable. "I'm sorry," I said, "for putting you away again."

"Your apology means so much," he said, "coming as it does after a second stint in storage immediately preceded by essentially the same words."

I considered disabling all his emotive programming, but even if that were possible, doing so would also render unbearably boring the one entity I could count on being able to talk to. Working with him was, I had to admit, a better choice than silencing him. "Here's the difference,"

I said. "This time I promise not to put you in storage if you can persuade me you can hide safely in orbit or elsewhere. Fair enough?"

"Yes, and now I accept your apology."

"Thank you. Now, load up another set of tourist shuttle codes and get us in the pack. We need to check out Xychek's HQ."

The company's ornate structure perched on a cliff so close to the heart of Bekin's Deal that urban sprawl had brought construction right to its border. The building was thus much, much closer to the city than Osterlad's, and much grander as well. Easily three times as wide as Osterlad's, its rock face featured the Xychek logo superimposed on what at first glance appeared to be irregular, raised asymmetric ovals in the rock. Upon further study, however, the carvings proved to be relief maps of all the solar systems where Xychek was active, their positions not true to light-year scale but at least indicative of relative distances apart. Under magnification Lobo's visual monitors revealed that what had appeared to be mere lumps in the orbits to mark the colonized planets were actually the faces of those planets, each face an accurate high-level map of an aspect of the planet as seen from its jump gate. Xychek had carved the entire surface of its structure from the native black cliffs, with the only additional highlighting being the degree to which its artisans had polished the various stone faces. The image struck me as the heavens might appear to a god holding the only light in creation after all the stars had burnt to black.

I understood for the first time why so many tourists opened their wallets for this view. Perhaps later I'd spend some time appreciating the other structures, but not now.

Now, we had to keep our focus on Xychek and learn what we could about Chung's habits.

Lobo kept image-matching programs running on every person who came out of the Xychek building, and I started my exercises, thankful that unlike when I've been on ground surveillance duty, in Lobo I could move around without concern.

After three days of flying the tourist shuttle rotation during the daytime and retreating to orbit each evening, I had to accept that kidnapping Chung during business hours was not going to be reasonably possible. He arrived every morning within ninety minutes of sunrise, his vehicle in the center of a heavily armed group of eight escorts, a number I felt was unnecessarily high and a sign of willingness to waste money on Xychek security's part. Chung came and went from the building frequently throughout the day to discharge his business and social duties, but the same escort vehicles always accompanied him. Other buildings stood right on the border of Xychek's, so Chung and his team always began each trip in a crowded area, and they stopped only at heavily populated spots. When he was on foot, guards stayed within reach at all times. I never caught them passing through desolate countryside during business hours.

Lobo had more than enough firepower to destroy his entire escort team, of course; they were bodyguards, not soldiers in battle-armored vehicles. A direct attack, however, would not only result in a lot of conflict with the bodyguards, it would also almost certainly yield a great many civilian casualties and enough collateral damage that the Frontier Coalition would have to join Xychek in hunting me down. With Osterlad's company likely to come after me once the new management settled in, and with Xychek already seeking me, I couldn't afford to attract any more pursuers.

I'd have to go after him in his home. To do that, of course, I had to find his house and scout it.

The first part was easy. As the light began to fade on Lankin and the last of the tourists were murmuring appreciatively about the great views as their shuttles cruised on long, lazy arcs over the ocean and back to the city, Lobo headed for the lowest fairly crowded orbit we could find. A bottom-feeder collection of relay sats, corporate spy and counterspy bots, weather monitors, and automated zero-gee fabs shared the orbit with us and provided adequate cover. The heat signature of Chung's escort team was distinctive enough that Lobo could track it with his onboard sensors, so we waited a couple of hours until the man finally headed home.

As we'd observed the previous days, he used exactly the same vehicle arrangement and headed initially straight into town. Each day, however, his course changed within the first few klicks away from the office; I appreciated the countersurveillance care his bodyguards were taking. From our vantage in orbit we watched as first one and then two more of the escort vehicles pulled aside at different points along the route and idled, engines and weapons at the ready. Anyone following from the ground would have to pass them all, so surface pursuit would end up in conflict with either the last standalone trailing vehicle or a rear-facing part of the main team. I revised my opinion of Xychek security: The eight vehicles represented more a practical paranoia than waste.

After about forty minutes of wandering in the city,
Chung's vehicle and his five remaining escorts headed
northwest out of town on a highway whose scattered buildings over the course of half an hour of travel time mutated
from city to suburb to widespread collections of large
houses and then finally to a forest dotted here and there
with estates. Chung and his team came to a stop at one of
the largest properties, a cleared rectangular chunk of land
that Lobo measured at a bit over eighty acres in size. An
outer rectangle of forest about a hundred yards wide surrounded the land. Three roads led into it: the one on which
Chung had entered, a second on the opposite side that
more or less continued the path of the entry road, and a
third on the left as you came onto the estate. The cleared
area glowed in the weakening daylight with a pure white
light from well-distributed and almost certainly redundant sets of spotlights, lights that made sure his team's
monitors missed nothing on the ground near the house.

We had the location of Chung's house, but we needed
a lot more data to be able to plan any kind of attack other
than complete destruction of the place. I didn't consider
that a viable option, both because of the attention it would
attract and because without talking to Chung I couldn't
know whether killing him would remove the bounty or
only raise it.

Getting more data wasn't going to be simple. The house
predictably read IR-neutral to Lobo, its shielding more
than he could penetrate from orbit; he wasn't built for
long-distance surveillance. So, we needed to find another
way to take a closer look. On Macken I'd gotten lucky:
Lobo had been deployed there as a local military reserve,
so he had sat friends, and the Gardeners never noticed

his surveillance drone because they were amateurs, bad amateurs. We knew no sats here, and I had great confidence that Chung's Xychek protection team was professional enough to immediately spot and shoot down any obviously military surveillance drone. Lobo's monitors had never tracked anything larger than birds flying over the place, so Chung and Xychek had probably paid local flight control to keep his airspace empty. I was also confident they possessed the weapons to make sure nothing flew too low over the house. On a transmission-heavy battlefield we could try a high-altitude flyover and dust the area with our own microsensor web, its activity sure to do no more than add to the electronic din that large-scale combat created. At Chung's estate, however, I had to assume his team had tracked and identified and was actively monitoring every transmission source in the area. Any change in the broadcast activity would trigger an alarm, an investigation, and possibly an evacuation.

The estate was secure against every modern electronic approach—and that, I finally realized, provided the opening we needed. I'd been thinking of this as a battle, the estate as a battlefield, where up-to-the-second data frequently played a major role in keeping you alive, but this wasn't a battle, and Chung's home wasn't a battlefield. I wanted surveillance data, not transmissions; the distinction was everything.

I told Lobo to keep us with the low-orbit gear and settled into a couch to sleep. In the morning, I'd send Lobo to rejoin the sats and continue his monitoring.

While he was at it, I'd pay a visit to Strange Kitty.

CHAPTER 14

Organic tech has delivered all of the serious progress in human augmentation. Gene therapy, growth-center manipulation, vat-grown organs—you name the technique for making us better or barring death from the door a little longer, and the odds are it's organic. Nanotech petered out, at least as far as the rest of the universe was concerned, after the Aggro accident resulted in an entire solar system no ship had ever been able to return from. Human/hardware fusion never took off, because whatever metal or silicon could do to help a body, cells inevitably proved to be able to do better. Hardware augmentation maintained its fans, however: people who indulged in machine-based enhancement as often and as severely as their lives and budgets would permit, all in the deep belief that one day metal-tech would break through the barriers of its previous failures and elevate them into immortal meat/machine gods. Their extreme-edge bioengineering counterparts rode the same rush but on a different vehicle, pushing the limits of organic tech as they constantly altered their bodies.

Queen's Bar attracted both fringes, of course, with shops where you could ride your augmentation tech of choice not only to the legal limit, but beyond. The metal- and meat-tech shops predictably occupied different zones in the area, each one's clients neither approving nor particularly accepting of the other's. For metal-tech, you wandered the southwest bits of the district; meat-tech clung to the northeast.

Strange Kitty managed a rare trick: Both the serious metal crowd and the severely bioengineered shopped there, and both groups ranked it the top place to go for pets with more. Its storefront/warehouse two-building complex joined popular favorites like the Busted Heart in the center of Queen's Bar. It filled most of a block, with the retail space opening on one street and the warehouse loading docks facing directly onto the other. If you wanted an augmented animal, you headed for Strange Kitty. What it didn't have in stock, its bioengineers could probably produce, and if they couldn't manage it, odds are nothing outside of the top-drawer conglomerate labs could do it either.

FC tech enforcers rousted the place on those occasions when some animal-rights group could grab enough public attention that the local government worried tax dollars might be slipping away. The raids never found anything outside the legal limits; for that, you had to know where to look or have the proper introductions. So, the unwanted attention never lasted long. The same groups would also sometimes make lackluster attempts at picketing the business, but protest rallies in Queen's Bar inevitably mutated quickly into parties, street fairs, or disorganized streams of fleeing ex-protesters, as vendors, pickpockets, and street hustlers of all types dive-bombed any crowd that would stand still long enough for them to catch it.

I paused for a few minutes outside the store to make sure no one was following me. A guy with metal chest-shield implants strolled out of the shop, all of his attention focused on a lizard he was holding with his meat right hand and stroking with his metallic left, the lizard's skin coruscating in the light in time with the passes of the metal fingers. A tall, elegant woman with waist-length straight brown hair followed with her acquisition, an amphi-basset, its prominent gills and blue/teal coloring marking it as anything but an ordinary hound. A trio of fashion-victim girls sporting identical body mods—wispy waists made possible only by elevated organs, thickened spinal columns supporting broad and relatively flat chests, legs rippling with muscle—emerged guiding a flat- and metal-nosed hundred-kilo dog on three identical leads, the animal's detachable metal legs moving perfectly in custom sockets. Neither the creatures nor, for that matter, the people were to my taste, but they, like the rest of the Strange Kitty traffic, were extremely unlikely to be working for Osterlad or Xychek.

I slipped inside in a seam in the outgoing crowd, air-break fans ruffling my hair as I moved through the semipressurized doorway. The smell crashed into my sinuses the moment I cleared the threshold. The odors

of fur, feathers, urine, dung, and sex recombined dynami-
cally as I moved through the room, an olfactory organism
in rapid multidirectional mutation. The doorway kept the
neighbors from complaining, but inside there was no
escape. Here and there I spotted nasal fetishists pretending to shop for as long as the management would let them
linger, their noses flared and eyes glazed. Most of the
customers, however, were focused, serious shoppers,
thickets of them standing in the midst of the creatures
that reflected their taste. Mammals, perennial human
favorites, owned the display space and most of the front,
where prospective buyers made unnatural cute noises over
cats, dogs, ferrets, various local rodents, and other animals I didn't recognize, each one a designer's custom work.
I made my way past them and into the reptile section,
pausing for a moment to admire plexi containers of liz-
ards with metal-barbed tails and snakes with additional
eyes—probably not functional but definitely decorative—
scoring their sides from the original pair backward for
half a meter or more.

After the reptiles, the room darkened a bit as I entered
the aquatic area. Filling this part of the store were tanks
of all sizes, from a few liters up to several huge containers whose capacity I couldn't easily estimate, plexi
enclosures that looked to be at least three meters deep,
five long, and three high. Everything from tiny, purely
decorative fish, to predators, to serious open-ocean racing
rays swam in the tanks lining the walls all around me.
The riotous colors and sheer variety of the fish and other
water creatures on display made the mammals and reptiles appear tame by comparison.

I finally made it to the back of the retail section, where

the store blended into the warehouse as the ceiling rose and the amount of customer activity dropped. In cages at eye level and in enclosed aeries that climbed from barely over my head all the way to the seven-meter-high unfinished ceiling, birds of all types perched, slept, flew, chattered, ate, and defecated. I've never been a bird fan, but that wasn't a problem; I wasn't shopping for a pet. Salespeople were scarce here, but that was fine, too; getting the help I needed would be easy. I stepped past the edge of the retail area and into what appeared to be a reception space fronting the vastly larger work and storage rooms behind it. I paused, knowing security was on the way, because with a quick IR scan I'd spotted some too-cool temperature-detection wall and floor sections, as well as a few failing motion sensors that shined as hot pinpricks; the owners needed to run physical-level maintenance checks on their security gear more often.

First to reach me was a short, thin fellow who moved with the precise jumpy motions of the over-stimmed, a man with neurochemical augmentations that rendered him deadlier than he appeared. Obvious security guys, hands on holstered weapons, followed a couple of seconds later. I stood very still, hands out from my sides.

"I'd like to make a significant purchase," I said.

"All our currently available merchandise is behind you," the short man said. He spoke like he moved: words clipped, phrases staccato, each sound precise.

"What I need is custom," I said.

"We strictly obey all customization laws," he said.

I laughed. "I couldn't care less. Nothing in the customization I want is, to the best of my knowledge, illegal for you to perform." I didn't have time to meet the right people in town, so I'd have to speed my way through this with brute conversational force. "What I do with my purchases is not your business. What is your business is what I'm willing to pay, which is well above your going rates." I pointed at my pocket. "I'm going to get my wallet."

He nodded his approval.

I pulled out the wallet and thumbed a link to my local bank. I'd priced the canine versions earlier, added a sizable premium, and set up an account that contained the result. I brought up the balance, obscured the account's number but left the bank's logo visible, and turned the wallet toward him. "This amount is ready to move to your local bank," I said, "once I have the animals I want—as long as I get them quickly."

He glanced at the screen, then at me. "What exactly do you want?"

"You engineer monitor dogs, right?" I said.

"Yes, of course," he said, "and cats and snakes and pretty much anything else you might like. It's generally standard stuff—organic fluid-drop-lens cameras bound into the eyes, transmitters feeding off the optic nerves—though it tends to lead to short lives for the pets." He shook his head. "What you showed me is way too much for monitors, even a herd of them."

"No," I said, "it's not. I need monitor birds—"

He cut me off. "Again, standard. What are you really—"

I returned the favor. "I need a flock of them," I said, "local, something common in the woods northwest of the city, plus enough controls to force them to follow a course I'll describe, and a wrangler to take them up and bring them back." I paused for breath, and this time he let me finish. "And I need it all without any transmissions of any sort, not for control, not for what they monitor. I need the absolute minimum amount of metal possible, onboard silicon or other nonmetal recorders, and all the recordings in my hands afterward; no one else sees the data."

"Pre-jump organic recorders?" he asked. "Why not simply transmit—" He stopped and waved his hand, stopping me before I could speak. "Not my concern, of course. After you're done with the birds?"

"I'll use them only once, and then they're yours—but the data is, as I said, exclusively mine."

He smiled for the first time. "The payment makes more sense. We've helped with similar work, of course, but nothing with tech this old. We also, as you might expect, want nothing to do with the end product of your . . . project, though as I think about it not having the data flow in realtime is only good for us."

"Yes," I said, "and I don't want you involved. It's a one-time run, then we're done. You take away the birds and do what you want with them."

"Fair enough," he said. "We can do business. Got a particular bird in mind?"

"No," I said. "As long as whatever you choose is common enough that no one tracking the flock will think twice about it flying overhead, I'll be happy."

He thought for a few seconds. "Blue-beaked moseys. They're everywhere outside the city, they move around frequently—a loud noise will send a flock flapping to a new location—and they fly at all times from first light until fairly late at night. They move relatively slowly, so the images should be clear. They'll home for multiple klicks after only a couple of feedings, so training is quick and range is good. Plus, they're easy to work on, with heads large enough that laser and cellular quick-heal techniques all work."

"Fine," I said. "One last complication: I need full-spectrum recording, visible and IR."

He smiled again. "You're new to working with animals. Of course you do; that's standard on this type of augmentation. When do you need all this?"

"This evening," I said, half statement and half question.

"Not a chance," he said. "A day to prepare and heal the flock, plus a day for the wrangler to work out his approach and do the homing training once you identify the start and end points."

I hated the delay, but he was right; it was never going to happen today. Maybe I'd get lucky in the interim and Chung would change his habits and give me an open shot at him. Unlikely, but I could hope.

"Okay," I said. "A quarter now, another quarter when they take off, and the remaining half when I have all the recordings."

"A third now," he said, "to help with up-front costs. Then take us to half when the wrangler's in position, and pay the balance when he hands you all the recordings."

He agreed so quickly that I realized I should have started with a lower offer and haggled, but the money pain was still tolerable. I needed Xychek to lift the bounty on me, and getting to Chung was the only way I knew to make that happen. I nodded my agreement, thumbed up a transfer of a third, and opened my wallet to accepting a destination code from his. "Done," I said. "Give me the account to transfer to, then we'll work out our communication protocols, and you can get me some birds."

⊠   ⊠   ⊠

Over the next three days, Chung kept to his routine, and Lobo and I clung to ours. We spent the nights in a variety of geosync low-orbit positions, Lobo maintaining transmission cover by echoing weather data or acting as a free public-data sat repeater, his sensors trained on Chung's house on the off chance that our target would surprise us with an easy opportunity. Chung didn't. In the days we flew with the tourist shuttle crowd, up and down the coastal cliff and outlying forest tour routes, Lobo's camo washing him with a different set of corporate colors every few hours. Chung's security team kept to its proven practices, and we never even came close to a low-collateral-damage shot at him. As the time wore on, the beauty of the cliff structures faded into unseen background, then eventually decayed into visual annoyance. Choose to look at a piece of art a thousand times, and each glance may reveal new beauty. Let a job force you to study it when you're aching to move on to the next task, and only those rare pieces that touch you most deeply will remain lovely.

I invested part of each evening in studying Lobo's low-orbit recon images of a fifteen-kilometer-diameter circle centered on Chung's estate, trying to balance my conflicting desires. For the obvious safety reasons, I wanted starting and ending coordinates that were as deserted as reasonably possible, but I also needed a flight line that passed over as many homes and businesses as possible. Should the Strange Kitty team be tempted to double-dip by offering intel about me to the possible targets, I wanted them to have to wonder which of many options I was scanning. Alerting all the possibilities would, I hoped, open them to more exposure than they'd like.

I finally settled on a not-quite-ten-kilometer path that started a couple of klicks off the road in a light-density forest and ran over three small business concentrations and five estates roughly on par with Chung's. The end-point was the far edge of the warehouse portion of one of the business areas—not ideal, but acceptable given that we'd be launching in the dying light of the day, when Chung would most likely be home.

I stretched out the route choice to maintain my focus on the task. I've never enjoyed waiting for a job to start. Waiting is fine when I can use the time to gather new intel. It can also be a pleasurable activity when I'm not working. I love idle time and can while away weeks observing a new starscape or ocean, as I'd been doing on Macken before all this started, but such lazy days are fun only when what I've chosen to do is be idle. I was on my first run up the coast one morning and way past ready to get to work when the Strange Kitty folks posted the sig-nal my birds were ready: an advertisement for a one-day, limited-quantity price reduction on mini-dragons with self-regulating homeostatic systems that would work in anything from a blizzard to a heat wave. I'd suggested a protocol that wouldn't risk costing them money, but my salesman had assured me that they'd overstocked the mini-dragons and would love it if the special offer boosted sales. To avoid attracting undue attention, Lobo and I finished the tour route we were running, called Strange Kitty, and worked our way cautiously to a location where Lobo could safely drop me.

Two hours before the projected launch time, I met the

Strange Kitty team, my salesman and the wrangler, at the coordinates I'd given them. They arrived in a heavily shielded company transport truck that contained my birds and a dozen other animals of various types, all sedated. The men sported Strange Kitty uniforms in ad-woven active fabric, images of augmented creatures of all types slithering over the clothing. Had anyone stopped them, they explained, they would have been able to produce a full schedule of deliveries. I nodded appreciatively at their caution. My salesman appeared exactly as amped as he had at the store. The wrangler, an even shorter man who was enough of a bird fan to have back feathers that peeked above the collar of his coverall, moved almost as if asleep—a by-product, he explained, of the chemically enhanced calming mosey pheromones he'd washed with before loading the birds.

"I'd like to verify the recording capability," I said. The air was hot, thermals playing almost visibly in the slow-moving atmosphere. This far inland we received all the heat of a tourist coastal city but none of the cooling ocean breeze.

"Of course," my salesman replied.

They opened the back of the truck and led me inside. Its rear half was a large cage full of moseys squawking and flapping and jumping about. As the wrangler walked over to the cage, however, the pheromone assault calmed the birds, and they settled on some of the many dark wooden perches that extended from the bars, walls, and ceilings of the caged area.

He took out one of the moseys and absently stroked its head, the bird lying as still and happy in his arms as a spent lover. A little under a third of a meter long and with a wingspan of over a meter, the mosey was bigger than I'd expected. At first glance as we entered the truck, I'd thought the moseys to be plain, basically gray animals with only the blue beaks to break up the color monotony. Now, with the time to look closely, I saw that their feathers eased through a gentle color transition from dark gray at the tips to a blend of lighter grays and finally to a blue so close to gray it was as if the merest few drops of blue pigment had fallen in a can of gray paint. Here and there on the bird's underside were flecks of white and black frequent enough that they invited the thought of a pattern, but not any pattern I could discern. Not showy animals, but ones that repaid close inspection, beautiful in their own way. I realized then, as I have at many such moments in the past, that the same has proven true of every living thing I've ever taken the time to study closely, a testimony to the wonder of creation. I know many people crave explanations for the glories of the universe, but I don't; what I crave is the will and the ability to learn to appreciate it all.

The wrangler interrupted my reverie. "It couldn't be simpler," he said. He parted the feathers on the left side of the bird's neck to reveal a small stud, pressed the stud, and pointed the animal's head at me. After a few seconds, he pressed the stud again, then hooked a small viewing port to it, the bird still happily pheromone-drunk in his arms. The screen snapped alive with multiwindowed images of me in visible, IR, and composite frequencies.

"They're trained for the end coordinates?" I said.

"Of course," said the wrangler, his pride obviously offended. As he put the mosey back in its cage, he continued. "We've made three other deliveries in that area earlier today. Each time, we fed them and established the destination for them. They're superb homing beasts, so that might have been enough. To make sure, though, we installed some of our proprietary tech—" he must have seen my eyes widen, for he quickly added "—nonmetal, of course—in every bird in the flock. They'll work, or you owe us nothing."

"And you'd refund my previous payments?" I said, addressing the question to the salesman.

"Of course."

"Excellent," I said. I counted the birds; nineteen were in the cage. I had expected more. "Why only nineteen?"

The wrangler's look ratcheted from offended to annoyed. "Because it felt right," he said, "for moseys, these woods, this time of year, this time of day. It felt right. It's what I do."

"My apologies," I said, meaning it. I'd asked out of reflex, not thought, and if I was going to question their expertise, I should have done the research in advance to be able to do so intelligently.

I took out my wallet, thumbed what I owed them, and showed it to the salesman.

After finishing the transfer, he said, "When do we launch?"

"When I call you," I said, "which will be in less than two hours. I want to be at the endpoint before you release them; no point in taking the risk of transportation issues messing up the schedule. Who from your end will be with me?"

"I will," the wrangler said. "Launching requires only opening the exterior cage access panel in the side of the truck, so he'll handle it. The moseys will handle it from there. I assume you can take me and my equipment bags; yes?"

"Yes." I didn't see him as a threat, and having a hostage could prove useful should something go wrong. "Let's go." To the salesman I added, "I'll call when we're in position and the time is right."

The trip to the endpoint went smoothly, no traffic and, to my delight, no probing chatter from the wrangler. I invested some of the available transit time in counter-ground-surveillance side trips and detours, and neither I nor Lobo, who was tracking me from one of his low-orbit posts, could spot anyone following. Lobo couldn't get detailed enough data for me to be completely comfortable, but that was fine; too much comfort in a mission is a dangerous thing.

As the sun was fading and the day's light deepening in tone and multiplexing in color, playing a visual symphony transitioning from unnoticed backdrop to in-your-face beauty, I made the call. The wrangler anticipated less than half an hour before the birds would reach us, so he began setting out food, harnesses, four pop-up cages, and another test viewer. I scanned the treetops on the other side of the parking area for signs of the moseys as Lobo kept me posted on what little he could discern. What appeared to be the flock was moving from the launch site toward me, its speed was consistent with the plan, and so on.

A little over fifteen minutes later, Lobo relayed the most important news: The flock had crossed Chung's grounds, and all nineteen birds were still airborne and heading toward us. I relaxed a little.

The vibrant colors of the sunset had begun to morph into somber, inky tones that would soon give way to night. The day was cooling quickly as the sun set. The moseys flew into view. The wrangler misted the air with a spray bottle I assumed contained more pheromones and put bits of additional food in the now open cages. The moseys circled us for a few minutes, enjoying the freedom of the sky and reluctant to surrender it. The chemical net of the pheromones and the installed Strange Kitty tech drew them down and into the cages. The last few hovered for a little bit just out of reach, moving in gentle spirals on wings working so slowly and perfectly you could almost believe they never really moved, but even those reluctant few finally settled into captivity.

The wrangler closed three of the cages and pulled one of the birds from the open fourth; it was as submissive as the one in the truck. A bit back from and below the control stud was a small flap of skin that covered a thumbnail-size recording module. He popped the module out of its socket and pointed to the module's connector. "Nonmetal conductor plug compatible with most milspec tech," he said. "They wear out faster than metal, so plug them in once, get what you need, and move the data to more stable media. Okay?" He handed me the module.

"Got it," I said, as I took the recording. I tested it in the viewer and watched the images at high speed, skipping forward quickly but seeing enough to confirm that it contained coverage of Chung's place. "Good enough," I said.

The wrangler nodded and went to work on the other birds. I again counted nineteen birds, and he delivered nineteen modules.

The salesman arrived ten minutes later. Lobo said he couldn't spot any pursuers. I paid the balance I owed and left as the wrangler was gently carrying the birds one by one into the truck's holding pen. The salesman stood calmly by, smart enough to realize there was no point in trying to rush this man with his charges.

We'd spent a lot of time in orbits near Chung's, so while we were analyzing the recon data I had Lobo park us in a fairly high orbit about as far away from Chung as possible, in a nice spot over the largely unsettled mountainous region on the continent on the other side of Lankin from Bekin's Deal.

I had to admire the quality of Lobo's analysis systems. He perfectly and quickly assembled all the recordings from the nineteen birds into a composite video and a set of stills showing images in various combinations of wavelengths. Predictably, no one bird had captured all the views I wanted, and most of the time the birds weren't looking directly at the estate, but their flight pattern was wide enough and slow enough, as the Strange Kitty crew had said it would be, that the composite images completely covered the estate. Almost two dozen of the most important still images filled Lobo's wall in front of me as I walked back and forth in his main open area.

No matter how long I looked at them, they told me the same basic story: Chung's estate was a fortress, more heavily armed than I'd guessed. Air-defense weapons, both missile launchers and energy pulse, squatted in plain sight about twenty meters from each side of the house. Image-match searches of Lobo's weaponry database pegged them as serious medium- and high-altitude killers, useless for targets below two hundred meters but deadly for anything above that height. At least two dozen guards were visible across the estate, some obviously carrying the smart missiles that conventional wisdom had long held were the best choice for combating low-flying attack craft. Lobo might be able to weather a hit from one of those missiles, but he also might not; I didn't want to find out.

IR views showed hot sensors scattered across the estate, with a ring of what I had to assume were overlapping area monitors covering the perimeter of the cleared grounds.

As I'd observed before, three gates, all staffed with guards, led into and out of the property.

The size of the estate, the multiple entrances, and the many guards and sensors combined to doom any possibility of a stealth attack with my nanomachines. I've never tried controlling more than half a dozen nano-swarms, and the clouds unavoidably move fairly slowly, certainly at nothing like battlefield weapon speeds, so I had no chance of individually taking down the whole place. Even if I did, explaining that much disassembled matter in a large city like Bekin's Deal would be impossible. I couldn't afford the attention.

I saw no way to do this job entirely on my own without enduring way too much risk.

Involving Lobo didn't improve my chances a lot. Even assuming he came in hot, my options were severely limited and incredibly unattractive.

The only one I was sure would work was a total-destruction missile and pulse attack from an altitude of about a hundred meters on the edge of the forest outside the house. Lobo could fly in quickly enough that only the gate guards would have time to attack, and from the images we had of their weapons his armor could handle the minimal attack those guards could muster before he killed them. Firing everything he had in one long screaming attack, he could take out the whole area, scorch the turf and everything on it, but that did me no good; I needed Chung alive.

Worse, that much destruction and death would tornado into enough news locally that the FC would have to come after me. They might be able to write off Chung's loss as a standard corporate casualty, part of the risk of operating on still-developing worlds, but some of his guards were bound to be talent recruited locally, with local ties, and their deaths would provoke an outcry the FC couldn't ignore. The FC would then use the Saw to get me, of course, and I doubted I'd live to walk away from that fight.

No, total destruction wasn't a reasonable option.

Any more finely targeted approach would, of course, leave Lobo open to the handheld missiles. Losing Lobo was also not an acceptable choice.

We could perhaps boost the odds of success by first blanketing the area with milspec sensor disruptors and hoping Chung's sensor web was old tech—not likely, but possible—but the guards would then take Chung and leave. Clusters of armored vehicles stood ready to roll at the intersection of each of the three roads with the house. I had to assume that these guys would use standard protection protocols, so at the first sign of attack all three sets of vehicles would roar out of there at high speed, and I'd have to guess which one held Chung.

The more I stared at the images, the more I was

convinced that I had to change the game's rules if I wanted to play at all.

"Lobo," I said, "I can't come up with a plan that doesn't involve massive casualties and that also guarantees we emerge alive and with Chung. Can you?"

"No," he said. "Quite the opposite. Logic dictates we can't guarantee success within the axioms you've set. Your rules don't allow us to destroy the entire place, so we're left with two of us to cover three well-spaced exit routes. This is obviously not possible."

"Yeah," I said, "it isn't. We can't do it."

I stretched out on a pilot's couch, the images on the wall blanking as I moved away from them. I had to stop avoiding the reality in front of me and accept the only real solution to the problem, or start running and hope Chung, Osterlad's team, and everyone else Chung contracted would eventually tire of searching for me. The latter was unacceptable. As little as I wanted to follow the only path I could discover that would get Chung, I had even less desire to spend all my days in heightened paranoia, even if the paranoia was justified.

"The answer," I said, "is just as obvious, but I hate it."

"What?" Lobo said.

"I have to get some help."

CHAPTER 15

The Saw recruiting center perched in the shadow of a skyscraper on the southern edge of Queen's Bar like a bird of prey waiting for rodents to crawl into the light. A plain rectangular building with clean, sharp lines displayed the Shosen Advanced Weapons Corporation name, icon—a gleaming serrated blade most of the way through cutting a rifle barrel in half—and motto, "The Price of Peace." The door stayed open around the clock. Inside, the honestly inquisitive visitor could always count on free drinks, food, and basic stimulants. The repeat moocher could equally reliably expect to hit the street face-first after fewer than three strides into the greeting room.

I counted half a dozen Saw troops on duty in the large open public area, their eyes constantly monitoring both their conversational targets and the room's access points.

About that many more were stopping by on a leave day to grab a bite to eat or enough uppers to keep them going as they fought to muster the stamina to spend the accumulated pay that was screaming for release from their wallets.

Standing to the side of the main information counter was an older man, a sergeant, whom the inattentive or the intoxicated could easily mistake for a friend's kindly uncle. A smile constantly played on his face, pleasant crinkles surrounded his eyes, and his hands moved with the unhurried ease of someone with not a care in the world. Bring even slightly trained vision to bear on him, however, and you'd note the master gunnery sergeant's stripes on his working blues, stripes that marked him as being as high a noncom as you'd find in the Saw; the complete lack of visible fat on a torso half again as wide and as thick as the bodies of most men his height; and the fine scar lines on his neck and hands, lines he kept despite the ease with which Saw doctors could have removed them, lines he used every campaign to remind him how easily and how quickly the drain could come out on any mission. An active-fabric patch on his chest alternated his name, "Gustafson," and the Saw logo. He made me while I was still figuring out that he was the one I needed. By the time I reached him, he'd shifted one foot forward and spread and lowered his stance, all in subtle movements you could easily miss. In my peripheral vision I caught three of the duty troops moving nearer the exits; should I get by him, they'd make sure I never left the building.

All around us the recruiting chatter continued. The locals, who were there to find out if the merc life might be for them, or if it really would pay enough to get them out of whatever trouble they were in, remained happily oblivious of the storm gathering wind across the room from them.

I stopped well short of Gustafson, spread my arms slightly, showed him my palms, and said, "Top."

"Looking to join up?" he said, the smile still fixed on his face.

"No."

"I didn't think so." The smile vanished. "What *do* you want?"

"No trouble," I said, "only to ask a question." Two more of the duty troops casually wandered closer. "I appreciate that you have to engage all the security," I tilted my head slightly toward the various gathering soldiers, "and I'd do the same in your job, but it's not necessary. Let me make this at least a little simpler. I served with the Saw for a decade, most of it under a captain named Tristan Earl, humping sector-to-sector on the ground in planets I'd just as soon forget. I opted out twelve years ago. Scan my fingerprints and retinas; unless the Saw has slid downhill enough since I left it to make me cry, I'll still be in the databases."

His expression didn't change, but he nodded his head in the direction of the recruiting desk. I walked up to it. He and the men accompanying me paralleled my path, never letting the distance between us change.

The woman who was leading the team at the desk, Schmidt according to her name tag, flashed me a smile that looked perfectly at home in a face pretty enough to make potential recruits want to sign up just so they could get to know her. Her sergeant's stripes, callused hands, and heavily muscled forearms suggested they'd end up spending more time fearing her than adoring her. She ran quick retinal and fingerprint scans, the skin scrape for the secret DNA test a little too obvious.

"You need to adjust the print scanner, Sarge," I said.

She cocked an eyebrow.

I smiled. "It accidentally scraped my finger."

She glanced at her display and straightened a tiny bit. "Thanks, Gunny. We will."

Gustafson stepped up, clapped me on the back, and led me off to a side room with a sofa, a few chairs, and a low table in the center of the seats. As we left the main area, the guys who'd positioned themselves behind me and those monitoring the exits all floated back into the swirl of the room.

He sat, and I did the same.

"What can we do for you?" he said. "Don't tell me you miss it."

I laughed. "Now and then, sure, I find myself thinking about it, but mostly because I liked being part of a group that knew what the hell it was about. Most of the time, though, no, I don't. Most of the time, I wish I slept better."

"I sleep fine," he said.

I stared at him, saying nothing.

He laughed. "Most nights." He shook his head and laughed again. "Some nights."

I laughed with him. "Fair enough."

"So," he said, "we've established we're a couple of guys with some obvious things in common. That's all fine, and if I were on leave I'd buy you a drink and maybe we'd get in a little trouble together, but I'm working. Again: What can we do for you?"

"I need to talk to the Old Man here on Lankin," I said,

"and I know trying to find out who he is and where he is will take a lot of time."

"Why?"

I shook my head. "Top, I have a little data to give, and I need a little data in return. Please trust me that I mean no trouble, and leave it at that."

He nodded, understanding. You don't make it anywhere near as far as master gunnery sergeant in any serious outfit I've ever seen without learning that you're going to spend a lot of your life acting without anything approaching all the information you'd like. The smile flooded back onto his face. "Who'd you say you served under?" he said.

"Captain Earl, Tristan Earl."

"Then meeting the Old Man will be a reunion for you," he said.

"Captain Earl runs the Saw here on Lankin?" I said. I'd always hoped Earl would receive the recognition he deserved, but I never expected it to happen so quickly. Then I realized it wasn't quick at all; sitting with a man in a Saw uniform, going back to those days even for a moment, the twelve years I'd been away seemed no time at all.

"Colonel Earl," Gustafson said. "When the FC awarded the Lankin deal to us, the colonel got the post. We've been here five years, and he's run the show the whole time. He's done a damn fine job of it, too, if you ask me."

"I would have expected no less."

"Stay put," he said, as he got up and headed back to the main desk.

I'd planned to improvise a bit with the local Saw head, because I needed to understand the FC, corporate, and

Saw relationships a bit better before I could know what was safe to say and what might land me in the brig. With Earl, though, improvising wouldn't cut it. He was too smart not to spot the game, and unless he'd changed a lot, too focused and too busy to have the patience to put up with it. I'd have to tread carefully but play it as straight as I could without putting either of us in a bad position.

Gustafson returned and handed me a small sheet of rich paper; the Saw's admin corps liked pomp. "End of business tomorrow," he said. "This will give you the details and a map."

"Thanks," I said. "I appreciate it. You won't regret it."

"I hope that's the case," he said, "because from your record I'd prefer to avoid ending up on the opposite side of any heavy action."

I shook his hand, and, as I was heading out, said, "Me, too." I meant it.

CHAPTER 16

The Saw station where I went to meet Earl blended
seamlessly with the many corporate fabs that ringed the
southwestern edge of the city. Surrounded by a few layers
of active-wire fencing that writhed like snakes when you
walked too close, fronted by gates bristling with both automated and human security, the cream-colored central
buildings appeared no more important or heavily guarded
than those of any of the fabs. Fabrication modules and
the design intelligences that guided them ranked as core
assets of all the corporations that dominated commerce
in this sector of space, so everyone expected heavy security around them. No one would give this facility's setup a
second thought.

When I torqued my vision over to IR, however, the
picture changed. Hot spots dotting the interior perimeter

at irregular intervals marked hatches covering weapons I could guess at but not see. Similar spots on the roofs and walls of all the buildings in the complex made it clear that the Saw had, as always, dug in securely and would make anyone trying to take their turf pay dearly for every centimeter.

I arrived early enough to make sure I'd be outside Earl's office a few minutes before our appointment; punctuality ranked high on the long list of societal conventions he considered vital. The guard made a show of checking for my appointment while the cameras and clearance systems did the real work. When I and the cab I'd hired had passed all the tests, the guard snapped me a small but polite salute, my record obviously visible in his pad. He beamed directions to the cab's guidance systems and waved me through. The vehicle dropped me in front of a central building that looked no different from all the others, then sped away as soon as I paid. Gustafson stepped out of a door a half-dozen meters in front of me.

"Good to see you again, Top," I said, "though I'm a bit surprised he has you on all these babysitting details."

Gustafson pulled on the outside seam of his right pants leg. The fabric parted to reveal an almost albino, hairless stretch of skin that ran as low and as high as I could see. "Still integrating the new leg and hip," he said. "Lost the old one on a dirtball a few jumps away that I'm not allowed to name and you probably wouldn't recognize anyway. I might have healed as fast, maybe faster, if I'd let them keep me in hospital, but I've always believed work is the best therapy. I posted for any station that would take me and let me do a job. Earl's unit offered the recruiting and admin gig, and here I am."

I nodded in understanding. I couldn't picture him waiting at some physical therapy station for a bunch of rear-echelon doctors to pronounce him fit. "So it's coincidence you're here to meet me?" I said.

"You know better than that. I understand you couldn't tell me why you wanted this meeting, but you have to know that your refusal left me curious. I can't believe anything that makes you feel the need to meet the Old Man is entirely legit, and he can't, either—which means he has to make sure nothing happens here that casts the Saw in a bad light with its employer. So, you get the pleasure of me joining your meeting."

I should have expected Earl wouldn't take the risk, physical or contractual, of even listening to me without a witness. The Saw and I could both fake recordings, of course, but I wouldn't have a supporting eyewitness on my side. This wasn't bad news—I'd known I'd need to be careful—but it did make caution even more important. I had personal history, a lot of it in sharp zones, with Earl; to Gustafson, that history earned me cordial behavior, but no more. I remained yet another guy who wasn't on his team.

I plastered on a smile. "I appreciate the honor. As I said before, I'm not here to cause the Saw any trouble. I'm only after information."

Gustafson led me through a door that I'm sure scanned me for weaponry, and then we entered the maze of busy, monitor-walled hallways that typified any active fort. The displays switched to images of the sky outside as I approached and failed to emit the appropriate clearance signals. After three turns, we came to a door the same dull gray metal as all the others we'd passed, but this time we stopped and waited for the door to clear and announce us.

About a minute later it slid open, and Gustafson motioned me in. Reflexes caused me to hesitate, my natural desire not to walk between two potentially hostile unknowns taking hold, but he outwaited me; we both knew I had no option if I wanted the meeting. I entered a pleasantly appointed conference space, five comfortable chairs covered in a local red-spotted leather surrounding a low table that held three glass pitchers. Gustafson followed, and I caught a momentary glimpse of the side of the door as it slid shut: It was thick and ran in a track on all four sides. I leaned on the wall to my right and nodded slightly at the firmness beneath its lightly patterned pale red wallpaper. They'd set the meeting in a containment room, its door armored, its walls thick with fused layers of metal and local composite, definitely reinforced, almost certainly laced with enough metal and active countertransmission circuitry that no electromagnetic data could enter or leave. I had to assume Earl could record in here, but I doubted he'd allow even his own devices to transmit—too much risk of transmission hijacking or piggybacking. The interior of the room operated entirely manually. The pitchers weren't for show: We had to pour our own beverages. Lobo might hate drink dispensers, but I would have been happy to see one.

A door in the wall opposite me swung open, and Earl walked in. Aside from the colonel's wings on his shoulders, he looked exactly as I remembered him, which was exactly the same as the day I'd met him over twenty years ago. Being able to look the same for decades is nothing notable; all but the very poorest and those choosing to live on new planets during their early colonization years have access to all the med tech they need to remain physically unchanged for at least fifty years. What is unusual is someone *choosing* to use med tech in that way. Most people grow bored with their looks, or decide to ride the wave of some passing celebrity-appearance fad, or simply opt to appease the desire of a new lover for a little customization. Not Earl. He wore his hair in the same combed style as always, neatly parted, never buzzed or shaved in the manner many in the Saw favored, but never long either. I doubted his weight wavered by more than a kilo plus or minus from what it was at the end of basic training, and he wore the same working blues he always had. I'd seen him in dress uniform only when informing families of the loss of their son or daughter and, on rare occasions, when a Saw Central Command general required it.

A good twenty centimeters shorter than I and considerably lighter and less muscular, Earl nonetheless was one of the men I'd least like to face in combat, because I knew he'd never be trying to fight, only to kill. In the years I'd served in his units, I'd watched him many times go to great lengths to avoid conflict, even to the point of appearing to retreat. When he finally judged conflict to be unavoidable, however, he acted quickly and committed completely, bypassing the small moments of hesitation common even in most highly trained fighters.

I started to salute him, but he waved it off.

"None of that, Jon," he said. "You're a civilian now, so this is strictly informal."

"As you say, Colonel Earl."

"Please, just Tristan." He pointed to a chair opposite

his, and Gustafson took one between us.

I smiled. "Sorry, Colonel, but some habits aren't worth breaking. And, though this is an informal visit, that doesn't mean it might not be of professional interest to you."

"Of course," he said, smiling. "I didn't think you came here just to tell me how much fun you were having since you left us, or how much you were enjoying traveling with your new PCAV." His smile never wavered, and he never looked away.

I matched his behavior, reminded of sitting at card tables with him while we waited for cleanup crews and scooping up the money of the newer officers and NCOs who were betting extravagantly in their happiness to be alive, to be anywhere but where they'd been. I'd assumed the registered transfer of any weapon half as powerful as Lobo anywhere in Earl's turf would attract his attention, but I'd half hoped that the fact that the Saw didn't have a contract for Macken might keep this information away from him. It was a dumb hope, but no matter; I'd left no other tracks he'd be likely to find.

"May we speak without a formal record," I said, "other than the one in Top's head, of course?"

"Yes," he said. He touched a spot on his sleeve. "All recording is off. Continue."

The notion that being true to one's word is a fundamental underpinning of a strong society either died or moved to life support centuries before I was born, probably centuries before mankind found and entered the first jump gate. For Earl, though, and for me and a few other men and women I've had the pleasure to know, the concept surged with as much vitality today as when Jennie first instilled it in me back on Pinkelponker. As a boy there

I learned the sad lesson that I shouldn't assume others placed the same value on their word as the two of us, but Earl was a proven exception. He said he wouldn't electronically record this meeting, so I trusted he wouldn't.

"Thank you very much," I said, slowing the cadence of my speech both for clarity and to give me time to choose my words carefully. "I appreciate how busy you are, so I don't want to consume more of your day than necessary. You also know me—knew me—well enough that I hope you'll recall how much I prefer getting directly to the point."

"I always liked that aspect of you," he said. "I wouldn't mind experiencing more of it now."

"I understand, but because I want to minimize any possible negative consequences for either of us, in this case I need to take a slightly more circuitous route."

He leaned slightly forward. "Negative consequences? Please don't tell me we're meeting so you can deliver a threat for some new employer. I'd hate doing what I'd then have to do, though"—he paused and leaned back, apparently relaxed—"you know I'd do it."

I waved my hands slowly, easily. "No, as I've already told Top, I don't want to be on the opposite side of the Saw. I simply need to understand how things work here so I don't accidentally cause problems for either of us by saying something wrong."

"Fair enough," he said, "for now. Go."

"I've canvassed the publicly available data about the Saw's contract with the FC for Lankin," I said, "but we all know how much that data is worth. I also know that Kelco and Xychek are the main corporate players here. What I'd like to understand are the limits of your contract with respect to conflicts that involve those two organizations."

"And for sharing this private data, I get what?"

"Maybe nothing," I said, "but maybe quite a lot you'll care about. I promise this isn't a game."

He nodded, knowing I was telling the truth. "We perform no police functions; the FC locals handle those jobs. We deal with any native fauna issues in new settlement areas, monitor and are on call to handle any serious armed insurrections, and, of course, make sure Lankin appears prickly enough to any governments outside the FC that it's not worth their time to attack. The two big corporations have the standard deal with the FC: They handle their own security and frontier action, and they pledge not to use their forces against each other or the FC. The FC—and we, as its enforcing agent—conduct periodic, scheduled and unscheduled inspections of their troops and weapons, and they report all weapons acquisitions and militia deployments. As long as they follow the rules, we run our inspections and otherwise leave them alone. The arrangement is classic post–corporate wars, the same one you've seen, the same one all the big conglomerates and governments have used for over a century, since before either of us was born."

No one, to the best of my knowledge, knew how old I really was, and I worked hard to keep it that way.

"What's your role when a conflict does involve one of the two?" I asked.

His eyes widened slightly, but he didn't press me. Yet. "Except for the standard small stuff the Lankin police might handle—theft, assault on individuals in the streets, that sort of thing—we have no role unless one of the companies requests our help. All local Kelco and Xychek staff maintain dual FC/corporate citizenship, so corporate security handles anything serious, as long as it doesn't endanger civilians." He poured a glass of a light green drink and offered it to me. "Local tea? Top?"

Gustafson waved off the offer, and I shook my head. "No, thank you," I said. "One more question, and then I'll start talking."

"Good," Earl said. He sipped the tea he'd offered me.

"To the degree that you can discuss or speculate about anything that involves your employer without violating your contract, how would you characterize the FC's relationship with these two corporations?"

"That's an easy one. I don't have to provide any private information. Layla Vaccaro, the ranking FC bureaucrat here and the Lankin rep to the FC council, is on public record with her discontent over the FC's role as the weak sister of the three. Lankin joined the FC after being developed initially by prospectors from the two companies, and the FC has been playing catch-up ever since. She hates the position it's left her in." He drank a bit more tea. "And now, as you said, it's your turn."

"Xychek's Jose Chung," I said, and paused until he nodded in recognition at the name, "has offered a bounty to anyone who captures or kills me."

Nothing in Earl's expression changed, but I could feel the force of his increased concentration. "Why?"

I hesitated, despite having known the conversation would reach this point. Answering him would lead to more questions. Eventually, those questions would take us to Johns and to Osterlad, and I didn't want to have to explain their deaths. Not answering would annoy him, but if I kept my focus on the matters that could affect him and the Saw, he might allow the omission. I had to try. "Nothing I did that motivated the bounty was illegal," I said, choosing my words carefully, "or deserving of that treatment, so Chung's motivation doesn't matter." Earl glanced briefly at Gustafson, so I hurried on before Gustafson could take the hint and ask the follow-up question Earl wanted him to pose. "What does matter is that Chung is buying weapons illegally from Osterlad, weapons I'm sure Xychek is not revealing in your inspections."

Gustafson sat up straighter and leaned forward. Earl didn't move, but tension lines in his face showed the effort the control was costing him.

"If this is true, the implications are significant," Earl said, "for all three major organizations on Lankin. I take it you can prove this?" Earl said, definitely a question, not a statement, despite the phrasing.

"Not yet," I said, "but my source is well connected, and I have no reason to doubt it."

"As I'm sure you'll understand," Earl said, a little frustration and anger audible in his tone, "no individual's word, not even the word of someone I've trusted in the past—" He paused to make sure I caught the tense, then continued, "—is enough justification for me to take the kind of action that proof of such a violation of a major treaty would motivate."

"I understand," I said, "which is the second reason I need to talk to Chung. After I finish my conversation with him, I have every confidence that he'll both fix my problem and give you all the information you need to act on yours."

"So talk to him," Earl said. "You don't need any action from us to do that."

"You're right; I don't. What I need is your inaction, and your advice." Earl raised an eyebrow in question. "As you'd expect, Chung isn't interested in having a friendly chat with me. To arrange a talk that I can be sure to live through, I'll need to . . . retrieve him, and I want to make sure that doing so won't bring the Saw down on me."

Earl nodded, clearly getting it. I waited while he considered; this was the moment when he'd decide.

After almost a minute, time during which he stared up and to his right, seeing nothing but his own thoughts, he focused his attention on me and spoke. "Not acting costs us nothing, as does advice. Some information, however, unavoidably carries almost viral risk when it moves from one person to another. Are you clear that if you tell anyone about any aspect of our involvement, even this conversation, we'll not only deny it, we'll also come for you?"

"Of course."

He nodded. "Okay. We've been covertly monitoring Osterlad Corp. as much as we could manage for some time now, because we have other reasons to believe it's been moving arms to a corporation, though I confess we thought the buyer was Kelco. No matter; either would pose a problem for us. Osterlad's death—" He paused, giving me time to react. I didn't, so he moved on. "—has prompted his company to push all its illegal business even further underground than normal, so now we're getting far less data than before. Obtaining firsthand information from Chung could be the break we needed. You'd have to be willing to bring him and the information not only to me, but to Vaccaro; as FC head here, she's my liaison, and she'd have to get them to support any Saw action in advance. She'd also demand to talk to Chung herself."

"Of course," I said. "Once I have the information, which I can't get until I have Chung."

"So we have a deal?"

"Yes."

"Good." He leaned forward, the hard part over and the fun part, the planning, now under way. "You asked for inaction and advice," he said. "I can do better than inaction. You can't be planning to go after Chung at Xychek's HQ, because you're not that stupid; you know doing so would cause more collateral damage than we could tolerate. Taking him in transit leaves too many chances that he could duck into any of the many civilian areas along his common travel routes, which would bring you back to the problem of collateral damage. So, you have to be targeting him at his home. I choose when we spring our inspections on the corporations, and how many of their troops we summon. Were you and Top here to start chatting every now and again, I wouldn't be surprised if on the evening you paid Chung a visit you encountered only a skeleton protection force at his house, with the rest of the force off-site at a major Saw inspection of Xychek's official weapons and troops."

Despite Earl's confidence, from what I'd seen of Chung's protection squad, they'd never cut below the number of personnel necessary to run exit groups through all three paths out of Chung's property. Still, any decrease in the force at the estate would be a great help. "Top and I get along great," I said, "don't we, Top?"

"You bet," he said, smiling.

"Then that's settled," Earl said. "The advice you wanted?"

"I can't do the job alone," I said. I didn't see any win from mentioning Lobo; if Earl didn't know how intelligent Lobo was, I had a small potential future edge should I one day need it. "So I want to hire some help. I don't know any of the right type of contractors in this area. I could find some, of course, but I wouldn't know more about them than I could find on my own. I assume you have a lot more knowledge in this area and might be able to recommend someone to me."

Earl thought for a bit, and I could almost picture the images and facts dancing across his inner vision. Gustafson appeared equally thoughtful. Finally, Earl looked at Gustafson, leaned back, and both men laughed lightly.

"I believe Top and I are thinking of the same person," he said.

"I'm sure of it," Gustafson said. "For what you want, and given that we can't recommend anyone in the Saw, she's far and away the best option in this entire sector of space."

"Yeah," Earl said, still chuckling, "she possesses strong mission-planning skills, has walked point on recon teams, worked as a long-range sniper, and done more than her share of damage in close-quarters fighting, with and without weapons. She even heads her own team, in case you need multiple people."

"So what's so funny?" I said.

"Because I'm involved," Earl said, "she might not want the work, and because of who she is, you might not want to give it to her." He stared intently at me. "You still don't get it?" When I didn't respond, he said, "You have been out a long time."

I nodded. "Yeah, it's been years."

"Alissa Lim," he said.

Her name evoked so many memories I had trouble focusing. She was one of the best, most competent soldiers I'd ever served with, everything in the field that Earl had said and more—but she was also one of the most violent people I'd ridden with, and one of the most potentially dangerous to her team when something tripped one of her several inner triggers. Our last assignment together had been rough . . . . I pushed back the memory, needing to maintain my focus on what was in front of me. "She's here," I said, "here but no longer with the Saw?"

"No," Earl said. "She's not here, and she left the Saw a few years ago. She's close, though, a single jump away, on an ancient piece of rock named Velna."

Velna wasn't a place I'd planned or wanted to visit. During our time on Lankin, I'd made it a point to learn at least the basics about each planet on the other end of all of this world's jump gates. As best I could tell, Velna was notable for two characteristics: It possessed the most seismically stable landmasses of any known planet, and in all other ways it was the least appealing world humanity has ever colonized. The first trait prompted both Kelco and Xychek to build all their most vibration-sensitive fabs there, so its populated continents abounded with nano-level manufacturing tech facilities that made everything from washing machines to optical and nanotube processor systems. Those fabs provided enough jobs that Velna developed a sizable population base, most of it long-term transient, because the second trait meant that no one wanted to stay there any longer than necessary to make the money they needed to go where they really wanted to be.

The sheer unattractiveness of the place also made it the number-one candidate for every new prison contract in the region; its prisoner population, most of which was hardcore and in deep storage, outnumbered its civilian populace. Lankin anticorporate groups protested that the corporations treated their Velna workers like slaves and dumped the waste from their fabs directly into the ecosystem, saving the huge clean-operation costs they'd incur on any other world. To hear those groups tell it, the FC didn't inspect the fabs or even lodge the feeblest of protests about them, because its prisons were the only places you could go that were worse than the corporate fabs. Nobody rocked the boat, and Velna kept absorbing the trash.

"What's Lim doing there?" I said.

"She left the Saw to start her own security company. Running a company is a lot different than working in the field, so it was rough going for her. The Saw won't do prison work outside of active combat detention, so we did her a little behind-the-scenes favor—one you'd do well not to mention—and helped her company win the contract for the largest FC prison there. It's not great work, but it's work."

"Lim is leading a prison team?" I said, having trouble believing it. "Amazing." Prison duty anywhere is dirty, nasty work that in my experience mangles everyone who stays with it. If Earl was as accurate as I expected, the prison work on Velna would be the worst of the worst. No one as willing to kill as Lim could afford the damage that kind of work would do to her soul. I wondered what she'd become, then recalled the way Gustafson had looked at Earl and Earl's comments about her. "What's her problem with you?"

"For some years before she quit," he said, "we'd been involved. She wanted me to go with her. That wasn't an option. She wasn't happy with me when she left."

Gustafson let out a breath loudly enough that it emerged as almost a snort, earning him a sharp look from Earl.

I was amazed that any woman who could get close enough to Earl to form a lasting relationship wouldn't know that his work always came first, but I was also generally amazed by women, having been unable to sustain an intimate relationship with one for more than a few weeks at a time.

"Any other recommendations?" I said.

"I can come up with more," Earl said, "but no one you'll know. Everyone you served with is either still in the Saw or no longer doing this sort of work." He paused and considered me for a moment. "You're the only one I know who's stayed anywhere near the same type of action." He shook his head. "Regardless, we both know Lim is the best you're going to find if you want someone whose flaws you know."

I nodded in agreement. He was right. Her skill set matched my needs perfectly. The bounty on my head wasn't going to vanish of its own accord, and I couldn't make it go away without help. On the other hand, when I'd last worked with Lim, she was given to almost psychotic rage and possessed an unsettling ability to kill with absolutely no remorse. Since that time, Earl had broken her heart, and she'd taken up prison work. Lovely.

My other option was to hire an unknown. I realized I had no excuse for hesitating: I had too much at stake to risk using someone I didn't know. Lim was a killing machine, but at least she'd be a killing machine on my team.

"Where can I find her?" I said.

"She's in Dishwa, a pit of a city on Velna," Earl said. He stood, and we shook hands. "Top'll get you the details. I'm sure you two will be talking."

CHAPTER 17

I instructed the cab to return to Queen's Bar via a long route with four switchbacks. I planned to spend another half an hour there in countersurveillance maneuvers on the off chance Chung's men had spotted me or Earl had Saw soldiers on my trail. As the vehicle skimmed over the highway, I sat back and pondered the logistics of approaching Lim. I could probably afford her fee straight up, but I was getting tired of pouring so much of my own money into simply staying alive. Besides, the more I thought about it, the more it seemed to me that discovering a corporate illegal arms deal and delivering it to the planetary government ought to be worth significant money. I didn't see the opening yet, but I resolved to examine the issue further over the next few days; money was lurking somewhere in all this.

Lim, though, presented the more pressing and immediate issue, so I returned my focus to her. Try as I might to think only about how best to recruit her, I couldn't avoid recalling the last time we saw action together. Willing down the hardcore sensory memories that cried for release in my head, I focused on the facts, hoping that by reviewing them I could leach some of the pain from the experience.

We'd been humping on Nana's Curse, a planet that spun around a young star three jumps from anyplace I'd ever heard of. A world of startling weather, with microclimates so extreme it dragged even the best forecasting technology out of its computational depth, the planet had been a place no large organization ever wanted to colonize. Over time, however, the extreme weather attracted dozens of the various nature-worshipping cults that had started on Earth and spread outward along with the rest of humanity. Despite their varying belief systems, these cults had managed to find enough common ground to live in peace in settlements scattered across the planet's largest continent. They'd even created a planetary government and joined the Frontier Coalition in the vain hope that formal representation might keep away the major corporations.

Then the Purifiers, the most militant and heavily armed of the many militant and well-armed one-god cults, discovered the world and its hordes of evil heathens, and all hell broke loose. I've never been a fan of dirt worshippers, but they were always either peaceful or so inept at violence as to not pose any problems for anyone other than themselves. The Purifiers, however, hated any religion other than their own. They pursued an ancient, simple approach to any place they found weak enough to attack: Convert those who'll accept the truth, and kill the rest.

The FC had contracted with the Saw to force the Purifiers off Nana's Curse, and in the process we'd spent months crawling from town to town, taking back those locations the Purifiers had overrun, burying the thousands of dead who'd possessed too much belief or too little sense to convert, and ferreting out the slash-and-burn squads that were purifying the smaller villages.

The villages. My last serious action with Lim was in one. I'd transferred to another unit as soon afterward as I could. Thinking of that mission, I suddenly found the cab hot, constricting, oppressive. My pulse quickened, the rush of the memory triggering the unthinking, unreasoning rush of aggressive, angry hormones I've fought most of my life, and I knew I couldn't beat back the memory. I closed my eyes and let it wash over me.

Rain drizzled out of a cloudless sky the color of water in a clear brook. The unrelenting heat overwhelmed the climate control in our fatigues and launched volleys of sweat down our backs, arms, and legs. Baker squad, my team, was fanned out across the rear of the village, ready to catch or kill any stray Purifiers. Data from the sensor webs we'd dropped via silent-opening delivery shells showed little motion and no active transmissions, so we figured no more than a few hostiles remained in the area. Lieutenant Earl played it safe, though, sending us to the rear position, then taking Alpha squad fast and hard, cocked and locked, right up the main path into the clearing in the village's center. A few shots and the ozone of arcing weapons cut the air; then Earl's voice, tight and clipped, barked out of my earpiece.

"Baker squad," he said, "hostiles controlled. Come to Poppa. Keep the newbs at the rear."

We formed up around my lead. For the raw meat in the squad the war on Nana's Curse was their first action, but we'd been here for months, so I couldn't believe anything in this collection of shacks could be bad enough to pose them a problem. Orders are orders, though; I motioned them back, and they fell in quickly. We double-timed out of the cover, over to the rear entrance road, and into the clearing.

I held up my hand, and the squad stopped. The moving people grabbed my attention first, and in a second's glance I took in the motion: Earl and a few of the Alpha squad men were leading four Purifiers—all oddly out of uniform, some missing their pants—to the front of one of the shacks near where the main road entered the clearing. A few more of Alpha squad stood off to the sides, several retching loudly. Lim paced in the center of the clearing, vibrating with energy, hands moving nervously, her close-cropped hair so drenched it resembled the surface of a black pool.

In the next second my gaze moved to the ground, and I understood Earl's order.

On the far side of the clearing an open door gave way to a meter-tall stack of bodies that filled a small clay and thatch building. Spread around the clearing in front of Lim were the tangled bodies of at least half a dozen children, the oldest barely a teenager. None was fully dressed; some wore shredded pants, others no pants at all, and most were missing their shirts. All were cut, broken, bleeding. The blood pooled in puddles bigger than I'd have guessed such little bodies could produce. Blood oozed from some and gathered under others, so much blood the sources were hard to spot, numerous cuts and hacks marring the half-naked corpses. The acrid smell hung in the moist air. My ears pounded with my own heartbeat. The scene tightened its grip on me, and I had trouble breathing, standing still, doing anything except screaming. I fought to maintain self-control, to keep it together.

"Listen up," Earl said.

I forced myself to look at him. Everyone else except Lim did the same. Her head pointed in his direction, but I caught a glimpse of her eyes: She was seeing only the images in her head.

"SOP with prisoners is to evac them to local brigs for questioning and then to POW storage." He slowly made eye contact with each of us, moving rapidly past Lim when he realized she wasn't yet focusing on him. "These men," he gestured to the prisoners, "do not deserve and will not receive that mercy. If anyone wants to discuss this decision, speak up; now's the time."

No one said a word to Earl. What mumbling I could hear was all angry agreement.

Earl nodded. He motioned to the men holding the prisoners, and they brought the four Purifiers to him. Earl pushed one to his knees. Three Alpha squad corporals followed his lead with the others. A few seconds later, all four prisoners were kneeling, hands restrained behind their backs with quick-application synthetic ties. Earl pulled a pistol from a holster on the rear of his belt.

"Lim, Moore, take your squads to our regroup point," he said. "I'll join you shortly."

"Sir, Lieutenant, sir." Lim's voice surprised me with its calm, careful, formal cadence. "Sir, I'd like to handle this, sir."

I was already moving, my squad behind me, and as I passed Lim I noticed her face was utterly calm, her expression serene, only the brightness in her eyes betraying any sign of the horror that surrounded her.

"Please, sir," she said.

Earl stared at her for a bit, then nodded his agreement. "Alpha squad, on my lead," he said. To Lim he added, "We'll wait for you. Make it clean and simple, one shot each to the back of the head."

I couldn't hear her answer over the sound of our feet on the road as we exited the clearing and double-timed for the rendezvous point a few hundred meters away. No one spoke when we reached it. I didn't bother maintaining formation once there; Earl would give us new orders shortly, and I figured we could all use a little time to deal with what we'd seen.

He and Alpha squad appeared less than a minute later. "Fall in," he immediately said. "Weapons and comm check."

The squads were slow to move, all of us trapped in our heads with the images of the village clearing.

"Now, people!" Earl yelled. "Inspection in ninety seconds!"

Everyone jumped to, Alpha squad left and Baker right. We all scrambled to check the status of our weapons, ammo packs, and comm gear. Between the seconds we lost to getting moving and the time it took to realign in formation, we were hard-pressed to complete all the checks by the deadline Earl had set. I finished barely in time, because Earl started his inspection with Baker squad, and I was first.

When he finished with me, I realized how wrong I'd been: Giving people time right now amounted to letting them dwell in a bad place they needed to leave. Keeping them busy was exactly right; they'd process what they'd seen later, certainly for days, probably for the rest of their lives. I vowed to remember this lesson for the future, even as I fervently prayed I'd never again need it—another battlefield prayer that went unanswered.

Earl was halfway through Baker squad when I realized Lim wasn't back. He appeared in front of me, as usual having recognized the problem before me.

"Moore," he said, "see if Lim needs assistance . . ." Lowering his voice, he added, " . . . and retrieve her."

"Yes, sir," I said.

I double-timed back into the village, energy rifle charged and at port arms, just in case we'd missed some hostiles. I froze when I entered the clearing and saw Lim.

With her left hand, she held one of the men by the hair. His mouth was taped shut. With her right hand she plunged her combat knife in and out of the man's chest and stomach, the whole time smiling and talking to him in a voice so low I couldn't make out her words. Blood and bile and bits of entrails hung from her blade. Two of the men were on the ground, body cavities ripped open, their insides exposed and partially spilled, clearly dead.

The fourth man appeared to have tried to crawl away. The blood pooling under his legs was the result of Lim's answer to that attempt. I threw up into my mouth, choked back what I could, and spit to clear the rest.

I saw with cold clarity exactly what I had to do, the

path so obvious it wasn't as if I were choosing at all. I was only doing what was inevitable, necessary, unavoidable. I put down my rifle, drew my pistol, and shot the fourth man in the head. Lim kept hacking at the man she was holding up. I quickly shot each of the two dead men in the head; Earl expected four shots.

When I turned to finish the third man, Lim stood between him and me, her knife pointed at me, the smile still on her face, her eyes wild. "You shouldn't have done that," she said. "I hadn't even started on the last one, and I'm not done with this guy."

"We're leaving, Lim," I yelled. "Lieutenant's orders. These men may have deserved—"

She cut me off. "*May* have deserved? What they deserved is more than we could ever do to them. This is only a taste."

I took one step closer to her. "You're done," I said. "We're leaving. You tracked down one who managed to run, then we tapped all four. That's how it happened. Got it?" I pushed past her, shot the last man in the head, and holstered the pistol.

Lim stared at me as the fire in her eyes slowly died.

"Clean your knife," I said. I headed out of the village.

She wiped it on the back of the shirt of the man I'd just killed, then caught up to me.

When she was even with me, I changed to double-time pace. She followed, and we entered the regroup point abreast.

"Problem?" Earl said.

"Nothing significant, sir," I said.

Lim nodded her agreement.

He stared hard at both of us for a two count, looked

away for another two beats, then turned back to the men, his internal argument resolved. "Fall in with your squads."

Only when we were heading out did I realize I was still shaking, my mind stuck in an image loop, the same composite frame screaming from the monitor inside my head, burning into its pixels until I became afraid it would never be able to show anything else: the dead, defiled, bleeding children in the background, the foreground a close-up of Lim's smiling face as she hacked and hacked and hacked at the prisoner's body.

CHAPTER 18

I shook my head to clear away the image. Though the years since then have done nothing to blur it, they have weakened its hold on me. The stories I'd heard of Lim since that mission all painted her as a fierce, fair, dependable fighter—as long as nothing sent her back to the dark, smiling place the clearing had either created or awakened. I didn't see anything in the kidnap of Chung to cause that reaction in her, and I needed a teammate I could trust to get the job done. Anyone new I recruited, even if trustworthy, would have flaws as well, but I wouldn't know those flaws. I wouldn't know that person at all.

I knew Lim.

I was still wasting time. I wasn't comfortable with Lim, but that didn't matter: As I'd agreed with Earl, she was the best option available to me.

Lobo and I were going to Velna.

❀   ❀   ❀

Once we slid into a low geosync orbit over Dishwa, I had Lobo tap into the publicly available data flows to see what he could learn. The combination of that data, what he already had in his store, and the information Gustafson had given me all painted the same basic picture. Dishwa was indeed, as Earl had observed, a pit. All the serious corporate manufacturing plants sat outside the city, their staffs freed only every few weeks. Corporate security was uniformly inward-looking, worrying only about protecting the fabs and their trade secrets, not about what the workers did when on R&R in Dishwa. From the nonstop flow of reports of thefts, fights, and other petty crimes, the Dishwa police didn't much care either.

The largest prison on the planet, the one Lim's group managed, hunkered down like a cancerous growth on the northern tip of the city. Well-behaved inmates earned wage-free jobs at local businesses after med techs laced their bodies with trackers and a variety of small explosive charges that would detonate if they strayed from the prison's controlling signals for too long. The pay they earned went toward prison upkeep. Those who caused trouble ended up in one of the slowly expanding sprawl of convict racks, buildings housing hundreds of fluid-filled tubes, one prisoner per tube, wires keeping their muscles fit while governmentally approved counselor voices whispered governmentally approved messages of good behavior, recovery, and repentance. Many hard cases figured the tubes for easy duty, but after a few weeks, most, when given the option, chose to go back to work. Those who stayed in the tubes for too long were rarely entirely right afterward, the voices never leaving them.

Dishwa served as the FC's tryout for the tubes, and nothing I saw made me believe this technology would last any longer than any other prison fad. The only way humanity has ever found to successfully solve the problem of prisoners is to avoid having them, to address the issues before people turn into convicts. No technology we've yet found succeeds at turning large populations of prisoners into contributing citizens.

"Another beautiful place you've taken me," Lobo said, after I'd gone through the information he'd amassed. "And whom are we here to kill?"

"Very funny," I said, "and the answer is, no one. We're here to recruit help. I think you'll like her; she likes big machines. In fact, she prefers them to most people."

"A woman of good judgment," he said.

"Call the prison," I said.

A reasonably convincing young male answering construct in a khaki uniform appeared on the comm display. "Dishwa central prison," it said. "We're tracing and recording this call. Speak."

Lim's personality had infected even the answering protocol; lovely.

"Jon Moore requesting an in-person meeting with Alissa Lim."

"Purpose of meeting?"

"Catching up on old times," I said. No point in marking this as confidential; she'd know I'd never visit socially. The construct vanished, and in its place an advertorial detailed the exciting and humane new therapy the prison was pioneering for the forward-looking Frontier Coalition. I tuned it out and waited while the construct tracked down Lim, gave her the message, and received her response.

After a few minutes, the construct reappeared and said, "Request granted at these coordinates and time. Please confirm." Lobo captured the location; we'd meet her about an hour before dusk.

When he showed me the spot on an aerial view of the city, however, I reconsidered; I had no desire to put down Lobo in such a highly populated area and no time to find a place to stash him and still make the meeting. "I need to land a Predator-class, fully armed assault vehicle," I said. "Is that acceptable at these coordinates?"

The advertorial resumed, and over the next several minutes the earnest faces of experts in psychology, criminology, and neurology explained why tube-tech was the prison wave of the future.

"Negative," the construct said when it reappeared. "No nongovernment craft of that class are permitted over our airspace. Request granted at these new coordinates and time. Please confirm."

Lim had changed the meeting location to a private shuttle facility twenty klicks from the prison and the time to a bit after dusk. I was pleased by her prudence. The Lim I'd served with would have either ignored the civilians or relocated us to the prison and set up for full combat there. The prison undoubtedly possessed significant self-defense capabilities, maybe not enough to destroy Lobo but certainly enough to consider taking the fight, so it wouldn't have been a tactically bad choice. I saw as a welcome sign of a calm maturity the fact that she was now factoring into her thinking both civilian casualties and the cost to her business of any action at the prison. I was even pleased that she was moving our meeting to a remote location, albeit one that I had to assume she was even now ringing with her own forces. Maybe this would work out after all.

"Thank you," I said. "We'll be there."

We landed in almost whiteout conditions, a winter storm having squatted over the shuttle facility and showing no sign of stretching its legs anytime soon. As we settled on the tarmac, I asked Lobo, "How bad is it?"

"I count twenty-four human profiles on IR," he said, "deployed in groups of three at various points in an irregular circuit around us, but no heavy weapons."

"Oh, the weapons are there," I said. "She's just shielding them and showing us the people. Transmission traffic?"

"Massive and heavily encrypted," he said. "Enough of it is hitting me that I have to assume we're being constantly monitored. My inner shielding is detecting no electromagnetic traffic, however, so we remain, as I would expect, secure."

"This should go smoothly," I said, "and all her precautions are understandable. Still, if anything happens that gives you any cause for alarm, leave immediately at maximum speed and track me from orbit. Don't hesitate."

"Affirmative," Lobo said, combat programming clamping down on the humor.

"Let's keep your innards as private as we can," I said. "Hover at a meter and a half, and on my command open a floor hatch. Seal it the moment I'm clear." As Lobo lifted gently above the ground, I put on a self-heating, light-weight, hooded jacket and crouched next to the section of Lobo's floor that would slide clear. "Now."

The same hatch I'd used for the stealthie on Floordin slid open, and I hopped out. I crouch-walked clear of Lobo, holding my arms straight out at shoulder height the entire time. The snow whipped at me, and the jacket struggled to keep up with the outside temperature. The sides of the hood extended enough past my face to form a bit of a barrier, but the cold still clawed at my skin. I counted on the jacket's IR profile to be so strong that everyone watching on any frequency would see I was approaching with caution.

A doorway opened in a building maybe twenty meters away. Someone dressed entirely in a white, floor-length coat walked toward me. The person was either quite over-weight or heavily padded. When it was close enough for me to see the face, I voted for heavily padded; it appeared to be Lim.

"Moore," she said, her voice confirming her identity.

"Lim."

"You're clean?"

"Absolutely," I said. "All I want is to talk to you about a business opportunity. I have no weapons and no bad intentions."

"What about your PCAV?"

"I own it, so I use it—but in this case, only for trans-portation."

"If it acts up at all," she said, "you won't live long enough to finish a sentence. We won't be anywhere that there won't be multiple sights on you."

"Understood. As long as they can't hear our conversation, we'll be fine."

"That sort of business?"

I nodded. "Of course."

"Fair enough," she said. "Follow me."

We returned to the building she'd exited and walked straight into summer, the space on the other side so over-heated I couldn't get the jacket off fast enough. The building was a hangar, currently empty save for a small table and two chairs in the center of its permacrete floor. Pockmarks and scorched streaks adorned its side and rear light-gray walls. The scent of fuel and oil hung in the warm air. When Lim wasn't using it to meet old comrades, this was a working maintenance facility. The four pairs of guards occupying stations in its black girder rafters were clearly Lim's additions to its standard equipment. When I pointed up at them, she smiled.

"Why all the security?" I asked.

Lim motioned to the chairs, and I followed her over, jacket in hand. She raised a gloved hand and ticked off reasons as she walked in front of me. "You ask for a meeting and won't say why. You arrive in a PCAV. We were never tight. And," she chuckled, "my people see so little action that I figured any excuse for a serious drill was worth taking. I made them think you are one seriously lethal ex-soldier."

She motioned me to sit, took off her coat, and turned to face me.

To the same extraordinary degree that Earl had stayed as he had been, Lim had changed. Even the standard-issue winter-white fatigues couldn't conceal the modifications to her body. When I'd last seen Lim, she'd been a little taller than most women and boyish, with close-cropped black hair sitting atop a wiry body you'd only realize was female if you saw it naked. This Lim was more gorgeous and astonishingly built than ninety percent of the women I'd ever seen in broadcasts, with large breasts over an obviously flat stomach and enough muscle mass that her uniform bulged at the arms and legs as she moved. She was taller, too, easily as tall as Earl. Where before Lim had shown signs of the mongrel stock from which almost all of humanity has grown, now her body glowed with trendy Asian chic, the folds of her eyelids perfect, the eyes themselves almost black, her lips full and wide, her skin tone an incandescent, perfectly consistent mellow golden hue. Her hair was still the flawless black of starless space, but now she wore it longer, a bit below shoulder length, and in a ponytail.

"You can close your mouth now," she said, laughing.

"I apologize," I said. "It's simply that you're amazing. I take it you've made a few mods."

"More than a few, and all from the best clinics I could find. Everything's organic, pure gene-driven work, nothing surgical." She studied me for a moment. "I can't say I ever bothered to look at you all that closely, but you don't seem any older. Had some work done yourself?"

One of the benefits of the combination of the changes Jennie made to me and the nanomachines the Aggro scientists melded with my cells is that I never appear to have physically aged past my early twenties. As long as I move around periodically, today's antiaging techniques make me no different from anyone else. Lim was more observant than she was suggesting, however, so I shrugged and forced a chuckle. "No more than the next guy. Who doesn't want to stay looking young?" I changed the subject. "Not that looking as great as you do isn't reward enough, but I never would have figured you for someone willing to drop that much money merely to be a sex bomb. Why?"

"Business," she said. "I don't have the resources, team, or armament—yet—to land the big bids against the Saw and the others. That reduces me to tracking down the small stuff, and no one remembers the small stuff at contract time. Everyone expects anyone running my kind of business to be a scarred-up old warrior, so I went for the opposite look. They all remember me, and that's my ticket in. Plus, even after thousands of years of lessons to the contrary, I find that most men and a surprisingly large number of women reflexively assume that anyone who looks as sexy as I do is stupid, and that's a negotiating edge I can use. The Law is a security company now, but that's only a start. We're going to be much more."

"The Law?" I said, laughing a little.

"The Local Area Weapons Corp.," she said, not even smiling, "my company."

"How do Earl and the other guys at the Saw feel about that name?"

"They hate it, think it's a slap at them."

"Is it?"

"Of course," she said, still not laughing at all, her face deadly serious. She leaned forward and looked straight into my eyes. "Now, what can I do for you?"

For a moment my mind jumped the business tracks and led me at high speed toward a contemplation of what this woman, this amazing body in front of me, could do for me, and then I more fully appreciated the power of Lim's approach. I looked briefly away, regained focus, and this time when I gazed into her eyes I made myself see only a person on the other side of a negotiation.

"You're right," I said. "Your look is a powerful tool. I lost focus for a moment, and immediately I forgot about you as a person and instead thought only about your body as a sex object. I have to work to maintain my focus even now."

She smiled and leaned back, waiting.

"In this building, I have no way to verify we're not being recorded," I said. "If we are, however, and you end up working with me, you'll have at least as much to lose as I will, and probably more, because your business provides services to corporations and governments. I honestly recommend you not record this; you can always decide later which of your team to tell."

"No recording," she said, the push of her cuff button so slight I almost missed it.

"I want to hire you."

"That's it? You could have saved us both a lot of trouble by saying so in your message. We have a rate card for our services and—"

I cut her off. "No," I said. "I don't want to hire your company. I want to hire *you*."

She shook her head slowly and exhaled loudly. "No," she said. "That's not what we do. We provide security and combat services. You choose the service, and I choose the appropriate staff." She studied my face for a moment. "I am curious, though. As I said earlier, we were never closer than any two other humps who served together, and as I recall the last mission we were on didn't end to your liking. So, why me?"

"I understand your company doesn't do this, but I don't want your company. I want you. The reason why is simple: I need one person, someone I know, to help me solve a problem. I can't afford the time to try out someone new."

"Your problem is not my problem," she said. "Why should I even consider this?"

"Three reasons," I said, ticking them slowly off on the fingers of my right hand in the same manner she had earlier. "First, money. Either I can pay you, or you can gamble, take nothing up front, and get half of a much larger amount if this works out the way I think it will. Second, the potential win for your company. If this goes well, the Frontier Coalition will emerge with more power than it has now, and helping it get that power should prove useful for you." I paused, leaned forward, and watched her closely. "Third, the action. Unless you've changed more than your body, part of you still craves it, and running prison security can't satisfy that craving." I slowly waved my arm to take in the men in the rafters. "This drill wasn't only for your company; it was also for you."

"Prison security is serious work," she said, "with the potential to run hot at any time."

"I'm not denying that," I said, "but has it gone hot since you've been on the job? When did you last get a chance to use your fighting skills?"

"I work out and shoot every day," she said, sounding defensive.

"I never doubted you'd stay in shape," I said, easing up my tone, leaning back. "If I did, I wouldn't have approached you. All I'm suggesting is that a little real action might interest you."

She thought for a few seconds, then put as much sarcasm as she could muster into her voice as she said, "And you expect me to sign up for some mysterious mission because you need someone?"

"Of course not. I'll run it down for you on two conditions."

She raised her left eyebrow in question and motioned me to continue.

"You tell me that you'll honestly consider it, and you give me your word not to tell anyone if you choose not to do it."

She was quiet for longer this time, either considering it or playing me; I couldn't tell which.

"Okay," she said. "I'll honestly consider it, and if I don't take it, I won't tell anyone."

"Fair enough," I said. "Here's the short form: For reasons I won't go into, Jose Chung, the Xychek head on Lankin, put a bounty on my head. That's my problem. He also has Xychek buying arms from a private dealer and not reporting those weapons to the FC in the inspections. If anyone could prove to the FC that Xychek was buying those weapons, Xychek would lose power in this region—and the FC would get correspondingly stronger. That's the big-play angle at the end. The answer to both problems is the same: We kidnap Chung. I persuade him to drop the bounty and confess to the arms deals, and everyone but Xychek wins. I'd do it alone, but I can't. I'll go over the setup if you decide to help, and you'll get to design the final attack plan with me."

"A snatch?" she said. "Of the head of one of the two biggest corporations in the region? Even if we succeed, no corporation will ever trust me after this."

"Sure they will," I said, "because you'll stay anonymous. Chung will know about me, but he doesn't need to ever see you. You remain a hired gun he never meets. We snatch him, I interrogate him and persuade him to help me, and then we turn him over to the right FC people."

She stood and grabbed her coat. "I'll consider it," she said, "as I promised. What's the timing?"

"As soon as you can get me an answer," I said. "If you're in, we'll go in Lobo—"

"Lobo?" she said.

"My PCAV," I said. "The AI's good enough that most of the time I think of it as a person."

"You need to spend more time around real people," she said. She headed for the door and motioned me to follow. "Call me in the morning. We're done until then."

I spent the night in Lobo in high orbit over an almost entirely desert continent on the other side of Velna. I'd considered taking Lim's advice and going into Dishwa to spend some time among people, but I decided not to push my luck in case Xychek security had a company-wide advisory about the bounty.

When I called Lim in the morning, the construct passed me straight through to her. Her face filled the display Lobo opened. I was struck again by her beauty and its effectiveness: Concentration was as hard as she wanted it to be.

"Earl backed your story," she said, the abruptness of the greeting at odds with the sweet look on her face. "He'd love to see us prove Xychek was arming illegally. You forgot to mention he was going to help."

"Not my place to tell his business," I said, appreciating at the same time how close she and Earl must have been for him to have told her of his possible involvement.

"So I'm in," she said, "but with three conditions."

"And they are?"

"One: If this goes right, I get half of any fee the FC

pays for the Xychek information, and you credit the Law with doing half the work. I'd love to get the FC to see us as useful for more than prison security."

"Fair enough," I said. Her desire to impress the FC had the potential to help me lower my exposure in this whole mess. "In fact, I'd be happiest if the FC sees the Law as having organized the whole affair and if I appear to be just one more member of your team—though I still get half of any fee."

"Even better," she said. "Don't bother to thank me for the opportunity for the low profile."

"Go on."

"Two: You don't tell anyone about my involvement without my prior permission, so if this plan goes nova, the Law had nothing to do with it. As far as my staff knows, I'm heading out on vacation with a heavily armed and more than a little psychotic ex-lover."

"No problem," I said. "If we blow this, I expect we won't be worrying about anything other than survival."

"Three: We don't go until we both agree on the plan, and I use my own weapons. I'm happy to supply you, too, but regardless of what you choose, if I'm going into action I'm using my own gear."

I paused, considering her demand. This one was tough, because small-team missions need single leads, and I already had strong ideas about how I wanted this one to go.

I must have pondered it longer than I realized, because she said, "None of these are negotiable, Moore."

"I have no problem with using your weapons," I said, "and I'm fine with both of us having to agree on the plan. We can work on it here, before we head to Lankin, because

Lobo has all the intel we need. But, you have to accept two key points."

"And they are?"

"When the mission goes live, I'm in charge, and we make this as nonlethal as possible."

She was quiet for a few moments, then nodded her head. "I can live with both of those," she said.

"Then we're on," I said.

"Deal," she said. "Pick me up at noon at the landing area where we met." The screen blanked.

"Rather abrupt, this woman," Lobo said. "Still, she is human, so I bet she won't end up in storage for any of the mission."

I was already looking forward to working with the two of them.

CHAPTER 19

Three days later, I was lying on my belly in the under-brush bordering the road about a hundred meters outside the main entrance to Chung's estate. Sweat ran down my back, arms, and legs as I sweltered in the heat-blocking camo blanket I'd wrapped around me. From the outside, I read as IR-neutral. Inside, I was baking, already missing the winter of Velna. Night was tamping down the last bits of daylight like a gravedigger smoothing the ground over a freshly buried casket. The climate control in the sealed suit Lim had provided was barely working, but I couldn't complain about its comm helmet: The faceplate shifted its light sensitivity with the setting sun so the scene in front of me remained clear and sharp at all times.

In the heads-up display I checked the small mirrors of Lobo's monitor and Lim's display. Lobo was necessarily too far away from the entrance behind Chung's estate for his sensors to be able to pick up much visual detail, but nothing they showed indicated any problem. Lim lay in a position much like mine but on the opposite side of the estate, and her display remained still and boring, exactly as it should be.

We weren't working silent, but we were keeping transmissions between us to a minimum, refreshing each other's displays on a random cycle ranging around every twenty seconds; no point in giving Xychek security a reason to skip the Saw inspection. Gustafson had said they would start it right after sunset, so the staff and vehicles that were attending it should be leaving soon. Our plan counted on minimum security at the house, so if Xychek security didn't send most of the estate team to the inspection, we'd have to abort and try another approach later.

On the principles that you can't be too prepared and you might as well make good use of the time available, I ran another complete weapons check. All sensors flashed green; I was good to go. I cranked up the resolution on the faceplate and focused it on the road in front of me. All ten of the urban disturbance mines I'd scattered on a twenty-meter stretch of highway clung to the road right where I'd put them, each the dull gray color of the pavement and a little thicker than a pair of pants, so inert without a detonation code that you could walk on them or even drive a wheeled vehicle over them without a problem. Transmit that code, though, and boom! Each would blow with enough power to tear a hole in a vehicle without an armored bottom. Every surface of Chung's vehicles would, of course, be reinforced, but the mines should pop with enough power to change their course, maybe flip them. Lim had set a similar group on the highway outside the exit on the other side of the estate.

I had the suit's audio pickups ratcheted almost as high as they could go, with external sensors in the blanket feeding them. The breezes sang a slow background harmony as the insects and rustling leaves and branches belted out a discordant lead vocal whose direction my mind kept trying unsuccessfully to predict. When the gate to the estate opened a few minutes later, the slight creaking of the moving metal played clearly in my ears. I took the faceplate's resolution back to normal, lowered the audio, and focused on the road in front of me. A few seconds later, the convoy of security vehicles slid past my position. When the last one had passed me, I forced a display update to Lobo so he'd have the count. He compared it to his earlier monitoring and almost immediately the number two appeared in my clone of his display. Perfect. They'd kept back the minimum, enough to give Chung two exit options.

At the appearance of the number, I set my time mark for ninety minutes. I sipped water from the tube built into the suit. I wanted the Xychek security detail heading toward the inspection to be far enough away that when the estate team yelled for help I could be sure none would arrive before we'd finished and escaped. Xychek's air support was, according to Gustafson, both minimal and the first thing on the inspection list, so unless something went wrong we should be able to count on at least one clear hour from the mission's start. That should be more than enough. I hoped.

I settled in yet again and tried not to look too much at the light-green countdown on my display.

Eighty-nine more minutes.

⌘   ⌘   ⌘

The timer wound to zero, turned red, and reversed direction, now displaying the elapsed mission time.

We were on.

My faceplate's copy of Lobo's forward video feed turned into a blur as he accelerated first downward and then at full speed as he skimmed the treetops toward the estate. The sensors would pick him up, but his low flight path would buy a second or two, and that was all we needed. After five seconds of approach, Lobo fired three small missiles at the gate on his side of the estate, then abruptly changed course and headed up, back, and away from the target, reacting as if he'd been unwilling to face the defense systems.

Each of Lobo's missiles mirved a second and a half after launch, changing from three fat tubes into a dozen slender rockets. The estate's automated defense systems did the best they could, but the hole our recon had suggested might exist in them proved to be real. The air-defense portion was designed for targets above two hundred meters, and Lobo had never been that high while in range of those weapons. The ground and low-altitude automated systems were solid enough for civilian or typical corporate attack-squad weaponry, but Lobo's milspec rockets overpowered them easily. By the time the defense system launched its three interceptors, it was facing twelve oncoming missiles.

Ten hit their targets. Via the relay of Lobo's long-distance video sensors I watched as two missiles turned the entire gate area into a cloud of smoke and the remaining eight hit the dirt along a hundred-meter-wide section of ground with the gate at its center. A split second after impact, those eight blew. A mountain of dirt and rock and small vegetation soared into the air and buried the gate and a long stretch of the wall on either side of it. The roar of the explosions shook the air. The helmet's audio system compensated quickly, lowering the volume then readjusting as the sounds died. No one in the estate would be coming out of that gate anytime soon.

I pushed the magnification on the Lobo relay as far as it could go, but even with the best interpolation the faceplate's processors could manage I couldn't see if any people were moving around; Lobo was too far away for his original feed to carry that level of detail. I'd insisted on an approach that gave the gate guards a chance at living, because I wanted this to be as nonlethal an attack as possible. My lack of information was the price of that insistence.

No time to worry about that now, though. I fought to control the adrenaline surge that begged me to regard the people in the estate as just so many more bodies, moving but already dead and not knowing it, existing only for us to finish them.

Lobo had already fired a second burst, this time a barrage of ten small missiles carrying transmission-clogging comm webs, thousands of grain-size modules that detected all active transmissions in their range and broadcast garbage across every in-use frequency. We'd set the cloggers to skip the hobbyist niche we were using and focus on the standard military and commercial bands. We risked our transmissions being recorded and decrypted if a civilian with a snooping hobby happened to be targeting the estate, but we'd kept the chatter down and our

encryption was strong, so the risk was minimal. Six of the
missiles made it through the defense systems and sprayed
their sensors across the estate before hurtling into the
ground just outside it.

"Team one, first group heading your way," said Lobo
in my left ear. "One vehicle, five humans. No way to tell
if target is among them."

"Got it," Lim—"team one" in case anyone did record
and decrypt our comm—said in my right ear.

"Trank 'em, don't kill 'em," I said.

"Already understood," she said, "but the roads are
murder." She'd taken great joy in pointing out that if
Xychek didn't armor its vehicles very well, our plan would
kill everyone in them. I had no answer for her other than
my belief that the vehicles would be strong, a belief born
of the respect I'd developed for Xychek's security squad
during the time Lobo and I had monitored them.

"Team two, second group heading your way," Lobo said.
"Also one vehicle, five humans, and no way to tell if target
is among them."

"Moving to position," I said.

I threw off the blanket and sprinted to my second mark,
a level spot behind a tree where I would have a good view
of anyone trying to get away from the vehicle. I pulled a
second camo blanket off the two guns I'd previously placed
there and aimed at the gate, and settled into sniper position in front of the bigger one.

"Second group has reversed course and headed for rear
exit," Lobo said.

We'd hoped the teams would split and take advantage
of the multiple exit points, so our plan focused on that
option. If the second team stayed with the first after what

was about to happen, we'd know the first team had Chung, and Lim would have to hold them both until Lobo could get there. I maintained my position; Lim had the best data on the action at her end, so it was up to her to make the call whether I should join her.

The first Xychek team reached the rear of the estate. My relay of Lim's display showed the escort vehicle jetting out of the barely open gate. Lim blew half her mines a second after the vehicle cleared the gate. The display image turned fuzzy with smoke. As the processors filtered the visual noise of the dust, the feed in my faceplate cleared enough to show the black vehicle flipping end over end in the air several times before it crashed to the road. Enough of the vehicle's internal systems were intact that it extruded disaster struts and righted itself, but two of the doors were hanging loose, their rear supports trashed by either the mines or the landing.

"Second group returning to original course," Lobo said. "Team two, assume the target is in your group. Team one, verify assumption."

First the front and then the rear of the crashed vehicle exploded as Lim placed armor-piercing rounds in both areas that might house the main drive engines. Armor shielding around the cabin was standard executive protection, so the occupants should survive the small explosions. Sure enough, all five people spilled out of the back of the vehicle, using its rear doors and the heavy dust in the air for cover. One peeked around the door and for that action earned a combo electrical disruptor and trank round in the meat of the shoulder; he dropped fast, twitching. Lim was as accurate as ever.

The sound of my gate opening yanked me away from

Lim's display relay. The escape group hit the exit point fast, and I blew half my mines. I'd planted them farther down the road than Lim, not trusting my accuracy as much as she did hers. The vehicle had been edging to the far right of the road, so the mines sent it spinning side over side into the air. It landed on its flank on the ground on the shoulder of the road opposite me, then righted itself. Both doors on my side sprang open, as did the rear door on the opposite side. The driver and the passenger nearest me spilled out and hid behind the vehicle as I shot an armor-piercing round into its front. These guys were fast: They fanned out to either side of the highway a moment after the front of the vehicle exploded. I switched guns, settled my breathing, and put a disruptor/trank round into the shoulder of the guy on my side of the road because he was the nearer threat. He dropped hard, body twitching on the way down. I swiveled the sights to my left and found the second guy. He was running fast and erratically, making it hard. I squeezed off three shots in rapid succession. The third hit him and dropped him.

I turned the sights on the open driver's door, but no one was inside. I scanned farther away from the car on the other side of the road and caught a glimpse of three figures running in a cluster, the front and rear each staying close to the center. The center had to be Chung.

They disappeared behind some trees.

"All five down," Lim said, her voice jagged, pumped. "Checking now."

"Three on the move," I said, my own voice as raw as Lim's, my breathing coming hard. "Opposite side of the road from me. Track if possible."

I abandoned the sniper rifles—they were no good on

the move—and sprinted across the highway, staying low, drawing a pistol loaded with disruptor rounds as I ran. I reached the vehicle's rear and used it for cover. I snaked up a video feed and panned it quickly across the area in front of me. All clear. I dashed to the tree nearest where the three runners had entered the woods, backed against it, and panned the video feed again. They had maybe ten seconds of lead on me, but the woods weren't dense and the ground was flat, so I found the men as they were angling out and away from the estate. I flicked the Acquire button on the video sensor, and my heads-up display gained a red tracking arrow. I took off on roughly the same course as the Xychek trio, following the arrow, running for all I was worth.

"Status," I gasped as I sprinted around trees, avoiding some bits of undergrowth and barreling through others. Lobo was to pick up the first of us to take down the assigned targets, then help the other person. If I didn't catch my runners, we'd be better off with all of us chasing, because we had to assume Xychek security had learned of our attack the moment we started and had teams coming our way. Our window was closing.

"Checked and confirmed," Lim said. "Target is not here. Repeat: Target is not here."

"Acquiring team one now," Lobo said.

I was gaining on the runners. Chung was almost certainly slowing them, the security guys both paid to stay with him no matter what. I pushed my pace, working to control my breathing, soaking in my own sweat, mentally cursing Lim yet again for the suit's inadequate climate control.

The rear guard slowed, turned his shoulder, and threw

something. I skidded into the back of the nearest large tree as a shrapnel grenade exploded in the air, blasting high-velocity shards of razor-sharp metal into the trees all around and in front of me. I lost three seconds to making sure all the shrapnel had found a home, then another couple as I snaked around a video feed to verify I could safely move. Anger coursed through me as I saw the damage the grenade had caused; it could have ripped me to shreds. If I'd permitted myself to bring lethal weapons, at that moment I would have drawn them.

I needed Chung alive, but I didn't need him happy. I holstered the trank pistol, pulled a screamer launcher from my rear pack, and sprinted after them. I could barely see them in the trees ahead of me, but the glimpse I got was enough. I forced off the suit's audio feeds, then fired the screamer over their heads and ran hard for them. I couldn't see the grenade's flight path, but I could tell when it neared them because they grabbed their ears and stumbled, then fell, as the intense pain shook their ear-drums and heads. I crammed the launcher into a side pocket and fumbled with my pistol's holster as I ran; they were already getting up. I drew within ten meters and stopped, aimed, fought the shaking in my arms, and fired four times, twice at each of the two men I could see, the center and rear runners.

So many things happened in the next second that only later could I reconstruct what I'd seen.

Lobo dropped from the sky fifty meters behind the runners, a side panel open to reveal the upper half of Lim.

The rear runner fell.

The center man, still standing, clutched at the man in front of him.

That man lifted and aimed a pistol at me.

The upward motion of the pistol dominated my vision. I dove to the ground, not wanting to have to rely on the suit's armor if I could avoid it, and rolled to my right. I looked up in time to see the front man drop, then Lim wave from Lobo's open hatch.

I scrambled up and ran to the remaining man. As I drew nearer I verified it was Chung; I'd looked at images of his face too many times not to know it well. He waved his arms and said something I couldn't hear; I realized then that the suit's audio feeds were still off. I grabbed him, pulled an injector from an arm pouch, and jammed it into the side of his neck. He collapsed.

I turned on the audio feeds in time to hear Lobo land, the sound barely audible over the pounding in my ears and the rasping of my breath. I released the helmet and shook my head, glad to be in the open air.

Lim darted out of Lobo, her helmet also off, hair tightly bound onto her head, face drenched in sweat, eyes wild, breath coming sharp and hard. She pointed at the man she'd taken down. "You owe me," she said between breaths. She smiled, eyes still shimmering madly.

I looked down at the men on the ground beside me, then nodded. I glimpsed myself in my helmet's faceplate: My eyes were as crazy as Lim's, and I was smiling, too.

I'd given in to it again, lost the battle for control, a fight so very easy to lose. Unless you were very lucky or very damaged, violence always consumed at least part of you. It ate through your civilized exterior like acid through cloth, uncovered the animal inside, and left you, if you were lucky enough to emerge alive, shaking and terrified and yet happy, juked from the conflict, your body still in it, part of you not ready for it to be over and another part elated that it was and that you weren't among the dead. This had been no big thing, as safe an action as an armed mission could probably be, the Xychek guys overmatched before it started, and yet the violence had spidered into me again.

Each time I put myself in this situation, I resolve not to do it again—but I always do. I consoled myself with the thought that I truly had no real alternative this time, that spending every day, days into months into years, running from a corporate bounty was no way to live. I shook my head slowly, fighting for calm, willing the juice of the moment to crawl back into the dark fetid pools it normally inhabited.

I grabbed Chung, lifted him on my shoulder, and headed for Lobo.

"Thanks," I finally said to Lim, nodding back at the man she'd shot. "What do you say we get far away from here fast?"

CHAPTER 20

We invested the next several hours in the tiresome but vital job of getting lost. With Chung stripped and strapped into a medbed that secured and sedated him, his possessions in a drawer in the medic area, and both Lim and me tucked into acceleration couches, Lobo took over. We rocketed out of the hot zone at tree level into the least populated of the nearby areas, then shot straight up into orbit, where we first wove among some of the busier sats, then came to an abrupt halt behind a large comm hub whose orbit we quietly mirrored for long enough to make me nervous. We then hopped up to a higher orbit, down and back up again a few times, pogoing across orbital loops, until we finally settled into one and eased our way slowly to the other side of the planet. Early on, Lobo identified himself as a Xychek comm sat. He changed his electronic identity half a dozen more times before he went transmission-silent behind a meteorological data-gathering sat.

With little chance of any of the estate's video sensors having captured Lobo or us, we were probably being overly cautious; after all, Xychek security had no reason to guess a space-ready PCAV was involved. Still, I didn't want to take any risks, because we were at the most exposed point in the mission: We had Chung, but not his confession, so neither the Saw nor the FC could or would back us.

After another hour passed with no signs of unusual orbital or earth-to-space activity within a few thousand klicks of us, Lim and I took turns cleaning up, then ate. I wanted to be calm before interrogating Chung, and the food helped consume some of the post-action hormones my body still had to digest.

Lim and Lobo monitored Lobo's tiny medic area, a room with the medbed in the center and an aisle around it so narrow that I had to walk sideways to fit. Chung obviously knew me well enough to put the bounty on me, so I saw no point in hiding my identity. Per my deal with her, Lim stayed back so Chung wouldn't ever see her.

Lobo kept two images running for Lim: a video feed of the room, and a display of Chung's vital signs. The latter also played on the wall behind Chung's head, where I could see it but he couldn't. Like so much in Lobo or anything of military origin, the room served multiple functions, both a place to heal the wounded and an interrogation chamber for the captured. Simple cleaning arms had wiped Chung's face and ears. Restraints over his waist, chest, neck, head, arms, and legs bound him securely to the bed. He'd be able to move his eyes to follow me, and he could wiggle his fingers and toes if he wanted to make sure they still functioned, but that was all; I didn't want to risk either of us doing something stupid. When I entered the room, Lobo instructed the medbed to inject Chung with a blend of a slight physical stimulant to wake him and a mood stabilizer to level his vitals. Deviations from the norms on the display would let us all know when he was lying.

I stood near Chung's head, leaned against the wall, and watched the display. As the stimulant brought him around, his pulse rose, and his respiratory rate climbed a tiny bit, but he didn't open his eyes. He quickly controlled the rhythm of his breath, kept it even, and neither moved nor opened his eyes. I smiled a bit in admiration. He was playing it like a pro, taking time to collect himself, gathering what data he could before he decided to let on that he was awake. If we were amateurs who'd kidnapped him for a ransom, the tactic might have bought him some potentially useful time and information.

"Jose," I said, using his first name both to annoy him and to show him we weren't going to abide by the usual corporate rules, "we both know you're awake, so we might as well talk." He continued faking sleep. I wasn't in the mood to waste time, so I added some positive motivation for him. "The sooner I get the information I want and we reach an understanding, the sooner you go home."

He opened his eyes and tried to move his head.

After he realized he couldn't, I stepped closer so he could see my face.

"Who are you," he said, "and what do you want?"

I opened my mouth to remind him again not to waste

time but stopped when the wall display caught my eye: Nothing had changed. He didn't know my face. That meant he'd placed the bounty on my name alone, probably using information the Gardeners on Macken had somehow gotten out of Barnes. I should have erred on the side of caution and not let him see me. I'd made a mistake, but I reminded myself that it changed nothing. My predicament remained the same: I needed him to remove the bounty.

"I'm the man," I said, "you placed a bounty on, and I'm also the man who knows about your illegal arms deals with Osterlad. You're going to remove the bounty and tell the FC about the arms deal. You'll probably lose your job, and Xychek will certainly pay heavy fines, but you'll walk away unharmed . . ." I paused a second. " . . . provided you don't make me hurt you."

"What are you talking about?" he said. This time, his vitals jumped, but consistently across the board, a pattern of agitation, not of attempted deceit. Maybe bounties were more common among the executive set than I'd realized, and he genuinely didn't remember all of the ones he'd set. That seemed unlikely but possible, so I decided to fill in the blanks for him.

"I called you once before," I said, "but you wouldn't talk to me then, so I had to arrange this conversation. I'm the guy who ruined your bid on Macken by returning Slake's daughter, Jasmine, to him. Remember me now?"

The calming drug Lobo had chosen must not have been very strong, because this time Chung's vitals raced up the display, every indicator elevated beyond the yellow caution lines the medbed had computed for him. His face turned red, and for a moment he shook with the effort of trying to move. "You're the one who gave him Jasmine again?" he screamed. "I'll kill you."

"All I did," I said, "was return her to her father."

"You're either a fan of sick games," he said, his body relaxing as he realized there was no point in struggling against the restraints, "or truly stupid."

I was getting annoyed at his attempts to distract me, but I did my best to keep the feeling out of my voice as I leaned over him and said, "You're wasting time again. Let's get back to the bounty and the arms deal."

He stared directly at me as he said, "Do you really not know what you did?" He looked at me intently for a few more seconds, then closed his eyes. "Jasmine is my daughter. I had no idea she'd ever escaped from Slake until you called."

This was a strange tactic, and I had no more patience for games. "Last warning," I said. "Stop playing games."

"Check my wallet," he said. "I had it when you kidnapped me." When I didn't move, he said, "Check it. What can that cost you?"

The sincere look on his face caused a pit to open in my stomach, and all my elation at the successful mission tumbled into it. I pushed back all feeling, opened the medic room drawer, and pulled out the wallet. I put it in his right hand, temporarily removed the restraint on that hand, and stepped away from his reach. "Open it," I said.

He thumbed it, tapped a security code, and held it out to me. I took it with my right hand, while with my left I forced his arm back down and snapped on the restraint; no point in taking chances.

I opened the wallet, found two microthin photo displays, and pulled out the first. It unfolded as I flicked it, and images of Jasmine blazed into life: Jasmine posing on the front steps of Chung's estate, Jasmine laughing and holding a woman I didn't recognize, Jasmine much younger and in Chung's arms, Jasmine with her eyes shut as she kissed Chung on the cheek. Jasmine, Jasmine, Jasmine.

I was breathing hard, the air pounding roughly in and out of me, loud enough that Chung must have heard it.

"Slake's people kidnapped her," he said. "He used her to force me to withdraw our bid for the Macken development project and for the new aperture there."

None of Chung's vitals showed the slightest sign of a lie. He was telling the truth.

I had returned an innocent girl to the man who'd arranged her kidnapping. An innocent girl, and I'd failed her.

I could clearly picture her face.

"The FC has no jurisdiction over intercorporate issues, so I couldn't go to them."

Her face as she awoke briefly in the cart, the fear as she spoke, a fear I mistakenly thought she felt toward the Gardeners.

"I couldn't afford to go to war with Kelco locally, because our board would never have granted me the budget."

Her face, which reminded me so much of Jennie.

"Besides, we knew Slake was dealing off the books with Osterlad and was better armed in this region than we were—but we couldn't prove it."

Jennie, another innocent girl I'd failed.

"So I abandoned the bid before the board could learn of the kidnapping. They would have sacrificed her if I hadn't. Instead, I stalled them with a flawed analysis that demonstrated that the bid would be unprofitable for us."

Just as I'd failed to see that Osterlad was playing me for a fool, claiming what I now realized was a bounty from Slake had come from Chung, sending me to do more of Slake's work by hurting Xychek further.

"Slake promised he'd give her back as soon as they'd completed the deal, but something happened to delay it a month."

Slake, who was holding Jasmine prisoner right now because my deal with Barnes had delayed the signing of Kelco's Macken bid by a month.

"I've hidden the kidnapping as long as I could by claiming she was with her other parents on vacation, but the board is bound to learn the truth soon. When they do, they'll fire me. I could live with that, though, if I could just get her back."

Slake, who'd recommended I go to Osterlad in the first place.

A catch in Chung's voice and the tears in his eyes dragged me out of my thoughts and back into the moment.

"If I could just get her back," he repeated.

Anger flushed through me with a purifying coldness that straightened me, focused me, directed me. I hadn't been able to save Jennie when I was young and they took her. I hadn't even been able to think of saving her. They took her, and her loss was at that time as inevitable and unstoppable as the wind. In the more than a century since then, I've learned a great deal, and I've tried not to fail others, but sometimes I inevitably have, and each time it hurt, hurt a great deal. This time, though, I hadn't merely failed; I'd let Slake use me to actively harm this young woman, this girl.

I've spent much of my life fighting to shove anger to the side, to keep it at arm's length until it could dissipate and become just so much more heat rising away from me. Not this time. This time, I didn't fight the anger. I welcomed it, I embraced it, I consumed it, I enjoyed the rich, purifying power of it.

I stepped to the med room's door, afraid to be near anyone until I could find my way back out of the rage that was, in this moment, all I wanted or needed. I said, as much to myself as to Chung, "You will get her back. You will."

CHAPTER 21

I stood outside the med room for several minutes, afraid to go up front and face Lim. The problem wasn't that I cared that she knew Slake had played me and used me; I've been a fool before and almost certainly will be again. What worried me was me, my own reactions. As angry as I was, anything she did, no matter how well-intentioned, might set me off, even though she wasn't the target of my rage. So I stood as still as I could manage, worked on slowing and controlling my breathing, and struggled to regain control. I didn't want to entirely abandon the anger—I knew I'd want it and need it to do everything I'd have to do to deal with Slake—but I had to harness it, to process it into fuel for action.

I slid down the wall and sat, wanting to stay alone and feeling I had nowhere else to safely go.

I realized then that I was letting my pain get the best of me, and that wasn't acceptable. Sometimes pain is necessary, and when it is, you should accept it and get on with the task at hand. I'd wasted enough time. I had work to do.

I got up, walked into the command area, and sat opposite Lim. "If it isn't obvious," I said, "the fact that Slake used me to hurt an innocent girl . . ." I paused, groping for words and finally realizing that saying the least I could manage would be best. " . . . upsets me a great deal. I intend to make this right, or, more accurately, as right as I can make it given what I did. I also intend to make Slake pay, and pay dearly, for all of this."

She nodded. I was glad she didn't say anything.

"You don't have to participate," I said. "I'll get you the fee we agreed on, and you can go."

"No way," she said. "You held out the hope of big money for this deal, and I still believe that's possible. Plus, I signed on to complete a mission, and it's not done. I'm in to the end."

"Fair enough," I said. I owed her the chance at more money. Staring at her, though, I also had to accept that she wasn't staying only for the money. I'd underestimated her loyalty, and consequently underestimated her. "Thank you. I appreciate this. The rules stay the same, though: You get to help with all the planning, and we'll do our best to agree before we proceed, but if we can't agree, the final call is mine. And, of course, I run all fieldwork."

"Understood and agreed," she said.

A black and sad weariness settled on me like night falling. As accommodating as Lim was being, I still found it wearying to deal with her. The problem wasn't her; it was me. I needed to get out, be alone, sort this out on my own without having to talk to anyone. "I need some time to think," I said, "time off Lobo. I'm going to have Lobo drop me outside Queen's Bar at a landing and storage area we've used. You guys can pick me up later; we'll set a time. While I'm gone, you take care of Chung and come up with some options for letting him go without getting us caught. We'll review the options when I'm back."

She nodded her head, studying me. "Okay."

"Lobo," I said, knowing he monitored everything that happened inside him, "plot an evasive path and take me there."

At Lim's urging I'd released Chung from the medbed. I returned his clothing and belongings, blindfolded him, moved him to a slightly larger but still locked holding area, and gave him some food. I reassured him we'd return him soon, then left.

I shouldn't have needed Lim to remind me to take care of him. I was making mistakes, being careless, and that had to stop. I'd kidnapped Chung to get him to remove the bounty and to make him confess to the FC so I could make some money in the bargain. The bounty remained, but at least now I knew its true source. The prospect of money from the FC also remained. This was a job, possibly a lucrative job, and I was behaving unprofessionally. I understood that what I'd done to Jasmine, the fact that I'd caused such harm to this young woman, was affecting me, but I also knew my best hope for success was to plan and execute her rescue carefully and professionally.

When I get lost inside the double helix of anger and self-loathing that to this day exercises such immense gene-level control over me, throwing myself into solitary work is the best remedy. It's why I've gravitated to confidential courier assignments. I couldn't go forward with this job, however, without planning, planning that would unavoidably involve both Lim and Lobo, and right now I couldn't trust myself to spend significant time with anyone.

That left me my backup option: losing myself in a city. Walking the streets, weaving through and around crowds of other people but never being part of them, eating alone, sitting outside humanity and studying it: A busy city afforded me a set of distractions and a form of solitude that would help me regain my focus.

Lobo was too small to be able to move at any useful speed without Chung figuring out that he was on a ship, so we abandoned any attempt to convince him otherwise. When Lobo could find no indication we were being tracked, he headed for the landing area at the highest speed we agreed wouldn't attract attention. We touched down in the middle of the morning of the day after the attack. I exited via the rear hatch, moving as casually as I could manage, and Lobo immediately took off again. We'd agreed to rendezvous a little after sunset.

I hadn't slept since the snatch, but I was too wired to relax, so I hired a taxi and had it drop me a couple of blocks away from the Busted Heart; that way, the vehicle wouldn't have a record of my exact destination should someone later try to reconstruct my path.

The image of Jasmine lying on the cart and waking in fear kept playing across my mental display. I walked slowly, aware I wasn't paying full attention and compensating with the slower pace.

As I turned the corner onto Dean's Folly, the Busted Heart in sight a block away, I felt bug stings, lots of them, more than I could immediately count, on my arms, neck, and back. I had time enough to realize I couldn't see or hear any insects, and then the world went black and I was out.

CHAPTER 22

I came awake slowly. My eyes opened before they could focus, and they focused before I could process what I was seeing. It wasn't much: a smooth white expanse, the whiteness blurry at the edges. I tried to roll over, but I couldn't move my body. I lifted my head and looked down my chest. I was lying on some sort of table, naked but not cold, the surface below me warm and my body wrapped securely in restraining plastic. An IV hung from each of my arms, the attached tubes running beside my body and behind my head to destinations I couldn't see. I felt nice, warm and secure, no worries, no troubles. I closed my eyes briefly and enjoyed the warmth, then opened them as I realized I missed the pretty whiteness, so soft and pure and far away. I smiled at it. I thought I saw it move, and when I squinted I was sure it was smiling back at me.

I realized it was a ceiling. It was a great ceiling, and I was happy to be there with it.

A pressure grew in the back of my head and distracted me from the whiteness. I didn't like the pressure, but it wouldn't stop, it wouldn't leave me alone, and then it burst into a thought, a realization that filled me: This was all wrong. I was drugged, and I needed to get away. Nanomachines. I needed to release some nanomachines to remove my bindings. I waded into the dense cloud of my brain, trying to concentrate, and then I heard a soft chime, a tiny faraway sound, and I was out.

I was asleep, and then I wasn't, the line between sleep and waking unclear and shifting, my eyes shut, then open, then shut again. I felt a smile, then realized happily that it was mine. My eyes cleared enough that I could see whiteness above me, and I remembered it was my ceiling. I smiled more broadly, glad to see it again. Right after the memory of the ceiling came the recollection of the lovely warm bed, the happy hugging plastic, and the tubes in my arms. I knew where I was: I was where I'd been before. I was glad I'd figured that out. I wondered why I'd left. There was certainly no reason to leave such a comfy place. I must have been acting silly. Yeah, that was it: silly.

I remembered something else silly: a tiny little chime, one I could hear but not see. I was happy to remember it. As I lay there thinking, I realized I was happy about everything, though everything wasn't very much: the ceiling, the chime, the bed, the plastic, the IVs, and me, all together, all part of each other, all happy.

Except the chime wasn't there, and that bothered me,

bothered me enough that I stopped smiling. Where was the chime? The question bounced around in my mind, a fuzzy ball ricocheting off the walls of the empty room of my brain, gaining speed until I realized I only heard the chime before I went to sleep. More knowledge followed that realization, a rapid-fire tumble of blurry recollection: I went to sleep after I heard the chime after I tried to concentrate after I figured out this was wrong.

This was wrong.

I remembered that I needed to focus so I could instruct the nanomachines to decompose the plastic and free me. Focusing was difficult, but I tried. I thought hard for what might have been a split second or an hour; I couldn't tell. Then I heard the chime again and just had time to figure out that I didn't want to go to sleep before I was out.

I realized I was awake when I noticed that instead of dancing swirls of yellows and red I was now seeing white, the white of the ceiling, the lovely ceiling.

Memories accompanied the vision of the ceiling: the warm bed, the warm plastic, the IV tubes in me, the bad chime. I remembered now: When the chime played, the ceiling vanished. Or did I vanish? One of us definitely went away; I was sure of that.

I lay still for a bit, enjoying the ceiling, happy in the realization I'd achieved, until a question shoved the happiness away: What made the chime play?

The chime. I repeated the word in my head, enjoying how it felt: chime, chime, chime, chime, chime.

The knowledge crept into my mind so slowly I couldn't be sure when it first appeared: I made the chime play.

Why would I do that?

I made the chime play, which made the ceiling go away, but I liked the ceiling. It was a puzzle, and puzzles are fun, but the pieces of this one weren't fitting right.

Like me, I realized, like the way I didn't fit here, not in the bed, not under the plastic, not here at all. I should leave. The tumble of memory—or was it imagination?—rolled over me. To leave I needed the nanomachines, and to get them I needed to focus, to think hard, and when I tried to do that, the chime rang.

More memory, or more imagination: I'd done this before.

I needed to know if I was remembering or imagining, but that could cost me. Still, I had to know.

I started a little song in my head, a gentle tune, two words repeating over and over: Concentration costs. Concentration costs. I tried to keep it going, make it something I couldn't forget, and then I focused on the nanomachines, focused as directly as I could manage. The ceiling vanished.

I woke with a song playing in my head, two words repeating: Concentration costs. Memories flowed like water into the bowl of my mind, filling me: bed, warm, ceiling, plastic, tubes, chime, concentration costs, concentration brings chime brings sleep.

I wanted to stay awake, so I stayed loose, kept my eyes open, enjoyed the ceiling and let time ease by, not focusing or concentrating but not sleeping, either. I kept my eyes open and let my thoughts dance in slow motion through my mind as I waited to see what was next. My awareness slowly increased. I noticed the slight pressure of the plastic covering, the contrast of temperature between my cool, uncovered face and my warm, plastic-wrapped body. Each time a thought tempted me to pay it more attention, I turned my attention away from it. Concentration costs.

"Very good," a voice said from all around me.

Another temptation, this voice was, another test, so I let the words wash through me but didn't allow them to send waves across the mental pond on which I was floating.

"We were wondering," the voice said, "how long it would take you to figure out that you had to stay completely relaxed. I'm sure you'll be pleased to know you beat our expectations."

It wasn't a nice voice, was nowhere near as nice as the ceiling, and that surprised me. Slowly new knowledge crept over me: The voice was harsh because it was the product of a cheap synthesizer, and it was all around me courtesy of speakers. I smiled and felt happy at the way my subconscious was injecting bits of information into me without requiring me to concentrate. Good subconscious; I wished I could pet it to thank it.

"I'm going to raise the brain-wave tolerance level slightly," the voice said, "but don't take this as an invitation to do anything. With the IVs we can knock you out in less than a second, and if that fails we can jettison the room you're in. You're in a low orbit, and we'd aim you into the atmosphere, so you wouldn't last long."

I fought to relax but an image of burning smacked into my brain and I suddenly realized I had to get out, to escape. . . .

The chime sounded.

"At this level," the voice said, "you get one warning tone. Let your brain activity rise much further, and we'll take you down again."

The voice paused. I used the quiet to calm myself further, shutting my eyes and grabbing at the edges of sleep without giving in to it completely.

"You showed us once that you know how to relax," the voice said. "Show us again."

I bathed in the colors on the inside of my eyelids, letting them wash over me and soothe me, then slowly opened my eyes and enjoyed the ceiling. Time passed, maybe another few seconds, maybe an hour; I couldn't tell, and I couldn't let it matter.

"Well done," the voice said. "Now we can begin."

I closed my eyes again, mentally crawling as far toward sleep as I could while remaining able to hear, knowing I needed to listen but not to concentrate on what I heard, the words a gentle shower I had to let rain on me.

"On Floordin," the voice continued, "you evaded security, stole a weapons control system, and escaped, while the man in charge went missing."

Floordin. The name rolled across the floor of my mind, accumulating debris as it went: Trent Johns vanishing, Osterlad setting me up, Lobo whole again.

"On Macken, you rescued a girl, and you did it, as best we can tell, without any real help."

Jasmine's face materialized in my mind, mouth open in fear as I took her on the cart to her kidnapper, to Slake. Slake, who was the man behind all my troubles, who was also, I suddenly realized, almost certainly the one who'd arranged my kidnapping. The two images assaulted me: Jasmine and Slake, pain at what I'd done and anger at being used, the two of them combining to generate more emotion and mental temptation than I could manage while remaining this calm. The chime sounded its sole warning.

"Relax, Mr. Moore," the voice said. "We simply want to know how you did these things. Something is unusual here, and we want to know what."

Paranoia joined the pain and the anger as I realized that if I lost control and talked then they'd know the truth about me and never let me go. I'd end up a corporate research guinea pig, because they'd know that nanomachine/human integration was not only possible but alive and well. I couldn't let that happen, I couldn't tolerate it, I had to get away, I had to—another chime sounded.

Awareness crawled over me like a foggy dawn, my mind waking up but remaining soft, fuzzy, and unfocused. Memories slowly took form, as where I was, what was happening, and what I had to do to stay awake congealed in the ooze that was my brain. I remembered the voice that surrounded me, but I couldn't recall whether I'd heard it once or many times, nor was I sure how many times I'd passed out from whatever drugs they were using on me. I knew I had to stay awake to have any chance of escape, so I tried to remain relaxed; perhaps more memories would return.

A door snicked open somewhere behind me. I heard the soft footsteps of someone entering the room and walking toward me. The person stopped far enough away that I couldn't see who it was.

"Mr. Moore," a male voice said, "because you've been unwilling to answer our questions thus far, my employer has decided to pursue a more aggressive option. Up to now, we've merely kept you sedated and used some drugs to knock you out each time you showed any sign of significant mental activity. I'm here to apply some additional incentives."

I felt the man's hands working on my head and neck, jabbing me slightly and sticking cold things to me. I kept my breathing light and avoided concentrating on anything in particular.

The voice I'd heard before flooded the room. "Mr. Moore, Jon," it said, the synthesized speech harsh and unpleasant, "I encourage you to answer our questions, spare yourself pain, and save us all time. How did you manage the theft on Floordin, and where's the man who was in charge there? How did you rescue the girl on Macken all by yourself? And, I must now add one more question: What has Jose Chung said to you?"

Images of the people washed across my mind: Johns, his head dissolving; Jasmine, her face drugged and afraid; and Chung on the medbed, anguished over Jasmine. I worked on my breathing and gently pushed them away, not wanting to focus so much I ended up asleep again. I alternated gazing at the ceiling with studying the colors inside my eyes, and time passed. I have no clue how much.

"Your choice," the voice said.

I heard the man behind me step away, and for a few moments I thought they might wait for me to make another mistake, cause the chime to sound, and be drugged into sleep again.

Pain smashed into my head. A jagged lancing sensation ripped through my neck and into my mind. I screamed, a long loud roar that hurt my throat, and even as I was screaming the pain increased. For a split second I wondered how they could hurt me without putting me back into sleep, but the pain shoved aside all thought and filled me, cut me, crushed me, my head and neck and shoulders flexing and tensing uncontrollably, my body spasming, my bowels emptying. I grabbed at the possibility that the pain would bring me focus and let me control my nanomachines, but as fast as the thought came it flew away. I couldn't think, couldn't do anything other than hurt, hurt, hurt.

Still the pain slammed into me, growing and filling me and pushing at my edges until I was sure I would explode. A higher, screeching scream erupted from me as if it were an animal fleeing a fire. The pain increased until it obscured all thought and I was sure I was dying, and then black unconsciousness overtook me.

I didn't want to wake up, though I couldn't remember why, so I fought to stay asleep, resisting awakening by clinging to wispy dream images that became more and more faint even as I struggled to maintain my grip on them. Despite my attempts, however, my mind came more and more aware, until I remembered with the fuzziness of a dying display where I was, what my captors were seeking, and the pain. The memory of the pain triggered an involuntary flinch, as I sought to run away even though at some level I knew I was restrained. No pain hit me now, however, so I quit resisting consciousness and opened my eyes. My body ached a bit, as if I'd been exercising strenuously for a long day, and my neck and head were tender, but I otherwise felt more normal than I would have believed possible under the onslaught of the torture. My skin was dry, and my groin and rear felt dry against the plastic and the bed. After a few moments, my fuzzy brain realized someone must have cleaned me. I was grateful for that courtesy, and I clung to the positive feeling of gratitude like a drowning man clutching a float.

"Welcome back, Jon," the voice said. "I really don't understand what could be important enough for you to endure this ordeal. We've studied what little data we can find on you, and nothing appears extraordinary. Your records begin less than forty years ago. You've worked for the Saw and a few other mercenary groups before it, you've acted as a rather expensive but apparently successful private courier, and that's about all we know. Explain the girl's rescue and the episode on Floordin, tell us what Chung had to say, and we'll stop all this."

I wasn't sure how much I could take. I'd sometimes imagined that I'd be able to resist interrogation by finding a mental safe house, a place to retreat within my mind, but in my heart I knew that I, like all other people, would break eventually. I had to get out before I did; once they discovered the truth about me, I'd never be free again. My mind seemed sharper than before, so I tried to focus enough to communicate with the nanomachines.

A chime sounded. Before the noise could fade, the pain stabbed again into my head and neck, filling my vision with a black-red darkness. One intense jolt, and then the pain stopped, but it was enough to make the point. I did my best to relax, to think of nothing, to exist but do no more.

"Jon," the voice said, "I hope you understand that I'm not enjoying this. None of us wanted it to come to this. Answer the questions, and we'll be done."

For a moment that seemed the most reasonable solution in the world, the residual shock waves of the pain in my body leaving me longing to make the voice happy. I opened my mouth to speak, ready to do whatever the voice wanted. Then the reality of what would happen flooded back into me, and I understood that the time might come when I'd talk without even realizing I had. That knowledge was, inexplicably, the funniest thing I'd ever thought. I started laughing, lightly at first and then wholeheartedly, my body twitching with laughter under the plastic. I laughed and laughed, unable to stop, unable to remember why I was laughing, and weaving among the laughter was a wispy thread: I was going crazy.

Maybe crazy was the safe place you went so you wouldn't talk.

"Jon," the voice said, "as you must know from your experience in the Saw, the issue isn't *whether* you'll answer; it's *when* you'll answer. I regret your choice."

The pain arced through me, cutting off the laughter as the muscles in my neck tensed so tightly my screams emerged as tight, compressed squeaks. More intense this time, so sharp I couldn't imagine anything else existed, the pain hit me and hit me and hit me, until I could take no more and passed out.

We continued in this manner, the voice and the pain and I, though I don't know for how many times and or for how long. I screamed sometimes, laughed others, and often cried, but the episodes blurred until each one began as if the first, a birth into pain, a new short life with no significant data from any prior ones, just awakening and then pain. After a time, I cringed as I awoke, enough memory lingering that I knew bad things were coming even though I couldn't remember what any of those bad things were.

I woke up and hid behind my eyelids, kept them closed as if by not seeing the world I could deny its existence, and tried to dig my way back into sleep. I failed, but as I lay there trying to sleep I eventually recalled the chime. That recollection led me to remember they had to be monitoring me, which in turn meant they had to know I was awake. I couldn't deceive them, I realized, and the thought filled me with despair. How could answering their questions, I wondered, make my life any worse than this? Even as I formed the question I realized that its existence marked a major step on the path to giving up.

I heard footsteps again behind me and opened my eyes, hoping for some sort of reprieve, knowing the hope was futile but harboring it anyway.

"The drugs I'm adding now," the voice said from behind my head, "represent the next stage."

I swallowed several times, until I thought I could speak. As I breathed deeply and slowly, staying unfocused and below the chime's threshold, I managed to croak out, "How long?"

The voice laughed, a sound filled with surprise and amusement and a hint of pity but no real humor at all. "How long for the drugs to take effect, or how long have you been here?"

Blackness crawled around the edges of my vision, and I couldn't tell anymore if my eyes were open or closed. Answering was beyond me.

"None of that will matter," he said, as the blackness completely filled my sight and crawled up my optic nerves toward my brain, "where you take yourself next."

CHAPTER 23

A light breeze tumbled off the ocean and up to where I sat high on the side of the central peak of our island. Carried on the wind were the strong smells of salt and fish and wet beach grass, filling my nose and letting me know I was home. The wind always blew on Pinkelponker, and the water always rolled fiercely back and forth along our shore. I couldn't remember a time when either had been still. In that way they reminded me of Jennie; she could never stay still, either. She was always moving something: her hands as she gestured or worked, her mouth as she spoke, her hair as the constant breeze played across its strands.

I couldn't remember walking here, or whether I was done with my chores for the day, but the sun was warm and bright in the sky, and the breeze and the ocean were as beautiful as I'd ever seen them. I was happy to be home. I shaded my eyes with my right hand so I could look far out onto the ocean and perhaps make out the next island. Sometimes you could see it on really clear days. My hand looked odd to me, too big but also not rough enough.

I forgot my hand and went back to enjoying the day.

Too bad Jennie's not here, I thought. She'd like this day. She'd like sharing it with me. She'd have some ideas for fun things to do.

And then she was there, beside me even though I didn't hear her walking up. I must not have been paying attention.

"Hi, Jon," she said, a big smile on her face.

I smiled back, but I didn't speak. I never needed to talk much with Jennie; she always knew. I liked that.

"So after all this time," she said, the smile disappearing, "you've finally come back for me?" Her expression was sad, lost.

I couldn't remember leaving, but I must have; Jennie always knew more than I did. "I'm sorry," I said, feeling sorrow but not able to remember why I felt it.

"You gave me to them," she said, her voice rising as she spoke. "You gave me to them, and then they took me away."

"I wouldn't do that," I said. "I would never give you away. I would never let anyone take you."

"You didn't let them," she said, and then we were heading down the hill, Jennie riding in a cart I was pulling and looking up at me, pain stretching the skin of her face. "You did it for them. You did it."

"No!" I screamed. "I wouldn't! I wouldn't!" I kept walking, though, pulling the cart and Jennie on it, but she wasn't Jennie now, she was Jasmine, Jasmine waking up, her eyes blurry, her face etched with pain.

"My father . . ." she said, as she passed out again and changed back to Jennie, who said, "You never came back, Jon."

"I couldn't," I said. I stopped walking and knelt beside her, tears seeping down my face. "I couldn't. They flew me away the day after they took you, and before I could even find a way to get back, I was on another island and then off the planet and on to Aggro and then everything went wrong and the whole system was blockaded and I couldn't." I gulped for breath. "I couldn't."

"My father . . ." Jasmine said from the cart as she struggled to wake up, then failed and fell asleep again.

"I'm sorry," I said. "I'm sorry." Louder this time. "I'm sorry." Screaming it at the sleeping Jennie Jasmine Jennie Jasmine Jennie. I felt like my heart would explode. "I'm sorry, sorry, sorry." I looked down and my chest was gaping open, blood pouring from it, my heart pounding out my life in apology and still it wasn't enough, not ever enough. "I'm sorry!"

I stood. The blood loss made me so dizzy I tumbled backward off the mountain, spraying red into the air as I fell and wondering why, why, why couldn't I save her. I fell faster and faster until I was plummeting so quickly the wind carried away the sounds of "I'm sorry" and still I didn't hit the water. I fell so long I wondered if the bottom would ever stop me and grant me release.

The ocean, still as far away below me as when I'd started to fall, extended tendrils of blackness that spread and rose until they wrapped around me and stopped my descent. I hung in the air for a split second, caught between the sky and the blackness. The tendrils accelerated me upward, higher and higher and higher, rocketing me toward the sun until its bright light filled my eyes and its heat burned my skin and all I could see was light. The light said my name, first in Jennie's voice, then in Jasmine's, and then in someone else's. It glowed brighter and whiter and louder until I screamed for it to stop.

And found myself awake, drenched with sweat under the plastic, trembling, heart pounding, the guilt over Jennie and Jasmine clenching my insides and contorting my face. As I finally internalized where I was, I tried to slow my breathing and my heart. I didn't want to hear the chime again. The noise in my ears dimmed enough that I could hear the sounds outside my head. The familiar voice was back again, talking to me.

"Jon," it said, "I certainly wouldn't want to have your nightmares. You, however, will continue to have them, and much worse, if you don't stop resisting us. Answer the questions."

The chime sounded, and I realized that the small effort of listening had cost me ground in my fight to bring my breathing and pulse under control. I clamped my mouth shut and breathed slowly and deeply through my nose.

"Nothing to say yet?" it said. When I remained silent, the voice laughed lightly, then continued, "On we go then. We both know where this process ends, but if—"

The voice stopped, and the room turned black. A moment later, emergency strips along the ceiling and floor glowed green into the darkness. The air stilled, a barely perceptible change I noticed only because I'd been enjoying its slight motion across my sweaty face. I pressed against the plastic, trying to move, but I couldn't; it held me tight. The floor shook, the vibrations strong enough that I felt them through the bed that confined me. I wondered if I was dreaming and hadn't really awakened, if all of this had been only another stage in my fall, and then the blackness of the room oozed over the green glow, filled my eyes, crawled into my brain, and carried me away again.

The long grass under my back was soft against my clothing and, where it touched my bare arms, tickled me lightly. Moving my arms slowly across it made me smile. The sky above me stretched cloudless and bright for as far as I could see in every direction. I'd finished my chores for the day and climbed to a nice flat spot not far from the edge of a cliff overlooking the ocean. Jennie was going to meet me later. I completed my chores about the same time every day, but Jennie's healing work never stopped at a particular hour. Some days, she'd be done before I was, maybe have to help only one or two people, and she'd bring me lunch and eat with me. Other days, she'd be healing people so late into the night that when she returned home to our little cabin she'd be almost asleep, barely moving, and I'd have to help her into bed and give her a little water to drink and some bread to eat.

Today, I knew she was on her way to meet me, so I stretched out and enjoyed the velvety grass, the clear sky, and the light breeze blowing the smell and taste and stickiness of the seawater over me.

Sounds like explosions or rockets tore through the air, but I couldn't see anything that could cause them. I wondered if a ship from another island was coming to get

Jennie to take her to work there. That had to be it, and that was sad, because it meant I wouldn't get to see her today.

Something large and shiny suddenly blotted out the sun way over my head. I wondered if it was Jennie's ship. I wanted to reach up for it, to try to persuade it to take me along, but I couldn't move my arms. The shiny thing headed toward me, and even though I couldn't move my arms I knew it had seen me, was coming for me. I heard it calling my name, the sound at first far away and then closer as the thing approached.

I smiled; maybe today I'd get to see Jennie after all.

Except the thing didn't stop coming, didn't stop or change course to land beside me, and I wondered now if it was going to smash me into the grass. I wanted to lift my arms and wave at it to move to the side, to stay away from me, but I couldn't; some invisible force pinned my arms to the ground. On down the thing came, until I knew it was going to crush me. The force of it shook me, then it called my name and shook me again. I closed my eyes so my last sight wouldn't be the thing that crushed me.

Pinkelponker vanished behind my eyelids. As its sky winked out, shreds of memory floated into my consciousness: the voice, the chime, the darkness, the emergency lighting.

I opened my eyes. A woman stared at me from only centimeters away. She wore a helmet whose visor covered her face entirely, but lights within the helmet illuminated her. I was confused, unsure what was happening. Was this Jennie again? Jasmine? No, the woman was neither of them. More memories flowed in, and I realized it was Lim. She shook me gently with one arm and called my name. I felt her other arm moving but couldn't tell what it was doing. Before I could answer her, my arms were free. I lifted my head for a quick look down my body. She'd cut the sections of plastic that had bound me to the table.

"Jon," she said, her voice harsh and forced, her breathing ragged, "can you hear me?"

I nodded and managed to squeak, "Yes."

"Good," she said. "We have to go. Can you stand?"

I heard her words. I could repeat each one. I even knew I should understand them. The problem was that I couldn't focus enough to make sense of them, to transform them from sounds into meaning. I squeezed my eyes shut in an effort to concentrate, and then she was shaking me again.

"Forget standing," she said. "Try not to move when I lift you. This'll be hard enough as it is."

She crouched beside the table, facing up my body, her head near my waist. She grabbed the far side of me and pulled me onto my side. She tugged me a little farther, and I rolled onto her shoulder. She grunted and dipped slightly as my weight hit her. Movement was strange, at first a freeing sensation and then a nauseating one. As my stomach hit her shoulder, I heaved and threw up.

"Lovely," she said. "The amount you owe me just went up."

Bracing herself with one hand on the table that had held me, Lim stood. I felt her arm holding me on her shoulder, and she leaned down on the side away from me. My nose smacked into her body with her first step, and without conscious thought I turned my face to the side. She walked carefully but quickly. I bounced with each step. The only colors I could see were the green glow from the emergency strips and the soft yellow of the thin tubes that ran down the other arm of the suit Lim was wearing and into the weapon that looked as if it had grown from her hand.

Lim kept me near a wall as we went, my body bumping into it every now and then. The bumps didn't feel good, but I also couldn't quite register them as pain; they were simply more sensations that my overloaded body interpreted as distant and irrelevant. We progressed along a hallway. Here and there in the darkness I caught glimpses of bent and scorched sections of walls. My nose itched from the smells of charred plastic and singed metal that thickened the air. Three times Lim passed men lying on the ground; none moved. I caught a clear view of only one. His head tilted at an angle that even in my condition I could tell was unnatural, and in his chest a hole bigger around than my arm was black and oozing, the smell so strong I vomited again as we passed him.

"Damn," Lim said, "you'll pay for this." The effort of speaking while carrying me caused her to pinch each word.

A few times everything went black. Each time I couldn't tell if we'd entered an area with no lights or I'd passed out again, and each time I have no sense of how long I remained in total darkness.

We rounded a corner and stopped outside a door that displayed both the usual green glowing strips and some additional red lights. I knew if I could clear my head I'd remember what those other lights meant, but I couldn't manage it.

"Open both airlock doors, Lobo," Lim said, her voice low and strained.

The door opened, and Lim stepped into a little room. A second door opened, and light slammed into me, everything so bright I had to shut my eyes. I felt Lim take a few steps forward; then she crouched and shoved me off her shoulders. I fell, for an instant alone in the air, and then I hit the floor. My stomach heaved again, but I was empty and nothing came up.

"Get ready to get us out of here," I heard Lim say. "I'll be back in two minutes."

Her voice was a whisper that reached me from what seemed an impossibly far distance. The world lurched, and I passed out again.

Sunlight warmed my eyes. I tried to roll over so it could work on my back, but I couldn't; my arms and legs were stuck. A torrent of memory erased the sun and tore me from Pinkelponker back to . . . where? I was lying down, unable to move, wondering if the voice would know I was conscious again, when the last strand of memory played across my mind and I remembered Lim and the rescue. I opened my eyes. I was indeed back in Lobo, in the small medical room, on the same bed where I'd secured Chung, held by the same restraints I'd used on him. An IV trailed out of my right arm.

I tried to call for Lobo, but all I managed was a croaking sound more like a cough than a word.

It was enough.

"I'm glad you're back, Jon," Lobo said.

Lim entered the room. "Finally," she said.

I closed my eyes, held them for a couple of beats, then opened them again. I was still in Lobo, and Lim was still standing there.

After a couple more croaks, I managed to say, "Water."

Lim swiveled a tube to my mouth. I sucked on it, gently at first, letting my mouth and throat reacquaint themselves with liquid, and then harder, drinking all I could manage. I turned my head away when I was done, and Lim removed the tube.

"Thank you," I said. The tube dripped a bit on my cheek.

"You're welcome," Lim and Lobo each said, Lobo a syllable ahead of her.

"I scanned you," Lobo said, "and found no implants or broken bones. All your organs are functioning at least tolerably, though you were dehydrated. So, we've loaded you with fluid and some broad-spectrum repairers, but only generics. Can you give us more specifics on what they did to you?"

"No," I said. "What you've done is all I need. Well, that and some time." I wanted to be better prepared the next time I encountered these attackers—and I was now convinced there'd be a next time. "Did you take blood samples?"

"Of course," Lobo said. "We were prepared in case my treatments proved to be inadequate to revive you and we needed to seek additional medical aid."

"Keep them," I said, "so I can study them later." When I had more energy and some private time, I could work with my nanomachines to provide my body with resistance to these drugs. Having more energy seemed a distant proposition; I felt very tired, as tired as I could remember ever being.

"Can you stand?" Lim said.

I nodded, then said, "Give me a moment."

I closed my eyes and focused on instructing the nanomachines. For the first time since my kidnappers had tagged me on my way to the Busted Heart, I could concentrate. I set in place a full body-cleaning regimen, something I've had to do all too many times in my life, and then took a deep breath. I was back. I'd hurt for a while as the nanomachines cleaned me and my body had to purge the waste, but as long as I drank a lot of water and rested, I'd be back to normal within a day or so.

I opened my eyes, looked at Lim, and said, "I can stand. Please let me up."

She removed the IV and undid the restraints, then stayed close as I sat up slowly. I put my hands on either side of my body and gently swiveled my legs so both hung off the side of the medbed nearest where Lim stood. I felt beaten, almost shattered, but in a dull way with no sharp pains, so I was confident no bones were broken. I rested for a moment. Lobo helped by lowering the bed until my feet touched the floor and my knees bent slightly.

I pushed off the bed and stood. I wavered for a few seconds, dizzy and weak enough that I closed my eyes unconsciously as I struggled for balance. The dizziness passed, and I opened my eyes again. I tried to step forward and almost fell; Lim's hands on my arm and shoulder were all that stopped me.

"Perhaps," I said, "I should sleep a bit more."

"Idiot," Lim said. "Of course you should sleep more. Get back on the medbed."

"No," I said. "My bunk." Lim scowled at me. "Please."

After a short delay, she said, "Okay, but you're definitely an idiot."

She ducked under my right arm, and I held on to her

shoulder as we made our way out of the small medic area and to my bunk. I moved like an ancient patient too proud or too stupid to let his nurse have the bed transport him, and in a humbling moment of self-honesty I realized that at the moment that was all I was.

When we reached my bunk Lim lowered me gently onto it.

"Thank you," I said, as I closed my eyes. "Really. For everything."

I fell into a deep sleep before she could respond, a sleep blissfully devoid of dreams.

CHAPTER 24

I awoke thirsty and ravenous. I drank a liter of water and ate quickly, staying alone, taking stock internally. I felt almost a hundred percent, the nanomachines and the meds having done their jobs. When I finished, I went up front, where Lim was scanning shimmering windows of information about Macken and Kelco's presence there.

"As you might imagine," I said, "I have a lot of questions. Let's start with the obvious ones. How long has it been since you dropped me off outside Queen's Bar? What happened to me? And, where are we?"

"About seventy hours, the last fourteen and a half of which you've spent sleeping," Lobo said. "You were kidnapped and interrogated by some Kelco staff, and we retrieved you. We're in orbit around Velna."

Lovely. Any time I want a simple answer from Lobo, I

can't shut him up. When I'd appreciate some details, he turns into Mr. Terse. I made a mental note to ask him sometime if there was a way he could display the amount of emotive programming at play in his answers. Having a sarcasm meter would be quite handy for dealing with him.

"Did you think you'd gotten here on your own?" Lim said.

I knew there was no chance she'd go for the sarcasm meter, so I didn't bring it up.

"No." I smiled and shook my head. I was feeling better. "As I believe I said before, thank you for rescuing me. I do appreciate it. I'm just trying to understand what happened."

"Fair enough," Lim said.

"I have, of course, recorded all the aspects of the mission that I could monitor," Lobo said, a note of pride evident in his voice, the added emotion suggesting that perhaps I had indeed read the earlier sarcasm correctly. "So, if you're interested you can view the logs of the rescue itself."

"It all started when you were late for the pickup," Lim said.

They took turns explaining to me what had happened, Lim doing most of the talking, Lobo speaking occasionally and providing the video log he'd mentioned. The story that emerged made me very glad I was working with them, sarcasm and all.

After dropping me off, Lim consulted Chung about how he'd like us to return him. She stayed out of his sight and used a voice scrambler, so her identity remained unknown to him. He was understandably angry, but he relaxed a lot when Lim finally convinced him that I hadn't intentionally put Jasmine in jeopardy and that he was going to walk away from this. After some negotiation, they agreed on a simple but safe plan.

Lobo invested some time in basic evasive maneuvers outside the atmosphere, moving among a few heavily populated orbits with no particular goal. Chung agreed to be sedated and took the pill Lim provided through a hatch Lobo opened. When his monitors indicated Chung was in deep sleep, Lobo used his camo capabilities to once again blend with the cliff tourist shuttles and fly the coastline. He landed with a group of them in time for the midafternoon tour-group switch.

Lim had brought more than work gear with her. Dressed in a color-shifting pantsuit, a blond wig falling loose around her face, huge sunglasses covering her eyes and most of her face, Lim looked every bit the trophy girl embarrassed at escorting her drunken husband off the shuttle and to the nearest restroom. She'd given Chung a mild stimulant to bring him up to a fuzzy consciousness, so he leaned on her and lurched along but would remember nothing. When Xychek security followed up, everyone who'd seen her would remember her, and the cameras would have captured a lot of good images, but neither the people nor the photos would provide a useful trail back to her. So many people passed through the station that her DNA trail wouldn't matter, either. She left Chung at the restroom door and got in line to board another shuttle. At the last minute, she appeared to change her mind and walked quickly down the strip to a different shuttle, one that happened to be Lobo.

Once they were airborne, Lim called one of her team

members who was on holiday on Lankin. He used an anonymous connection at a comm joint in Queen's Bar to send Chung's location to Xychek security. Lim and Lobo, trusting the quality of Xychek's team, hadn't followed up on Chung, but the worst case, they felt, was that Chung awoke in the restroom robbed and sick; no one at a tourist shuttle site was likely to bother to kill him when they could have his wallet for nothing.

Lobo landed a few minutes before sunset, correctly planning to minimize his time on the ground. At precisely sunset, he started monitoring the frequency of my transmitter to see how long they'd have to wait for me.

When three minutes had passed without him detecting a transmission, Lobo knew something was wrong and told Lim. On the chance that I'd been coerced into revealing our pickup plans and to generally minimize risk, Lobo immediately took off and blended in with the last of the tourist shuttle crowd. From there he started the search.

They swept along the coastline up to the northernmost corporate headquarters, but with no luck. Lobo flew a slow series of parallels up and down the continent, starting with the area over the city, until he was about a quarter of the planet away. When he still hadn't detected even a trace of a signal, he headed up to the highest orbital plane on which he could find recent signs of ship or satellite activity. He plotted a cylinder with its center over Bekin's Deal and a radius equal to the peak range of the transmitter, and started sweeping it for a signal. The search was maddening, Lim said, a blind trawling exercise that over the course of many hours reminded her just how much empty space exists around every planet.

After moving down one radius of the cylinder to a lower

orbital plane and shifting a radius westward of the city, Lobo picked up my signal. He traced it to a small, gray, logo-free satellite floating unobtrusively among a group of FC weather sats and Kelco comm relays.

At this point I'd been missing over twenty-eight hours.

Per our previous agreement, Lim took command. First priority was intel. Aside from the occasional short bursts from my transmitter, the sat was electromagnetically inert. Nothing about it read as military, and it sported no obvious signs of armor. Lobo and Lim monitored it for almost an hour before it engaged in a short bidirectional comm link with a source on Lankin. Lobo traced the link back to Kelco headquarters there, so now they knew they had to hit fast and hard or Kelco would launch serious corporate security in pursuit.

With no more data available, Lim opted for as much of a crash-and-trash approach as was feasible given that I was aboard. Lobo copied the markings of one of the FC weather sats and over the course of an hour moved slowly into a position with a clean line of sight to the target. During that time, the sat didn't communicate with Kelco on the ground.

When the next communication began, Lobo moved a bit closer, and Lim suited up.

Right after the sat broke contact with Kelco corporate, on the assumption that no one on the ground would be likely to contact it again for a while, Lim gave the go.

Lobo fired an EM disruptor missile. It moved in fast, hit the sat, and sent a pulse through the vessel. If the structure was milspec and armored, the disruptor would fail, but they had to bank that the small satellite wasn't up to those standards. Lobo followed the missile in and docked hard with the sat, broadcasting interference waves to block as much as possible any communication with the ground. Lobo opened his airlock, and Lim stepped in.

From that point on, they had multiple AV streams for me: the output of feeds from Lim's forward camera and mic, the in-helmet camera and mic focused on her face, and the body-function monitors Lobo maintained on her. The sound from the forward mic, mixed with an undercurrent of Lim's initially steady breathing, filled the room from Lobo's speakers. The forward camera's output, the images of the camera on Lim, and the standard personnel vitals played across Lobo's wall displays.

Darkness bathed the sat's interior, the only lighting a soft green glow from the emergency strips. Lim plugged a lead from Lobo into the airlock's manual-override port and waited while Lobo hacked the switch, impatience showing in her elevated heartbeat and her gloved left fist occasionally smacking the wall. The sat was definitely not milspec; anything modern and military would have launched virus attacks against Lobo and used stronger encryption than his processors could defeat in any reasonable period of time. At just under two minutes into the mission, the door indicator glowed ready. Lim pushed it open, staying behind Lobo's wall as she did.

A shower of projectiles hit Lobo's inner airlock wall. Lobo flashed to Lim's heads-up display the data from a forward video feed: An unarmored guard stood across from the airlock, bending around the corner carefully, exposing only part of his head, his hands, and the projectile rifle he held. Lim ordered Lobo to take him out, not trank him. Lobo fired an energy beam mounted beside the camera. Lim watched in her heads-up display as the exposed portion of the guard's head turned into a fine mist.

She smiled and said, "Good work."

Lim ran in and flattened herself against the wall the guard had been peering around. Two halls led away from her position, one toward the guard and the other into blackness on the opposite side. She tossed a sensor grenade down the hall with the guard, then threw another down the other hall. The grenades sprayed microsensors as they first flew through the air and then fell and rolled along the floor. No weapons hit them, so with the lack of armor on the vessel Lim decided to risk that it was pure civilian issue and unlikely to have any significant automated defense systems. Lobo collated the IR and temperature feeds from each hallway's sensors and fed the results to two new images in Lim's display. Both halls were empty, so Lim backtracked the guard and headed down his passageway.

Lim moved carefully and slowly in the soft green glow, keeping her own lights off and using only the strips to guide her way. After eight steps, Lobo flashed her an alert: Another guard was coming down the opposite hallway. She sprinted back, pulled a short projectile rifle out of the harness on her back, thumbed it to full auto, and crouched beside the body of the first guard. When the sensor-web output in her display showed the second guard was less than three meters away, she leaned into the hall at knee level and shot the guard in the chest until the clip was empty. Her respiration rate and pulse skyrocketed, and she was smiling, eyes bright with effort and excitement, as she killed the guard. I'd wanted to avoid killing, and I wish she'd tranked the guards, but I also understood how she felt: When it's them or you, you is an easy choice, and in that moment survival is the most intense treat you can imagine.

Neither sensor-web display showed any additional activity, so she headed back down the first hallway, reloading the rifle on the run, moving faster this time on the theory that if more guards were available, they most likely would have joined the pursuit. She approached a room on the outside wall, the first doorway she'd seen. Staying to the side, she pressed the Open button. The door slid aside. Staying low and out of the line of sight of the room, she tossed in a handful of self-dispersing sensors. Lobo collated the video feeds immediately: The room was empty.

She passed two more outer-wall rooms and repeated the process. No sign of any hostiles.

The small sat contained a total of five outer rooms, a hallway that wrapped around its center, and a large central area with a pair of doors spaced a hundred and eighty degrees apart. She dropped sensors outside the first door to the central area and kept moving around the hallway. On its other side she found the remaining two outer rooms, both also unlocked and empty. She dropped sensors outside the second door to the inner area, checked the feeds from the first—still clear—and pushed the Open button.

The door stayed closed.

Her pulse rose, and she grimaced. I understood how she must have felt, the seconds of the mission piling up like weights on her chest.

She reached into her pack and pulled out a pair of acid crawlers, purely mechanical, limited-range versions of the squidlettes I'd encountered on Floordin. She attached both to the top of the door, a roughly thirty-degree angle separating their paths to the floor, thumbed them into action, and stepped to the side. They worked their way down the hatch, spewing an acid mix as they crawled, eating away a centimeter-wide strip of the dull gray alloy, until they reached the bottom and all that held up the door was a wispy web of smoking metal they hadn't quite dissolved. Lim stayed outside the line of sight of the door and fired a single round into its bottom left corner. The round was enough to dislodge the door. Its bottom flew backward into the room, and its top crashed into the hallway.

A flurry of widely dispersed rounds smacked into the hallway wall opposite Lim. The shots covered a large area in a random pattern that suggested the shooter wasn't a pro. Lim dropped to her side, facing the room, rifle held along her body, and tossed in a handful of sensors. The shooter, now visible in Lobo's new feed to her as a man who appeared petrified, fired at the sensors. As he did, Lim pushed forward and emptied the rest of her clip in a tight cluster in his chest.

Lim's display showed a room full of storage areas but empty of any life, a single door on its opposite side the only other way in or out. That door opened easily, and though she of course took the time to carefully check the connecting room, the only person in it was me.

Watching her carry me out was strange, the images in front of my eyes colliding with my hazy memories of the same events. I winced as I saw myself hit the floor inside Lobo, where Lim dumped me. "Get ready to get us out of here," she said. "I'll be back in two minutes."

She grabbed a waiting pack and headed into the sat. She moved swiftly and with no wasted motion through the halls, barely slowing as she tossed one charge from the pack into each outer room and, on her way out, the rest of the pack into the center room with the dead man. She was back in Lobo in well under two minutes. He closed the airlocks and detached from the satellite.

Via a recording from an outside camera, I watched as the distance between the sat and Lobo grew until the sat appeared only as a small gray dot in space. The dot turned bright white as Lobo triggered the charges, which blasted the sat into small pieces of debris, many of which would one day succumb to Lankin's gravity, find their way into its atmosphere, accelerate, and burn up, leaving virtually no physical evidence of the torture I'd undergone.

I shivered as I recalled the pain my torturers had caused me, the happy images of Pinkelponker that morphed into nightmares as I once again failed both Jennie and Jasmine, the desperate feelings that gripped me on that table, and the even worse knowledge that soon I'd have told them anything, given up every secret I'd hoped to keep, failed myself just as I'd failed Jennie and Jasmine. I understood intellectually that everyone succumbs to torture in the end, but that knowledge was as nothing next to the gut-deep sense of my own weakness.

Not for the first time, I wished some memories could encounter the same easy fate as the satellite's remains. I knew, though, that instead they would be with me forever, sharp and dangerous debris waiting in the places inside me that were as dark as the blackest space between stars.

"Did you have to kill them all?" I said, regretting my tone as soon as the words left me, realizing too late that I was taking out my mood on Lim.

She stared at me for a few seconds before answering. "Yes. I was working alone, in hostile territory with no definite count of the opposition, and I assumed time was critical." She walked a few steps away from me, then stopped and faced me. Her face was tight, her amazing beauty replaced by naked aggression. She rubbed her hands on her shorts. "First, I have to hope you're simply not thinking clearly yet, because you shouldn't have needed to ask that. Second, it was my mission, so it was my call, and you have no right to question it. Finally, I saved your carcass back there, so fewer questions and more gratitude would be appropriate."

I knew she was right, but the force of her stance and her words hit me like an attack, and I wanted to hit back. I took a step toward her, and immediately and probably unconsciously she responded, shifting her weight to her rear leg and raising her hands slightly to her sides.

What was wrong with me? I forced a long, slow, deep breath and closed my eyes. Before I opened them, I raised my hands, palms outward, and backed up slightly.

"You're right," I said. "I'm wrong." I lowered my hands and stared directly at her. "I'm hurt, frustrated, and sick of the killing." I shook my head. "I've caused one mess after another since this whole thing began, and I left you the problem of cleaning up part of it. I have no right or reason to criticize. You did everything right."

I paused as I pictured her face on the monitor and realized I was lying. What bothered me wasn't the killing but rather her pleasure in it, and what she did wrong was to feel that pleasure. Yet I'd known she'd respond that way when I approached her, so I had no right to chastise her for it. Worse, I realized then that I really would have done the same, and that I, too, would have opted for lethal force. No, I made myself face it directly: I would have killed them, and as each died I would have been glad it was them and not me. The differences between Lim and me were subtle: I would have found no joy in the killing per se, and I would have felt bad about it afterward. Did those differences really matter? Certainly not to the dead men or their families. In the end, though, valid or rationalization, real or illusion, they mattered to me. Looking at Lim, I knew there was no point in discussing any of this.

I also knew, when I forced myself to confront the truth, that part of me was happy she'd killed the people who'd tortured me.

Most of all, I was glad she was on my side. Hurting someone on my team was stupid, and stupider still was punishing them for doing the right thing—however they felt about it while they did it. I shouldn't have questioned her.

"I'm sorry for what I asked," I continued, "and I'm sorry for questioning your choices. You're right that I'm not back to normal yet, and you're also right that the mission and the choices were yours to make. I greatly appreciate the risk you took to save me. I owe you."

She studied me, searching for any trace of irony, and as much as I wanted to turn away I continued to look at her, trying not to hide my feelings, willing her to know I was telling the truth. For a few oddly intimate seconds we stood like that, the gulf of anger between us evaporating, our feelings exposed and connected by the experience and its intensity, and then she visibly relaxed and even forced a smile.

"So get better, okay?" she said.

She turned away again and headed to the small room Lobo had formed for her use. Over her shoulder, she added, "And do it fast, so we can figure out how to pay back Kelco and make some real money."

I'm not sure how long I sat in the pilot couch, staring at the stars and dozing occasionally as my body finished cleansing itself of the drugs. The visions of Pinkelponker still trickled through my mind each time I lost consciousness, and each time I awoke with a start. Honest longing accompanied each bad dream, and in each one I wished with all my heart that I'd somehow been able to stop them from taking Jennie and that I had never returned Jasmine to Slake. At some moments in the dreams, I yearned for this longing to count for something, to have value, to make things at least a little better, but I knew it didn't, at least not to Jennie or to Jasmine.

Jennie was long gone, vanished over a hundred years ago, her path unknown, even the very existence of her and our home world uncertain.

Jasmine, though, remained in a different situation entirely, a captive of Kelco still imprisoned because I was foolish enough to let Slake manipulate me. As I recalled his approach to me I started to get angry again. I embraced the anger as the old friend it was. The more I considered the situation, the angrier I got. I'd been a pawn since this whole mess started, constantly walking on a path Slake and others in his employ were charting, reacting as they wanted and ultimately doing nothing in my own service. The anger spread inside me and cleared my thinking like a cool evening shower settling the dust of a hot day.

I resolved to save Jasmine and to make Kelco and Slake pay in as many ways as possible for using her—and for using me.

I walked back to Lim's room and knocked. She stepped out, a wary expression on her face.

"Yes?" she said.

"I'm fed up," I said. "I'm done letting Kelco control me, and I'm done helping them. No more. We're going to get Jasmine back, and we're going to make them pay."

"About time," she said. "I particularly like the pay part."

"We can't do it alone, though," I said. "Now that I understand how many Kelco resources Slake can bring to bear, I realize we're going to need to involve some others."

"Fine," she said, "as long as their take doesn't come out of my paycheck."

"It won't," I said, "because I believe I've figured out how all of us can make money in different ways, so everyone except Slake can win." I stepped slightly back from her. "There is one potential problem, though."

"What?"

"One of the groups we need to help us is the Saw. We have to go see Earl, and we have to work with him."

She stiffened, but she kept her face calm. "If what you want is an armed team, then the Saw isn't necessary. My group is more than capable—"

"That's not the point," I said, cutting her off. "We do need soldiers, but what we need more are Earl's contacts, his relationship with the FC."

"You have no better options?" she said.

"None," I said. "We need the Saw and the FC, and Earl is our only way into both."

"Then it's not a problem," she said, the look on her face not at all agreeing with her words. "It's just business, right?"

"Absolutely," I said.

"Then set it up," she said. With a smile she added, "I'm sure he'll be as happy to see me as I'll be to see him."

CHAPTER 25

When I strolled into the Saw recruiting center this time, Gustafson was waiting for me, standing by the door to the side room in which we'd met on my first visit. His readiness wasn't a good sign, because it meant either the people or the software scanning the exterior monitors were watching for me. I supposed it couldn't be helped, but it was one more reason to consider a major change in location when this was all over. I gave Gustafson a genuine smile—I found it hard not to like him—and followed him into the room.

He seemed less happy to see me. "I haven't heard from you," he said, "and that wasn't the way this was supposed to work."

"How secure is this area?" I said.

"Secure enough for us."

"Maybe not. Top, I haven't been in contact because my plan lasted about as long as a new private's enthusiasm."

"I take it, though," he said, "that you still want something from us."

"And I have quite a bit to offer," I said. "We're talking business, not charity. Trust me, I haven't been on R&R."

He studied my face for a bit, then nodded, rubbed his hands on his pants, and sat back. "Fair enough. Sorry for the welcome. We've been wondering what was happening."

"We need to meet with Earl again," I said.

"You and I can't handle this?"

"I'm quite sure we can't," I said.

"Okay," he said, nodding his head again. "How soon?"

"As soon as possible. In fact, the earlier today, the better."

"He won't like that," Gustafson said. "I hope you know him well enough to understand exactly how little he'll appreciate having to change his routine."

"I understand, but enough's at play that we have to meet, and it has to be somewhere completely secure physically and with extremely secure comm links. As near as I can tell, with Earl's level of caution that means we'll have to use a Saw facility on the base."

"Of course."

"You can give him some positive motivation," I said.

"What's that?"

"The opportunity for the Saw and the FC is quite possibly greater than before."

Gustafson laughed. "Every time somebody offers me an opportunity, I scan for escape routes. What's this one going to cost us?"

"If we go with my plan," I said, "a little more risk and a little more involvement."

"Oh, he'll love this," Gustafson said. "I think I'll save that part for you to explain."

"That's only fair," I said, "but there is one other change I think you'll want to warn him about."

Gustafson raised an eyebrow in question. "And that would be?"

"Lim is in this all the way," I said. "I owe her. She has to be in the meeting, and she and her people and the Saw will probably have to work together before this is over."

He laughed. "Well that's just perfect. I'm sure the colonel will be thrilled to see her."

I raised my hands and shrugged in the ages-old "what can you do?" gesture. "Sorry."

Gustafson stood and smoothed the front of his uniform, which was already flawless. "Nothing to do but do it," he said. "Call me in an hour, and I—" He paused and chuckled. "—or my replacement should have the particulars for you."

Two and a half hours later the afternoon sun was high in the sky, the air was warm and smelled slightly of the ocean on the other side of Bekin's Deal, and another gorgeous summer day was in full swing on Lankin. Lim and I were missing the day's beauty, physically together in the cab but mentally in separate, private worlds. The guard at the Saw base gate processed our IDs quickly and waved us through. The cab dropped us at a building that looked exactly like the one I'd visited last time but which sat far closer to the center of the base.

Gustafson walked out of the nearest door as soon as the cab pulled away.

"Gunny," he said to me.

"Top."

"Lim," he said.

"Top, is it going to be like that?" she said with a smile. She wore a simple coverall, having abandoned a Law dress uniform at my request, but even the coverall couldn't conceal her figure. When she smiled and turned on the charm, she might as well have been a princess in jewels, as incandescent and hard to gaze at directly as a sun. She opened her arms and stared straight at him.

Gustafson melted, though I couldn't tell whether it was the act of an old friend abandoning a forced distance or the foolishness of just another male who flew too close to her and couldn't resist the heat. He hugged her and said, "Not out here, Alissa. Not out here."

They held the hug for a few seconds, then both said, almost in unison, "Good to see you again."

Gustafson stepped back. "And you," he said. He nodded to the building behind us. "In there, though . . ."

"I understand," she said. "I'm no happier about being here than he is about seeing me, but it's business, that's all."

"You know that doesn't help," he said. "If anything, business has been the problem all along."

"You're not starting with me, are you?" she said.

Gustafson held up his hands in surrender. "Not me. I know better." He turned to me. "Anything else I need to know before we meet with the colonel?"

"No," I said, "and certainly there's nothing we need to discuss out here."

He nodded, turned, and headed to the door. "Then let's not keep him waiting any longer."

We followed him inside and passed through three isolation areas, each one, Gustafson explained, running a
different type of weapons and comm gear check. After
the third, we walked down a long windowless hallway and
turned to a burnished blue sadwood door on the left near
the end. Gustafson rapped twice with his knuckles. The
resulting sound was so muted I was sure the door was
thick enough that no one on the other side could possibly
have heard his knock. What they could hear didn't matter,
of course. The knock was a formality; the staff manning
the hallway monitors would decide if and when we could
enter.

The handle clicked so quietly I barely registered the
sound. Gustafson pulled open the door and waved us in.

We stepped into a conference room that was about as
thematically far as it could be from the tiny containment
area in which Earl, Gustafson, and I had sat. Where that
space had been casual, almost intimate, this one was formal and large, at its center a conference table of the same
polished sadwood as the door. Eighteen chairs, each a
blue leather that perfectly complemented the wood, surrounded the table, one at each end and eight along each
side. The walls were floor-to-ceiling displays, some currently acting as subdued wallpaper, others showing Saw
logos, images from past campaigns, and maps of major
worlds—Lankin the visually largest among them—for
which the Saw currently held contracts. Aside from the
walls, the room was devoid of machines; no doubt Earl
used human attendants to make the visiting brass feel
important. I've never particularly liked formality, but I
had to admit the space was impressive. I assumed this
was where Earl met with the FC and the local corporations

when they had formal reviews; no one organizing a Saw staff meeting would ever have booked a room like this.

Earl hadn't worried about anything more than security when he'd first met with me, so either he was showing off for Lim, which I considered unlikely, or he wanted home-turf advantage. My bet was it was the latter.

One feature I was sure this room shared with our previous meeting place was security. Any group that Earl considered important enough to meet here was one he'd consider dangerous enough to contain electronically.

I glanced at Lim to gauge her reaction. Her smile remained, but it was tight now and lacking in any real warmth. I hoped Earl had also wanted to put some distance between them.

A section of the wall opposite us slid open, and Earl walked in. Dressed in his standard working blues and walking with the same perfect posture as always, at first glance he looked far less nervous than I knew Lim was. As I watched him approach, however, I realized he was uncharacteristically not looking Lim in the eyes, and his back and expression were rigid, set in place by force of will. I have to give him credit, though: He never slowed or faltered. He walked up to Lim, shook her hand, and said, "Lim." He shook my hand, said "Moore," and headed to the center of the left side of the table. The way he spoke to me wasn't a good sign—I was "Jon" in the last meeting—but I should've expected it.

Gustafson sat beside him. Lim and I took seats opposite them.

"Before you explain why we're meeting," Earl said, staring at me, "I have an obligation to address certain complaints the FC has tasked me to handle. Specifically,

Xychek's local security chief, Larson, has asked us to investigate the kidnapping of Jose Chung, their executive in charge here. He apparently satisfied himself that neither Kelco nor any other corporation is involved, so he believes that makes the issue our problem. Technically, he's correct." I opened my mouth to speak, but Earl held up his hand. I stayed quiet. "In addition, a Kelco R&D security man, Amendos, who to the best of our ability to determine is normally stationed on Macken, visited here to tour one of their small research sats."

Amendos. The name took a moment to register, and then I had it: the auditor I met at the Macken jump station. No way could this be a coincidence; he had to be Slake's man in this affair. As I tuned back in to what Earl was saying, I realized I'd missed a couple of words.

" . . . unable to complete his tour, it seems, because something attacked and destroyed the sat. He also could find no sign of corporate involvement, so he went to Vaccaro, who promptly called me." He leaned back in his chair and looked casually around the room. "I don't suppose either of you could help us with those investigations."

"Why are you—" Lim said, stopping only when I touched her leg and shook my head.

"I'm simply doing my job," Earl said, leaning forward again, "as I think the head of any security group, even a small one, would understand if she wanted the group to stay in business."

"You—" Lim said.

I cut her off, raising my voice a little. "Is this room completely secure?" I said.

With visible effort Earl turned his attention back to me. "Of course."

"Are we being recorded in any way?"

"No," he said. "Based on your comments in our last meeting and your request to Top for this one, we're secure and off the record, at least at this point."

"Then let me answer your questions," I said. "As you knew from our last meeting we would, we kidnapped Chung. We later returned him unharmed, a fact I hope Larson mentioned." Earl nodded, and I continued. "Lim destroyed the Kelco satellite after rescuing me from it."

"You appreciate, I assume," Earl said, "that though our last meeting left certain possibilities open, having you directly confirm these accusations places me in an awkward situation."

"That's garbage," Lim said. "I know how much flexibility you have, and unless Jon has misinformed me, you also understand the opportunities this situation offers all of us, the Saw included."

"You may be able to make up the rules when you're dealing with minor policy issues in a jail," Earl said, "but when one has a planetary security contract, one has to treat a great many matters much more formally."

"That's total—" Lim said, before I cut her off again.

"Colonel, Lim," I said, trying to keep my voice level and my tone formal. "I appreciate that this meeting is uncomfortable, but I assure you that it is both necessary and worthwhile for all of us." I faced Lim. "You understand completely what's at play, and you chose to participate." I turned to Earl. "The stakes I mentioned in our last meeting have not lowered, though they have mutated." I paused a moment, then continued, "We're all professionals, so I've assumed we could work together successfully. If I'm wrong in making that assumption, please tell me now and save us all a lot of time."

I glanced at Gustafson. He'd pushed slightly back from the table, so he was no longer in Earl's direct line of sight, and his face was a carefully composed neutral.

Lim's cheeks were taut and slightly flushed, but she stayed quiet.

After a few moments, Earl said, "You said the stakes have changed. What exactly is different now?"

"The capsule version is this," I said. "I blamed the wrong person and the wrong company. Kelco, not Xychek, has been buying arms from Osterlad, and Slake, not Chung, put the bounty on me. I learned some of this from questioning Chung, and some of it from the fact that Kelco kidnapped and tortured me."

Earl chuckled and rubbed his hands on his trousers. "So Kelco was already after you," he said, "and now Xychek is, too. Lovely. Are there any more highlights I should know? Anyone else you've managed to antagonize?"

I hesitated, not wanting to talk about Jasmine, but then realized there was no way my plan could work if everyone here didn't have all the relevant data. "Slake kidnapped Chung's daughter, took her to Macken, and used her to force Chung to withdraw the Xychek bid. A group on Macken grabbed her from Slake. I rescued her—well, I thought I was rescuing her—and returned her to Slake." I paused a second, then added, "And as you might imagine, Chung wasn't too happy to learn all that."

Earl laughed outright this time, and Gustafson joined him, shaking his head in wonder. Even Lim smiled and chuckled.

I could see the humor in what I'd said, but I couldn't

feel it; memories of the torture and images of Jasmine's face kept crawling to the edge of my consciousness. Their laughter triggered a reflexive anger, but I shoved it down and stayed under control; the job was to get the Saw's help and rescue Jasmine, and the job was what mattered most now.

"Exactly how," Earl said, "did you manage to so royally fubar this situation?"

"By screwing up one thing at a time," I said, "in a long sequence of nothing but missteps."

Earl stopped laughing and turned serious. "I think it's time you ran it down for us," he said. "As you noted, we're all professionals, and as such I'm sure we all want as much information as possible before we decide what we're going to do."

I couldn't decide if he was trying to provoke me, getting in his licks, or simply saying exactly what he meant, but his intent didn't matter. He was right: They needed all, or nearly all, of the information. "Okay," I said.

I walked them through what had happened, omitting only my killing of Johns and Osterlad and my use of my nanomachines. None of that information was vital to the mission at hand, and I didn't trust *anyone* enough to expose myself to the kinds of problems those data points could cause me. When I was done, I sat back and waited for Earl to process the story.

It didn't take him long. "So why not walk away?" he said. "What's in this for you?"

"Several things," I said. "Most of all, I want to return Jasmine Chung to her family. The Gardeners might've done that eventually, but I stopped them. Slake and Kelco have caused me a lot of pain, and I want to make them pay for that. And the money, of course. I still believe we can all profit from this."

"Is that really the order of your motivations," Earl said, "or are you just looking for a big payday?"

I felt my face flush, and I gripped the arms of my chair. "Colonel, I know it's been a long time since I reported to you, but I hope you remember enough about me to know that I've never done anything only for the money. Yes, the income potential here is high, and, yes, I'd like to get paid. But whether there's any money in this or not, and whether anyone helps me or not, I'm going to rescue that girl. And as much as I'd like to make Slake suffer for all he's done to me, that's nowhere near as important to me as saving Jasmine."

Earl studied my face, then nodded and turned to Lim. "And you?" he said. "What's in it for you?"

She shrugged and said, "Mostly the money, but also finishing the job. I told Jon I was in to the end, and the job's not over, so I'm still in."

Earl nodded again and looked at me. "Fair enough. I understand your motivations. What are mine? Perhaps more importantly, what are my employer's? If the Frontier Coalition doesn't win, I can't believe my bosses will let us get involved."

"You told me before that the FC was tired of being the weak third party in this quadrant," I said. "We handle this situation correctly, and Kelco will lose its exclusive rights to the new Macken gate and also end up with a great deal less local power in the process. If no corporation has exclusive rights on Macken, the FC will have to play an arbitration role there. That role will bring them involvement and more power."

"And the Saw?" he said. "What will we get out of this?"

"A stronger relationship with the FC, more presence in the region because the FC would have more power, and a chance at another planetary contract, this time for Macken. With two actively competing conglomerates there, the FC will want a continuing peacekeeping force."

"Macken is still a developing world," he said, "so the FC might well not have enough need to warrant the price we'd demand."

"Then you'd control the subcontracting," I said, hoping Lim would see the potential opportunity as motivation for playing nice, "and make at least the usual small profit in the bargain. Even if there's no direct money in it for the Saw, you'll still win because you'll have stopped an illegal arms buildup. Keeping down the local corporate weapons inventory has to be in your best long-term interest."

Earl pondered the situation for a few minutes. I knew the gains I was offering the Saw weren't huge, but the potential for the FC was large, and anyone as skillful as Earl could turn being the agent of such a win for a client into a positive factor in that relationship. Lim had clearly picked up on the potential subcontracting role, because she looked like she wanted to jump in and try to persuade Earl further. I caught her gaze and shook my head slightly; we needed to give him all the time he wanted to think, and we definitely didn't need his feelings about her coloring the whole pitch.

When Earl finally spoke, his manner had changed, and it was clear he was with us. We were no longer selling him; he was helping us plan. "I don't think we need to burden Vaccaro with most of the details of what's happened in the past," he said, "because if we did she might feel obliged to order me to get involved. By omitting those details, however, we'll leave you, Jon, without any apparent motivation. You mentioned money, which she'll certainly understand. She will, however, wonder the obvious: Exactly which group will be paying you?"

I sat forward a bit, excited that Earl was on board. "Xychek. I believe I can persuade Chung to pay both a fee for Jasmine's return and another for helping him gain access to the new gate on Macken."

"So where do we start?" Earl said.

"I call Chung," I said. "I don't think he needs to know about your involvement at this stage, and on the chance that he turns me down, it's better for you if he never learns we met. Can you set up a private call from here?"

"Of course," Gustafson said. He tapped on the desk in front of him, murmured a few instructions and made some adjustments, then pointed me to a section of the wall at the far end of the table. One large panel showed a close-up of my face; the other glowed a soft, sleeping black. "The left is what he'll see. You'll view him on the right."

"Xychek tracks every call," I said, "so they'll be back-tracking the moment we initiate. How long will I have before their software finds us?"

Gustafson and Earl looked at each other and smiled.

"Gunny," Gustafson said, "either you've been away longer than I thought, or you've forgotten a lot. First, do you think there's any chance we'd use less capable software than a corporation? Even if you do, do you honestly believe there's any chance I'd propose this call if I didn't know for damn sure that the line was secure?"

"My error, Top," I said. "I tend to be overly cautious."

"Fair enough," he said. "Do you want to call his direct

number, which we have, or wade through the software flak catchers?"

"He might wonder where I got the number," I said, "but I see that as only good for me, so let's save the time. Call him."

The voice that answered was as perfectly appealing as the previous time I'd contacted Chung's office, and the face that went with it was so flawless it had to be a construct. "Mr. Chung's office," she/it said. "May I help you?"

"I'd like to speak to Mr. Chung," I said.

"As I'm sure you can appreciate," she—the construct was too gorgeous not to deserve the pronoun—said, "Mr. Chung receives a great many communications, so he asks us to handle them if we can. May I perhaps help you?" This was the same greeting as last time; apparently Xychek wasn't a slave to the current corporate "back to people" trend, in which a company demonstrated how successful it was by wasting money placing people in human-facing jobs that software could just as easily perform.

"No. Please tell Mr. Chung that he and I met on his recent outing and that I'm calling about Jasmine."

I didn't need to give any further instructions this time. Chung was clearly waiting for me to contact him, because he appeared within a few seconds. He was also better composed than last time, so he must've decided that I might have some value to him. That was good; negotiating is vastly easier when everyone involved starts out calm.

"Thank you for calling," he said. "When I last saw you, you said I'd get Jasmine back. I hope you're calling to explain how that will happen."

"Yes. I want you to know first, though, that if I had

fully understood the situation I would never have taken her back to Slake." I might be the only one who cared that I made that statement, but I had to make it, if only so I'd told him directly.

Chung's eyes, so much larger than life on the wall display, stared impassively at me. If I had looked only at them I might have believed he wasn't upset. The tension in his cheeks and the way he clipped his words when he finally spoke told me otherwise, and I admired his effort at control. "If you need me to make you feel better about what you did," he said, "and if that's what it takes to get my daughter back, I'll try." Even his eyes gave him away now. "What matters to me is getting her back."

"No," I said, "I don't want that. I'm not only going to return your daughter, I'm also going to get Xychek shared rights to the new gate on Macken." I leaned forward. "And you're going to help."

"How?"

"By cooperating, and by paying."

"So this is all about money after all?" he said.

"No," I said, "it's not, but money is a part of it."

He nodded. "Isn't it always? Tell me what you want me to do."

"He'll stick to the plan," I said after the call was over.

Earl nodded in agreement. "He's got the most to win, and almost nothing to lose. I agree."

"One more call," I said, "and you start this one: Vaccaro."

"She'll need to understand your role," Earl said, "and Lim's."

"Portray us as consultants and informers," I said, "as

well as former Saw soldiers. Tell her whatever you think
will work to get her involved, but make it clear that we
can't risk attacking Slake directly on Macken. The only
real evidence of any wrongdoing that we could produce
is Jasmine Chung, and we don't want to give him any reason to dispose of her before we can find her."

"So you want me to sell her on this whole thing?" he
said.

I laughed. "No, Colonel, I most definitely do *not* want
you to try to sell her. With no offense intended, I've never
considered sales your strong suit."

"Good," he said, "and for whatever it's worth, I'd only
be offended if you did think sales was what I was best at."

"What I need you to do," I said, "is to let her know you
vouch for us and that you're signed up for the plan that
I'll then explain to her. I'll take care of the rest."

He turned to Gustafson. "Top, please take them outside for a few minutes. This will go a lot better if I don't
have to worry about anyone else being in the room."

I considered protesting, because I hated not hearing
what he said to Vaccaro, but I knew he'd be most comfortable talking to her alone. For this to work at all, I'd
have to trust him at some point, so I figured I might as
well start then.

Gustafson stood and motioned us to the door.

When Earl led us back into the room, Vaccaro's face
was staring at us from the wall opposite the door. She was
beautiful, a very different kind of beautiful than Lim but
definitely beautiful. Thick blond hair framed an oval face
with large blue eyes, a fine, straight nose, and perfectly
shaped lips. Her skin shone with the whiteness of the

Macken beaches. I might have misjudged Lim: Heavily engineered beauty might be the new corporate norm. I wondered if cosmetic software was refining her image or if her skin was really fine enough to appear this perfect at such large magnification. I forced myself to look away and composed my thoughts as Earl motioned to us to sit.

Vaccaro waited until we were all in chairs before she began. "Mr. Moore," she said, "Colonel Earl has given me a very brief update, but he's left the particulars to you. I'm listening." The voice that came out of the speakers warred with the image. Her tone was harsh, and her voice sounded far older than her face looked.

"We have an opportunity to tilt the balance of power in this region toward the Frontier Coalition," I said, "and in the process to make some money and even do some good. Kelco's been illegally buying arms from Osterlad, and it's also used kidnapping to stop Xychek from getting any new-aperture or commercial rights on Macken. With a little help from you and a bit more from the Saw, we can expose Kelco, return the kidnap victim, and open the rights to the new aperture."

"So far you've painted a picture I'd love if I worked for Xychek, but I don't. I work for the Frontier Coalition."

"Jose Chung has agreed to back a proposal for a peace-keeping force on Macken and for Coalition forces to monitor and tax the shared gate access for a period of time you two will need to iron out. When we prove what Slake and Kelco have done, they'll have no choice but to back this offer and pay their part of the bill or risk losing all rights on Macken. Any other choice would put them in direct conflict with both you and Xychek, and that would ultimately be both very expensive and destructive for everyone."

"What do you need from me to make this happen?" she said.

"Almost nothing. In a few days, Kelco is due to seal the deal for the gate rights on Macken. I assume the Coalition will have someone present to witness the signing."

"Of course. We'll do more than witness it, however. We'll verify that both corporations have agreed to the arrangement, approve the language and limits of the agreement, and so on."

I reminded myself never to use a term like "witness" with a government official. Bureaucrats, even the highest-ranking ones, always need to inflate their roles in any activity. "Attend the meeting personally," I said, then added "please" as her eyes narrowed slightly. "Please also demand that Slake and Chung appear there, so you three can discuss, oh, I don't know, important issues concerning future uses of the new aperture, their firms' recent complaints to the Saw—any agenda worthy of a long in-person meeting involving the three of you. I just need you to get everyone together and keep them there for a day and a night."

"Easy enough," she said. "What else?"

"If this works, the Saw either gets the contract for the force on Macken or has the first right to subcontract it."

"Colonel Earl already explained that part," she said. "As our existing partner in this region, the Saw would be our natural first choice in any case."

"That's it," I said.

"What do you want from the Saw?" she asked.

"I lack the level of expertise that you and the colonel possess when it comes to your agreements with the corporations in this region," I said, trying to use the type of indirect bureaucratic discourse I normally find distasteful, "but I believe this is a discussion you might do best to allow to occur without you."

She laughed. "Of course. I can't see a reason in the world I'd want to join former comrades-in-arms talking shop." She turned slightly to look at Earl. "I'm sure the colonel and I will be speaking again soon."

"As often as necessary, of course," he said.

She nodded, and the wall blanked.

"What's next?" Earl said.

"Lim has to run the lead team on the ground in Macken," I said. I looked at her. "I owe her, and more importantly she'll have more freedom for some types of action than your troops can officially possess."

He thought for a moment. "Under my command," he said.

"No," Lim said. "I don't work for you."

"I'm certainly not putting my troops under your command," he said.

"We all agree to a plan in advance," I said, "and each of us runs our parts of it independently." I turned to Lim. "If the wings come off, all of us, and I do include myself, defer to Earl, because the Saw's the official power here." I turned back to Earl. "But only if the wings come off. If the plan stays within specs, we operate as equals." I pushed back slightly from the table so I could easily watch them both. "Deal?"

Neither spoke. Neither looked at the other. Gustafson studied some dust on his trousers.

"Yes," Earl said, finally breaking the silence, "that's reasonable."

"Deal," Lim said.

"So what do you really want from the Saw?" Earl said.

"I assume your troops here have trained for work in all elements, including the ocean," I said.

"Of course," Earl said, sounding a little put out, "or haven't you noticed the amount of water on this planet?"

"Does the Saw still provide vacation transport for troops on R&R?"

He nodded. "Though only on existing shuttle routes, as always."

"To Macken?"

"When the Coalition needs us to run FC staff or supplies there, we provide protective transport."

"It's a shame about your transport repair team," I said.

"They're the best in the business," Earl said, "as you should know. Those soldiers are—"

I held up my hand to cut him off. "It's a shame," I said, "that they've been so busy that none of the smaller shuttles are operational right now, and that you're having to fly big ships on even the small routes for the next few days. I expect some of your pilots will be complaining publicly about having to take big tugs on every single run, even the hops to little planets like Macken."

Earl smiled. "I expect they will," he said. "Tell me more."

CHAPTER 26

Gustafson's conservative civilian dress—working pants and standard business shirt, both in muted browns and perfectly laundered, his gig line ramrod straight—screamed undercover trouble to the crowd at Strange Kitty. A third of the customers lost interest in shopping and fled out the front door as we walked slowly to the back of the store. By the time we reached the warehouse entrance, it was locked and blocked, four security guards backing the same small, nervous salesman I'd met before.

"May I help you?" he said. I had to give him credit: He acted as if we'd never met, his eyes showing no obvious signs of recognition. I hadn't gone into the details of my recon of Chung's estate in my briefing of Earl and Gustafson, so I had no reason to reveal my past Strange Kitty business now.

"I believe so," I said. "We're interested in assisted ocean sports, specifically in the racing rays I saw in the rather large tanks just before the aviary. My understanding is that ray racing is an increasingly popular sport."

"It is indeed," he said. "We've augmented the rays for both surface and underwater races, though most of our clients prefer the underwater variety."

"As do I. I'm looking for one creature with enough power to easily handle a rider weight of as much as a hundred and fifty kilos, and I also want top-notch speed and control."

I caught his odd look at me.

"Several of us will be sharing the ray," I said, "and some of my friends are very large." Gustafson coughed as he fought to suppress a chuckle. I reminded myself, as I'd already done many times since he and I had met outside Strange Kitty, never to try to pass him as a civilian again. "We plan to race strictly underwater. Surface breathing ability isn't at all important to us, nor is price." I paused a moment to make the point, then realized with a guy this adept I was wasting time; he'd caught the hint the moment I made it. "Speed augmentations, on the other hand, interest us greatly. We're not planning to participate in any sanctioned races, so I don't care whether we stay within stock specs."

"We're certainly capable of meeting the highest hobbyist demands," he said, "but you must understand that there are fines for using out-of-spec creatures in official competitions."

"I do, but as I said before, we have absolutely no intention of entering any such races."

He bowed slightly. "Very good. I'm sure we can help

you. Other than racing augmentations, is there anything else you'd like?"

"Yes," I said. "Two things. First, we're planning some travel, so any modifications you could make to help the ray thrive in other seas would be most useful."

"Easy enough," he said. "We've yet to encounter an ocean our gill adaptations can't handle. Of course, you'd be responsible for dealing with the local animal import authorities on each planet and for complying with all local regulations. We don't ship off-planet."

"We'd take full responsibility, of course, for all the relevant licenses," I said.

"And the second thing?"

"A tank, one suitable for long-distance and off-planet transport."

"As you'd expect," he said, "we have such tanks, but with the size of the rays—their wingspans run to two meters, so each needs a tank at least three meters wide— and their desire to move almost constantly, any such tank would be extremely expensive."

"As I said, price doesn't matter."

He smiled. "When would you like the ray and the tank?"

"I need you to deliver both in the morning. I'll also want you to conduct a brief training session with me at the drop-off."

For the first time, my salesman showed alarm. "With so little time, we could get you only the best of our in-stock rays," he said.

"Fine."

"We could not, however, build you a tank."

"Aren't any of your in-store tanks suitable for my purposes?"

"Of course," he said, "several are, but they're in use, and freeing them would be difficult, time-consuming, and—"

"Expensive," I finished for him. "We're happy to pay for your inconvenience. Our timetable, however, is not flexible."

The salesman smiled again, no longer alarmed. "Let me work up something for you." He headed into the back, two security men parting just long enough to let him through the door.

While we waited, I showed Gustafson some of the racing rays. Magnificent creatures, the largest were wider than I was tall, their sleek bodies a dark purple color that would vanish in the depths of Lankin's oceans. Light-blue fluorescent lines along their backs gave the impression of small fish moving through the water, a tactic that helped them lure prey. At their turns at the ends of the tanks I occasionally caught glimpses of tow cord jacks and metal receptor webs woven among the skin cells around their heads. I also spotted a pair of additional ports of some type I didn't recognize. Given how good my experience with the birds had been and the number of mods I could spot on these rays, I was confident that the best of Strange Kitty's stock would be more than adequate for my purposes.

"I've always preferred working with machines," Gustafson whispered. "Even the worst of the AIs is less likely to flake on you than an organic."

"We've been through this," I said.

"It's your ass," he said.

"Yes," I said, "it is."

We studied the rays some more. Gustafson walked alongside one that was moving languidly down the tank, its body undulating slowly and gracefully. Their faces were at once fierce and impenetrable, clearly not human and yet teasingly familiar, as if with the tiniest bit more understanding we could fathom the minds behind them.

"I have to admit it," Gustafson said. "They are beautiful, in the way that any well-designed machine is beautiful. They give the impression of caged energy begging for release. Quite hypnotic."

Our salesman found us and handed me a display with a detailed quote glowing beneath a Strange Kitty logo. "This should cover everything," he said, "including tax, delivery, on-site training tomorrow morning, and loading into the cargo carrier of your choice."

Without even checking the total I handed the quote to Gustafson. "Sold," I said. "My friend will take care of this." I admired the rays a bit more, their undulating motion both lovely and menacing. A useless question sprang to mind, and I indulged myself. "Does the ray you're considering for us have a name?"

"As I assumed you understood, all ray control is via electrical impulses from a remote. They don't respond to names."

"I understand. I'm just curious what you call the one we're purchasing."

The salesman tilted his head and gave me the largest smile I'd seen in a while. "Bob."

"Perfect!" I said. "We'll keep the name."

Gustafson finished studying the details of the quote. He couldn't stop shaking his head. "He's going to kill me," he said as he handed back the quote and pulled out his wallet.

I clapped him on the back. "Nonsense," I said. "I'm sure our friend will love Bob."

❈   ❈   ❈

It was Gustafson's turn to laugh. My discomfort at being in a private's blues must have been obvious, because every time he caught sight of me he turned away quickly to cover a chuckle. Wearing the outfit was bad enough—I'd hoped to never again put on a Saw uniform—but being marked as a private, well below my old rank, hit a nerve I didn't know I still had. I'd worked hard to earn the stripes I once wore, and not having them on my sleeves made me feel I'd lost ground. The uniform was necessary, however, because by working as a crewman on the *Hathi*, the largest of the Saw's matériel carriers stationed near Lankin, I attracted no attention from the Kelco and Xychek security people who we had to assume were monitoring the Saw launch facility. The well-leaked breakdown of the smaller personnel carriers covered our use of the *Hathi* for the R&R run to Macken.

Lobo rode inside the shell of a large dirt mover the Saw was delivering for the FC. Bob's tank sat inside Lobo, and Bob swam to and fro in his tank. The ray in the tank in the PCAV in the mover in the transport: It struck me as a chain of key words from the sort of children's story Earl might make up for his kids—if he could ever bring himself to have children, and if he could overcome his reaction to what Bob and the tank had cost. Gustafson would be sharing tales of that reaction, which I gathered had involved equal measures of amazement and obscenity, with other noncoms over drinks for years to come.

I had to hand it to Earl, though: He was a resourceful manager. He was already getting back some of the mission's cost by transporting the dirt mover for the FC, which he'd convinced to pay secure-cargo rates on the grounds that anything as powerful as the dirt mover was a potential weapon. The huge mechanical beast was hollow now, its main chassis a shell hiding Lobo, but once we hit Macken and smuggled Lobo out of it, some of the "vacationing" Saw troops who were actually transport mechanics would reassemble the giant construction machine.

As we closed on the Lankin gate I made my way to a private viewing lounge for a better look. The *Hathi* shared the spare design, emphasis on functionality, and drab gray color of every Saw transport I'd ever ridden. Stay in any one area, and you'd have no way to tell if you were on a platoon shuttle or a major freight hauler. The five-meter-wide window in the viewing lounge was a rare exception, added, I'd heard, to appease the FC dignitaries the Saw had to transport from time to time. Though *Hathi* was huge, she wasn't slow: In the few minutes I stood in the lounge, the Lankin gate grew from a purple speck barely visible in the distance to an enormous pretzel of grape-colored aperture frames and connective pieces, the whole gate a humbling construct reeking of otherness.

Gustafson appeared at my shoulder. "Always amazing, aren't they?" he said.

"Yeah," I said, "I never tire of looking at the gates. They're like the oceans or the forests on a new planet, before any of us arrive to mess them up: inhuman yet usable by humans, awe-inspiring, somehow beyond us." I thought about the unspoiled beaches of Macken and the construction happening along them. "Too bad no ocean or forest ever proves to be beyond us for long. Give us enough time and let enough of us go after it, and we can shape, mold, change, or destroy anything nature can create."

"Except the gates," he said.

"Except the gates." I turned to look at him. "Of course, we don't know if nature created them."

"Don't tell me you're a Gatist," he said. "Do I need to leave you alone to worship?"

I laughed. "Hardly. I don't have any idea whether some god or nature or even aliens we've never found created the gates, and for the most part I don't care. What matters most to me is that they *are* and they *work*, in the same way that the rest of the universe exists and works. It does, and that's good enough for me."

We both stared again at the parts of the gate we could see; we were far too close now to be able to make out the whole thing. Each twist in the pretzel was thicker than Lobo was long, and most of the apertures dwarfed even the ships of *Hathi*'s size. I couldn't tell the Macken aperture from any of the others, but when we settled into line behind a small Kelco transport it was clear we were on our final trajectory toward the gate. Intellectually I understood that we were moving under control, gravity systems working, everything smooth, but for an instant I felt almost as if I were falling, falling through the gate into Macken, into conflict, into whatever that conflict would bring. Once you've been on a few missions, you realize that no matter how well you plan, you're never in total control.

"Can you remember," I said, "how you thought it would be when you first signed on, before you'd actually been in the field?"

"Of course," he said. "I make it a practice to remember my stupidest moments, so I can avoid repeating them."

"And then you go on the mission, and if you're lucky enough to make it back you learn the truth," I said, "or at least you learn the truth of your own experience and reactions."

"Or you die," he said, "or you go crazier than the rest of us because you can't find any other way to cope."

I nodded, then waved my hand at the aperture growing before us. "Yet here we are again," I said.

"Yeah, here we are." Gustafson clapped me on the back and headed out.

The aperture slowly grew larger in the viewport, as the ships in front of us took turns vanishing into it, each replaced in alternation by a vessel coming the other way, a procession of humanity passing from one strange place to another via a mechanism they might never understand, men and women jumping into their futures with absolutely no way to see what those futures held for them, and then it was our turn.

CHAPTER 27

We landed on Macken far up the coast from Glen's Garden, at a construction site a few klicks north of the spot that had hosted the fireworks display I'd seen and that sat well away from any current settlements. The Saw team quickly and efficiently unloaded the dirt mover and its hidden passengers. I ducked into Lobo to grab a hand-gun, a small carry-pack of supplies, and a comm hookup we'd need in the next stages of the mission.

"How do you like Bob?" I said, regretting the flip question almost as soon as I asked it.

"He's lovely company," Lobo said. "The frequent bubbles, the constant motion, and the accompanying gentle waves in the tank: What more could a being of my intelligence and firepower want from a companion?"

"We'll be working soon enough," I said. "I have to go."

"I so enjoy these little chats," Lobo said. "It's the quality of our time together that matters, not the quantity."

If I came out of this mission alive and well paid, I was definitely going to look into the cost of customizing Lobo's emotive software.

Next stop for us was the terminal at Glen's Garden, which we reached via one of *Hathi*'s personnel shuttles. The shuttle dropped us and headed straight back; it would be in *Hathi* and on the way home to Lankin within an hour. I split from the Saw troops and changed out of my uniform at the terminal, then grabbed a taxi to the rental agency I'd used before.

Enough had happened since I'd been here last that I expected the town to have changed, but of course it hadn't; less than a month had elapsed. The town was the same sleepy oceanfront village I'd left. I was pleased to learn that my previous rental agreement had barely expired and the house was still available. I paid for two weeks, the minimal rental period, and set out to find some food.

The streets were wide and quiet, the air warm and lazy and rich with salt and ocean smells, the sky clear, another quiet coastal town on another perfect coastal afternoon. Each time I visit such a place, I find myself relaxing, my pulse and my pace slowing until I realize I'm doing almost nothing at all. The longer I stay, the more I wonder why I don't simply settle down and enjoy life.

That question nagged me for decades, until I finally had the time and money to try it. After a few months, I drifted into work, never really intending to go back to it but doing so nonetheless. The nature of most of the jobs I take is that, like my seemingly simple rescue of Jasmine, they turn complicated and frequently end up causing me to have to relocate. Now, I enjoy these towns each time I visit one, but I know I'll never be able to stay for very long.

I navigated the streets by following the noise, an approach that's never failed me in party towns—and beach towns are almost always party towns. Soon enough, I found a corner bar, shutters open on three sides to let in the air, the building spilling music and laughter and conversation into the intersection it faced. A singer on a small stool in the back played a guitar and sang ballads with an accent so foreign to me and so thick I couldn't understand his words. The rest of the noise drowned him out, but he labored away gamely. Every now and then, the credit gauge he'd set on the floor would light up as someone sent him a tip. I made my way past a clump of locals, five Saw off-duty troops still in uniform, three more soldiers not in uniform but easy to spot by the way they moved and their tendency to hang near the uniformed group, and a handful of Kelco security people wearing identifying tags. I did my best to let them all get a good look at me before I forced myself onto the end of the bar nearest the street.

When I finally gained the bartender's attention, I ordered the special dinner and some water, then leaned against the wall so I could watch in all directions. As I expected, the special proved to be a fish sandwich. I was pleasantly surprised at how good it was, warm and tasty despite being greasier than I typically prefer. I chewed slowly and kept my face to the crowd, giving plenty of people all the time they could use to study me but also scanning the many faces at the same time. If the Kelco security team was on the lookout for me and their staffers in this bar were at all competent, they'd spot me. If they failed to notice me, I had to hope they were monitoring property rentals and would find me that way.

After I finished eating, I headed into the street for a stroll. I stayed on roads with plenty of other pedestrians, and I kept a suitable distance from all of them. I figured the Kelco staffers couldn't have known about my presence long enough to have set up any kind of snatch they could execute in a public place, but at the same time my experience on Bekin's Deal reminded me that they could surprise me.

One of the main streets, Wharf, ended at a largely ornamental wharf with only a few small boats moored at it. A four-deep crowd clung to the sides of the road as flying autocams recorded whatever they were watching, so I eased closer for a look. Vaccaro, Barnes, and Slake were walking the street, ostensibly talking and reviewing the progress of construction in town, more likely simply creating media moments that showed the locals that their government and corporate leaders were working hard for them. I suppose there must have been an era in which it was so difficult to get information about how organizations really functioned that people fell for these staged shows of management at work, but I couldn't imagine such a time. Everyone knew what was going on, but for no reason I could understand the chance to see the FC leader for this region of space working hand-in-hand with the head of the only large corporation with a serious local presence was still enough to draw some people away from their homes and jobs. The three bureaucrats would spend the evening providing a good show for the public, then eat in the main municipal building's private dining room. They'd all spend the night there, because Vaccaro had provided entertainment and insisted they make a long, bonding night of it.

I was glad Vaccaro was making her presence public, because it smoothed the cover story. I also needed her to keep Slake away from his house; it wouldn't be good for the FC if anything happened to him while I went after Jasmine. Other than those interests, however, I had no reason to care about Vaccaro's actions at this stage, and I didn't want Barnes, Slake, or any of their people to get spooked, so I strolled away down a side street.

Night was coming on, the sky purpling and the temperature dropping. As soon as I'd wandered a couple of blocks from Wharf, I grabbed a taxi to my rental house. I'd hoped going there might feel like coming home, somehow relaxing or soothing, but instead it was more like returning to the scene of a crime. Before I got out of the taxi I ordered it to go off-road—at an extra fee, of course, such charges being a common way to gouge new-world tourists for a little extra money—and circle the house. I didn't spot anyone in the building or for as far as I could see around it, even when I cranked up my vision to include IR, but I was still concerned; I'd been here long enough now that Kelco should have been on to me.

I paid the taxi, sent it back, and walked to the side of the house farthest from town and closest to the forest. I stood close to the wall and tuned in to the machines inside. The washers were, as usual, chattering away nonstop. Vaccaro's visit had already made an impression on them, because apparently Barnes had instructed his staff to show up in their dress best, launder every piece of fabric Vaccaro might see or touch, and so on. The washers sang the praises of this special work. Instead of going with the usual rough settings, the users chose the gentlest options for their good clothes, and those options were vastly more interesting to the washers. I suppose that information might come in handy should I ever want to spoil a washing machine with kindness, but it didn't help me right then. I gave up on the washers and tried the other kitchen appliances, but they also had nothing of value to say. As best I could tell from them and the washers, the house had stood empty since my last night in it, and they were all quite bored.

I checked the lighting control system next. It was complaining about the two men who'd visited the house less than half an hour ago. Apparently, these two callous souls had turned on only a few lights and hadn't even touched the options on the viewing window, depriving the lighting system of any chance to strut its stuff. The control complex sulked, both disappointed and annoyed. More importantly, the lighting controller had been forced to deal with minor electrical disruptions caused by some work the men had done on the front door.

Kelco had behaved as I'd expected, which was good. The problem now was that I wasn't sure what those men had done to the house. I could simply leave, but then I wouldn't know their intent. I wanted to understand whether they were out to capture me again or to kill me, because the difference would matter later. To know which it was I needed to either look at what they'd installed or trigger it remotely. The house's security system covered the doors and windows, so those were out as possible entries. The floors and ceilings lacked any motion sensors or other protection, so I could easily use some nanomachines to create a hole in the floor and climb inside, but if the Kelco visitors had left any motion-activated grenades, something I certainly would have done in this situation as a backup for any door-linked explosives, then those would go off the moment I set foot in the house.

I settled for remote activation. It wouldn't yield as much information as entering the place, but the data I would get would have to do. I liked this house, so I hoped they weren't planning to kill me, because if they were they'd probably blow up the whole thing. I'd left almost all the weapons on Lobo; all I had with me was the small projectile handgun. I paced about twenty meters from the front of the building toward the beach, crouched, took aim at the door handle, and fired, one round at a time. I was out of practice, so the first few shots thwacked into the door and the walls around it, missing the handle entirely. I made a mental note to practice my handgun shooting if this all ended well. Then I got the range and started hitting near the handle. I did enough damage that on the sixth shot the door swung inward.

As the door opened, the entry hall visibly filled with a milky cloud of gas. I hadn't heard the release mechanism, but my ears were still adjusting from the sound of the gunshots so that was no surprise. The room grew cloudier, and some of the gas floated out the front door. I left the gun and ran to the edge of the ocean, in case I needed to seek cover, but the gas dissipated quickly.

I couldn't know for sure without taking the risk of exposing myself to the gas, something I was unwilling to do even though the nanomachines might have been able to handle it, but the fact that the men seeking me had used gas instead of explosives strongly suggested they wanted to capture me again. Good; for a change I agreed with Slake on something: I wanted Kelco to want me alive.

I didn't, however, want them to capture me now, and I had to assume they were on their way. I retrieved my gun and headed into the woods. As soon as I was a few meters in, I called Lobo.

"It's so nice to hear from you, Jon," he answered. "Bob and I are having a lovely time waiting in orbit."

"Not now," I said. "I'm in motion and facing possible attack. Slake's men must be on the way. Do you have my position?" I jogged as we talked, heading into the woods on a rough diagonal line away from the house.

"Yes." Lobo's tone shifted instantly to pure work, all sarcasm gone.

"Do you have the coordinates for the place I waited for the Gardeners the night I went after Jasmine?"

"Yes."

"Scan it—"

Lobo interrupted me. "The satellite I'm using shows the area clear under visible light and IR checks, and there's no signal activity of any type."

"How does its IR signature compare to that of the surrounding area?"

"No difference. If I didn't already know its coordinates, I wouldn't spot it on IR."

I'd assumed the pit would have changed to a normal profile for the area in the time since I was in it, but I wanted to be sure. "Direct me to it. Use an evasive course."

I continued jogging, moving more slowly among the trees and through the light undergrowth than I would have liked. Lobo gave me course corrections as necessary. The pit was far enough into the woods that there was little likelihood Slake's men would find me there.

When I reached it, I took a rope from my pack, tied it around the same tree the Gardeners had leaned against when I'd confronted them, and lowered myself into the hole. I pulled a nearly transparent insulating cloth from my pack, wrapped it around my torso, and sat in a corner of the pit. "How's my IR profile, Lobo?"

"Almost invisible," he said. "On the best imaging the satellite can provide all I can see is a spot so small I'd take it for a large rodent. It's nothing anyone would investigate."

"Good," I said. "I'm going to stay here and rest until I need to leave to meet you at the rendezvous point. Wake me in six and a half hours. Until then, monitor the surrounding area, and alert me if you see any activity."

"As if I would do anything else," he said.

Back to the sarcasm. Great.

"Jon," Lobo continued, "why do you waste time during missions asking questions to which you already know the answers?"

Our start time was less than eight hours away, so I wasn't in the mood for this. "Why are we having this discussion?"

"Because," he said, "you asked me if I knew your position when we'd already agreed I would track you." With no emotion that I could discern coloring his words, he continued. "You asked if I knew the coordinates to this pit, when you know I never delete mission logs. You asked me to plot an evasive course, when you know I would automatically do that when you're under pursuit and the pursuers are still far enough away to make that an effective strategy. You asked me to scan this area and alert you to any intruders, when you know I do that automatically per our previous discussions."

I thought about what he was saying. To my chagrin, he was right. "I was wasting time," I said. "I could and should have realized everything you said." I've worked with many different individuals and groups in the past, and even in the Saw I was never able to fully trust anyone else to protect me. I always trusted exactly as much as the mission demanded, and never more. Whenever I could put safety nets and double-checking procedures in place, I did. "The only way I can stop myself from asking those questions," I told him as I realized it myself, "is to trust you, and I've never been good at trust."

"Given my nature," Lobo said, still with no emotion in his voice, "trust would be the most efficient option."

"You're right," I said. "I'll work on it."

"Good," he said.

This time, I could swear there was a note of petulance in Lobo's single-word response, and I found it both annoying and oddly reassuring.

Night had settled in. The forest played a symphony that blended small animal sounds with the soft swishes of branches and leaves moving in the gentle breeze. The old light from distant stars brightened the sky, and for a moment I felt old myself, back again in a place I never sought but all too frequently found, in a jungle waiting to go into battle. I hadn't consciously intended to join this fight, at least not initially, when all I thought I was doing was rescuing a girl in trouble, but whatever my motivations had been, I had to accept that my own actions had led me to this point.

I pushed aside those thoughts and focused on the plan. I could analyze the past all I wanted when this was over, but right now I needed to rest and make sure I could perform my role as well as Lobo was performing his. Whatever I did, the night would deepen, the time to go to work would come, and I'd either follow the plan or . . . or what? I couldn't even conceive of not trying to make this situation right, so there was no point in pretending to consider alternatives. Nor was there any value in punishing myself about what I might have done. I was here now.

What I would do next was all that mattered, and what I would do next was rescue Jasmine and make this whole mess better—or die or get captured in the attempt. Regardless of how it all turned out, I knew that as surely as Lobo could not forget the coordinates of this pit, I could do nothing else but try my best to succeed.

CHAPTER 28

As I waited near the water for Lobo, I soaked in the magic of the night. Oceans transform under starlight and reveal their true power and mystery; daylight paints them as less than they are, as friendly and understandable creatures we humans might one day tame. The illusions of daytime vanished as I watched the black waves sprinting to shore and listened to them crash into the land. For a brief time, I felt I was comprehending at last the full extent of a gigantic alien beast, its shape and power normally beyond my ability to discern. Clouds covered Macken's moons and obscured almost all of the starlight, so the water undulated in darkness, bits of soft gray here and there marking the moving surface. I leaned against a tree barely a meter inside the forest line a couple klicks up the beach from my rental house and stared as if hypnotized at the ocean. For as far back as I can remember, oceans have held a special power over me, and I never tire of watching them.

A pair of blinking red lights up the beach to my left interrupted my reverie. The lights approached at high speed and in a rapid forest-to-beach-to-forest pattern, as if running toward the water, finding it too scary, and jumping back to the trees, over and over. Under the sound of the ocean I heard the low roar of Lobo skimming with baffled jets along the sand.

"I see you," I said. "ETA?"

"Ten seconds."

"Ready."

Lobo cut the running lights as he pulled beside my position and opened a portal. I ran in, and he closed the door and headed back the way he'd come.

"Surveillance?" I said.

"Nothing from the sats," Lobo said, "because Kelco doesn't yet have monitoring rights to the planet."

I realized I'd been wrong when I'd told Barnes that delaying the Kelco contract for a month would do no good: The FC had taken advantage of the delay to limit Kelco's satellite surveillance capabilities, and those limits were now helping me.

"The house, though, is another story," Lobo said. "Security personnel and portable sentries are monitoring its perimeter and exchanging reports on randomly changing frequencies with more encryption than we have time to break."

"Anything different on the ocean side?"

"No," Lobo said.

We ran about twenty klicks up the beach and shot across

the water, flying low enough that waves were splashing Lobo's hull. Without sat coverage, we should be invisible to Kelco. "Show me," I said.

Lobo opened a display with a map of the shoreline and the ocean, the house at the shore's center. A wavy but roughly semicircular line with the house at its center and a radius of a little over fifteen thousand meters stretched from the shore on either side of the house into the ocean. The semicircle contained hundreds of red and purple dots. The red dots marked sensors from which Lobo or his sat friend had detected transmissions; the purple ones denoted intelligent mobile mines working in a redundant grid to stay roughly in line despite the ocean currents.

"The sensors' transmission intervals have shortened," Lobo said, "so they've definitely tightened their security."

"As we expected," I said. "Lim and Earl?"

"Both have checked in and are moving into position per the plan."

I inspected Bob's tank. He swam back and forth, with no more apparent concern for the future than when the Strange Kitty team had delivered him. They'd again proven to be professional in all areas: The new tanks on either side of his head matched his body perfectly.

"It's our turn," I said. "Give me ten minutes to change and check the gear, then take us to the drop point."

"One minute to drop," Lobo said.

Though the combat dive suit was as flexible and thin as modern technology could manage while offering some minimal armoring, it was still warmer than I'd have preferred for land work. It covered me completely, a tight mottled black and gray shroud that blended perfectly with the nighttime water and provided reasonable camouflage on land as long as I stayed to the shadows. My eyes and the skin around them were visible when I lessened the tinting on the built-in mask, but I could run with it almost totally black and use the mask's night- and IR-vision facilities to navigate. The suit and mask sacrificed some processing power for thinness and the ability to function underwater, but not much; it maintained a full comm link with Lobo, and all I needed of the mission profile resided in the suit's local storage. The small air-processing tubes and the backup tanks were also built into the suit, the air-processors running on either side of my neck and the tanks along my back, so I presented as little water resistance as possible. Some drag was, of course, unavoidable, because I bulged from the dive weights and the waterproof cases holding the weapons: the rifle on my back, the pistols strapped to my thighs, and the knives belted to my calves. Carrying the extra weight would slow me, but only a little, and I was happy to pay the minimal speed penalty to have them. The remote for Bob was so small I didn't count it.

"Five seconds," Lobo said. "Opening."

A hatch slid aside in front of me, and I jumped feet-first into the darkness. I hit the water almost immediately; Lobo had flown as low as I could have wanted. I treaded water, fighting the dive weight I'd later jettison, and watched with night vision as Lobo, the side door already closed, rolled upside down. A hatch opened in his top; then the lid of Bob's tank slid back, and Bob fell a meter or so into the ocean. Lobo's hatch closed, and he accelerated away from me, righting as he went.

I gave Bob thirty seconds to acclimate himself to the Macken ocean and stretch out, then summoned him. He'd run farther than I'd expected; it took him over twenty seconds to reach me. He bumped my feet gently, then went a bit deeper and circled my position lazily, the blue lines on his back giving the impression of a small school of fish swimming slowly beneath me.

I dove to Bob and grabbed the rider handles hanging on cables from the mounts on his back. With the handles I directed him down to about three meters and oriented us toward the midpoint of the Kelco house's security arc. After making sure my grip was secure, I used the remote to tell Bob to go.

True to his racing training, Bob shot forward quickly and accelerated for several seconds before he settled into a pace far faster than any human could swim without assistance. With IR-detection cranked way up I watched his powerful wings flap in the water. Riding above and slightly behind him, seeing his wings work and feeling the rush of the ocean against my body as we sped through it, I realized I was smiling and having a wonderful time, all the cares of the mission washing away for a few seconds in which I was flying, in the water but still flying, the primal rush of moving at high speed joining with the inevitable juice you get when you move fast in darkness. It was an absolutely wonderful experience. I understood the appeal of ray racing now; maybe I'd try it again if all of this went well.

We came to a section of the reef that paralleled the coastline on most of this side of the continent, and the ocean burst into life below us. With IR I saw fish in all directions, hundreds of them, maybe thousands, sea creatures of so many different sizes and shapes I couldn't even begin to log the varieties, all schooling through rock and

coral and plants large and small. If I switched to the
normal light spectrum, most of the fish disappeared, but
here and there schools of glowing bodies moved in the
watery darkness like light beams magically slowed in space
and available for close inspection, almost but not quite
within reach. I alternated the views a few times, then
settled on IR as we passed over and beyond the reef, the
life below us rapidly thinning and then vanishing. The
only creatures visible now were the occasional larger fish
keeping to the depths, eager to stay away from the huge
intruder speeding above them.

An alarm chimed as we drew within fifty meters of the
nearest of the Kelco sensors, and a representation of this
section of the sensor line appeared in my display. From
the data Lobo was able to gather about the sensors and
the information Gustafson had provided us about current
milspec tech, we estimated the upper limit of the effective sensor range to be thirty or so meters. Past that, they'd
be able to discern at most movement and provide at best
some rough IR images. None of that data should cause
me any trouble, because Bob's profile and my position
relative to him created the impression of a very large sea
creature or at least something odd—but nothing that
resembled an attack team or ship.

I stopped Bob at about forty meters out and used the
breather's exhaust to let some saliva into the water. I set
the nanomachines in the saliva to the task of replicating
from the water for a little over a minute, then sent the
new mass toward the sensors. Unless we'd misinterpreted
the data badly, the sensors were maintaining their approximate relative positions via tiny water jets and making
gentle coordinate adjustments as necessary based on data

from others in the communicating grid. I'd instructed the nanomachines to disassemble and repurpose anything metal they touched, then use the resulting larger mass to dispatch more swarms left and right in search of additional metal. I'd given them instructions to disassemble as much as possible themselves and stop operation after fifteen minutes, more than enough time for them to do what I wanted.

I turned Bob left and started him moving in slow, easy circles about twenty meters in diameter, just another large fish out for a swim. If the Kelco security team monitoring the sensors spotted us, they'd at least have to wonder why we were taking our time in the water, swimming to and fro with no apparent destination.

In my display the sensor closest to me vanished, leaving a break in Kelco's security line; the nanomachines had reached it and done their job. I kept Bob moving in the same pattern but now risked a call to Lobo. "Confirm sensor loss," I said. I needed to make sure the data my suit provided was reliable and not hacked or fed to me by Kelco.

"Confirmed," Lobo said, his voice clear on the encrypted channel. "Continue holding."

The last bit was our backup protocol; if Lobo hadn't added it, I would have known someone else had compromised the communication. The technique is simple and ancient, but sometimes an old method is the right way to go.

Two more sensors and a pair of mines winked out in my display. The hole in the Kelco line was now almost forty meters wide. The lost sensors would definitely grab Kelco's attention. I changed Bob's course so we angled toward the sensor-free area. The route kept us more than thirty meters away from both of the two nearest sensors as we slowly drew closer to where some of the disassembled devices had floated only moments before.

Two more sensors and multiple mines disappeared from my display. The hole was now almost sixty meters wide. The edges of the line now extended past the range of my suit's sensors, so I had to risk getting live data from Lobo. I opened my comm link. "Lobo," I said, "switch to feeds."

The first one—a complete image of the line with the size of the hole indicated on the display—appeared a few seconds later. We'd agreed that Lobo would send me updates on a quasi-random basis centered on a ten-second update interval. To confuse matters further, he emitted a wide-beam broadcast that swept over a three-hundred-meter-wide area.

My display flashed a new update: The hole in the sensor line measured over eighty meters wide.

"Lobo," I said, "what can you read around the house?" Kelco had shielded the house so it yielded little to remote visual or IR probes, but we could still check the surrounding area and, of course, monitor the level of transmission activity; we'd already learned that the place served as a communications hub for Slake.

"Additional people have left the house and deployed to various locations along the water and around the perimeter of the grounds," he said. As he spoke, an aerial IR view of the place appeared on my display. A couple dozen red dots spread around the building. A large red splotch sat in the middle of the landing facility. "Transmission levels between the sensors and the house have increased.

They know something's up and are trying to learn what. I see no transmissions in your area at this time."

"What's the ship in the landing area?" I said.

"The IR signature is inconclusive," Lobo said, "as are the visible-frequency images the sat has provided. The available data suggest a midsize corporate near-space fighter, probably four times my size and significantly more heavily armed and shielded than I. Whatever it is, it appears to be squatting hot, ready to run."

From what I'd seen on Wharf I had reason to believe Vaccaro had managed to keep Slake off-site. The ship could be for his security team to use for air defense, or it could be an escape vehicle. Either way, it wasn't a factor we'd anticipated. Fortunately, the ship's size and Lobo's guess suggested it wasn't built for air-to-ground work, so as long as they didn't use it to take away Jasmine, it shouldn't cause us any problems. "How many people are stationed near the ship?" I asked.

"None we can spot with the available imaging," Lobo said.

"The rest of the team will have to watch it," I said.

"Already warned," Lobo said.

I had no more questions. I felt a rush of adrenaline as I realized we were done with the preliminaries. It was time to go in.

I steered Bob to the center of the sensor hole on my display. From here on, speed of approach was vital, because if I gave Slake's men time they'd train monitoring gear on this area and get a solid fix on me. With Bob's remote I checked the booster tanks; both showed operational. According to the Strange Kitty trainer who'd shown me how to use them, the tanks were the latest in racing ray speed mods. They coupled a rapid increase in blood oxygen levels in Bob—courtesy of a blend of nitrogen, oxygen, and some nerve-friendly trace chemicals they injected into his bloodstream—with direct electrical stimulation of Bob's neural system. The result was supposed to be a great increase in speed at minimal cost to Bob's health, as long as I didn't keep it running for more than a few minutes.

As we headed toward shore, I activated the booster tanks. Nothing happened for several seconds; then Bob's wings picked up speed and we accelerated. The force of the water against my face was strong enough even through the suit's mask that I turned my head downward to avoid the impact. Staring at the muscles in Bob's back in IR I saw the effect of the additional exertion as we shot through the water toward the house. That was all I could see. The sheer speed of our passage combined with the almost complete lack of any visible input to turn this into a joy-ride of such raw intensity that I whooped loudly and repeatedly inside my mask. I couldn't recall the last time a mission had included anything that was as much fun as riding with Bob. Most of my mind knew I was headed into a dangerous situation, and the primitive part of me had responded with a liberal injection of adrenaline. At the same time, some of those very same primitive parts were both scared by and greatly enjoying the sheer speed at which we hurtled through the dark water. The combination of all these sensations was heady, and for two minutes I gave myself over to it and simply held on for the ride.

Data feeds from Lobo continued to refresh my display as we approached the house. A flashing note indicated we were five hundred meters from the shore, and a course-correction alarm almost immediately joined it in the display. Lobo had plotted a path as far down the coast as we could go and still stay out of the range of the sensors my nanomachines hadn't disassembled. I steered Bob onto the new course, and we sped onward. I aimed for roughly where the line of trees separating the house and the landing area would intersect the water if the trees had grown down to the ocean's edge. The joy I'd taken in the speed of the ride faded as we drew closer to the moment at which I'd have to leave the water.

A hundred meters from shore I slowed Bob. We came to a full stop about sixty meters out. Even with the high tide we'd counted on to reduce the distance from the water's edge to the house, the ocean was shallow enough here that we stayed as close to the bottom as Bob could manage. I steered him in a small oval pattern with its long side parallel to the beach. The glowing lines on his back would be visible to anyone very near us, but I hoped they wouldn't show to observers on the shore. If they did, I wanted his movements to resemble those of a small school of fish playing in the nighttime water.

I let go of the handles and slid off Bob. For an instant he stayed still, either trained to wait for his rider or surprised not to be carrying a load any longer. I used the remote to hit him again with a tiny shot of the stimulant. A couple of seconds later, he jetted sideways along the shore and then turned out to sea, picking up speed rapidly. He raced out of view of both IR and visible light scans in less than ten seconds. If everything worked out well, we'd retrieve Bob later and return him to Lankin; Strange Kitty would take him back, though my salesman had hastened to add that there'd be no refunds. If the mission went nonlinear, then Bob would at least get to while away the rest of his days in the ocean here on Macken, a much better fate than the rest of us would have suffered.

I swam to shore, staying under the ocean's surface as long as I could, until the sandy bottom pressed my back out of the water. I raised my head and looked around. The nearest Kelco guards were at least forty meters down the shore. Even with the suit's shielding and the cooling water around me, I'd show up on any IR scan that covered my position, so I wouldn't be alone for long. I unsheathed the rifle on my back and rose to a crouch. Despite the suppressor on it, the rifle would make enough noise that the guards would hear it, but that shouldn't matter if I focused their attention properly. I sighted on a spot along the shore about sixty meters to my right and fired. The grenade shell exploded in the sand almost instantly, a massive burst of light and sound that illuminated the beach all around it and drew shouts from guards. I stood and rapidly fired four more times down the beach, placing each round five or so meters past the previous one. A line of blazing light now made that section of beach brighter than a cloudless summer day. Guards converged on the burning rounds from multiple directions.

I dropped the rifle and sprinted for the cover of the trees that separated the house and the landing area. Any members of the security team who looked my way as I ran would see me, but I couldn't help that; I had to hope the rounds would buy me the seconds I needed.

I reached the trees and stood behind one, forcing myself to slow my breathing. I peeked around the edge of the tree and checked the house. I had a clear line of approach with no guards in sight. Lights mounted on the edge of the building's roof bathed the area in a pale white light. The ground was an uneven mass of soft earth, with only the occasional scrub bush dotting the expanse of dirt; neither the landlord nor Kelco had gotten around to planting the area. I didn't have the time to take out the lights, so after a quick check showed the beach guards were still occupied, I sprinted for the house.

Before I'd made it halfway there, the ground in front of me shook and six guards in low-thermal-signature combat suits sprang to their feet. Covered completely in black, even to their black hoods and tinted displays, the soldiers resembled wraiths that had clawed their way back from the underworld to seek revenge on the planet they'd been forced to depart. Each pointed a rifle of some sort at me. The weapons were black and draped with black cloth, so I couldn't make out what they were. They knew what they were doing. No one was in anyone else's line of fire. No one's weapon wavered. I stopped as quickly as I could and raised my hands in the air.

They had me.

So far, so good.

All I had to do was hope I'd correctly interpreted Kelco's attack on my rental house and they really did want me alive.

CHAPTER 29

As much as I'd realized the Kelco security team would capture me, as much as I'd needed it for the plan to work, and as much as I'd visualized this moment, the reality of standing alone in front of a squad of armed troops and doing nothing was much more intense and upsetting than I'd expected. In the past, I've fought more than my share of battles with bad odds, but I've always been doing just that: fighting. I've always worked to secure the best position, hamper the opposition, do whatever I could to assure my side would win. I've never offered myself as defenseless bait, and even though doing so was part of a plan I'd crafted, I didn't like it.

No one spoke, and no one moved. Time slowed, as it always did in situations in which one misstep could prove fatal. Each little movement carried the weight of enormous potential significance. I focused as hard as I could on paying attention and not missing anything. A guard in the center nodded his head first left and then right. The two on either end of the group fanned wide and moved slowly behind me. Each kept his weapon trained on me, and each stayed out of the other's line of fire. They walked well behind me, past where I could see them any longer, and then I heard them approach. Hands gripped each of my arms and wrenched them behind me, straining my shoulders. I felt a tie snap around each wrist. One guard moved beside me on my left, where I could see a tiny bit of the side of him in my peripheral vision. He grabbed the back of my neck with one hand and held a knife to the front of my throat with the other. The second patted me down from behind, working slowly and systematically and missing nothing. In about a minute I was weaponless, and both guards were behind me. Simultaneous kicks in the back of my knees knocked me flat on my face. I tried to fall only to my knees, but the kicks were too hard. They pulled me up so I was kneeling. One grabbed the top of my head; the other cut my suit at the neck and ripped off the headpiece.

Without the suit's night-vision amplification the world I stared into was much darker than it'd been a moment before, so I shut my eyes for a few seconds to acclimate to the lower light. I could switch to IR on my own, but I'd lose so much of the nuances of the situation that I preferred to work with what I could see in the minimal available normal light.

With the mask and comm unit gone, I'd lost my two-way link with Lobo. Hundreds of strands of microtransmitters laced my Saw combat suit, so theoretically Lobo should be able to monitor the whole situation as long as I was wearing even a ten-centimeter-long strip of the garment. I hoped the theory held.

The two troops on either end of the four in front of me fanned out further, their weapons still aimed at me. The two who remained in the center motioned me to follow them and backed slowly to the side of the house. The blazing grenades I'd launched earlier finally fizzled out, and all but one of the lights on the side of the house winked off. Their thinking was obvious: If anyone later asked what had happened, they'd answer that they'd suffered a false alarm, fired a few rounds, and resumed their normal routines. The guards in front of me backed all the way to the house and then moved carefully to their right, until they stood at the edge of the area the remaining roof-mounted light illuminated. They motioned me to stop and rapped on the wall outside the lit area. A door opened. The guards who'd been leading me stepped to either side of it. They motioned me to follow, then backed into the house in single file, one crouching and the other standing, both keeping their weapons trained on me.

I was vaguely pleased at the star treatment they were giving me, because it confirmed my belief that Kelco still very much wanted to know how I'd rescued Jasmine and escaped from Floordin with Lobo's weapons control system. Of course, the care they were taking also meant they could shoot me many times before I could mount any kind of attack at all, so I walked slowly and carefully and did my best to broadcast complete cooperation and surrender.

We proceeded this way up a short flight of stairs and emerged into a large kitchen. The lighting was so bright that after the time outside I had to squeeze my eyes nearly shut to deal with the glare. I opened them slowly as they adjusted. As I did so I realized much of the brightness came from light reflecting off the wood that composed the floors, walls, and cabinets, a wood so nearly white I'd have taken it to be some sort of composite were it not for the beautiful, ethereally blue grain running through all of it. Two doors on either end of the wall opposite me led elsewhere in the house. Judging from where we'd entered the building, the kitchen was a couple of rooms behind the foyer in which I'd given Jasmine to Slake. Beyond that guess, however, I had no clue as to where I was.

The two guards in front of me held up their hands. I stopped. The two behind me moved so quietly that even though I was listening for them I could barely hear them step closer. Another pair of kicks to my knees sent me to the floor again, and this time the fall hurt, even though I curled my shoulders forward to absorb some of the impact and lifted my head to keep it from banging into the floor. A hand from behind me grabbed my head, fingers digging into my forehead, and pulled me to my knees. I wanted to shake my head to clear away the little shocks of pain running through my skull, but the hand held me steady. Resisting it seemed a bad idea.

The door on the right end of the wall in front of me opened, and a man walked in.

"Mr. Moore," the man said, "I'm pleased we'll get to continue our discussion."

Though he obviously knew me, I didn't recognize him at first. He gave me time, apparently in no hurry to proceed. His short blond hair and willowy frame struck me as familiar, but the black combat suit was the same one the others wore and so added no information. Something was missing. I finally realized what it was: the moving Kelco tattoos he'd been wearing when I met him.

"Amendos," I said. "Are you still auditing Slake? If so, Kelco maintains much stricter financial controls than I'd ever have guessed."

It was his turn to look confused, but only for a second. He smiled, shook his head, and said, "Not that conversation. I'm talking about the one aboard the satellite, the one you somehow interrupted a few days ago."

"Of course," I said. Of course I should have known that anyone Slake ordered to get information from me wouldn't give up merely because I didn't satisfy his curiosity the first time.

"We can save a lot of time and pain, Mr. Moore, Jon"— He smiled as he used my name—"if you'll answer my questions without any additional motivation. You've experienced a few steps of the interrogation process, but I assure you there are many, many options we've yet to explore. You know you'll answer me eventually, so why not now?"

I couldn't afford for everyone monitoring and recording Lobo's transmission relays to wonder about Osterlad and Johns and how I rescued Jasmine, because otherwise some listener might end up asking the same questions as Amendos. Chung and Xychek were on my side now, but I had no reason to believe they'd stay that way. I've often wondered if I should be more trusting when it comes to people, but with corporations and governments I never have such doubts. You can't trust them for any longer than the brief periods of time when their interests and yours are in perfect alignment, and even those times are almost always shorter than you expected.

"Not now," I said. "Not ever. Where's Jasmine?"

He pulled a tiny pistol from a pocket in his pants and motioned to the right with his head. The hand holding my head pulled it hard to the left as another hand pressed down on my right shoulder, exposing my neck fully to Amendos.

"You can choose not to answer me now," he said, "but we both know you'll answer eventually. In fact, I think we'll take your hint to speed the process and involve Jasmine in your interrogation." He raised the pistol, took a step closer, and aimed. "You'll see her in a few hours, after you wake up."

He fired. The pain in my neck faded as I lost consciousness.

I couldn't have been out for even a minute, because when I awoke two men were carrying me, one with his arms under my shoulders and the other lifting me at the knees. Most security forces stock and employ a very limited number of sedative weapons, because for each trank type you use you also have to keep on hand an antidote; rounds of all types go wild during fights. Kelco had stayed with what had worked previously, and the combination of the antidote the Saw lab had prepared for me and the action of the now-prepared nanomachines in my body had cleared my head quickly. I kept my eyes shut and my breathing shallow. If I let them know the trank had failed, I had no doubt they would use another of the many options they almost certainly maintained. Those options would be either ones for which I was not prepared or, worse, deadly. They banged my head into a wall as they turned a corner, and I fought to keep from showing any reaction.

"Watch it," one said.

"Why?" said the other. "He's going to get a lot worse soon."

"Do *you* want to explain to the boss why you accidentally broke the guy's neck?"

"Good point."

We reached level ground, went straight for at least fifteen paces, turned right, and walked another ten or more paces; counting the footfalls with my eyes shut was more difficult than I'd have guessed. Because I'd been unconscious for an unknown amount of time, I wasn't sure where I was, though a basement under the house seemed a pretty safe bet. I heard a door open, and we turned. They placed me on a slightly giving surface, pushed my back against a wall, and wrapped a tight enclosure around each of my ankles.

"Do we have to stay?" one of the voices said.

"Nah," the other answered. "Like Amendos said, he'll be out for hours. Let's go report we're done, see if we can get off for the rest of the night, and grab some sleep."

I heard steps, a metallic thump, and more steps. When the area stayed quiet for several seconds, I counted off an additional minute, just to be safe, and opened my eyes enough to peek through my eyelashes. They were bound to be monitoring me, so with luck I'd still appear to be unconscious.

I was lying on a narrow platform in a room with metal bars on three sides. Though I couldn't see it, the wall behind me felt solid enough. Kelco must have either purchased the house or leased it for a long time, because otherwise they wouldn't have bothered to install their very own mini-jail. My cell formed part of one side of a long, narrow, dim hall. Only a few tiny lights spaced along the

wall opposite me broke the dark. A small food dispenser
was built into that same wall a bit down from my cell. No
security cameras were visible, of course, but I had to
assume they were there, watching me. I arched my back
a little and moaned slightly, as if I were having a bad
dream, and glanced down the hall in the direction of my
head. At least two more cells followed mine. As best I
could tell from my narrow viewport onto the world, the
one next to me was empty.

The cell beyond it was not.

Someone stood at the bars on the side facing me.

I moaned again and arched my back even more. From
what I could see in the faint illumination of the miniature
hall lights, the person was a woman.

"Are you okay?" the person asked in a distinctly female
voice.

The voice sounded familiar. It could be Jasmine's. I'd
heard it live only once, though, and I wanted it to be her,
so I couldn't trust my memory to be accurate.

"Can you talk?" she said. "I can't reach you to help."

I had to continue feigning unconsciousness, so as much
as I wanted to confirm her identity, I couldn't respond.
Lobo should be able to do a decent voice match from the
few words she'd spoken. We couldn't risk any audio transmitter the Kelco men who searched me might find, but
Lobo could alert me by using the communication fiber in
my suit and the protocol we'd established.

Sure enough, a few seconds later a twenty-centimeter-
long strip of the suit warmed my stomach in response to
a signal from Lobo: The voice was Jasmine's. We were
ready to go to the mission's final stage. I had one minute
to call off the attack.

I used the time to tune in to the food dispenser across the hall. It probably wouldn't be able to give me a lot of information I could use, but it should be in the house's appliance network and so hear the news when Lim's and Gustafson's teams moved in. Sure enough, like almost all modern machines, it was babbling incessantly. I picked it up in midrant.

"—this one might eat something more interesting than bowls of protein and carbohydrate slop that I wouldn't use to test a dishwasher. If you ask me—and of course they don't, why would they, I'm nothing more than a glorified delivery chute to them—you don't need a complete food preparation and delivery system of my caliber if all you're going to do is ship down the same rehydrated garbage from the kitchen day after day. Oh, if they'd give me a chance I could show them what a meal, a real meal, should look like, one with multiple courses, each composed of actual food, and I could cook it, too. Sure, I don't mind working with the processors and dispensers in the kitchen—we're a team, guys, don't get me wrong—but every now and then they should give me an opportunity to show off what I could do on my own. And plating! Don't get me started. Do they have any clue how much plating intelligence I possess? Why, I could show them presentations that—"

I tuned it out momentarily and let out another low moan, this time curling in slightly to bring my hands as close to my feet as I could without giving away that I was awake. When the moment came, I wanted to be able to move as quickly as possible.

I focused again on the food dispenser, which was still, as far as I could tell, engaged in the same rant.

"—as I would tell them if anyone would ask, or even listen for that matter, a lumpy cream soup on a plain white plate is as boring to the eyes as it must be to the palate. Speaking of eyes, I have to assume that if they actually cared at all about my food they'd give me something better for sight than these off-market cameras so dumb they can barely carry on a conversation."

"That's not nice," said another appliance, which I had to assume was the vision system. "We can too talk."

"Talking is not the same as carrying on a conversation, you sorry excuse for a machine," the dispenser said. "The mere ability to speak is no more a guarantee of conversation quality than—what's that?" I'd never been able to pick up purely wired appliance conversations or even wireless ones that weren't close to me, so I had to assume the dispenser had just received information from appliances in the rest of the building. "Someone is attacking the house? Oh, dear. Are they coming down here? Have they hurt the kitchen? Will our staff perhaps desire a fortifying snack?"

I didn't need to hear any more. Appliances are generally self-centered enough that it was a safe bet that all the rest of the information it would provide would focus only on the small parts of the building that affected it directly. On the chance that someone might later review the security log of my cell, I pantomimed pulling something from the back of my left calf, bent down, and acted as if I were using an acid dispenser to dissolve the clasps of the cuffs on my ankles. Instead, I spit into my left hand and rubbed it first on the clasp of the left ankle's cuff and then on the right's. I instructed the nanomachines to decompose the clasps. In about ten seconds, enough was gone that I was able to force open the restraints.

Faint sounds of the attack wafted down the hallway: high notes from shrieks, low thumps from shells and explosions, the sounds of people running overhead.

I stepped to the cell door and repeated the pantomime act, focusing on the section of the door and lock that kept it closed. The door contained dense metals, so the nanomachines proceeded more slowly on it than on my ankle cuffs. As the lock slowly disappeared, the security lights brightened.

Jasmine stood in the corner of her cell closest to me, her eyes wide, not speaking but waving her hands to get my attention. I ignored her and focused on the door. I pushed hard on the bars above and below the lock. I needed to get out of there before Amendos or his men came to get us.

The door popped open, and I stumbled out. I sprinted the few steps to Jasmine's cell.

"Get on your bed so I don't accidentally hurt you with the acid!" I said.

"What's going on?" she said.

"Now!" I said. "Move it!"

"But—"

"Move it!" I yelled.

She backed onto the bed and rolled into a ball on top of it, obviously scared. I had no time to worry about her feelings; we could deal with them later, if we made it out of this.

I worked on her door, hunching over to hide from the cameras as many of my actions as possible. As soon as the small cloud of nanomachines started working, I grabbed two bars and pulled as hard as I could. As I strained, I stared down the hallway to my right, hoping not to see anyone and trying to figure out where to go if I did. Maybe I could make it to the cover of the bed in my cell. I listened closely for footsteps. Maybe if I heard them in time I could reach the corner before whoever was coming turned it.

The door popped open, and I fell back against the wall on the other side of the corridor.

"Out!" I said. "Now! We're leaving."

Jasmine turned and looked at me but stayed where she was. "Who are you?" she said. "You look familiar"— She shook her head—"but I don't know for sure."

I ran into the cell, grabbed her arm, and yanked her to her feet. "I'm helping your father, and I'm helping you." I pulled her toward the door as I spoke. "Do what I say, and do it fast."

"I don't understand," she said. "What are you doing? I—"

I grabbed her shoulders, wrenched her close, and cut her off. At another time in another place, I might have cared about how scary I appeared to her or how roughly I handled her, but not then. "Do exactly what I say, and don't speak unless I ask you a question. Do anything else, and I'll knock you out and carry you." I let go of her right shoulder, made a fist, and raised my hand. "Decide now."

She looked in my eyes as if trying to solve a complex equation entirely in her head, and then she stared at my fist. She nodded her head.

I grabbed her right hand and headed out of the cell at a jog. "Stay behind me, and keep up!"

At the end of the hall to the left of my cell, I pushed her against the wall and motioned her to stay still. I dropped to the floor, inched my head around the corner long enough to take a peek, and pulled back to cover. I saw no one, so I risked a slightly longer look. A dark hallway stretched down to a stairway that ran straight up for eight steps, then turned right and headed up again. The ceiling obscured the top of the stairwell, but light streamed onto the stairs from above; probably an open door. The hallway was about four meters wide, with several closed doors on the left and stacks of boxes against the right wall. Visible light was dim, so I tried IR but gained no more information; the hallway still appeared deserted.

The familiar sounds of urban combat—bangs, sizzles, thumps, and occasional screams—grew louder. Already the smells of the fight were drifting down, the air rich with residue from explosive shells and energy beam shots. I was confident Lim's and Gustafson's teams would win in time, but I had no way to know how long that would take. In the meantime, our mission clock was ticking. No matter how well Vaccaro insulated Slake, he either already knew about this attack or would hear about it soon. Earl would be able to keep him in the government building for some time under the guise of protection, but Slake wouldn't stay there indefinitely. I had to get Jasmine out of here.

I jumped up and faced her. "We're heading into a mess. Stay close behind me—very close—and you should be okay. I'm taking you back to your father."

Her eyes widened in fear. "Now I remember you. You brought me back here. You—"

I cut her off again. "That was a mistake," I said, "and we're making another one now by wasting time talking.

Last warning: Follow me closely, or I'll have to knock you out. We'll be in a lot more danger if I have to carry you."

"Okay," she said.

I turned the corner toward the stairwell. Jasmine stayed on my heels. I ran a few paces and stopped suddenly as I heard a foot hit a step. The sound of gunfire rang from the top of the stairs. Whoever was there had paused to fight. I wasn't sure we could make it back around the corner before the person on the stairs saw us. An old-fashioned door with a handle stood closed on our left. I pulled it open. Inside was a small storage area with shelves on the sides and rear wall and stacks of boxes in the center. There was enough open space for Jasmine, but not for both of us.

I pushed her into the closet. "Stay," I said, "and no matter what happens, don't make a sound. If anyone else opens the door, hit 'em with something and hope for the best."

She nodded. I closed the door quickly but quietly.

I heard another footfall on the stairs and ducked into the darkness on my right. I had no cover. My only hope was that whoever was coming wouldn't be wearing IR gear and wouldn't have adjusted to the dim light of the hallway.

More sound from the steps, and the person started coming into view: boots, legs, waist, part of the torso, the upper torso as the person turned the corner—and a Saw logo. The person took a couple more steps downward and entered a shaft of light that fell from the doorway above. I recognized his face: Gustafson.

I stepped out of the darkness. I felt the smile stretching across my face, my heartbeat slowing, my breathing easing, all my muscles relaxing. "Top," I said, "good to see you." Black streaks ran across his face, his wide eyes shined with the barely controlled lunacy of battle, and his breathing rasped uneven and ragged. He looked as good to me then as another human could.

"You, too, Gunny," he said as he ran to me, "but let's save the hugs and kisses for when we're out of here. We haven't finished up there, and we've got to get you—"

A sizzling sound electrified the air, and Gustafson suddenly stopped talking. A look of surprise crossed his face, his eyes stretched wider than I would have thought possible, and his throat constricted in a scream that began guttural and arched up to a screech in seconds. He pitched forward onto me. I was so unprepared that we both went down, Gustafson on top, his head facedown over my right shoulder. The smell of burning flesh rushed over me. Small moans told me he was still alive. I worked my hands under his shoulders so I could roll him off my chest.

"Don't," a voice said. "Don't move at all."

CHAPTER 30

I lifted my head to look over Gustafson. Amendos walked slowly toward us, an energy pistol held at the ready. His beam had cut most of the way through Gustafson's right leg and almost completely severed the bottom section from the top about five centimeters below the knee. Both pieces oozed where the cauterization was incomplete. All that kept the parts of Top's leg together were a thin wedge of skin and muscle and the front of his uniform; the beam hadn't cut quite all the way through.

Amendos walked past my head, turned so he could watch us, and backed down the hallway. I had to bridge upward to keep him in sight. He glanced down the hall with the cells, turned back to me, and ran to my side.

"Where is she?" he said.

I forced myself to stare at him, only him, so I wouldn't give away anything.

"Who?" I said.

He smiled slightly and shook his head. "I don't have time for this, unfortunately," he said.

He fired a tiny burst at Gustafson's other leg. Gustafson arched his back, screamed, and passed out completely. His face hit the floor with a soft breaking sound; his nose had shattered. The smell of burning flesh intensified.

"From what I overheard," Amendos continued, "this guy is a friend of yours. Jasmine is nothing to you. You don't even know her—and if my time with her is any indication, I doubt you'd like her very much if you did. She's just some girl. Save your friend, and save yourself. Where is she?"

He was right. I didn't know Jasmine. Yeah, she reminded me of Jennie, but she wasn't Jennie, and saving her wouldn't make me feel any less guilty about Jennie. If Jasmine had never been kidnapped from Kelco by the Gardeners, or if Slake hadn't conned me into taking her back from them, I'd never even have met her. If Osterlad had simply sold me Lobo's weapons control system, I'd never have tracked him down and gone after Chung.

If, if, if.

You could build a life on ifs, but what would it mean? Where would it get you? All we really ever have is the world as it stands right now, and all we ever get to do is make the best of that. The rest is either long gone or still to come, if it comes at all. That doesn't mean we should stop planning, hoping, and dreaming, because those plans, hopes, and dreams help direct our actions now. Ultimately, though, we face what's in front of us. We take the situation and the data at hand, make the best decision we can, and jump into the future.

I didn't know Jasmine. She was just one of the billions and billions of humans alive in the universe.

But she was my responsibility now.

Top had known the risks when he'd signed up for the mission. So had I.

I stared into Amendos' eyes and shook my head.

"Your choice," he said. He pointed the pistol at Gustafson's head. "I think he'll go first."

"Stop!" a voice screamed from the direction of the stairs.

Even as I realized the voice belonged to Lim, so much happened in such a short time that I could barely track it all.

Amendos swiveled toward the sound and fired.

Lim returned fire as she dove off the stairs.

Amendos fell backward as the round from her weapon hit him in the stomach.

The stairs crackled, and several steps shattered.

Lim rolled behind some boxes.

Amendos scrambled to his feet, clutching his abdomen and gasping. Though his armor had stopped the round from killing him, his breath came hard.

Lim fired again but missed.

Amendos dashed down the hall and around the corner toward the cells.

Lim shoved the boxes aside and got up. She stumbled forward, her face set, her gun raised.

I rolled Gustafson off me, stood, stepped in front of her, and yelled, "Stop!"

Lim turned toward me. Her face was crazy, twisted with rage, scraped and bleeding in several places. She shook with anger. "He's getting away!" she yelled. "He shot Top and he shot at me and now he's getting away!"

"I know," I said, "but if we don't get Top and his legs to the medics, he might not make it. And, we don't need to get Amendos to finish the mission. We have all we need." I didn't mention Jasmine yet, in case Amendos was still within earshot.

Lim froze for a few seconds, visibly torn between her deep-seated desire to kill the enemy and her training to follow orders. "Okay," she finally said. "You're right."

"Check down that hall and make sure he's gone," I said. "No one else should be there."

Lim ran to the corner of the hall, pulled a grenade off her belt, and tossed it around the corner. A few seconds later, the grenade detonated with a roar followed by the screeching of flechette rounds smacking into walls and metal bars. Lim dropped to the floor, pulled her combat mask over her face, and craned her head to check the hall.

"No one in sight in visible light or IR," she said. "This thing curves after fifteen meters, so he's somewhere down there."

"What med supplies do you have?" I said.

She ran back, pulled off her pack, dug into it, and tossed me a roll of self-stick bandage and a tube of an organic antibiotic/glue combo. "That's all that's useful," she said.

The slice that Amendos' second blast had carved in the back of Gustafson's leg was about two centimeters deep and cleanly cauterized.

I squirted the glue into the cut and motioned to Lim.

"Push his leg up," I said.

She held the parts of that leg together as the glue hardened and I wrapped the area with the bandage.

Both parts of his right leg continued to ooze, and his uniform was now the only thing keeping them attached. I coated the raw ends of the two pieces of his leg with the glue, jammed them together as best I could, and nodded toward them. Lim kept them in place while I wrapped first the connection point and then up and down his leg with the bandage until I'd used it all. I squirted more glue around the outside of the bandage. If we were lucky, the pieces of his leg would stay together until we got him to a medic with reasonable microsurgery capabilities.

The whole process couldn't have taken much more than a minute, but time was moving too fast, sucking the air out of the mission.

"Can you carry him?" I said. "I've got to get Jasmine out of here."

"Is your memory that short?" she said.

As she checked his legs to be sure the glue was set and started working him onto her shoulder, I went to the closet.

"Come on out, Jasmine," I said.

No answer. I stood to the side and pulled the door open, in case she remembered my instructions. Nothing. I looked inside. She'd worked her way into a corner, her back to the door. Her shoulders shook as she whimpered almost soundlessly, the barest hint of sobbing audible only when I leaned close enough to touch her shoulder.

"We have to leave now," I said.

She turned around, then recoiled into the corner as Lim came into view, carrying Gustafson on her right shoulder, a gun in her left hand.

"Grab my other pistol," she said to me. "Let's move."

I pulled the weapon out of its holster and turned to go.

Jasmine didn't follow. I grabbed her arm and yanked her next to me.

"Same as before," I said. "Keep up and stay right behind me, or I'll knock you out and carry you."

She nodded.

I took off, Jasmine behind me. Lim trailed, moving slower under the weight of Gustafson and her constant checking over her shoulder for Amendos. I stopped at the landing halfway up the stairs. Jasmine bumped into me, but I kept my focus on the top of the stairwell. No one was in sight, so I walked most of the way up, motioned the others to stop, and stretched out on my stomach across the remaining stairs. I heard sounds of fighting, but they were distant; the house around us was quiet. I risked a look around the corner. All clear. I turned around, went to Lim, and pulled off Gustafson's mask. I put it on and started broadcasting.

"Moore here," I said. "Cargo in tow, one down. Need status of my area and transport."

A voice I didn't recognize responded almost immediately. "Interior secure. Cleaning exterior sides and rear. Exit front. Will alert transport."

I stepped around the corner, pistol at the ready. I stood in some sort of informal meeting room. It was a wreck, furniture shattered and walls ripped. I ran to the doorway at the far end; Jasmine and Lim stayed right behind me. On the other side was the living area where I'd met Slake before. I headed for the front door, which was on the ground in pieces. Up here the fighting sounds were louder, but they all originated from the sides of the house. I almost collided with a sergeant in a Saw uniform as he stepped inside from the front porch.

"Your transport's on the way, sir," he said. "Who's down?"

"Top," I said. "One leg cut in half, the other with a deep wound. We did what we could, but he needs work right now."

The sergeant turned and yelled out the door. "Haul it in here," he said. "Top's down. Rush him to the medic."

"We'll take him from here, sir," he said to me. The respect and affection for Gustafson was evident in his voice and his eyes.

Four men rushed in, two carrying a stretcher. They gently took Gustafson off Lim's shoulder and put him on the stretcher.

"Let's go, Lim," I said.

"Thanks," she said to the medics. As soon as they left with Gustafson, she collapsed. "I can't," she said to me.

"What's wrong?"

She pointed to her other shoulder. "Small stuff," she said, "but enough that I'll only slow you down."

I looked closer and saw a burn through the top of her combat suit and a blackened gouge in the skin of her shoulder. The part of the wound on her back was freshly torn and bright red, blood oozing from it down her body.

"Oh, hell, Lim," I said. "I'm sorry. You should have let me carry him."

"No way," she said. "You were in the best condition for point, and you have to get the girl out of here." She nodded toward the front of the house, where the beach glowed faintly. "Go."

"Okay," I said, "you're right." I stood. "Another down," I said to the sergeant.

"Got her," he said.

I didn't wait to make sure they did. I grabbed Jasmine's arm, and we dashed onto the now well-lit beach. In the glare of the spotlights of a ship flying toward us at high speed the beach might have been warming under an afternoon sun. The light was bright enough that the instant I entered the illuminated area I couldn't see anything outside it.

"Moore here," I said. "With the cargo and in front of the house, ready for pickup."

"Touching down in twenty seconds," Lobo's voice said. "Hostile ship airborne and banking over town. Board quickly."

Lobo, a side hatch already open, settled to a hover less than fifty centimeters over the beach. I ran to him, dragging Jasmine behind me.

"Where are we going?" she said.

I didn't take the time to answer. I pushed her inside, jumped in myself, and pulled her back from the opening. Lobo closed it as soon as she was clear, turned sharply, and headed out over the ocean.

We needed to get to the government center, so I started to ask Lobo why we were flying in almost exactly the opposite direction. Then I remembered his admonitions in the forest and instead forced myself to assume he knew what he was doing. I was surprised how hard it was to trust.

I pushed away those thoughts; they were no help now. "Status?" I said.

"Colonel Earl has mission recordings from all personnel and my message that you and Chung are aboard. That's enough for him to hold Slake, but only for the rest of the day. The Kelco fighter is hovering over the town, so we must assume whoever is commanding it has figured out our plan and is positioned to intercept us."

Amendos. The other end of the prison hallway must have led to the landing area. "Course?"

"One hundred and eighty degrees opposite the line formed by the house and the fighter, altitude two meters. Pending your instructions."

The fighter should have trouble tracking us at this altitude, but we couldn't afford to stay this low forever; we had to get Jasmine to Earl. If we lured the fighter out to sea, we could engage it without having to worry about collateral damage to the town. "What are our chances in a battle with the Kelco ship?"

"Effectively nil. We'd win only if it possesses none of the weapons or defense systems typical of ships of its design."

"So you've saved me just so they can kill me?" Jasmine said.

I'd focused so much on the situation that I'd forgotten she was listening. I needed to maintain that focus. "I don't have time for this," I said. I grabbed her arm, ran her to the room where Lim had stayed, and shoved her in. "Buckle yourself into the acceleration couch." I backed out. "Lock her in." The door whisked shut. I dashed up front.

"Can we outrun it?" I said.

"Almost certainly not. It should be faster, though not by more than approximately twenty percent—provided Kelco hasn't customized it. In the atmosphere, we should be able to outmaneuver it, but just barely."

"Enough for you to lead it away from town, then circle back briefly to drop us?"

"No. Before I could decelerate enough that you could get off, it would destroy us."

"We should have stayed on foot," I said, "and taken our chances with the Saw team protecting us."

"Only if you assume the fighter would have refrained from attacking you on the ground," Lobo said. "Update: The fighter rose, spotted us, and is now on its way to us."

We couldn't outrun it, and we couldn't outgun it.

"Incoming communication from the Kelco ship for you," Lobo said. "Accept?"

"Yes."

Lobo opened a display on the front wall. Amendos' face filled it. "Mr. Moore," he said. "One option: We dock, you give me the girl, and we let you and your PCAV go. Otherwise, we destroy you, which though not as good an outcome for our company as maintaining control of the girl still leaves no proof of anything other than an unjustified Frontier Coalition attack on a corporate headquarters that quite understandably and quite legally defended itself. We'll catch you—"

"Stop transmission," I said to Lobo, cutting off Amendos.

We couldn't outrun it, and we couldn't outgun it, but we weren't dead yet. I strapped myself into the pilot's couch.

"Take the fastest course to Trethen," I said.

"The fighter will catch us long before we get there."

"I know," I said. "Remember your lecture to me about assumptions? Do it."

"I executed your order as soon as you gave it," Lobo said. "I was simply supplying additional data."

"How long until the fighter exits the atmosphere?"

"One minute."

"Thirty seconds after it does, fire half of your missiles at it," I said. "Put up a tracking display."

A three-meter-wide schematic display blossomed on Lobo's front wall. Macken's surface, the end of its atmosphere, and Trethen appeared at appropriate scale. A yellow line marked our course; we were a small red dot on it. A black dot farther from the small moon than Lobo tracked the same course. The scale of the display made it almost impossible to tell from moment to moment that the black dot was gaining on us, but I knew it was.

Lobo shook slightly as he fired. The ride would only get rougher.

"You know that at this range the missiles are entirely useless," Lobo said, "because the fighter's defenses will have more than enough notice to dispatch them easily."

"You're doing it again," I said.

"No, I'm simply keeping you informed."

I ignored his comment. "Time for the missiles to reach the fighter?" I said.

"Four minutes," Lobo said. "Our lead has already shrunk."

"Is Jasmine in the acceleration couch?"

"Yes."

"Lock her down," I said. "I don't want to have to worry about her getting hurt because she started roaming around at the wrong time."

"Done."

"What do you know about that fighter's guidance system?" I said.

"I have no data about that craft per se," Lobo said. "It appears to be a standard five-year-old model, designed for low-orbit and midrange space combat, though with minimum in-atmosphere capabilities. The sat images suggest corporate customization, so I assume it offers more amenities than its pure military counterparts."

"Guidance systems and weapons?"

"Both are almost certainly milspec. Likely weapons include pulse-beam cannons and a variety of missiles. What level of detail would you like?"

"That's enough on the weapons. We know it can destroy us once it's close enough that you don't have time to deal with its attack."

"Correct."

"Is its guidance system likely to be on par with yours?"

"I have reason to believe that my level of intelligence is extraordinary among battle craft," Lobo said with what sounded like pride in his voice, "so the fighter is unlikely to match me in that area. Otherwise, however, our systems are from the same time frame and so should be similar."

"You'll have to tell me about that reason sometime," I said.

"No," Lobo said, "I don't. My programming doesn't mandate that."

I wanted to pursue this topic further, but now was definitely not the time. "Sorry," I said. "Go back to the fighter's guidance system. What alerts are automatic in deep space?"

"Collision, incoming missiles, and ship status," Lobo said.

"Anything else?"

"Such as?" Lobo said, and again the emotion showed, though this time he seemed peeved. Before I could answer, he continued. "Missiles entering range of fighter's defenses in three, two, one, now."

"Record but do not encode the following message," I said. "Arriving highest speed with Jasmine Chung. Under pursuit from Kelco fighter. Request covering fire."

"Done."

"Send it on all frequencies to the secret Saw base on Trethen," I said. "Use a laser pulse transmission as well."

"There is no Saw base on that moon," Lobo said.

"Pick a spot on the side of the moon facing us and pretend," I said. "But send that transmission now."

"Done," Lobo said.

"Missile status?"

"All but one destroyed by the fighter," Lobo said. "Last one under attack and," he paused for a few seconds, "now gone."

"How much time did we gain?"

"The fighter slowed for fifteen seconds," Lobo said, "and has now resumed full speed. Best estimate is that we gained five seconds."

"Amendos won't think we spent those missiles well, will he?" I said.

"Not unless he's far less competent than he appears."

"Perfect. Is there any reason to believe the destruction of the missiles would have covered our transmission?"

"Of course not," Lobo said. "Are you that unaware—"

I cut him off. "Just making sure," I said. "How long until we reach Trethen?"

"We won't reach it before the fighter gets us," Lobo said.

"Hail the fighter."

Amendos made me wait almost a minute. When his face appeared on the wall display in front of me, he was smiling and visibly more relaxed.

"Reconsidered my offer?" he said.

"No," I said. "I'm offering you a chance to surrender.

Return to Macken, wait for Saw troops to take you into custody, and you can come out of this alive."

A wave of emotions washed over him, his face shifting in rapid sequence from bewilderment to amusement to anger. Anger stayed. "I'd thought better of you, Moore," he said, "but now I realize you must simply have been lucky so far, or perhaps you benefited from the help of friends who are far more competent than you. No ship left Macken in pursuit. You're alone."

"We'll be within range of the defense systems of the Saw base on Trethen before you can hurt or capture us," I said, "and they'll destroy you."

"That's pathetic," he said, "as was your transmission. There's no base on that moon."

"There's no base that *you're* aware of," I said, working hard for the annoyed tone of a lecturer addressing a particularly dim student. "I wouldn't have told you about it, but we'll have to reveal its existence anyway when we explain what happened to you. Last chance."

"We would know if—"

"Shut it down," I said to Lobo, cutting off Amendos again. The display winked out.

"We're now at the extreme edge of the range of the fighter's missiles," Lobo said.

"But you could handle them at this distance," I said.

"Correct, which is why he won't fire them yet. He'll wait until he's close enough that I can't deal with all that he can send our way."

"How far are we from Trethen?" I said, ignoring Lobo's prodding.

"Roughly one hundred ninety-eight thousand kilometers and closing," Lobo said.

"Superimpose on the display an arc three hundred thousand kilometers from the jump gate."

A pale green line the color of Macken's gate appeared on the display. It arced between us and the fighter.

"How long until the fighter crosses that line?" I said.

"Two minutes," Lobo said.

"How long until the fighter is close enough that you can't stop its missiles?"

"Two minutes thirty seconds."

"Slow gradually to quarter speed," I said. "Don't rush it. Hail the fighter. Tell me privately on machine frequency when it crosses that line."

"Executing," Lobo said.

Amendos answered more quickly this time, and he made no attempt to hide his annoyance or confusion.

I didn't wait for him to speak. "I don't want any more people to die," I said.

"Give me Jasmine Chung," he said, "and no one has to."

"You're not listening," I said. "I'm giving you a chance to save your life and the lives of any crew on your ship. Turn around, go back to Macken, and you'll walk away."

"Even if there is a base on Trethen," he said, "and I don't believe there is, it can't stop me. I can destroy you and get away well before we're close enough that anything it could shoot at us could hurt us."

On the display beside his head, the black dot was still on the other side of the line. I had to buy more time. "Amendos, you kidnapped and held captive a girl whose only sin was to have the wrong father. You tried to bribe me. You tortured me. You shot my friends. Despite all that, I'm sick enough of killing that I'm trying to save your life. Take this offer seriously. It's your last chance."

"You're the one who's dooming that girl," he said.

I didn't respond.

"The fighter is over the line," Lobo said to me, the machine-frequency interruption a jarring noise in my head in the midst of human conversation.

"Goodbye, Moore," Amendos said at almost the same time. The display vanished as he cut the communication.

"Can your visual sensors pick up the fighter yet?" I said.

"Yes, on extreme magnification," Lobo said. A second display opened next to the first. In the center sat a tiny image of the fighter.

"Time to pray," I said.

"To what?" Lobo said.

"Not to anything. Pray simply that things work as they should."

I climbed out of the couch and stood closer to the new display. "No matter what happens, do *not* defend us."

For the second time in a matter of hours I was helpless, bait for an opponent. I didn't like it any better this time than the first.

"Missiles are away from the fighter," Lobo said. "They'll reach us in less than one minute. I might be able to destroy some—"

"No!" I said. "Wait."

The fighter grew bigger in the display as it hurtled toward us. Streaks of exhaust discoloration marked the passage of the missiles as they accelerated at us.

Almost exactly two seconds after the fighter launched the missiles, the heavens glowed a light greenish white and sheets of light arced across the display. The light sliced through the positions of the missiles and the fighter, and then they were gone, disappeared from the display with no wreckage or other trace that they'd ever existed. The fighter and the missiles simply vanished, the space where they'd been now empty.

Macken's jump gate had worked as it should, refusing to tolerate any weapons fire within its neutral area by destroying both the missiles and the ship that had launched them. How the gate had destroyed them without leaving any traces remained the mystery it had always been, but that didn't bother me. I don't need to understand something to have faith that it works.

I let out a breath I hadn't realized I was holding.

"The gate," Lobo said.

"Yes," I said. I laughed, the tension leaving me as my body figured out what my head was still accepting: I had survived. I was alive, and my enemy was not. I knew I should feel bad about Amendos, about having added more deaths to the list of the lives lost since this all started, but I didn't. He was a jerk who'd tortured me, and I'd given him a choice, which was more than he would have given me.

We'd fought, he'd lost, and I was still standing.

Nothing could have been sweeter.

CHAPTER 31

The first time I walked by the main Frontier Coalition building on the edge of Bekin's Deal, I might not have noticed it had Barnes not stopped me and taken me inside. This time, though, the squad of Saw soldiers guarding the entrances and patrolling the perimeter clearly stated that this was a very important place. Jasmine seemed unimpressed despite the troops. Since Lobo had released her from the couch, she'd barely spoken, her attitude wavering between scared and petulant. For a while, I found it annoying; then I reminded myself that she was almost certainly new to kidnapping and battle and entitled to cope as best she could. More important, my feelings about her didn't matter. What mattered was finishing the job and making right what I'd messed up earlier.

A Sergeant Schmidt, who was standing at parade rest

at the entrance and scanning the people passing by the building, spotted us before we reached the front door and hustled us inside. Fresh scrapes on her face and a tendency to favor her left arm marked her as someone who'd participated in the earlier action. As we walked into the building's foyer, I remembered where I'd seen her.

"Sarge," I said, "why'd they let you out from behind the recruiting desk for this one?"

She smiled. "Top told me what was up, and I could hardly let him go it alone." Her tone changed as she dropped her voice and shook her head. "Not that I ended up doing him much good." She obviously shared at least the same affection for Gustafson that all the troops I'd seen had shown, though I thought I detected more than collegial concern and respect in her voice.

"If anyone's to blame," I said, "I am. He was saving me when he was shot. How's he doing?"

Schmidt rode with us in an elevator to the top floor of the building. "He'll recover fully," she said, "though he's in hospital right now and will spend some time in rehab."

"Other people were hurt rescuing me?" Jasmine said.

Anger welled in me, and I wanted to scream at her that of course people were hurt, men and women always paid a price to save the innocents, but I stayed under control. I could try to make her understand, but to what end? I let it go.

Schmidt stopped, stared hard at Jasmine, shook her head, and turned to face me. "As for fault, Gunny, from what he told me, if anyone's to blame, he is. He didn't watch the entrance points, and he knows better. Besides, we both know that if you want to play, you always pay, one way or another."

"Yeah," I said. "Thanks for helping."

She smiled as she motioned us forward again and down a hallway to the right. "It's my job."

We came to a pair of old-fashioned wooden doors built expressly to impress, each composed of large, weighty panels with small carved trees running around their perimeters.

"This is as far as I go," she said. As she knocked, she leaned closer to me and whispered, "Stick it to that Kelco jerk." She snapped a quick salute and headed down the hall before I could return it.

A Saw corporal I didn't recognize opened the door and stood aside to let us in. The room offered the best the Frontier Coalition could manage on Macken: rich wooden walls decorated here and there with active-display panels showing scenes of sections of the planet from various altitudes, a large wooden conference table, and various supporting pieces of furniture I didn't take the time to identify.

Instead, I focused my full attention on Slake, who was leaning back in a chair on the opposite side of the table and giving the room his best bored look. His expression didn't change when he saw me, but when Jasmine entered Slake sat up and transformed from bored to business in the space of a heartbeat. Earl, who sat next to Slake, smiled and pushed a little back from the table when he noticed me. Jasmine hid behind me when she spotted Slake.

Vaccaro, who naturally occupied the head chair in an FC conference room, turned to me and said, "Thank you for joining us, Mr. Moore."

Chung had his back to me but turned quickly when he heard my name. His face fought a losing battle with anger and frustration until Jasmine stepped from behind me, and then he scrambled out of his chair and ran to her. She met him halfway. As they hugged, they murmured to one another. I couldn't understand what they said, nor did I want to.

After almost a minute, he leaned back from his daughter, still holding her, and looked at me with wet eyes. "Thank you," he said.

I nodded at the Saw soldier and Earl. "They did most of the work," I said, "they and Alissa Lim's team. I just drew the visible assignment."

He nodded and said, "Thank you all. I cannot tell you—"

Vaccaro interrupted him. "Mr. Moore, where did you find Jasmine Chung?"

"In Kelco's local headquarters," I said, "which is also Mr. Slake's residence."

"And you have witnesses?"

"Multiple," I said, "and I'm sure some Kelco employees could be persuaded to testify about her kidnapping. Not all the Kelco employees involved, however, are available." I turned to face Slake. "Ryan Amendos, the Kelco security chief who last spoke to me about Jasmine and who tried to negotiate her return to Kelco's custody, is dead. So are all the members of his crew on the fighter that was docked next to Slake's house." I realized I was enjoying this and felt guilty for a moment—but I didn't stop. "Oh, and that ship is also gone."

Fury tightened Slake's face and widened his eyes. He stayed totally focused on me and didn't notice Chung circling the table toward him.

"You killed these people?" Vaccaro said.

"No," I said. "The jump gate everyone is so excited about destroyed the ship and everyone aboard it. Amendos showed the poor judgment to ignore my warning and fire missiles too close to the gate."

Chung, who was now on the other side of the table, ran screaming at Slake. "You kidnapped my daughter! I'll—"

Moving with the same quiet speed I remembered, Earl appeared between Chung and Slake, grabbed Chung, spun him, and clamped an arm around his head and over his mouth, muffling his screams.

"What I'm sure Mr. Chung was about to explain," Earl said, "is that this unassailable evidence of criminal activity on the part of Kelco has the potential to lead to enormously expensive and time-consuming legal actions, during which all corporate activity on Macken would necessarily have to cease." Earl sat Chung back in his chair and stood beside the still-livid father, his hand on the man's shoulder. "I believe Mr. Chung was also going to suggest that instead of all of us wasting resources on such actions, we instead agree that Xychek and Kelco will evenly split the commercial rights to Macken and its new aperture, with the Frontier Coalition also owning a small piece and acting as a mutually agreed-upon dissent arbiter ad infinitum." Earl looked at Chung. "Did I get that right, Mr. Chung?"

"Daddy," Jasmine Chung said, "you're not going to let this man—"

"Jasmine," her father said, his voice cracking with the effort of resuming his corporate persona, a persona I was now sure his daughter had never understood existed, "Colonel Earl's men will help you to a room where a doctor will examine you and help you rest."

"Daddy!" she yelled.

"Jasmine," he said, "I'll see you shortly."

The corporal led her out of the room.

"We already have a contract," Slake said, "and I see no reason to renegotiate it."

"Sure you do," Vaccaro said. She looked at Earl. "Turn off all recordings." When Earl nodded, she turned back to Slake and said, "We settle this right now, and you deal with your bosses however you want, or I will make it my personal mission to tie up Macken for the next fifty years and ruin your career. You know I'll do it, and you know I'll win in the end."

Slake sat completely still for several seconds, glaring at me.

I smiled in return. None of this seemed like enough of a punishment for what he'd done, but I knew that the ramifications of this loss for his company would hit him over and over for weeks, maybe years, to come. His corporate life would never be the same. If I wasn't willing to kill, I had to learn to accept these alternative punishments.

Slake faced Vaccaro and smiled slightly. "I believe I'm the only one here," he said, sounding as if he were choking on each word, "who doesn't already possess the details of the new arrangement. Please outline them for me."

As Vaccaro explained, Chung came over to me and stuck out his hand. We shook. "Thank you again," he said. "I don't meet a lot of men who keep their word. I'll keep mine: You'll get paid."

"You're welcome," I said, though his last words stung. They were reasonable, and they told part of the truth, but they weren't enough of the truth. They didn't speak at all to the heart of why I'd done this, and the difference mattered incredibly, at least to me.

I left before I wasted my breath by explaining or wasted my opportunity by hitting him.

CHAPTER 32

I spent the rest of that day and all night sleeping in my rental beach house. I hadn't expected to ever see the place again, so staying there a final night brought me a soothing sense of closure. With all of this over, I was finally able to relax—though I kept Lobo in low orbit monitoring the house and ready to alert me at the first sign of trouble. I had no way to be a hundred percent sure I was safe as long as I remained on Macken and Slake was here, too.

The next morning, I walked on the beach, admired the ocean a last time, packed a small carry bag, and took the house's shuttle to the government center. The Saw guard on duty directed me to Earl, who in keeping with his nature occupied a small office as far away from the bureaucrats as he could manage. To my surprise, Lim was there with him, the two of them talking congenially over a desktop display. Earl wore his usual working blues. Lim generally appeared back on duty, her Law uniform crisp and her boots polished, but her hair was down. The only sign of her injury was a slight hitch in her movement as she turned when I knocked.

"I'm heading out," I said, "but I wanted to thank you both before I left."

"Don't thank me," Lim said. "I got paid more than we'd ever planned, we saw some real action, we did a little good, and I gained a contract in the bargain."

I raised an eyebrow in question. Lim looked at Earl.

"As part of the three-way agreement for commercial and aperture development rights on Macken," he said, "the FC will maintain a small monitoring force here. Putting a team of that size in a remote location doesn't fit Command's business model, so the Saw is subcontracting the assignment to Alissa's team."

"Yeah," Lim said, "Tristan and I are working together again. Not what I expected, but I think it'll be fine. I'll stay on-site for a while to make sure everything is shipshape." She laughed lightly, her voice as charming as her looks when she wasn't in battle or under stress. "Living one jump apart should be just about right for the two of us."

Earl smiled but wisely said nothing in response.

"How's your shoulder?" I said.

"No serious damage," she said. "A small price to pay."

I shook hands with Lim, then put out my hand to Earl. "Thank you, Colonel."

We shook. He held on an extra few seconds as he said, "Of course. As Alissa said, we did something worth doing, and we'll all profit. And, as you said you would, you saved the girl. Well done."

From anyone else I would have found the comment

patronizing, but not from Earl. He said it sincerely and, I suspected, with a real understanding of what it meant to me. I felt good to hear him say it.

He paused as he stared intently at me. "I'm pretty sure I'm wasting time by asking this, but it won't take much time: Any chance you'd be interested in joining us again?"

I laughed, and to my relief after a few seconds he laughed with me. "My joining days are long over," I said. "If I were ever to sign up again, though, it would be with the Saw—but I prefer to work alone."

He nodded. "Fair enough. Does working alone mean I could interest you in selling back that PCAV? Now, we could use it here."

"Sorry, but no," I said, deciding the less I talked about Lobo the better. "It's proven to be a handy machine to have around."

"Well, one of the newer models will cost the FC quite a bit more," he said, "but with what Kelco is paying in penalties, they can afford it." He looked at Lim, who was again studying the glowing data. "We better get back to work."

As I left, they huddled over the display and began talking about inspection timings and reporting intervals. Though no frontier planet ever likes the presence of law enforcement, Macken had definitely improved its lot by moving from being under Kelco's sole control to operating as a multicorporate world with Lim's team ensuring that both companies obeyed the rules.

Barnes grabbed me before I reached the exit.

"She'd like to see you," he said.

I motioned for him to lead and followed him into what

I immediately recognized as his old office; the view was as lovely as before. Vaccaro sat behind his desk, the room now hers. After Barnes ushered me in, she waved him away. He closed the door behind him as he left.

"Mr. Moore," she said, "are you leaving us already?"

"Yes."

"This is an unofficial meeting," she said, "and it's not being recorded."

"I didn't know we were meeting." I regretted being so sharp as soon as the words left my mouth, but as always, dealing with a bureaucrat put me on edge.

She ignored the tone. "As this incident and others have demonstrated, there are occasions in which unofficial freelance help can be very useful to any government—and very profitable for the freelancer. Check your wallet."

I did. Everything Chung had promised that Xychek would pay, along with a bonus from the FC, sat in my local account. I moved it to a different account immediately; no point in not being careful. "Thank you for the bonus. Though it wasn't necessary, I appreciate it."

She waved her hand, dismissing the topic.

"It's almost nothing," she said, "compared to what's possible if you continue in this sort of relationship with the Coalition."

I ignored the bait. "Xychek's payment is also in my account," I said. "Would you happen to know where Chung is, so I can thank him and say goodbye to him and Jasmine?"

"They both left yesterday," she said, a slight smile playing across her face. "He wanted to meet with his key staffers on Lankin, and she begged to get away from this world as quickly as possible."

I hadn't realized I'd expected more from Jasmine, but the hollow feeling in my stomach told me I had. I knew it was illogical to want her to thank me for remedying a mess I'd helped create, but that thanks, I now had to accept, was indeed what I'd wanted—that and a bit of forgiveness from Jasmine for returning her to Slake in the first place. I've lived too long not to see the obvious connection—Jasmine forgiving me would be a bit of cheap emotional salve for the open wound left by my inability to find and save Jennie—but sometimes knowing what's happening has absolutely nothing to do with being able to stop it from occurring.

"Mr. Moore," Vaccaro said, bringing me back to the present. "Would such a relationship interest you?"

"Thank you," I said, "but no. I'm looking forward to a long vacation."

She turned back to her work, dismissing me. "Very well. Please understand that offers such as this don't stay open long."

Until this conversation, I'd known only that I *wanted* to get away from this region. Now, her tone convinced me that I *needed* to go very far away. She struck me as the sort of person who saw the world as composed entirely of people either with her or against her, and I'd just joined the wrong team by refusing to be on hers.

I let myself out.

Barnes was waiting. He followed me to the building's exit and out into the sort of clear beautiful day I hoped to find on another planet somewhere many jumps from here.

"Almost a month ago, you told me the time you'd bought us wouldn't do much good," he said, "but it did, and I thank you for it—and for everything you've done.

This is a great planet. I'm hoping we can all work together to keep it great even as we populate it."

I wasn't sure how much I believed in humanity's ability to manage any planet well, but someone had to nurture the belief that we could and work to prove it was justified. I was glad he was willing to try.

"Good luck," I said. "I hope you succeed." I stared at the forest beyond the cleared perimeter, sniffed the rich air that blended the smells of trees and the ocean, and basked in the gorgeous day. "It is a beautiful world."

I had to hand it to the FC: It did hospitals right. The one where Gustafson was recovering looked to be as modern as any facility I've seen—and I've been inside far more medical buildings than most. Gleaming, self-cleaning walls, robotic crawlers working tirelessly on all surfaces to minimize infection spread, monitoring and treatment equipment I couldn't begin to understand: Everywhere I looked, the hospital practically trumpeted the triumph of technology over illness and injury. Of course, the discreet entries on the building's nav displays for the coroner's office and the morgue reminded the close observer that technology didn't win all the time.

Top was stretched out on a bed in a private room with a Saw corporal standing guard outside. A wall-sized window afforded him a great view all the way to the ocean. Schmidt sat beside his bed. Wires ran from two different machines to his legs, which twitched under a sheet as the system worked his muscles.

"Gunny," he said when he spotted me, "it's good to see you. I hear we won."

"Gunny," Schmidt said.

"We did indeed," I said. "I'm sorry it had to cost you so much."

"This?" he said, laughing and pointing to his legs. "I have more problems with the new hip than with the reattachment they've done here. The first shot hit below the knee, and the second got only meat, so I was lucky. I should be as good as ever in a couple of weeks. I didn't even need any new parts this time."

"Back to Lankin then?" I said.

He looked at Schmidt, and for a few seconds his expression was the softest I'd seen on him. "Nah. The colonel's okayed some R&R." He looked at her again, then back at me. "We're going to spend some time here, do a little swimming, take it easy, you know." They both smiled broadly at the last bit.

Their smiles were infectious; I found myself smiling, also. "Sounds good," I said.

"What about you?"

"I'm taking off as soon as I leave you. I feel a strong need to be somewhere far away."

"I understand," he said. "I told the colonel you wouldn't be interested."

I opened my pack, pulled out a small box and an entry card, and put them on the bed beside him. "I thought you might enjoy these."

"What are they?" he said.

"The card is for my beach house. It's paid in full for almost two more weeks, so someone might as well use it. The box contains the tracker and the remote for Bob. He's strong enough to pull two of you, and I'm here to tell you, swimming with Bob is one heck of a ride."

Schmidt looked at him. "Bob is that ray you've been talking about, isn't it?" she said.

Gustafson actually blushed. "He's a magnificent creature," he said to Schmidt, "and if you spend a little time looking at him, I think you'll feel the same way." He faced me. "Thanks, Gunny, for both. I appreciate them."

I nodded and turned to leave.

"Will I see you again?" he said.

"Don't take this the wrong way, Top, but I hope not."

He laughed. "Fair enough. If I do see you, I hope you're beside me."

"You can bet I don't want to be across from the Saw in any action," I said, "so that much you can count on."

One ship remained between us and the jump gate.

Lobo was freshly fueled, and we'd topped off his supply and weapons stores, courtesy of the Saw tab that Kelco was paying.

The green light of the gate bathed the transport in front of us as it slipped into the aperture, disappearing bit by bit until it was, I trusted, in the Lankin system. About a minute later, a large vessel, an FC hauler by its size and nose logo, poked through.

Our turn was next.

"You still haven't decided where we're going after Lankin," Lobo said.

I pondered the options again. I needed to get away from this region of space, because Kelco, Xychek, and the FC all had reasons they might want to find me. Osterlad's successors might also decide having their founder killed by an outsider was bad for business.

What I should do next, however, remained a mystery.

I could try to get back to Pinkelponker to see if Jennie was still alive, but I had no more plan now for reaching my old home world than I had in the past, and the blockade around the single jump-gate aperture that reached it was reported to be the toughest in the galaxy.

I could check out the rumors of another survivor of the Aggro experiments, but I'd seen the disaster and didn't believe anyone else could have survived it. Even if another person had made it out, did I really want to find him?

I could try to find a job, because I'd need to work eventually, but for the foreseeable future I was set for money.

When I can't understand the big picture, which is most of the time, I focus on the bit I can see in front of me. I needed to be away from here, and I needed to be difficult to track. The fastest path to those goals was a crooked one.

I watched as the last bit of the hauler emerged from the gate.

"Jump randomly," I said, "at least six times, and don't go to the same gate twice. We'll figure out the next step when we get where we're going, wherever that is."

"Will do," Lobo said, "though that's not much of a plan."

I was so glad to be leaving that I didn't even mind his sarcasm.

We eased forward, moving closer and closer to the aperture until its utter blackness filled our vision and blotted out the heavens. In that perfect black I could see a dark and dangerous universe, but I could also see worlds yet to form, an unwritten future waiting for me to fill it with the bright colors of days to come.

In that moment, I hoped for brightness.

We jumped.

The following is an excerpt from:

SLANTED JACK

by

MARK L. VAN NAME

Available from Baen Books

July 2008

CHAPTER 1

Nothing should have been able to ruin my lunch.

Joaquin Choy, the best chef on any planet within three jumps, had erected his restaurant, Falls, just outside Eddy, the only city on the still-developing world Mund. He'd chosen the site because of the intense flavors of the native vegetables, the high quality of the locally raised livestock, and a setting that whipped your head around and widened your eyes.

Falls perched on camo-painted carbon-fiber struts over the center of a thousand-meter-deep gorge. You entered it via a three-meter-wide transparent walkway so soft you were sure you were strolling across high, wispy clouds. The four waterfalls that inspired its name remained visible even when you were inside, thanks to the transparent active-glass walls whose careful light balancing guaranteed a glare-free view throughout the day. The air outside filled your head with the clean scent of wood drifting downstream on light river breezes; a muted variant of the same smells pervaded the building's interior.

I occupied a corner seat, a highly desirable position given my background and line of work. From this vantage point, I could easily scan all new arrivals. I'd reserved and paid for all the seats at the five tables closest to me, so a wide buffer separated me from the other diners. In the clouds above me, Lobo, my intelligent Predator-class assault vehicle, monitored the area surrounding the restaurant so no threat could assemble outside without my knowledge. I'd located an exterior exit option when I first visited Choy, and both Lobo and I could reach it in under a minute. Wrapped in a blanket of security I rarely achieved in the greater world, I could relax and enjoy myself.

The setting was perfect.

Following one of my cardinal rules of fine dining— always opt for the chef's tasting menu in a top-notch restaurant—I'd forgone the offerings on the display that shimmered in the air over my table and instead surrendered myself to Choy's judgment, asking only that he not hold back on the portion size of any course. Getting fat is never an issue for me. At almost two meters tall and over a hundred kilos in weight, I'm large enough that I'd be able to eat quite a lot if I were a normal man, and thanks to the nanomachines that lace my cells, I can eat as much as I want: They decompose and flush any excess food I consume.

Spread in front of me were four appetizer courses, each blending chunks of a different savory meat with strands of vegetables steaming on a glass plate of slowly changing color. Choy instructed me to taste each dish separately and then in combinations of my choice. I didn't know what any of them were, and I didn't care. They smelled divine, and I expected they would taste even better.

They did. I leaned back after the third amazing bite and closed my eyes, my taste buds coping with that most rare of sensory pleasures: sensations that in over a hundred and fifty years of life they'd never experienced. I struggled to conjure superlatives equal to the food.

The food was perfect.

What ruined the lunch was the company, the unplanned, unwanted company.

When I opened my eyes from my contemplation of that confounding and delicious blend of flavors, Slanted Jack was walking toward me from the stark white entrance hallway.

Slanted Jack, so named because with him nothing was ever straight, had starred in one of the many acts of my life that I'd just as soon forget. The best con man and thief I've ever known, he effortlessly charmed and put at ease anyone who didn't know him. When he eased through a room of strangers, they all noticed. He was a celebrity whose name none of them could quite remember. Maybe ten centimeters shorter than I, with a wide smile, eyes the blue of the heart of flame, and skin the color and sheen of polished night, Jack instantly cornered the attention of everyone around him. While weaving his way through the tables to me he paused three times to exchange pleasantries with people he was almost certainly meeting for the first time. Each person Jack addressed would know that Jack found him special, important, even compelling, and Jack truly would feel that way, if only for the instant he invested in sizing up each one as a potential target.

While Jack was chatting with a foursome a few meters away, I called Lobo.

"Any sign of external threat?"

"Of course not," Lobo said. "You know that if I spotted anything, I'd alert you instantly. Why are you wasting time talking to me when you could be eating your magnificent meal, conversing with other patrons, and generally having a wonderful time? It's not as if you're stuck up here where I am, too high to have even the birds for company."

"It's not like I could bring you into the restaurant with me," I said, parroting his tone. I know he's a machine, but from almost the first time we met I've been unable to think of him as anything other than "he," a person. "Nor, for that matter, do you eat."

"You've never heard of takeout? I may not consume the same type of fuel as you, but I can be quite a pleasant dinner companion, as I'd think you'd realize after all the meals you've taken while inside me."

I sighed. Every time I let myself fall into an argument with Lobo when he's in a petulant mood, I regret it. "Signing off."

"You don't want to do that yet," Lobo said.

"Why?" Just when I think I understand all the ways Lobo can annoy me, he comes up with a new one.

"Because I was about to alert you to an internal threat," he said.

"Let me guess," I said. "The tall man who recently walked into the restaurant and is now talking to some people not far from me."

"Correct," Lobo said. "I did not consider the threat

high both because other humans have stayed between you and him since he entered and because his two weapons are holstered, one under his left arm and the other on his right ankle."

Jack was armed? *That* was unusual, the first thing he'd done that didn't fit the man I'd known. Jack had always hated weapons and delegated their use to others, frequently to me. I don't like them either, nor do I like violence of any type, but both have been frequent hazards of most of the kinds of jobs I've taken over the last many decades.

"Got it," I said. "Anything else you can tell?"

"That's all the data I can obtain from this distance, and even that information required me to force enough power into the scan that the restaurant's skylights are now complaining to the building management system about the treatment they have to endure."

I kept my eyes on Jack and tuned in to the common appliance frequency. Restaurants employ so many machines, every one of which has intelligence to spare and a desire to talk to anything that will listen, that tapping into their chat wavelength was like stepping into the middle of a courtyard full of screaming people. The sonic wall smacked me, the sounds in my head momentarily deafening even though I knew they weren't really audio at all, just neurons and tweaked receptors firing in ways Jennie and the experiments on Aggro had combined to make my brain interpret as sounds. I sorted through the conversations, ignoring mentions of food and temperature until I finally found a relevant snippet and focused on it.

"Radiation of that level is simply not normal for this

area," one pane said, "though fortunately it is well within the limits of what my specs can handle."

"All of us can easily handle it," said another pane. Household and building intelligences, like appliances, are insanely competitive and desperate for attention. They spend most of their lives bickering. I listened for another few seconds, but all the chatter was between the pieces of active glass; the household security system didn't respond to the windows, so it clearly didn't consider the burst from Lobo's scan to be a risk. I should tell Joaquin to upgrade his systems.

"If you see that man reach for either weapon," I said, "alert me instantly."

"Of course," Lobo said. "Must you constantly restate previous arrangements?"

"Sorry. Humans use reminders and ritualized communications during crises."

"I appreciate that, and I sometimes don't mind, but he's one man, he's made no move to suggest aggression, and so I hardly consider him a crisis."

Lobo clearly didn't appreciate the trouble a single man could cause, much less a man like Jack. Jack had finished with the foursome and was now leaning over a couple at a table adjacent to the first group. "Now signing off," I said.

I blended bits of food from a pair of the plates into another bite, but I couldn't take my eyes off Jack; the charms of the appetizers were dissipating faster than their aromas. Jack would require all my attention. He and I had worked the con together for almost a decade, and though that time was profitable, it was also consistently nerve-racking. Jack lived by his own principles, chief among which was his lifelong commitment to target only bad people for big touches. We consequently found ourselves time and again racing to make jumps off planets, always a short distance ahead of very dangerous, very angry marks. By the time we split, I vowed to go straight and never run the con again.

"Jon," Jack said as he reached me, his smile as disarming as always. "It's good to see you. It's been too long."

"What do you want, Jack?"

"May I join you?" he said, pulling out a chair.

I didn't bother to answer; it was pointless.

He nodded and sat. "Thank you."

He put his hands palm-down on the tablecloth, so I said nothing.

A server appeared beside him, reset the table for two, and waited for Jack's order.

"I throw myself on Joaquin's mercy," Jack said. "Please tell him Jack asks only that he be gentle."

The server glanced at me for confirmation. Jack wasn't going to leave until he had his say, so I nodded, and the server hustled away.

"Joaquin truly is an artist," Jack said. "I—"

I cut him off by standing and grabbing his throat.

"I'd forgotten how very fast you are for a man your size," he croaked. As always, he maintained his calm. He kept his hands where they were. "Is this really necessary?"

I bent over him so my left hand was on his back and our bodies covered my right hand, with which I continued to grip his neck tightly enough that his discomfort was evident. "Carefully and slowly put both weapons on the table," I said. "If you make me at all nervous, I'll crush your throat."

"I believe you would," Jack said, as he pulled out first

a small projectile weapon from under his left shoulder and then an even smaller one from a holster on his ankle, "but I know you would feel bad about it. I've always liked that about you."

"Yes, I would," I said. When the weapons were on the table, I pushed back Jack's chair, released his throat, and palmed both guns. I put them behind my chair as I sat.

Jack stretched his neck and pulled his chair closer to the table. "I really must locate a tailor with better software," he said. "You shouldn't have been able to spot those."

I saw no value in enlightening him about Lobo's capabilities. "What do you want, and since when do you travel armed?"

Jack assembled bits of all four of my appetizers into a perfectly shaped bite, then chewed it slowly, his eyes shutting as the tastes flooded his mouth. "Amazing. Did I say Joaquin was an artist? I should have called him a magician—and I definitely should have dined here sooner."

He opened his eyes and studied me intently. The focus of his gaze was both intense and comforting, as if he could see into your soul and was content to view only that. For years I'd watched him win the confidence of strangers with a single long look, and I'd never figured out how he managed it. I'd asked him many times, and he always told me the same thing: "Each person deserves to be the center of the universe to someone, Jon, even if only for an instant. When I focus on someone, that person is my all." He always laughed afterward, but whether in embarrassment at having been momentarily completely honest or in jest at my gullibility is something I've never known.

"We haven't seen each other in, what, thirty years now,"

he said, "and you haven't aged a day. You must give me
the names and locations of your med techs"—he paused
and chuckled before continuing—"and how you afford it.
Courier work must pay far better than I imagined."

I wasn't in that line of work when I last saw him, so
Jack was telling me he'd done his homework. He also
looked no different than before, which I would have
expected: No one with money and the willingness to pay
for current-gen med care needs to show age for at least
the middle forty or fifty years of his life. So, he was also
letting me know he had reasons to believe I'd done well
since we parted. I had, but I saw no value in providing
him with more information. Dealing with him had transformed the afternoon from pleasure to work; the same
dishes that had been so attractive a few minutes ago now
held absolutely no appeal to me.

I decided to try a different approach. "How did you
find me?"

He arranged and slowly chewed another combination
of the appetizers before answering. "Ah, Jon, that was
luck, fate if you will. Despite the many years we've been
apart, I'm sure you remember how valuable it is for someone in my line of work to develop supporters among
jump-gate staff. After all, everyone who goes anywhere
eventually appears on their tracking lists. So, when I made
the jump from Drayus I stopped at the gate station and
visited some of my better friends there, friends who have
agreed to inform me when people of a certain," he looked
skyward, as if searching for a phrase, "dangerous persua-
sion passed into the Mund system. Traveling in a PCAV
earned you their attention, and they were kind enough to
alert me."

I neither moved nor spoke, but inside I cursed myself. During a recent run-in with two major multiplanet conglomerates and a big chunk of the Frontier Coalition government, I'd made so many jumps in such a short period that I'd abandoned my previously standard practice of bribing the station agents not to notice me. Break a habit, pay a price.

"Speaking of your transport," he said, "is that a show copy or the real thing?"

I said nothing but raised an eyebrow and forced myself to take another bite from the nearer two plates. With Jack silence was often the best response, because he would then try another approach at the information he wanted, and the tactics he chose frequently conveyed useful data.

"There's no shame in a good copy, Jon," he said, his curiosity apparently satisfied. "I spent a couple of years recently brokering the machines to planetary and provincial governments in this system. The builder, Keisha Li, was this munitions artist—and I mean that, Jon, not merely a manufacturer, but an artist—who found her niche on Gash but couldn't ever hit it big. Her dupes were full, active transports that could handle any environment their originals could manage, though admittedly they were slower—and, of course," he chuckled, "completely lacking firepower. I helped her grow her business. We sold a couple of PCAV clones, though they're pricey enough that they were never our top sellers. Less expensive vehicles provided most buyers all of the intimidation value they sought." He leaned forward for a moment, his expression suddenly sad. "The worst part is that it was completely legal, an indirect sort of touch that I thought would be perfect for me, the real job I've always wondered if I could hold, and it delivered no juice, Jon. None." He sat back and threw up his hands as if in disgust. Jack always spoke with his whole body, every gesture calculated but still effective. "Oh, we made money, good money, the business grew, and we were safe and legit, but I might as well have been hawking drink dispensers." He took another bite, savored it, and then shook his head. "Me, selling machines on the straight. I mean, can you imagine it?"

As engaging as Jack was, I knew he'd never leave until he'd broached his true topic, so I tried to force him to get to it. "Jack, answer or one of us leaves: What do you want?"

He leaned back and looked into my eyes for a few seconds, then smiled and nodded. "You never could appreciate the value of civilized conversation," he said, "but your very coarseness has also always been part of your appeal—and your value. Put simply and without the context I hope you'll permit me to provide, I need your help."

Leave it to Jack to take that long to give an answer with absolutely no new content. If he hadn't wanted something, he'd never have come to me.

"When we parted," I said, "I told you I was done with the con. Nothing has changed. You've ruined my lunch for no reason." I stood to go, the weapons now in my right hand behind my back.

Jack leaned forward, held up his hand, and said, "Please, Jon, give me a little time. This isn't about me. It's about the boy."

His tone grabbed me enough that I didn't walk away, but I also didn't sit. "The boy? What boy? I can't picture you with children."

Jack laughed. "No," he said, "I haven't chosen to

procreate, nor do I ever expect to do so." He held up his hand, turned, and motioned to the maître d'.

The man hustled over to our table, reached behind himself, and gently urged a child to step in front of him.

"This boy," Jack said. "Manu Chang."

—end excerpt—

from *SLANTED JACK*
available in hardcover,
July 2008, from Baen Books